MARRIAGE REUNION WITH THE ISLAND DOC

SUE MACKAY

AN ER NURSE TO REDEEM HIM

TRACI DOUGLASS

MILLS & BOON

First published in Great Britain 2024
by Mills & Boon, an imprint of HarperCollins*Publishers* Ltd,
1 London Bridge Street, London, SE1 9GF

www.harpercollins.co.uk

HarperCollins*Publishers* Macken House, 39/40 Mayor Street Upper,
Dublin 1, D01 C9W8, Ireland

ISBN: 978-0-263-32154-8

03/24

This book contains FSC™ certified paper
and other controlled sources to ensure responsible forest management.

For more information visit www.harpercollins.co.uk/green.

Printed and Bound in the UK using 100% Renewable Electricity
at CPI Group (UK) Ltd, Croydon, CR0 4YY

Sue MacKay lives with her husband in New Zealand's beautiful Marlborough Sounds, with the water on her doorstep and the birds and the trees at her back door. It is the perfect setting to indulge her passions of entertaining friends by cooking them sumptuous meals, drinking fabulous wine, going for hill walks or kayaking around the bay—and, of course, writing stories.

Traci Douglass is a *USA TODAY* bestselling romance author with Harlequin/Mills & Boon, Entangled Publishing and Tule Publishing, and has an MFA in Writing Popular Fiction from Seton Hill University. She writes sometimes funny, usually awkward, always emotional stories about strong, quirky, wounded characters overcoming past adversity to find their for ever person. Heartfelt Healing Happily-Ever-Afters. Connect with her through her website: tracidouglassbooks.com.

Also by Sue MacKay

Single Mum's New Year Wish
Brought Together by a Pup
Fake Fiancée to Forever?
Resisting the Pregnant Paediatrician

Also by Traci Douglass

The GP's Royal Secret

Wyckford General Hospital miniseries

Single Dad's Unexpected Reunion

Boston Christmas Miracles miniseries

Home Alone with the Children's Doctor

Discover more at millsandboon.co.uk.

MARRIAGE REUNION WITH THE ISLAND DOC

SUE MACKAY

MILLS & BOON

This story is dedicated to the Raro girls, Vicki, Lenore, Joy and Kerry.

Great friends to spend holidays with in Rarotonga—along with our husbands.

CHAPTER ONE

'WOULD ALYSSA COOK please come to the check-in counter?' came the request over the intercom at Nelson Airport.

Alyssa headed across the room. Hopefully this meant her flight to Rarotonga was sorted. Being delayed here meant she was going to miss the connecting flight from Auckland to the islands, but fingers crossed there was a seat going spare on the next one.

'Hi, I'm Alyssa.'

The woman behind the counter looked harried. The airline was dealing with a lot of annoyed passengers because one of the pilots for the Nelson to Auckland flight hadn't turned up for work and there'd been a hold-up getting a replacement.

'Good. You're probably aware you won't be catching your flight out of Auckland, but we have put you on the one later in the afternoon. You won't get to Raro until around ten tonight their time.'

'Which means a whole day hanging around the airport.' Not a lot she could do about it, and at least she would still fly out today, and wouldn't miss out on too much of the things the girls had planned. 'Thank you for sorting it out for me. I really appreciate it. Even nicer that you called me over and didn't just ping my phone.'

Seemed the personal touch wasn't completely out of fashion.

The woman's shoulders drooped and a small smile appeared. 'Thank *you* for not biting my head off.'

'It's hardly your fault this has happened.'

If only she could grab some shut-eye somewhere comfortable, but that was unlikely. She'd knocked off work on the cardiac ward after a double shift two and a half hours ago, rushed home for a shower and to grab her gear, thinking she'd sleep on the flight to Rarotonga. That might still happen, only a lot later than planned.

'You'll be boarding your flight out of here in a few minutes,' the woman told her.

'Then I'll send some texts now.'

Two other nurses from the Nelson hospital where she worked had overnighted in Auckland and would wonder what was going on when she didn't turn up for the flight they were catching to Rarotonga. Damn, she was going to miss the party tonight with some of the girls. Thank goodness the wedding they were going to was still days away.

In Auckland Alyssa walked from the domestic terminal to the international one to fill in some time and get fresh air. Once through Immigration she found a café and had breakfast before doing the rounds of the duty-free shops. Time dragged and when she finally looked down at the well-lit runway at Rarotonga airport she'd lost count of the hours since leaving Nelson. A sigh slid over her lips. At last. She'd made it. Now the fun could really start.

Though what she wanted most was a hot shower followed by a cold drink beside the pool at the resort she was staying at along with the others from work. Despite being exhausted, she wouldn't be ready for sleep for a little while. It felt good to be going on holiday for the first time in what seemed like for ever, and falling into bed wasn't the way to kick-start the break from the pressures of the job as Head Nurse of the cardiac ward. A doctor and a nurse who was a close friend, from the same ward, were getting married on the beach, which promised to be stunning and a whole lot of fun. Even better, she was here for a whole fortnight. Fourteen days with nothing more to do than relax and enjoy herself. Unheard of lately.

The queue inside the terminal wound up and down the small space, roped-off lines keeping everyone crammed together, but no one seemed to be in a hurry to get through Immigration. Like her, they were already in holiday mode. She grinned as she watched an elderly man sitting on a raised platform in the corner playing a banjo and welcoming everyone to the Cook Islands in a low, crusty singing voice.

Perfect, Alyssa thought. Checking her phone, she found a photo of the happy couple, Collette and Jamie, on the beach outside the resort, laughing their heads off as one of them took the shot.

Alyssa had a momentary pang of envy. When she'd married after a whirlwind romance, it had been in a register office with two other couples and the parents of her husband-to-be witnessing the ceremony followed by a meal at a local restaurant. She'd been unbelievably happy despite the glares from her in-laws. These two had family and friends joining them for the celebrations in an idyllic location. She wished them all the best and a happier, longer-lasting marriage than she'd experienced. Jamie and Collette hadn't rushed to get married, and had taken time to really know each other, unlike her. Wham bam, married. Then separated a year later after some acrimony at the end.

'Next,' called the officer behind the immigration counter.

Alyssa stepped up.

'Welcome to Rarotonga,' said the woman as she stamped Alyssa's passport.

'Thank you.' Now that she was through the barriers she couldn't wait to get started. Her back tweaked when she lifted her case off the carousel. Too much sitting around airports and on planes. A long walk would help, but not happening tonight when she knew nothing about the area.

A woman wearing a blue and white floral dress was welcoming passengers as they made their way out into the open-air arrivals area. 'Where's the rental car office?' Alyssa asked. Preferring to be independent, she'd booked a car for her and her friends to get around in even though buses ran every thirty minutes and took only about an hour to circle the island.

'Depends which company you're using. One's open, the other closed after the last flight left.'

When Alyssa named the company the woman grimaced. 'Sorry, that's the one that's shut. You'll have to come back in the morning. Do you want me to get you a taxi?'

'You're kidding, right?'

'Unfortunately I'm not. When your flight was delayed in Auckland the girl who should be working had to go home to look after her child as the father had to go out on his fishing boat.' The woman's face crinkled into a smile. 'That's how it is here.'

Alyssa drew a deep breath and counted to ten. No point in losing her temper. Nothing she could do about it. 'It's all right. Where're the taxis?'

'Come with me. Keep the receipt from the driver and you'll be reimbursed when you pick up your rental.'

Within minutes she was ensconced in the back seat of a well-used car heading to the resort, the driver talking non-stop about the sights she'd see more clearly in the daylight. Thankfully she'd soon be in her room and pouring a glass of champagne from the bottle that was part of the accommodation package.

'Miss Cook, welcome to Seaview Resort. I am Pepe.' The young man behind the desk smiled. 'You are very late.'

'Yes, my flight was delayed from Nelson so I missed my connection in Auckland and had to wait ten hours for the next flight. So, I'm looking forward to getting to my room. I did send an email advising you.'

'Yes, we got that, thank you, but I have to tell you there's been a problem with your booking.'

No, don't do this. Not today.

Alyssa snatched her phone from her bag and tapped the screen. 'There can't be. I have a copy of the confirmation right here.' She pushed the phone across the counter. 'See?'

'I know you have a booking but you were late arriving and the couple who were previously in your room have to stay another night because their flight to Australia has cancelled due to bad weather in Brisbane.'

Of course it had been. She'd have been surprised if there'd been any other outcome. 'So I don't have a room? Is that what you're saying?' No car, now no room. What next?

'Please, we have made arrangements for you.'

Her patience was running out. 'They'd better be good.' What were the chances?

A huge smile lit up the man's face. 'They are very good, Miss Cook. We have bungalows next to the main building and you are to have one of them. You will be close to the pool without everyone being able to see into your room. All your breakfasts are free and you're to stay there for the first week you are with us.'

From the research she'd done, Alyssa knew the bungalows were wonderful, and she'd have loved one except she couldn't justify the expense when she was saving every dollar she could to buy her own house. The only downside to the bungalow was she wouldn't be on the first floor with the rest of the gang, but hardly a problem. A bungalow was a no-brainer. 'Thank you very much.' It did sound too good to be true, but tonight she wasn't asking. She'd take what was on offer and sort things out in the morning if necessary.

'I'm glad you are happy. The cleaners are still preparing the bungalow as the last occupants only checked out two hours ago. The concierge will take your bag across now but you'll have to wait in the bar for a little while longer.'

How long did it take to clean a room? But this was Rarotonga and she'd heard the place ran on island time. Right now she'd be happy with a shower and a single bed in a wardrobe so she could begin unwinding from weeks of extra shifts and difficult cases. 'Do you sell champagne by the glass?' she asked, because if she'd wanted one before, she was desperate now.

'They do in the bar. I'll ask them to pour you one. On the house.' Pepe grinned.

Suddenly she laughed. She was here, in the islands, on holiday. Everything could start going right. Looking around, she realised the bar was barely twenty steps away. She headed across.

A sound from long ago reached her as she leaned against the counter waiting for her drink to be poured. Whipping around, she stared at the apparition sitting on a lounger beside Jamie, the groom. Got that wrong, didn't she? Lots more had just gone wrong. Really wrong.

Leighton?

Couldn't be. She must have brain fade from almost no sleep in more than thirty-five hours. Leighton could not be here. Not after all this time. She was not prepared to see her ex-husband. Didn't want to. They were over and done with.

Turning her back on whoever that lookalike was, she reached for the glass being placed on the counter and took a big gulp before pointing at the glass and saying to the young man, 'Another, please.'

Don't wait until I've emptied this one.

She took another mouthful and the glass was nearly empty. She was on holiday, remember?

A shiver tripped over her. She had to know. Had to make sure she was wrong and that it wasn't Leighton sitting only metres away. She'd had a day full of let-downs. There weren't any more to come. There couldn't be.

'Hello, Lyssa. Long time, no see.'

Only one person had ever called her Lyssa. And that voice was so familiar it was lifting the hairs on her bare arms. Her head spun and she gripped the counter. Leighton was for real.

Leighton Harrison held his breath in an attempt to calm the pounding in his chest. Lyssa was on the island. After four years of not seeing her, or knowing anything about what she was up to, here she was, looking even more stunning than he recalled. So much for thinking he remembered everything about her, right down to the moment when she'd walked out on him. She'd be twenty-seven now, right? Naturally she looked more beautiful. Her face had matured and those eyes that had haunted him for a long time appeared greener and more intense. As for her mouth—still sensuous. More so. Proof of that was in the tingling in his hands where those lips often used to caress him.

'A very long time,' Alyssa said, staring as though caught in headlights. Then she blinked and took a step towards him.

Automatically he reached to give her a hug, and instantly regretted the move as the scent of citrus and exhaustion caught him. So damned familiar it hurt. It shouldn't. He was long over her. Well and truly done with them as a couple. So why hug her? Because he'd moved without any input from his brain. Some things hadn't changed. Dropping his arms without touching her, he stepped back. That was different. 'You here for something special or taking a break?'

Alyssa looked around the room before coming back to him. 'I'm here for Collette and Jamie's wedding. I see you're sitting with Jamie and some of the others I work with. Have you just met them or do you know one of the group from home?'

'Just Jamie.'

My half-brother you never knew about. A huge part of why I withdrew from you and became less than the man you married.

Seemed the truth had a way of coming through no matter what. He'd try to dodge that bullet for a little while longer. Jamie didn't know Lyssa was his ex, either, because he never talked about her. Losing her had hurt too much. He'd loved her deeply and then failed her big time by not being open and honest after what he'd learned about his family after they'd married.

Hey, Lyssa failed you too by packing her bags and leaving without trying to find out what was going on with you.

'If you're working with these people I presume you live in Nelson.' He hadn't tried to keep up to date with her life during the years since their marriage fell apart. No point. They'd rushed into marriage and fallen out just as fast. Cracks had formed in their relationship with him working long hours and Alyssa going out with her mates a lot, though nothing serious to raise concerns she mightn't be happy with him.

Soon after she'd gone he'd learned the truth about the other immoral thing his father had done. Make that what his father had tried to do, but, Alyssa being Alyssa, she'd thrown the offer of money if she refused to marry his son back in the old man's face. He'd been furious with his old man. So much for being close all his life, and being teased for being so alike in many ways. He hadn't had a clue who his father was. Learning what he did made him fear Alyssa would think he was capable of the same hideous things his father had done.

Lyssa had loved him. Yeah, and she'd left anyway without mentioning what his father had done before they married, breaking his heart along the way.

Add in the secret about his brother that his parents had kept from him, and his life had turned upside down and inside out, leaving him uncertain of who he was and what to do about the future. He felt as though he'd lived a lie all his life and needed Alyssa to love him unconditionally.

Except he'd been opening a Pandora's box of ugly truths and painful emotions he was struggling to cope with and did not want to share. He'd been the strong one in the relationship, supporting Lyssa with insecurities brought on by her past, and he hadn't wanted her thinking he wasn't as tough as she'd believed. So he'd hidden behind his work, using it as an excuse for not being at home with Lyssa as often as he should've been. If only he'd overcome that fear and kept the lines of communication open, things might've turned out differently. Crunch time had come when he'd forgotten her birthday and while she'd packed her bags she'd yelled at him that he was selfish and didn't care about her.

Which couldn't be further from the truth. He had loved her but apparently not enough. He'd lost focus on his wife and their marriage while spending too much time brooding about his stuffed-up family and what they'd done to him and Jamie. He hadn't deserved her. Or, more bluntly, she deserved a hell of a lot better. But it'd still hurt when they split. He'd needed her support even when he hadn't told her about his father's duplicity. She had been quick to leave when life hadn't been all fun and laughter. He sighed. Unfortunately there was no undoing the past.

'I'm the charge nurse of the main hospital's cardiac ward.' Pride spilled out of her. She'd always had ambitions to be the best at what she did, and now it seemed she'd achieved at least one of those. No surprise there. He looked closer. She appeared so much more confident than the woman he'd married. The haunted look in her eyes had gone, those shapely shoulders were upright, not drooping, her spine was straight. Interesting.

'Here's your drink, Miss Cook.' Pepe held out a glass of champagne.

Leighton winced. Miss Cook. She'd dropped his surname. That shouldn't hurt, but for some unfathomable reason it did. He'd think about it later. Along with what he had to tell her about Jamie, because no way could he ask his brother to keep quiet when he had his own issues with their father. It would be impossible anyway. Some time in the next few days someone would mention them being brothers. It was time to put it out there without explaining why he hadn't told her four years ago. He wasn't going to give her all the details, just the basics.

'Thank you, Pepe.' Lyssa took the glass in a shaky hand. Turning back to Leighton, she frowned. 'So you're here for Jamie's wedding?'

'I'll be at the wedding, yes.' He wouldn't say he was the groomsman in case she already knew that was the role of Jamie's brother. A memory struck. Jamie saying, *'There's a nurse coming to the wedding on her own. You two will hit it off perfectly. She's just your type.'*

Great. He ground his teeth in frustration. That nurse had to be this one, his ex. He just knew it. He needed to talk to Jamie fast, and then Lyssa first thing in the morning. He was putting off the inevitable, but it was late and she looked shattered. She didn't do empathetic when she was overtired. Or she didn't used to. Nor had she stood so straight before. Something to be aware of. She'd changed and he had no idea who she was any more. They'd both have grown up a bit, having been quite young when they married.

'Alyssa, you finally made it.' Jamie joined them.

'It's been the day from hell but I'm here and all's good.' She gave his brother a brief hug. 'Where're the girls?'

'Collette's hit the sack. Says she needs her beauty sleep to look good for the wedding, though why she thinks that when she's beautiful I don't know. Some of the others are on the party bus that goes to various bars in town every night. They can't be far away.' Jamie was looking at him with a grin.

Leighton shook his head. It was not happening. 'Got a minute before I head home?'

Jamie frowned. 'I guess. Alyssa, those of us in the bar are about to head to our rooms but if you want company while you down that drink I'll be with you after I've heard whatever Leighton's got on his mind.'

At least he hadn't said 'my brother', Leighton thought with relief.

'Home?' Alyssa asked. She was quick. Again, no surprise.

'I'll be over with the others.' Jamie stepped away.

Leighton wasn't sure whether to be pleased or not. 'I've been here for five months working as a locum at one of the general practices.' She wouldn't know he'd left the medical centre he'd joined when they were together, and opted to work as a locum in general practices up and down New Zealand. There were lots of things she wouldn't know, and no doubt wouldn't want to. For her, finished had meant exactly that. It had for him too, though there'd been plenty of days he'd struggled to believe it because she'd always wanted so much of him. When he hadn't been trying to deny it, he'd missed her so much it hurt. Now the past had come back to bite him on the backside and he had to talk to her sooner rather than later. Maybe he should dive into it tonight, get it out of the way.

Alyssa's eyes had widened. 'You didn't keep the partnership in Remuera Medical Centre?'

'No. I'm working all over the place and enjoying it.'

Her smile was disarming. 'Go you.'

A fraction of the tension eased. 'It was a good decision.' He didn't have to get to know people too well and learn later he'd got them wrong.

A racket of laughter and music drowned out her reply.

'That's the party bus pulling in,' he said. The rest of the wedding party returning gave him the excuse he needed to escape. Now that his ex-wife had turned up he wasn't in the mood to sit around casually chatting. He'd be constantly on alert for anything Lyssa said. Alyssa, not Lyssa. That was in the past along with everything else.

Except technically they were still married as neither of them had filed for divorce. A kernel of hope for the future he'd deny if anyone asked kept him from finalising it. Why Lyssa hadn't done something the moment the two years required before a divorce could go through were up was beyond him. It had to be because she was busy and didn't need it, not because she was waiting around for a second shot at them getting together. Presumably she hadn't met someone else she wanted to marry. Hope rose, then disappeared. What was he thinking? They were finished. Over. But—she was beautiful and filled him with happy memories. There were plenty of those as well as the others.

'I was meant to be on that bus with the others,' she said. 'Never mind. We can party now.' Then she yawned and grimaced. 'Maybe not so much. It's been quite the day. With a double shift beforehand.'

The urge to wrap her in his arms was so strong he spun around and charged back to where he'd left his beer at the table Jamie was sitting at. He was not touching her. No hugs. No idle chit-chat. Nothing. They were long done for. She hadn't stayed around to support him when he needed it. Now he wanted to hug her? Get real, man. She should've known him well enough to understand something was wrong and that he needed her. He'd loved her, but had he really *known* her? Do it again and he'd lose his mind. She'd only let him down again and there was no way he'd manage the pain of that.

His gut cramped. So much for being over her. Of course he was. It was the shock at seeing her walk in catching up. Strange how he still felt that instant attraction to her after all that had gone down between them when they broke up. She'd stolen his heart the moment he'd set eyes on her five and a half years ago, sitting on a stool in the cafeteria, talking and laughing with other trainee nurses as though she hadn't a worry in the world. Which was untrue, as he'd come to find out over the next few months as they'd got to know each other. She had a lot of insecurities after losing her mother while still at school. There'd never been much money to go round and Lyssa had struggled financially. Naturally he'd helped out when they'd got together and she'd been studying to become a nurse.

Aren't you forgetting something?

Forgetting how at first she had tried to find out what his problem was and support him, but he wouldn't tell her what was going on, wouldn't share his pain and refused to let her in, no doubt making her feel worthless. He'd grappled with what he'd learned about his father and that had devastated him further. He'd told her he couldn't take any more. What he should've said was that he'd learned his parents weren't the people he'd believed them to be. But he was still trying to come to terms with that. The man he'd done so much with as a child and enjoyed fishing and hiking with in his teens was an out and out bastard.

Alyssa had never asked for a share of their matrimonial property when he'd sold it, or any of the possessions, all of which he'd bought because she hadn't had a dollar to her name. His family were wealthy, and he earned a good income that he'd happily shared with her. When he'd tried to deposit her share of the property finance into her bank account he'd learned she'd closed it. He mightn't love Alyssa now, but he certainly admired her for her fairness.

The beer suddenly tasted sour. Of course he hadn't forgotten any of what went down back then. Nor had he forgotten how much it had hurt when she left. He'd loved her with all he had, and still kept her at arm's length.

'So you already know Alyssa?' Jamie asked when he joined him.

'She's my ex-wife.'

Jamie stared at him. 'Hell. I knew you were married when we met but as I returned to the UK shortly after I never met your wife. Nor have you ever talked about her.' Now he was looking thoughtful. 'Wish I'd known.'

'What does it matter?' They still struggled talking to one another about anything that had gone on in their lives before they'd learned the other existed. Opening up about his family life when Jamie had missed out on knowing his father was difficult because *he* had been so happy growing up. It was just as difficult to talk about Alyssa.

Jamie crossed his legs, uncrossed them again, picked up his empty glass. 'Unfortunately there'll be no avoiding each other at the various evening events leading up to the wedding. We haven't got such a huge crowd of guests for you to hide amongst,' he added.

'Don't worry, we'll cope. We're adults.'

'What were the odds?' Jamie shook his head. 'I did think you two would get on great, but I'm a few years too late.'

'Ironic, huh?' Sadness filled him. He had loved Alyssa so much. Just seeing her brought back a load of memories and until those final months they were all good ones. Better than good. Wonderful. Sexy and caring. Sharing and fun. 'I'll see you tomorrow,' he said. 'I need to hit the sack.' He needed fresh air and quiet time to think about what Lyssa's appearance meant. 'I've got an early start tomorrow.'

Early in the Cook Islands meant any time after a late breakfast, though he was usually at the medical centre by eight. Mainly because there was nowhere else he had to be, or anyone to be with. Now he sounded sorry for himself. Better keep a straight face though. He couldn't have Alyssa seeing he wasn't totally engaged in the life he'd worked so hard to achieve. Bet she was wondering why he'd sold out of the medical practice he'd busted his gut to get into.

'We're meeting at the wharf at eleven,' Jamie reminded him.

Not that he needed it. The guys' fishing trip would be fun. He'd been out fishing once since arriving here and thoroughly enjoyed the experience. It was great how most of this week one of the other doctors was covering for him so he could spend time with Jamie. It *had* been perfect and then Lyssa had walked through the door. Now he was hurting when he had no reason to. So much for being over her. But he was. Wasn't he? Better be. He wasn't going through that pain again.

'See you at the wedding,' Lyssa said as he walked past her.

His head spun. She had no idea. 'I guess so.' There'd be no getting away from her over the coming days. Tomorrow the women were going out to the reef in a glass-bottomed boat while the men were fishing, but there was a barbecue arranged for everyone here at the resort, hopefully with the chef cooking any fish the guys caught.

'Leighton.' She had followed him.

He paused, needing to know what she might say, yet wishing she weren't here. After all this time the fear of rejection still nagged.

'You're looking good. I'm glad you're happy with your work choice.' Then she walked away, leaving him startled and with too much to think about. Which he didn't need right now, or ever.

Yet he couldn't take his eyes off her as she strode out

of the bar, head high, shoulders tight, and that sassy ass as curvy as ever, and making his body tight. Then she was gone, and he could inhale some air. Alyssa had come back into his world. However temporarily, it was going to be awkward. Might be interesting. No doubt about it. She'd changed. The new confidence suited her and made him want to learn more about who she'd become.

A man appeared in front of him. 'Dr Leighton, can you come? A lady fell off the bus and is bleeding.'

'Sure, Amiri.' Nothing like a bit of medicine to distract the mind. 'Is this woman a guest at the resort?' Hopefully not one of the wedding party. Thankfully Collette had opted to stay in for the night.

'No, she's not,' Amiri said as they headed outside. 'Here's the doctor. Let him through.'

Leighton reached the woman sprawled over the tarmac and winced. Alyssa was ahead of him, already dropping to her knees and taking a wad of tissues from someone to press onto what must be a head wound causing the bleeding. 'How bad?'

Alyssa's eyes widened, but all she said was, 'The bone's exposed.'

Crouching down, he tapped the woman's shoulder. 'Hello, I'm Leighton, a doctor. Can you tell me what happened?'

'I was pushed off the step by someone trying to get back on the bus after realising he was at the wrong hotel.'

'What's your name?' Alyssa asked.

'Michelle.' The woman blinked, looking confused.

A man crouched down beside them. 'She's Michelle Hopkins. We're staying at the family resort near the airport. She's my sister,' he added softly. 'I'm Andrew.'

Concussion was top of the list for injuries given she'd slammed her head onto something hard resulting in the injury. 'I'm going to do a quick look over her before driving her to the medical centre where I can fix her up.'

Alyssa shot him a startled look. 'No ambulance? She's not going to the hospital?'

'Things are done a little differently here.' He wasn't explaining the health system in front of the crowd of onlookers, but sometimes seeing a patient who was a visitor to the island in the medical centre saved hassles with insurance and the airline if the patient needed to return home in a hurry. Unless they were in a serious way, that was.

'I need some more tissues or paper towels.' Alyssa looked around and her eyes lit up. 'Pepe, can you get me some?'

'I'll be right back.'

'Is she going to be all right?' the brother asked. 'Wouldn't she be better going to the hospital?'

'I work at the local medical centre and we have all the equipment necessary to look after her.' As up to date as any in the hospital anyway. 'Your ankle's twisted, Michelle.'

'Leighton,' Alyssa said quietly. 'Her ear?'

It was torn away from the side of Michelle's face where more bleeding was going on. 'Are you on any medications?'

'Blood thinners,' Andrew answered for his sister.

That made perfect sense. It was going to take more than tissues to slow the bleeding. 'You'll need to stop taking them for the next two days so that the wound can start healing.'

'Is it safe to do that?' Michelle asked. Her thinking seemed to be getting clearer.

'Yes. It's no different than if you were to have surgery. The doctors would get you to stop taking the thinners to prevent haemorrhaging. Right, let's get moving. Alyssa, are you okay here while I get my car?' At least he'd called her *A*lyssa. Surprising when one look at her evoked so many Lyssa memories.

'Of course.'

Silly question, but he was being practical, not denigrating her medical abilities. 'I'll be right back.'

Their patient pushed up onto her elbows. 'Let me go. I want to get back on the bus.'

Alyssa gently pressed her down. 'I wouldn't recommend it. You've got a serious cut on your head that needs stitching.'

'You can't stop me going on the bus.'

Andrew leaned in. 'Sis, calm down. The bus is leaving and the driver doesn't want you on board like this.'

'I'll only be a minute,' Leighton said to anyone who was listening. His car was parked on the road outside the main entrance.

'I'm coming to the centre with you,' the brother called after him.

'No problem.' It'd be good having another pair of strong hands to lift the woman if she struggled to walk to the car.

It was also handy having Alyssa around. She was competent and unflappable, which always made things easier with difficult patients.

Fifteen minutes later they were at the medical centre and Michelle had become very subdued.

'Are you all right?' Alyssa asked her.

'Yes.' She nodded. 'Feeling stupid though. I've had a bit to drink.'

'That's the nature of a party bus.' Alyssa smiled. 'Now we have to get you fixed up. Leighton's got some sewing to do.'

He nodded. 'Take her through that door on your left while I get the equipment I need.'

'I'll wait out here,' Andrew told them. 'You don't want another patient on your hands if I faint.'

'You've done all right so far.'

'I wasn't looking.'

Lyssa laughed, sending inappropriate ripples of longing down Leighton's spine. He headed to the equipment room, glad of some space for a moment. Being around Lyssa wasn't easy, though he couldn't think of a better nurse to have at his side in this situation.

You have no idea what she's like when it comes to nursing.

He'd never worked with her, but she'd handled Michelle calmly.

Thirty minutes later the taxi he called drove away with Michelle and Andrew and his phone number, along with a list of instructions about taking care of the wound and ankle and signs of concussion to look out for, and Leighton sighed. 'I'll give you a ride back to Seaview, Lyssa.' Alyssa, not Lyssa, he reminded himself. Old habits.

'Thanks. I've got a rental car booked but the office was closed when I arrived. I'll deal with it in the morning.' She headed outside without waiting for him.

'Big day?' he asked once they were on the road.

'Very. At least I'll be able to sleep in.' She tipped her head back and closed her eyes. Conversation over.

He'd go along with that. There wasn't anything to talk about anyway. Other than his brother. But he wasn't doing that when she was half asleep. He needed to be sitting down looking at Alyssa with his wits about him when he told her about Jamie. Right now he was more in need of sleep than an argument or trying to explain himself. As if sleep would be possible. His body was firing up on all cylinders with Alyssa this close.

Of course, sleep wasn't an option when he got home. Alyssa's sudden reappearance in his world wound him up tighter than a coil so he took a mug of tea out onto his deck and sat staring into the distance, hearing the waves crashing on the reef as he fought the picture of his wife now front and foremost in his mind. Thinking about making love to her. How she'd cry out his name as she came. One touch from her light fingers and he'd be gone. Yeah, his body could remember those touches. Her heat. Her body accepting his.

Jamie had hoped they'd naturally gravitate towards each other because he was into matchmaking and thought everyone should be as happy as he and Collette, but to believe Alyssa would be right for him made Leighton shiver.

He'd laugh, only it was painful even thinking about her.

Because unfortunately his brother was right. He and Alyssa had been made for each other, until reality had got in the way.

Reality as in learning that he had a brother he'd never known about. More reality had come to the fore as he'd found out how his father had paid Jamie's mother to keep quiet about his role in bringing Jamie into the world. His father had had an affair with his wife's best friend and Jamie was the result. He'd become the financial provider for Jamie as long as the boy never learned his identity. Jamie's mother had gone along with the deal because she'd wanted Jamie to have every opportunity possible in life, but she'd left a letter to be given to him on her death that named his father and why she'd sworn to keep his name a secret.

When he'd found all that out Leighton had been stunned, and hurt. He had a brother he hadn't known existed. It had explained the state of his parents' marriage and the sometimes awkward atmosphere between them.

But it was no excuse for not being open with Alyssa so that she could've had the opportunity to support him. He hadn't made it easy for her to stay. He'd been hoping she'd understand he needed her without being told, which was ridiculous really. By not talking he'd done what he'd most wanted to avoid—become secretive like his parents.

It was that more than the hurtful things she'd said that had kept him from asking her for a second chance. She hadn't known his true family. If she'd found out about Jamie and his father's affair, would she have believed him to be like his father in every respect? He couldn't face finding out. After she'd gone, the first bombshell about Jamie had been followed by another when he'd learned his father had also treated Alyssa appallingly and he'd been ashamed to be the son of a man who hurt women. Worse, by refusing to talk to her he'd done much the same. He could still see the anguish in her face when she'd packed her belongings and left, accusing him of shutting her out of his life. What cut deep was that she'd been right.

Now she appeared to have moved on with her career and made new friends along the way. From what he'd observed while helping Michelle she was different: stronger, self-assured, focused. It could be a front to keep him at arm's length, but he doubted it.

He'd left the medical centre to take on locum jobs, moving all over the country, unable to settle anywhere for long. His own ambitions had gone down the drain along with his belief in his family. Not only his father's appalling behaviour but his mother's acceptance of it had riled him.

Where had Alyssa been over the past four years? In the beginning he'd heard she moved to Perth, Australia, but after that her whereabouts were unknown to him. There was nothing he could have done for her, other than tell her the truth and he hadn't been prepared to do that for fear she'd despise him by association with his father.

But the time had arrived when there was no avoiding the truth, which just made it clear he should've got it out of the way right back when it mattered the most, because once Lyssa heard what he had to say she'd be even more glad she'd left him.

CHAPTER TWO

ALYSSA OPENED HER eyes and rolled over to look around the bungalow. Sun streamed in around the edges of the blinds and the temperature was toasty. She'd been so exhausted she couldn't remember getting into bed last night and had no memory of taking a shower but the damp-looking towel on the rail indicated she had. Not even Leighton running around in her head had kept her awake. Unbelievable because his presence last night had shocked her to pieces.

Loud knocking on the door grabbed her attention. Was that what woke her?

Go away. I'm on holiday.

But she scrambled out of bed and snatched the resort bathrobe off the back of the door because it had to be one of her friends. She tripped. Or Leighton. She so wasn't ready to see him. Anyway, why would he be here?

'About time.' Collette laughed when she opened the door. 'We gave up waiting for you to join us for breakfast by the pool, but you can't sleep the whole day away. We've got a boat trip starting in under two hours.'

'What's the time?'

'Ten fifteen.' Collette stepped around her to gaze at the accommodation. 'I heard you got an upgrade. Well done.'

'Is coffee supplied? Or do I need to ring for some?' Coffee was the only thing that would get her moving. Her body felt like concrete.

'It should be here any second.' Collette's smile slipped. 'I'm here before the others gatecrash your peace and quiet because I've got a confession to make.'

A chill touched her warm skin. She had no idea what Collette was talking about but something about her stance suggested she wasn't going to be happy. 'Let's sit on the deck in the sun.'

'Here's the coffee.' Collette took the mugs Pepe held out. Did he work everywhere, every hour? 'Thank you.'

'Did you sleep well, Alyssa?' Pepe asked.

'I was unconscious all night.'

'That's got to be good in the circumstances,' Collette murmured as she headed for the deck and Pepe left them alone.

The first two mouthfuls of coffee went down fast and Alyssa started to come alive. 'Come on, spill. You look like you've swallowed a lemon.'

'You're not going to be pleased with us.'

Us? 'You and Jamie?' The picture was becoming clearer. 'This is to do with Leighton, isn't it?'

'The thing is we didn't know you used to be married to him.'

So Leighton had told Jamie. No surprise. It had to come out some time. 'Why would you? I didn't know Leighton and Jamie knew each other, and even if I had I wouldn't have mentioned him. We're finished, been separated for years.' The second man to abandon her, even if she had been the one who'd left.

She'd never known her father. He did a runner before

she was born and apparently died in a boating accident when she was about eight. She'd clung to her mother even more after that. Despite the lack of money everything had been fun if her mother was involved. Except cancer stole her mum away when Alyssa was seventeen, leaving her with a burning desire to become a nurse after caring for her mother over the last months of her life.

Words poured out of Collette. 'Jamie's been up to his old matchmaking tricks. We arranged for you two to sit together at the wedding dinner. He really thought you'd hit it off.'

She'd have laughed, except it wasn't funny. 'He's a bit late for that.' More coffee went down her throat. Great. Her ex would be beside her at the wedding. They could be civil to each other. They'd managed with looking after Michelle last night without getting in each other's face. They'd do it again, and this time there would be lots of laughter and fun going on around them to make it easier. 'It's all right. Honestly.' She'd do her darnedest to make sure it was.

'Thanks.' Collette stared over the pool. 'You never talk about your past relationships.'

'What's there to say? We were happily married, then it went belly up and I'm running solo.'

'You don't think you'll try again?'

'With Leighton? No, I won't.' Once hurt was more than enough.

'There are other good men out there.'

'Alyssa?' Leighton stood with a woman beside the deck. 'Kara's from the car rental company. Can she come through?'

'Of course.' The coffee regurgitated in her stomach. What was he doing here?

'I brought coffee but I see Collette beat me to it.' Worry filled Leighton's eyes as he glanced at her friend. Wondering what Lyssa's reaction was to learning they had to share a table?

'Think I need to get dressed.' A shower would have to wait. 'I'll be quick.' Alyssa headed inside without waiting for anyone's comment. So much for a slow get-up on the first morning of her holiday. There was a crowd out there. One person in particular was very attractive and disconcerting.

Damn you, Leighton. We're long finished. I shouldn't feel anything for you.

When she returned outside, Kara held out a set of keys. 'Hello, Alyssa. I'm sorry we were closed when you arrived last night, but Dr Leighton told us you're staying here. Your car's now parked outside the resort.' The young woman looked uncomfortable. 'I just need to get you to sign some paperwork and show me your licence.'

Leighton organised this? Why? They weren't a couple, not even friends. 'That's kind of you to bring the car here. I could've gone in and got it. Please don't worry about last night. It was probably better I wasn't driving anyway. I was very tired.'

'Thank you.' Kara smiled softly.

Leighton looked relieved. Did he think she'd give Kara a telling off for not waiting for her to arrive? If so, he didn't know her very well. Then again, he'd probably forgotten more about her than he remembered. If only she could do the same, but it seemed there were a lot of things she was suddenly remembering. Like how a kiss could turn her into jelly. Or the way he'd generously make sure she always had enough money in her account not to have to go without anything, because sharing was his nature. The times he'd helped her with her study leading up to the nursing finals. His hands on her hips as he pulled her over him to make love.

Her body slumped. He had been perfect. Until it all went wrong. She reached for the paperwork. Time to stop thinking about the past. She no longer needed propping up on the difficult days. Having grown a backbone, she did that all by herself. Having to totally rely on herself for decisions about everyday things had strengthened her resilience big time.

Ten minutes later she'd signed the rental papers and was looking over the yellow sporty-looking car with its top down. Swinging the keys in her fingers, she grinned. 'Awesome. I'll take it for a spin shortly.' The air blowing through her messy hair and over her face would clear the cobwebs from her mind. And the heat brought on by Leighton from her body.

Collette appeared beside her. 'Don't go without me. I'll be by the pool with the others. They'll want to come too.'

'Let's go now.' So much for thinking they'd have a chinwag.

'Leighton's waiting to talk to you.' Collette looked everywhere but at her.

Dread filled her. 'What's going on?'

'Nothing. I'll see you later if we don't have time for a car ride. We're meeting out here at midday for the van that's picking us up to go along to Muri for the boat trip.' Her friend headed into the resort's main building at a fast clip.

The dread increased as she returned to the bungalow. 'Leighton, why are you here?' she demanded the moment she stepped onto the deck. 'I need a shower and then want to take the car for a spin before going out with the girls.' Being sidetracked by Leighton's good looks and gorgeous eyes wasn't an excuse for sitting around. 'I don't have time to chew things over with you.' They didn't have anything to talk about. They were history.

Then she recalled the look on Collette's face and knew she was wrong. 'What's going on?'

'Here's another coffee if you want it.' He handed her the paper cup he'd brought with him and went to stand by the railing, staring out over the beach beyond the pool area.

He was so still and quiet, she was puzzled. And worried. This was nothing like the man she'd known, who was always under control, taking charge. He looked uncertain. Definitely not her Leighton. Worry bells began ringing. What had happened? Did he need her support about something? Could she give it to him after what went down years ago? Yes, absolutely. There was no way she wouldn't. No matter what they'd said to each other back then, she still cared enough to want to be there for him if needed. He was the only man she'd ever loved. There'd always be a place in her heart for him, no matter how awful their break-up was. She sank onto a chair, not taking her eyes off him for a moment. 'Leighton?'

He turned to face her. 'Jamie's my brother.'

That wasn't a problem between her and Leighton that needed sorting. Phew. Then what he'd said hit her. 'Jamie and you are brothers? But—' She stopped before she said something inept and stupid. There hadn't been a brother in sight when she knew him. There had to be more to this. 'Go on.'

He drank some coffee and stared at the deck between them. Then he crossed to sit beside her. 'We're half-brothers. My father had an affair with my mother's best friend and Jamie's the result. I never knew until Jamie turned up on our doorstep.'

The coffee was warm on her tongue, but what Leighton said made her blood boil. She'd loathed John Harrison for how he'd treated her, he'd never felt she was good enough for Leighton or their family, but this was far worse. For Leighton *and* Jamie. 'What happened for Jamie to come and tell you?'

'His mother died. That's when he learned who his father was, and, after some research, found me. He came from the UK where he was specialising to tell me the sordid details, even brought DNA results as proof. All those years as kids that we missed out on.' Leighton drained his cup before turning to her with such despair in his eyes that the urge to hug him swamped her.

She held her cup tight in both hands. She was not hugging Leighton. She'd never let him go. Not a good idea. 'Continue.'

Drawing a deep breath, he rushed on. 'You were at work the day he turned up at home. It was a deliberate move as he didn't want anyone else to know until he'd talked to me. I think he was afraid I'd send him packing, and if you were there you might have stood up for me and undermined everything he had to say.'

Quite likely. She wouldn't have accepted the news without digging into the proof first. 'You never mentioned any of this.'

'No. I am so very sorry I didn't.'

The lights were starting to go on in her head. 'This happened around the time we stopped communicating so well by any chance?'

'Yes.'

'If only I'd known.' What difference would it have made? For one, she'd have helped Leighton deal with the shock by being there with a shoulder to lean on and letting him talk it through uninterrupted. It must've been hell, at the very least. Then she'd left him—because he hadn't seemed to care for her or them any more. Maybe he hadn't. He had a brother he'd known nothing about and parents who'd betrayed him.

But, 'We were married, Leighton. In love and supposed to share everything, not just how the day had been or who we'd seen.' What else had he kept from her? She was getting angry. He'd had no right to hide this from her. She'd been his other half. Or so she'd believed. But when he'd withdrawn from her she'd been reminded how her father hadn't wanted her and she'd started protecting her heart too.

'Yes.'

'That's it? Yes.' When he said nothing, she continued. 'Our marriage fell apart because you withdrew from me. You'd spend hours at work studying or doing extra hours in the medical centre and not coming home to have a meal with me or go to bed to make love and curl up together. I felt redundant.'

'Really?'

'Yes, really.'

'I see.' He still wasn't really talking to her. He'd covered the basics and that was it.

Not good enough. She'd loved him, and would've done anything for him. The old her might've let him get away with this, but not any more. 'I need more, Leighton. Why didn't you tell me?' she snapped. Seriously? How could he not have talked to her? Enough so she'd understood why he was so withdrawn. They might've saved their marriage. 'I deserved better. So did you.'

He stretched his legs out in front of him and studied the view beyond as if it were about to disappear for ever. 'I was angry at Dad for never telling me I had a brother. Like, *really* angry. Jamie should've been a part of the family scene even with his mother being my mum's friend. I also felt hurt and bewildered. Dad wasn't who I'd believed.'

'That would've been very awkward for everyone.' Leighton's mother would've been hard on Jamie. She was an unforgiving woman at the best of times so to accept Jamie on the scene would've been impossible, and who could blame her? Alyssa was beginning to understand the woman a little better. Her husband and her friend had had an affair and produced a son along the way. Appalling. 'I do understand you missed out on so much with Jamie.'

'Mum has had nothing to do with her friend since she learned about the affair.'

'But she stayed with your father.' The woman did like the comfortable lifestyle, but that much?

'No comment.' The bitterness in his voice said more than any words could.

Alyssa dropped the subject of Leighton's mother. It was only rubbing in salt. 'You and Jamie seem to get along fine.' Funny that she'd never heard Leighton's name mentioned whenever she was with Collette and Jamie.

Then again, Jamie was usually working when she and Collette did anything together outside the hospital. Besides, she never mentioned Leighton to anyone.

'Unbelievably well considering. I readily accepted Jamie. Once I saw the DNA proof there was no argument, and I was glad he'd sought me out. Having a brother is special.'

Again her blood heated.

I wasn't told any of this.

'You really didn't believe in us. In me.' Or surely he'd have talked to her about Jamie and the impact it had on him? They'd been married, loved each other. Didn't that mean they should have shared everything? So much for thinking he couldn't hurt her any more. He just had. Badly. Any trust she might've had when it came to sharing her heart had flown out of the window. Why did he marry her in the first place?

He gulped. 'I struggled to take it all in and accept I'd been lied to all my life. My emotions were all over the place. When I approached Dad with the news that I'd met Jamie he blustered, said he didn't know what I was talking about, then when I showed him the proof he went ballistic, accusing Jamie's mother of breaking the contract she'd signed where she'd accepted payments every month until Jamie turned twenty-one on the grounds she never told him or anyone else who his father was.'

John Harrison was a wealthy man and believed money was the answer to all life's problems. 'No surprise there.'

Leighton turned to her and touched her hand gently. 'He also said that you were stupid for turning down his offer of a payment to go away. I was stunned. You never told me that, Alyssa. Why?'

'It was between your father and me. To tell you would've put pressure on you. You adored John. I didn't want to make you feel you had to choose between us. Don't say you wouldn't have had to, because knowing he'd offered me money to leave you and how much I loved you would've raised barriers between all of us.'

She'd spent many hours considering the ramifications of telling Leighton, and it had always come back to the fact he thought his father could do no wrong and she didn't want to be the one to destroy that. It wasn't her fault John was rotten to the core but it wasn't her place to tell his son. She'd loved Leighton so much she hadn't wanted to hurt him, but she had to acknowledge what he'd be thinking. 'I accept you might be upset I didn't mention it. I'm more upset that you didn't talk to me about Jamie. Why didn't you?'

He swallowed. 'I know I should've approached it differently, but at the time it wasn't easy.'

'And now?'

'I accept I stuffed up, okay? But we weren't getting on great before Jamie turned up. You were spending more and more time with your friends.'

'Because you were never there,' she snapped.

'I was busy with work and studying, then had to grapple with my father's deceit on top of that. You obviously didn't notice anything was wrong. Or you didn't care.'

'What?' she gasped. Of course she'd cared. She'd loved him. This was unbelievable. She spun away, turned back to stare at him. Had she ever really known him?

'Alyssa, I'm sorry. That came out wrong. I know you loved me.'

'You just put it all back on me and then an apology is

supposed to fix it?' She pointed at him. 'You could've sat down with me and got everything out in the open. I'd never have left you to cope alone. Never.'

He stared at her, raw pain in his eyes. 'We weren't getting on well,' he said defensively.

She shook her head. 'I don't believe you didn't trust me enough.' Her chest ached and her head spun. This was too much to deal with.

His mouth flattened. 'I'd better go. We need to cool down before we say anything else to hurt each other.'

'Sure.' He was running away. But she did need space to absorb everything he'd said—and what he hadn't said. 'Just remember I'd never have left you to go through that alone.'

She might've left him in a fit of anger, but he hadn't talked to her much for weeks, even months prior. It'd been like living with a flatmate who worked opposite hours. Had she been fair? She'd had no idea what was going on and thought he'd fallen out of love with her. It had felt as if those who were meant to love her left her one way or another. What if she had insisted they talk? Would he have told her everything? Would they still be together? Her heart slowed. Was she just as much at fault?

'I mean it,' she snapped at his back as he left. She wanted to say more but let it go. Nothing to be gained by revisiting all the angst of those days.

Watching him walk away, she suddenly felt she was missing out on love. Leighton had been her love. Now he was here and winding her up in every way possible, and still her heart did a dance at the sight of him.

The coming week was going to be difficult with this anger sitting between them. She had to put it behind her fast. They were separated. Though not divorced. Why Leighton hadn't filed was beyond her. He usually kept on top of things, didn't like leaving anything hanging over him. She hadn't done anything about it either. She'd been busy with her career, but it would've only taken one visit to a lawyer to get the ball rolling. Hadn't she wanted to divorce him? Had she been hoping deep down that they might still love each other? Not likely. And less so now.

Her morning had gone belly up and now she needed to put aside her distress while out with the girls. They were not going to know about this.

'Lyssa.' Leighton was back at the gate. 'I know I should've talked to you about Jamie. I am truly sorry for not doing so.'

'My name's Alyssa, not Lyssa.' Not any more.

That was special between us and special has gone.

Alyssa wouldn't forgive him easily, if at all. Leighton kicked a stone lying on the kerb and cursed the blue sky grey. Did it matter? They weren't together any more, weren't in love and thinking happy families in the future.

But it still mattered what she thought about him. No getting away from that.

He couldn't believe how much he wanted her understanding and acceptance for screwing up. It had been a difficult time and he'd blown it. Not everything had been his fault though. Once Lyssa, no, Alyssa—yes, he had heard her say that—qualified as a nurse she'd changed. She'd wanted to have the fun she'd never had as an adult, while he was still training as a GP, which had involved long, exhausting hours at the medical centre or in front of his computer. Truly, she had deserved to let her hair down after all the study, and the year spent nursing her mother. They couldn't get it right to be able to spend time together and strengthen their relationship. They'd crashed at the first hurdle, looking out for themselves instead of joining together and growing as a couple. If only he'd had the guts to tell her everything.

His father had put pressure on him to stay away from Jamie, saying it would only hurt his mother. As if it were his fault his mother had been hurt, and nothing to do with the result of his father's infidelity. She never talked about Jamie when he tried to find out more. Instead her stiff upper lip only got stiffer. He'd never felt unloved by her. They just had a different relationship from the close one he'd had with his father. Not that he blamed his mother, considering what her friend and husband had done, but he'd never understood why she stayed with his dad. Not even the fact she came from a poor background should've been enough to continue with their marriage. It wouldn't be for him. But then he wasn't an expert on making a marriage survive the pressures of everyday life. He and Alyssa hadn't made the grade, which had him wondering if he was cut out for love and commitment. Especially after learning how shallow his parents' relationship was and how the life they'd led had hidden a lot of ugly truths, and made him question how genuine their professed love for him was.

No wonder he moved around for work so much these days. He didn't feel he belonged anywhere with anyone. Now catching up with Lyssa had him wondering if deep down he'd been looking for her.

'You want a lift to the wharf?' Jamie called out.

Turning, he saw his brother and the other guys standing

by the van taking them to the fishing boat. No, he didn't want to go along and act as if he were happy right now. There was a hole in his heart that needed plugging, put there by the shock and disappointment that had crossed Alyssa's face while he'd been talking about Jamie. He still cared about her. More than he'd have thought when he'd got out of bed yesterday morning with no idea who was turning up that night. That he did have these feelings rattled him. They'd already argued, and there was more he should tell her. Until he did she'd turn her back on him if he showed he cared.

'Leighton?' Jamie stood in front of him. 'Get a grip. You're still in one piece. Alyssa now knows everything and you can put it behind you.'

'You're so practical,' he growled. Jamie was wrong. Alyssa didn't know everything. It wasn't that easy to tell her. She was such a huge part of his past dreams that seeing her again upset the deliberate calm he held over his emotions.

Laughter from the resort foyer had him turning. There she was, that gorgeous long blonde hair falling over her shoulders as she talked animatedly with her friends. He used to run his fingers through her hair, soft and silky against his skin, lighting him up and making him want her in an instant. Damn, how he'd loved her. His hands tingled with a yearning to touch her.

Spinning around, he headed towards the guys getting into the van. There was some fishing to do. Nothing like a big fish fighting the line to take his mind off annoying memories. That was all these thoughts were. Memories of a time when he'd been in love and happy and thinking he had nothing to worry about. Memories of a wonderful smile that could light up his bleakest moods, of being held tight after watching a patient bleed out on the table in front of him and not being able to save the person.

Memories being overtaken by a more mature and beautiful Alyssa who was getting to him as she did the first time they met. Her sweet smile had become confident and beguiling. Those green eyes that used to fill with caution in an instant now full of laughter and self-belief. She was so intriguing—and tempting, which was a worry as he was not following up on these feelings.

'Hey, Leighton, isn't this better than checking some patient's blood pressure and telling them they need to be more careful about what they eat?' asked Dan, a cardiologist who worked with Jamie. He looked as if he was trying to make Leighton forget whatever was bothering him.

'You bet.' These guys were a good lot, and he'd become a part of their group without any effort. He owed it to them to give the same back. 'Or it will be when I catch the biggest fish of the day.'

'Oh, right, here we go. Our local GP thinks he's going to show us up, guys.' Dan laughed.

'When was the last time you went fishing off the reef here?' Jamie asked with a grin, and with concern in his eyes.

Leighton squeezed into one of the back seats. 'A month ago. It was a bit of a fail, but I've heard a lot of success stories in the bar over a beer more often than I can remember.'

'Beer and a fishing story? Expect them to be truthful?' Dan rolled his eyes.

'Good point, but I'll give you a big story to take home with you,' Leighton retorted. Hopefully. 'Or I'll shout the first round when we get back.' He'd set himself up for a fall, but all in good fun. It was time to let Alyssa and the past go. Again. But hell, she was gorgeous. He got in a twist just looking at her. A very familiar twist he hadn't experienced in years—since she left him. There'd been the occasional fling to scratch an itch but not a woman to sidetrack him enough to think about a future relationship.

CHAPTER THREE

'I'M GOING FOR a spin. Anyone want to join me?' Alyssa asked her friends. There was a little time to spare and she needed to do something, anything, so she could stop thinking about Leighton and what he'd told her. Having Collette in the car with her wouldn't be a problem. Her friend knew when to keep quiet. She wasn't someone to talk for the sake of it, and she'd understand how Leighton's news would've rocked her. 'We've got an hour before we need to be ready to go to Muri for the boat trip.' She'd exaggerated the need to get ready when talking to Leighton to get him out of her space while she grappled with his news. A look around the island might help calm her down.

'Yes,' was the answer all round.

'We're going to look cool in your car.' Collette laughed. Moving closer she asked, 'You all right?'

'Yes.' Be honest. 'And no. There's a lot to take in, but nothing's changed. Our marriage is over, and that's not going to be any different.'

'That's a pity. I reckon Jamie's right. You two are right for each other.'

Hearing that raised something like hope. Alyssa's head banged on the inside. She wanted to shove a sock in Collette's mouth. When she wasn't angry with him Leighton was still capable of heating her from top to toe with only a smile. Thankfully there hadn't been too many of those moments or she'd be a puddle by now. His honesty about Jamie had been too late, but there'd been pain as he'd talked and that opened her heart some, making her want to get closer to support him. She felt he had more to tell that could hurt her. A good reason to remain cautious.

'Cut it out, Collette. There isn't a hope in Hades we could get back together. Apparently I wasn't there for Leighton when he needed me, and he couldn't trust me enough to tell me what was going on.'

Not that she'd realised how bad he was feeling. Had she been too into her own need to get out and catch up on having the fun she'd missed out on growing up? During her final year at high school she'd looked after her mother through the last months of her life as cancer ate her away. She'd missed out on socialising with friends, instead spending what spare time there was working on school assignments to gain good marks. Her teachers had supported her, encouraging her to do her best. She'd done well enough to get into nursing school and had studied hard to make her mum proud of her even though she'd never know. It had been difficult, and then she'd met Leighton and fallen in love. Everything had been wonderful. Except there'd been holes in their relationship she hadn't seen.

Collette climbed into the front seat. 'I think Leighton's pleased to see you despite everything.'

'Sure.' As if Leighton had any reason to want to get back in her good books. He'd always been a good guy at heart, but it'd be going too far to think he might want to spend time with her. She'd believed he'd been glad to see the back of her four years ago. As far as she was aware nothing had happened since to make him think differently.

But then she wouldn't know, would she? They knew nothing about what the other had been up to in the intervening years, and she didn't need to know now. He might have a partner, for all she knew. She swallowed the spurt of jealousy. He was free to do as he liked. Damn it. Or he could be like her and focused mainly on his career by running solo. Wishful thinking?

'Where should we go?'

'The main road does a circuit of the island. Follow that and you'll get an idea of where everything is. It only takes about forty-five minutes, so we'll still be in time to meet up with Mum and my sister for the boat trip,' Collette answered. 'We're being picked up here so if we're a few minutes late they'll wait for us.'

'Let's do it,' Alyssa said with a grin, all feelings of exhaustion gone. To hell with her past. For now.

'Better warn you the speed limit is very low all over the island,' Collette said as they pulled out of the car park. 'But we're in Rarotonga and everything's great,' said the happy bride-to-be.

Again a feeling of longing struck Alyssa. Her wedding day had been quiet as it'd been a long weekend and most of their friends had already made plans to be away when they made the sudden decision to marry before Leighton's final exams six weeks later. They'd opted to get married by a celebrant in a restaurant where they had a superb lunch with their few guests before heading to an upmarket hotel that they didn't leave until Monday night.

She'd missed her mother more than ever that day. She'd have adored Leighton and been proud of her daughter. It didn't help Alyssa that she wasn't welcome in Leighton's family, but she'd known that from the beginning because John Harrison had told her she wasn't good enough for them, and Jean had kept reminding her she had no taste in clothes or anything else. When John had offered what was to her a small fortune to disappear out of Leighton's life she'd been shocked, then angry. She'd told him where to stick his money and received an even bigger offer, which had only made her more determined to see the man lose the battle. Though he'd won in the end without spending a dollar.

'Is that the medical centre you went to last night?' Andrea asked from the back seat. 'Looks like the one Leighton said he works at.'

'Yes, that's it.' It was modern and practical. She still couldn't see Leighton working here even if only for a few months. Being laid-back was one thing, but Leighton had to be kept busy or he got antsy. That was the man who'd always got her in a twist with a look. Not a lot had changed in that respect. She'd been in a twist when she first saw him last night, and again when he'd walked onto her deck with coffee in hand this morning. But it was possible he no longer had to keep busy every minute of his day. And night. That was one busy thing about him she'd loved. His hands were always touching, caressing, lighting her up in ways she'd never have dreamed of before she met him.

'Wonder if they need a nurse? I could handle working here.' Gina laughed.

Alyssa tuned out from the light banter going on

amongst the others, instead concentrating on driving and noting places to return to over the coming days. There were cafés and bars everywhere. Plenty of beaches too. She wouldn't be short of things to do, though once this lot returned home it might be a little quiet. Unless she dropped in on Leighton. Great. That was not the best idea she'd had.

'The resort's around the next corner,' Collette warned her.

'That went fast,' she said. 'I'll have to do the loop again to really get my bearings.'

'There's the van for the boating trip.'

'I haven't got my gear together,' Alyssa said. 'I'll be a couple of minutes.'

'We should've changed into our bikinis before you took us for a drive. Would've looked the part in this car.'

She was more than glad she hadn't changed earlier when Leighton was still around. She might have given him something to choke over if he'd looked her way. There again, he probably wouldn't care one way or the other. The red bikini she'd bought last week left little to the imagination. Much the same as the other two she'd bought after being told by Collette she'd spend a lot of time in or beside a pool or snorkelling in the sea looking at the colourful fish and turtles.

'See you back here shortly.' She needed to throw on a little make-up and loads of sunblock, and she'd be ready.

'Bring your underwater camera,' Collette called.

'Will do.' Plus her phone, sun hat and towel, and a shirt for when she cooled off—if she ever did. Racing to the bungalow, she felt happier than she'd been in so long. Suddenly not even the idea of bumping into Leighton was hindering her fun. She was truly on holiday and going to enjoy every moment. Starting now. Really? Really.

'First we're having a barbecue lunch on the islet on the Muri lagoon,' the boat captain told them all as the boat left the beach at Muri. 'My men are already there setting up.'

Judging by the delicious smells wafting through the air when they all clambered ashore the men had been there for a while. 'That's making me hungry.' Collette laughed.

'So we're having two barbecues in one day?' Alyssa grinned. 'As long as the guys catch some fish, that is. Where were they going?'

'Out beyond the reef somewhere. Jamie wasn't too sure about the details as Leighton arranged it all. Like he did almost everything for the week, including this trip we're doing.'

Leighton… Leighton. There was no getting away from him. After so long apart it was strange how easily he came to life in her head. Tall, broad shoulders, slim hips and thick dark blond hair made him good-looking and interesting. The very first time she ever saw him she'd felt a moment of panic, as though her life had changed for ever. Turned out that was true, if not in the way she'd expected. They'd hit it off immediately and were hardly ever out of each other's lives from then on. Only work had kept them apart and the catch-up afterwards had been hot and heavy and wonderful. Six months later they'd married and her world had been a garden of roses. Sweet smelling, colourful and glorious.

'You okay?' Collette asked. 'It must've been a shock

seeing him at the resort last night.' She knew where Alyssa's mind had gone.

'Can't say it wasn't. But I'm good.'

'I hope so.'

'This week's about you and Jamie, not me. I'm making the most of not having to prioritise patients and staff. I can't believe it's been more than two years since I had a proper holiday.'

'Let's celebrate with a cold drink.'

'I'm sticking to water until we're back at the resort. Call me boring but I prefer to be safe than sorry.' Champagne would've been great but there'd be plenty of time later for that. At the barbecue with the guys, and Leighton. See? Leighton was always there, whichever way she looked or thought.

'Lemonade for me,' Collette said.

The steaks and salads were as delicious as they'd smelt and then they were back on the glass-bottomed boat heading out to the reef where numerous colourful small fish soon came into view.

'Right, ladies, you can go overboard and swim with the fish. They won't be frightened away. Take lots of photos to show your families back home and then they'll come for a visit too.'

When it was her turn to slip into the water, Alyssa dropped off the edge of the boat fast and seemed to go down for ever.

Where's the bottom?

All around her the other women seemed to have paused, as though they'd reached the bottom while she kept going. Panicking, she began clawing at the sea, trying to get back to the top. Nothing happened, she was suspended in the water. Kicking hard, she gasped and swallowed a mouthful of salt water.

Don't cough. Kick again.

Finally she began rising to the surface. When her head burst out of the water she gasped mouthfuls of air while spitting out the salt water. Grabbing the side of the boat, she clung on tight.

'You all right?' a crew member called out.

'I want to get back on the boat,' she cried and took the hand reaching down to her. A moment later she was sprawled on the deck, coughing hard, bringing up salt water.

'What happened?' Andrea was beside her.

'I don't know. I kept going down and down and I swallowed a mouthful of water and started to panic.'

'Are you all right?'

Breathing in deep, she realised she was despite the knocking under her ribs. 'I'm fine.'

'Drink this.' The crewman held out a bottle of water. 'It's not very deep, but if you're not used to jumping into water above your head you can get a shock,' he said.

She hadn't jumped, she'd just let go and dropped down. 'Scary.'

'I'll stay with you for a bit,' Andrea said.

'No way. Go and see the fish.' She wasn't spoiling someone else's afternoon.

'Truth is I don't like being in the water,' Andrea told her. 'I nearly drowned as a kid and have hated swimming ever since.'

Coughing up more salt water, Alyssa nodded. 'I can understand that.' But she was all right, and there were fish to be seen. 'I'll go a lot slower next time.'

Everything was fine when she did, though she stayed close to the boat to be able to grab hold if she panicked again.

'Leighton, can you check on Alyssa? She swallowed a bucket load of salt water when she jumped off the boat.'

Thanks, Collette.

'I didn't jump in and I'm fine now.' They were back at the resort where the guys were celebrating a successful fishing trip with some beers. 'I'm going to have a shower and get changed into something more comfortable.' The bikini was fine out on the boat but not here in the bar with Leighton hanging around. It made *her* so aware of *him* when she was meant to be wary. All back to front. Go figure.

'I'll come with you.' Leighton was moving towards her.

'I am fine,' she reiterated.

'You probably are but I won't relax until I know for certain.'

Her stomach dropped. She did not want him in her bungalow. It was cosy but not when the second person was Leighton. 'I'm fine,' she repeated, getting nowhere because Leighton followed her inside anyway.

'What happened in the water? Did you gasp and take in a lungful?'

'I went over the side of the boat too fast and got a fright. When I returned to the top I spat out water a few times. That's all.'

I was scared silly but that's for me to know.

'Hold out your wrist.'

'My pulse is fine. Andrea checked it.'

'I want to be certain, Lyssa.' He swallowed hard. 'Sorry, Alyssa.'

Sorry? That hurt. Shouldn't, but it did. Holding out her wrist, she tried to ignore the warmth emanating from his fingers, heating her where she didn't need it.

He focused on his watch as he counted her pulse, almost as though he were practising on a dummy. Too focused, as in aware of her and not wanting to be?

Her pulse was probably going crazy. Not because she'd swallowed too much salt water but because of standing this close to Leighton. Too many memories came with those firm fingers. Memories she'd thought were long forgotten. Or was this new? Was she seeing him through new eyes? She shivered. Surely not?

'Your pulse is normal. Have you been coughing a lot since getting out of the water?'

'No. I told you, there's nothing wrong. I was surrounded by nurses who all had to check me out.' None of them had let her back on her feet before they did.

Leighton nodded, looking far too serious to be thinking about what she'd done. 'You're right. You're good to go.'

'Then I'll get ready for the barbecue.'

In other words, go back to your mates and leave me in peace. I need to get my head under control.

'Right.' He didn't move.

Her arm brushed his chest as she squeezed past him to head out to the deck in an attempt to make him leave, then she had to sit down because her legs were a little shaky. 'Did you catch any fish?' she finally asked to fill the void growing between them. Why was he still hanging around?

'We brought back two. Right now the cooks are preparing one for our dinner, and the other one is to be shared by the staff. Can I get you anything?' Definitely not in a hurry to leave. 'A drink perhaps?'

She should go in and have that shower, but she didn't know if she had the strength to stand. Not while Leighton was here, getting to her in ways she'd never have believed. So much for thinking they were done and dusted if he could rattle her this easily. She might as well have a drink and hopefully start to relax. He'd probably tell her she shouldn't but too bad. 'A glass of bubbles would be great. There's a bottle in the fridge.'

'Not a problem.'

She blinked. What? No argument from the doctor. Or had he moved on from the doctor role? To what? A friend? An ex wanting to keep an eye on her because he still cared a little? It made her head pound harder thinking about everything. 'Thanks.'

His laugh sounded hollow. 'There's nothing wrong with you and you're on holiday. Why shouldn't you have a drink?'

'Do you want to join me?' she asked, and instantly regretted it. She needed space between them, not Leighton sitting within a few feet of her.

'I'll take a rain check. I'm going home to get clean and put on some less fishy clothes for the barbecue.'

Relief warred with disappointment, which she couldn't explain other than he messed with her head. That was all. That was enough. 'I'll see you later.'

Did she want to? There was nothing to be gained by getting too friendly. They'd given marriage a shot, and failed. A second crack at it would only lead to more heartbreak. She would struggle to trust him to be open with her, and he'd probably always be looking for her to let him down. Her body needed to quieten down. They weren't hooking up.

Back at his place Leighton headed down to the beach instead of going inside. Anything to get away from the image of the despair in Alyssa's eyes that morning bringing back memories of them arguing. It wasn't there when he was checking her out after swallowing the salt water, but he knew she'd be thinking about it often. That was Alyssa. She always thought things through more than once before moving on. He should've told her about Jamie right from the get-go. Part of him had been well aware he was being selfish, but he'd wanted to absorb the news and look at it from all ways before putting it out there for someone to say he was stupid to think Jamie was there for anything but money and the family name.

Though Alyssa wouldn't have said that. Not in a million years, but he hadn't wanted to see compassion or sympathy in her eyes either. He was supposedly the strong one in their relationship. Though learning how she'd turned his father's offer down flat after she'd left him proved him wrong there.

Raking his hand through his hair, he swore. Alyssa had been everything he'd wanted in a woman. Warm, funny, kind, and generous. Especially loving. His heart had never stood a chance. There'd been some neediness about her too, but he could live with that. She'd lost her mother to cancer when she was seventeen, and there'd never been a father in the picture. Her mother had remained single and raised her daughter without any help, working two jobs to pay the bills. Alyssa always said she had the best upbringing, but she did want a family and to be loved again by someone special since her mother had gone. He'd had no problem with that. He'd loved her and could give her what she wanted with his parents at her side too. Got that wrong, hadn't he? Another blunder he was accountable for.

He couldn't have loved her enough or they'd still be together. He hadn't trusted her to support him when Jamie appeared on the scene, or to see he was different from his father. He'd been in a bad place, not getting to grips with who his father really was. Another mistake to overcome if they were to at least be friends. Yet when he'd told Alyssa about Jamie that morning she'd been accepting although angry because he hadn't explained years ago. He understood. He'd used his battered heart as an excuse.

He skimmed a small flat pebble across the water.

His father had disowned him the day he'd told him how gutted he was not to have known about his brother. Apparently his loyalties should lie with his parents, and not Jamie. He wasn't supposed to share himself around. Was that why Dad tried to pay Lyssa off? Afraid she'd steal all his love?

Leighton stared over the water to the far horizon. No wonder he no longer called Auckland home. There was nothing there for him but sad and bitter memories. His wife had gone, his parents were distant, and Jamie had been living in England, though he was now back in Nelson, settled in permanently. Which was why Leighton was considering moving south. He owned a house in Auckland that he returned to between locum jobs but it did nothing for him. It was a house, not a home.

He was lonely. Keeping busy didn't fill all the gaps in the day. Until now he hadn't realised how much he'd missed Alyssa. He'd never have believed it, but then he'd been determined he wasn't going after her to beg for a second chance. She deserved better than being a part of the Harrison family, however remote that had become to him.

She still does.

He'd hurt her all over again explaining how he'd avoided talking about Jamie when he first found out he had a brother. Seemed hurting her came too easily. Something to remember over the coming days. She still distracted him far too quickly. That was his to deal with. He had to remain vigilant. She got under his skin far too easily so the barriers had to remain up.

Whatever he felt when around her, he did not want to get back together. This morning had shown there was too much hurt between them to forget the past. Both had made mistakes: Alyssa not sticking with him and him keeping quiet. They both deserved better.

His phone vibrated.

Jamie. 'Get your butt back here. The beer's getting warm.'

Turning back the way he'd come, he strode back to the house for a quick shower. Hopefully Alyssa had fallen asleep and wouldn't be at the barbecue for a long while, if at all.

He really didn't need to see her right now, or any time until the wedding. Even then he didn't *need* to spend time with her. No denying the heat that flared whenever she was near though. As soon as the wedding day was over he'd get back to his normal steady but quiet life as a GP.

Jamie and Collette's family and friends would leave the island. All except Alyssa. Apparently she was staying on for another week. Their paths didn't have to cross then. She'd be a tourist, checking out the market and cafés, seeing the sights and visiting the bars. He'd be at the clinic or the house he called home for now.

Perfect. They had a history. They weren't getting a future.

Alyssa knotted her blouse beneath her breasts and sucked in her stomach. Her skin was too pale, since it was winter back home. Time by the pool every day she was here would go some way to fixing that.

Laughter reached her from the main deck where the barbecue was happening. Everyone was happy and enjoying the pre-wedding events. Tomorrow she and the girls were going to have massages and facials. Talk about dream living. She'd never pampered herself before. Cautious with money, doing something decadent seemed extravagant. Growing up, there'd never been spare dollars to have some fun, and she'd carried on much the same way as her mother had with her hard-earned money—which was why she was getting close to putting down a deposit on her own home.

Home. A place to feel safe and secure. Like she'd had as a kid with her mother supporting her in every way possible. Not quite how home had been with Leighton. They'd bought an apartment on Auckland's North Shore and they'd made it cosy, but as time had gone by they'd spent less and less time there together and it had begun to feel less like home and more like a house anyone might've owned, but not them.

'You joining us or what?' Jamie stood in her doorway, a sympathetic look on his face.

So he understood she was struggling with Leighton's presence. 'Just coming,' she lied. It would be easier to stay at the bungalow than face up to Leighton and the way he set her tingling all over, but these days in Raro were about her friends, not herself.

'I imagine it astounded you learning about Leighton and I being siblings. It came as a surprise to realise you two had been married too. Small world, eh?'

'It's okay, Jamie. I'm over the shock.' No harm in a little fib. 'Really, what does it matter? If anything, I'm glad you both have each other. Leighton often said he'd felt lonely growing up as an only child.' Whereas she'd been more than happy being her mother's one and only.

'I've told Collette we're having a brood of kids.' Jamie laughed.

'Nappies and bottles on their way,' she responded. Kids. Hard to imagine what having one of her own would be like. She and Leighton had talked about having a family one day and she'd been excited to think she could be a mother. But they'd agreed to wait until he'd qualified as a GP and by then their marriage was falling apart. Maybe a baby would've kept them together, except that wasn't a reason to stay in a failing relationship.

'Not this week,' Jamie warned.

'Here I was thinking I'd figured what to get for your wedding present,' she said as they made their way across to the group.

'Get this into you.' Collette handed her a cocktail. 'It's your favourite.'

'A margarita? You're a gem.' She really had the best

of friends, and if Jamie knew she was struggling with Leighton's presence then Collette would be more than aware. But it was their special occasion and she wasn't going to spoil that for anything. Lifting her glass, she grinned. 'Here's to the happy couple and a fantastic wedding.' It really was wonderful being here, like the fun times she'd hoped for when she'd married and qualified.

'I'll drink to that,' Dan said and then everyone was raising their glasses and toasting their friends.

'Have I missed something?' Leighton asked from the edge of the deck.

A shiver went through her. She'd missed his arrival. Which had to mean she wasn't so caught up in his presence as she'd thought. Good.

'We're toasting Collette and Jamie.' She took another sip. Without them she'd be back in Nelson still working her butt off and not enjoying the sunshine and that beautiful beach with the reef beyond where the waves pounded incessantly. She glanced that way and blinked. 'Hey, is that a whale leaping out of the water beyond the reef?'

'Quite likely,' Leighton answered. 'There are always some about.'

'I'll have to watch out for them.' Needing to put space between her and Leighton, she inched closer to Andrea. 'You got a bit sunburnt today.'

'Don't know how when I put plenty of sunblock on. How're you feeling? Not coughing up any more salt water?'

Leighton turned to look at her, obviously waiting for her reply.

'Not a drop.' She didn't need him looking out for her.

He's being caring, as he would for anyone.

She wasn't anyone special in his book. Though he had always been caring towards her until those last months. Had she acted in haste when she left? It was starting to feel like that. Not a good feeling. What if she had done a bunk too soon? Broken Leighton's heart along the way? She'd never forgive herself. He'd been her heart's desire and she'd believed he'd always be there for her. Sounded naïve now. Despite wanting to be there for him, she'd packed up and left when the going got tough. No one was perfect. She groaned. This was getting harder to take by the hour. But for everyone's sake, including theirs, they had to get along and not spoil the fun.

'At least you got back in the water,' Andrea said. 'I wish I had the courage to go in and see those fish. They looked so colourful and pretty through the glass.'

'I'll flick you some photos, though it's not quite the same as swimming with them.' The aroma of fish cooking on the barbecue reached her and her stomach sat up, reminding her she hadn't eaten much lunch. 'That smells delicious.' Then she laughed. 'Fish for dinner when we spent hours watching others swimming over the sand.'

'None of those would've been Mahimahi,' Leighton said.

'What he's not saying is I caught it.' Jamie laughed. 'He was certain he'd be the hero of the day and catch our dinner. He didn't even get a bite.'

'Had to let someone else have a chance,' Leighton quipped.

'I don't remember you being into fishing.' Alyssa instantly wished her words back. Talking about their past was irrelevant at the moment. Or at any time, come to think of it.

He looked surprised. 'It's something I'd like to do more often but never seem to get around to. I used to fish when I was younger. One of the doctors here at the hospital dragged me out once and I'm always hopeful we'll go again one day.'

'You'll be able to continue on the Hauraki Gulf when you return home. Snapper's yummy.'

'If I go back to Auckland.'

'Are you considering staying here permanently?' That didn't sound right. He liked to immerse himself in work and from what she understood it wasn't that busy here.

'No, not at all. I take locum positions up and down the country, only returning to Auckland in between jobs. But I think it's time to look elsewhere for somewhere to live. I'm well and truly over the big city.'

Really? He'd been an Aucklander through and through with no inclination to move anywhere else. 'What's made you change your mind?'

He shrugged as he studied the beer bottle in his hand. 'I'm ready for a change. I want to connect with people and feel at home somewhere. I haven't got that in Auckland.'

Hello? Is this Leighton? The guy who told you in no uncertain terms right from the get-go that Auckland was home and he was never moving?

'It doesn't sound like you're there much anyway.' A trickle of excitement warmed her. Leighton excited her? To be brutally honest, he did. He was different and talking about a different life from what he used to want. And more intriguing, with his matured looks and well-honed body. Give over. His body had always been a turn-on. Nothing new there. Just as the heat coursing through her now was nothing new.

'Perhaps that's why.'

Her hand shook as she sipped her margarita. How honest could he be? With her, at that? It wasn't like the Leighton she'd known. What was going on here? Had the fact he'd never talked to her about Jamie changed how he approached people? 'I know I'll never go back there.' She could do honest too.

'You like Nelson?' A tightness appeared at the edges of his mouth as if her answer was important.

'Love it. After Perth I travelled around Oz a bit, then returned home. I didn't even stop in Auckland. There was nothing there for me.'

Leighton winced. Not the answer he was hoping for? Or expecting?

Guilt sneaked in. All very well being blunt, but she didn't have to hurt the man who'd stolen her heart and then given it back. His shoulder felt muscular under her palm. 'That wasn't a dig at you, Leighton.' He had been a part of why she didn't return to Auckland, but not the whole picture. 'I still miss Mum but she's not about Auckland even though I grew up there. My closest friends have all moved away and the hospitals are so big there's nothing personal about working in them.'

You aren't a part of my life.

'You didn't used to speak your mind quite so clearly.' There was a wry smile on his face.

She probably hadn't known it so clearly. Guess they'd both changed. She'd grown up a lot, probably much the same with Leighton. That damned smile hadn't changed though. 'Maybe I should've. You might've had a clearer understanding of my needs.'

'There you go again. Saying what you think. I like it.'

'If you're not keen on returning to Auckland, where do you think you might go?'

Don't say Nelson.

It was her home town now.

'There's a certain appeal about Nelson.'

Her heart slumped.

No way, Leighton.

'Have you ever been there?'

'I've visited Jamie a couple of times since he returned from England. It's a lovely place with lots of outdoor attractions. Though for me the biggest attraction would be having family nearby.' He watched her intently. 'By that I mean Jamie and Collette. I have very little contact with my parents these days.'

'Since Jamie came into your life?'

He nodded slowly, as if wanting to steer the subject away from his parents. 'I'll see what's on offer workwise when I'm through here before making any major decisions.'

'You always knew exactly what you wanted and got on with achieving it.'

Her arms ached with the need to hug him, to take that sadness out of his eyes. If only she could do it without having to worry that he might see it as more than it was. He had always been a kind, caring man with a big heart. Leighton deserved to be loved. Just not by her. They'd tried and failed. It would be pointless to try again. As well as painful. She'd never fully trust him to be open with her about everything, and in hindsight she knew she'd let him down too.

'Guess you've got some decisions to make before you return home.' She was being glib, but this was getting too intense, which she did not want. Their time for that was long over.

He shrugged. 'I'm working on it.'

'Keep me posted. I'd like to know what you decide and where you end up living.'

'Really? Why?'

Because I've missed you.

Her drink sloshed over the side of the glass. She had? Surely not. They'd broken up because they weren't getting along, couldn't even hold a conversation without getting into an argument, and she'd missed him? Yes, she did, and probably had all along. Missed the funny, caring, kind man she'd fallen for. Not the withdrawn, 'don't share my feelings' guy who never came home for dinner or to make love.

'Now we've caught up again, I'd like to know how you're getting on.' Did that come out all wrong? Would he think she wanted to get close again? 'Sorry, I'll shut up now.'

'Nothing to apologise for, Lyssa.' He reached for her glass. 'I'll get you a top-up.'

'Thanks.' Lyssa. Seemed he still thought of her as Lyssa and not Alyssa.

'I call you Lyssa in my dreams.'

He'd told her that after he kissed her the very first time, and had never stopped using that version of her name all the time they were together. Lyssa. Her toes curled thinking about how 'Lyssa' sounded deep and sexy when he was making love to her and she was about to explode with desire. Her heart lifted recalling how 'Lyssa' was full of concern when he carried her to the couch after she tripped on the stairs of their apartment and sprained her ankle in the resulting fall.

Loud talk and laughter interrupted her thoughts. She looked around, suddenly remembering they were at a barbecue with friends. Everyone had moved to the long table, where they sat together as though there'd been a mutual agreement to leave her and Leighton in their own little space to get along. They probably meant well, but she wished they'd mind their own business and leave her and Leighton to decide if they wanted to spend time together or not.

Right now she felt bewildered. Listening to him open up about his home had her wondering what he actually wanted for his future. She'd always thought he knew exactly what he wanted, so either their break-up had affected him a lot more than she'd imagined, or something else had gone down in the intervening years. Jamie arriving in his life would probably have a lot to do with how he looked at things.

'Come on. We'd better get amongst it.' Leighton held out her refilled glass. 'Enough serious talk for one day.'

Enough for the rest of her time in Rarotonga, more like. It did her head in hearing him say he didn't know where he wanted to live. It underlined how much he'd changed. The idea of him even considering Nelson gave her goose bumps. She was getting her own house there to settle down for good. It was her town, not his.

'Cheers.'

But it could prove interesting if he did move there and they were getting along.

CHAPTER FOUR

ALYSSA WALKED ALONG the beach, enjoying the sand pushing between her toes. At least it would wash off easily, whereas her hair was going to be a problem. The humid air was making it frizz around the edges despite the can of hairspray the hairdresser had used. Great. She was going to look like some toddler's stuffed toy after it had been left out in the rain. It didn't really matter. Today wasn't about her. Except she did like to look her best. She'd bought new clothes for every occasion planned for the days leading up to the wedding, going a little crazy with her overtime pay, but it was good to spoil herself for a change.

Then there was the gorgeous dress she'd got for the wedding hanging on the back of the door, ready to slip into when she returned to the bungalow. She was not thinking she'd like Leighton to see her all spruced up and looking hot in the dress with its narrow straps and long lines accentuating her breasts and hips. And her butt, one feature he'd always said was so damned sexy he could never resist her.

She wasn't.

Who gave a toss what Leighton thought?

Try again, Alyssa. This morning you spent hours

preening yourself in front of the mirror because you're sitting next to him at the wedding dinner.

True. She had. The silly thing was, it seemed she'd never quite got over Leighton. She'd moved on from their marriage heavy-hearted but determined to be true to herself, and she'd done okay, but there'd never been another man to replace him. The few she'd known since just hadn't come up to his standards. That could be because she'd loved Leighton so much—and believed he'd felt the same—that when they broke up she didn't believe she was lovable.

Or because she hadn't stopped loving Leighton.

If he could walk out of her life so easily then he couldn't have loved her half as much as she'd thought.

You walked away too.

Yes, she had. Better that than stay and become even more disillusioned about their marriage and how it seemed so different from what she'd expected. Or so she'd believed. But she might've been too quick to give up. When he wouldn't talk, she'd got angry, not sympathetic, feeling as rejected as she had when she'd learned her father had wanted nothing to do with her.

The turmoil brought on by catching up with Leighton was too much at times, which was why she was out here and not sitting on the deck with the other girls counting down the final hour until everyone gathered together to witness Collette marry the man of her dreams. She was ready, apart from the sand on her feet and the dress to put on, but the agitation about the man who'd once been her dream grew with every minute she had nothing to keep her busy.

If someone had told her Leighton could get her in such

a hot, flustered state as he used to she'd have laughed and told them to get a life. Except it seemed she was the one needing to do that. There was still some unfinished business to deal with about when Jamie turned up in his life that she was clueless about. Other than that there was no reason why he was messing with her head so much. She'd thought she was over him, and here she was getting hot and bothered over that sexy smile and lean body.

The sound of a racing motor scooter came from the road fifty metres beyond the beach, followed by a loud thump. Screams rent the air.

Almost relieved at the disruption to her walk, Alyssa ran towards the noise. What happened? Had someone been hit by the scooter?

Shouts and more screams.

Scrambling up the low bank, she tore across the lawn to where others were aiming for. Running around the corner of a house, she gasped. 'What happened?' she asked aloud as she noted a woman sprawled on the ground with the scooter imbedded into the wall and the back wheel pressed into her stomach. The woman wasn't moving and blood was oozing from the back of her head.

'If it's anything like what Sarah did yesterday I'd say she used the accelerator instead of the brake by mistake,' another woman said. 'It's easy to do. The controls are on the handlebars. One to brake, one to accelerate. Sarah's mixed them up a couple of times. She's my friend,' she added.

Would've been better to have stayed off the scooter, Alyssa thought but kept it to herself. Dropping to her knees beside the woman, she said to anyone listening, 'I'm a nurse. Is anyone else a nurse or doctor?'

Apparently not, judging by the sudden silence.

'Can someone phone for the ambulance?'

'I'm doing that now,' a local man told her. 'They won't be long. Is there anything you need in the meantime?'

Alyssa looked at the scooter. 'We need to get the wheel off her. Is there any way to move the scooter without causing any more problems?'

Two men carefully checked to see if the scooter was moveable. 'I think we can do it,' one said.

'Let me check Sarah's abdomen first,' Alyssa said. 'We don't want to cause further bleeding.' If the wheel was pressing on an internal injury it might still be haemorrhaging. But first, 'Sarah, I'm a nurse. Can you hear me?'

No reply. The pulse in her throat was rapid, but at least there was one.

She tried again. 'I'm Alyssa. I'm checking you over for injuries. Does it hurt where I'm touching your head?'

Silence.

'Hey, there's Doc Harrison,' someone said. 'Over here, Doc.'

Relief filled Alyssa. Having a doctor helping with this was going to make everything easier. He'd make the call on what was happening and what needed to be done. Only difficulty she had was it was obviously Leighton. Even better, he was calm under stress. That much hadn't changed.

He was already kneeling beside her. 'Where did you spring from?' he asked.

'I was walking on the beach when I heard the scooter slam into the house.' She shuddered at the memory. 'It sounded terrible.'

'I bet it did. What've we got?'

We. She liked that. 'I can feel a softness in her abdomen where the wheel is pressing. There's a head injury and she's not responding to my questions. Her name's Sarah.'

'The ambulance just left the hospital, Doc.'

'Good. I wonder if she hit the wall with her head or shoulder,' Leighton said as he began working his hands over Sarah's skull. 'The left shoulder looks dislocated.'

'Impact to the shoulder would be better than her head,' Alyssa said. 'These two men are prepared to remove the scooter when we give the go-ahead.'

'We're going to need to do that sooner rather than later.' Leighton's hand moved around Alyssa's as he felt for any injuries. 'That's where you felt a softness?' he asked.

'Yes. Shall I put pressure on it as the wheel is lifted?'

'Yes, but be prepared to have to shift the pressure as the wheel might be hiding the true extent of the damage.' Leighton looked around. 'Hey, Manu, Jacko, glad you're here. I'll give you a hand to lift the scooter away. What we have to do is lift it directly upwards, not drag it sideways at all.'

'Onto it. You tell us when, Doc.'

'On the count of three. One, two, three.'

The wheel was gone, the bike lifted over Alyssa's head and put aside.

She was instantly pressing down with one hand while checking for further injuries. 'Can't find any further problems,' she told Leighton. This was intense. They'd done a lot of things together in the past, but never worked on a patient until the other night, and this was far more serious than Michelle's injuries. He was calm, focussed, doing what was required without making a fuss. Leighton to a tee. He was often too calm for her liking, contained, not relaxing and doing nothing over a beer or a book type of calm, but right now he was perfect.

The friend moved closer. 'We're due to fly back to New Zealand tomorrow. What's going to happen to her? Is she seriously hurt?'

'She'll be taken to the hospital, where a doctor will attend her. Depending how serious her injuries are, she might be flown back to Auckland tonight.' Leighton was lifting Sarah's right arm. 'Shoulder's definitely dislocated. I'll try to put that back before she goes in the ambulance, otherwise she'll require surgery once she's back home.' He glanced at Alyssa. 'We don't have an orthopaedic surgeon, but there's a general surgeon I'll phone to let him know what's going on.' He pulled his phone from his pocket. 'Keep that pressure on, Alyssa.'

An ambulance pulled up, and she felt happier. Sarah needed to be in hospital fast. Then it dawned on her. 'Leighton, you've got to get ready for the wedding.' He was wearing denim shorts and a tee shirt, not wedding attire. Not for the best man.

He nodded abruptly and turned away to talk on his phone, presumably to the surgeon he'd mentioned.

The surgeon had better be available. Leighton couldn't miss his brother's wedding. He had to be there. It was important to both men. They'd gained so much when Jamie came into Leighton's life. Her heart squeezed. And she'd lost Leighton, though she couldn't blame all that on Jamie's appearance. If their marriage had been strong they'd have got through the difficulties and still been happy and in love.

'That's sorted. Phil will meet us at the hospital.'

'Us? You can't go. You've got to get ready for the ceremony.' Blood had splattered across his arms. He needed a shower.

Glancing down, she realised she did too. So much for having one earlier.

'I'm going in the ambulance with Sarah. The ambulance crew aren't paramedics,' he said quietly. 'Once at the hospital Phil will take over and I can come back to the resort for a shower. Would you mind following in my car so I've got a lift back?'

'Sure.' She took the keys he was holding out in her free hand. 'Who's going to take over from me here?'

'Annie will do that. Annie, this is Alyssa, a nurse here on holiday. She'll show you where we need to apply pressure and you can take her place.'

It was busy for a few minutes while Annie replaced her, and Sarah was put on a stretcher before being lifted into the ambulance. The door was closing when Alyssa suddenly called to Leighton. 'You'd better call Jamie and tell him what's happened in case you're late getting to the wedding. Or do you want me to do it?'

'I'll do it once Sarah's at the hospital. My suit's in the car. I'll need a bathroom.'

'Use mine.'

Good thinking, Alyssa. You need a shower too.

The unit wasn't large when it came to two people using the bathroom and getting dressed for a wedding at the same time. She shrugged. They'd manage. She didn't have to worry about doing her make-up as she and the other girls had been to the spa earlier in the day before getting their hair done by a hairdresser who'd moved over from Wellington to set up a wedding business.

Leighton nodded and disappeared into the back of the ambulance.

Alyssa crossed over to his car. They just couldn't avoid bumping into each other. When she'd first found out he was part of the wedding proceedings she'd assumed she'd only see him whenever everyone got together for a meal or to go somewhere. Showed how wrong she could be. Leighton had a knack of turning up everywhere she went. She enjoyed his company, but mostly she wanted to keep her distance because her heart did feel vulnerable. This was supposed to be a holiday where she relaxed and had fun with her friends, and yet she was starting to look out for Leighton wherever she went.

'I *have* missed him,' she said as she swung the car around to follow the ambulance. 'More than I knew.' Was it because she'd been so busy with work she hadn't had much time to get to know a man, or give one more than a passing glance, and Leighton was here and she knew him and didn't need to go through the basics of finding out more about him?

Don't forget he let you down in the end.

They'd let each other down, but that didn't give him a 'get out of jail free' card. He'd hurt her with his endless hours of work and study. Now she knew there'd been far more behind it, it was still hard to accept that was reason enough to keep her at arm's length. Then there was the way his father had behaved, as though he'd done nothing wrong and it was everyone else's fault. Typical John.

How that must've devastated Leighton. He believed in his family, and had loved them wholeheartedly. As he'd claimed to love her. But with the revelation about Jamie and what his parents had done to keep that a secret, he'd hidden his feelings and hurt from her. He hadn't put the facts out there for her to be able to reassure him he'd still mattered to her, that she'd still loved him as much as ever.

While she was wondering why he didn't come home for meals or want to spend time with her, or go out with their friends, he was avoiding her because of his problems. They'd both thought they weren't what the other wanted any more. She'd been playing catch-up after spending years studying and had wanted Leighton to be a part of that. She hadn't liked it when he was always too busy to be with her, yet she should've understood. He was only working hard as she'd done. What would've happened if they'd just sat down and talked through their concerns? Would they still be together? Or would they have decided it was too tough and still broken up? Lesson for the future—always talk about problems.

Following the ambulance up the tree-lined, narrow, windy road to the hospital, she shook her head. It was still hard to imagine Leighton living in Rarotonga, even if only temporarily. It was a wonderful place and she knew she'd be back again in the not too distant future for another holiday, but, for a man who liked to be non-stop busy, the laid-back lifestyle of the islands didn't fit him. But she was thinking about the man she'd known four years ago. Leighton today seemed more relaxed and accommodating of others. As though it wouldn't matter which side of the bed he slept on, only that he had a side. She sighed. 'Oh, Leighton, who are you?'

Pulling into a parking space outside the emergency department, she got out of the car to cross over to the ambulance where medical staff were crowding around to offload Sarah. Leighton stepped down and began talking to a man in scrubs, most likely the surgeon he'd spoken to on the phone. Lucky for Sarah he was available as there weren't many specialists in any field working here.

Another car pulled into the parking area and Sarah's friend leapt out. 'How is she? Is she going to be all right? Where are the doctors?'

Alyssa answered. 'They'll take her in the emergency room. I think that man talking to Leighton is the general surgeon and he'll see to Sarah.'

'This is awful. I told Sarah to be careful. She should've handed the scooter back when she made the mistake of accelerating rather than braking the first time, but she's so stubborn.'

'Take it easy. These things happen, and now you need to focus on being strong for her. Go inside and I'm sure the nurses will keep you posted on what's happening.' She walked beside the distraught woman until she veered off to head for the entrance to the department.

'All the best,' she said but doubted she was heard. It was hard for anyone to see their loved one in serious trouble as Sarah was, and knowing the local hospital wasn't set up with all the modern equipment for every scenario only made it more difficult to deal with.

'Thanks, Phil. If you're sure you don't need me, I'd better get cracking. Time's speeding by.' Leighton turned to her, looking relieved. 'I'm not needed.' He wouldn't want to miss the wedding, but if there hadn't been a doctor to take over with Sarah he wouldn't have hesitated to step up. Being the best doctor possible was always a big part of his make-up, one she'd admired and was glad hadn't changed.

'Here.' She passed him the car key. 'You're going to have to rush getting ready. Time's running away on you.'

'On you, too. I know you want to be there for Collette as much as I do for Jamie.'

Yes, she did, but it wasn't quite the same being Collette's friend as Leighton being Jamie's brother and groomsman. 'Let's go.'

The main road circling the island was busy with locals and tourists in cars, on scooters, walking along the roadside. The speed was slow and Leighton's frustration was rising.

'Did you call Jamie?' she asked.

'Yes. He said don't panic. They'll hold off until we get there. As long as we aren't going to be hours.'

'I'll send him a text to let him know you're on your way and that you need a thirty-second shower and you'll be ready.' Her fingers flew over the keys.

'That long?' He flicked her a quick smile. 'How long are you allowing yourself?'

'I don't have to be there as soon as you, so I'll take a minute.'

Leighton slowed for a turning car, accelerated away again. 'I'm not going without you. Collette will murder me if I leave you behind.'

'The bungalow's only a hundred metres from the wedding site on the beach. I'll be right behind you.'

'You'll be beside me, no argument.'

She shook her head. This was more like the old Leighton. He was going out of his way to make sure she understood she was turning up with him. She wasn't asking why. She mightn't be able to cope with the answer, though it was probably because he felt guilty for dragging her to the hospital so he'd have a car to get back here. It wasn't as though he'd want her on his arm whenever he wasn't with Jamie. Which was a shame. It would be fun, and exciting.

Stop it.

They were turning into the resort car park as her phone pinged.

'Jamie says not to panic. Everyone's relaxed and having a glass of bubbles while they wait. Sounds idyllic. Bring it on.'

'You're relaxed about this,' he said with a smile that touched her heart.

He was right. She did feel comfortable with him and the urgency to get ready for the wedding wasn't bothering her.

'Whatever.' She shrugged and headed to her room to get ready with Leighton right behind her. There went the relaxed feeling. Her muscles were tightening. He was going to share her minuscule bathroom, her bedroom and the very air she'd be breathing. Things were looking up.

Leighton was buttoning up the white shirt that was the same as Jamie's for the wedding as he walked out of the bathroom after a fast shower. He stumbled at the sight before him.

Lyssa was stepping into her dress, her lace-covered breasts standing proud and reminding him how he used to cup them in his hands as his fingers caressed her nipples.

He gasped.

She spun around to face him full on, her face reddening instantly. 'Leighton, I thought you were still in the shower.' Then she blinked, and turned away.

Her back was satiny, her skin another memory long buried with all the pain of the past. Only these memories were firing him up fast. One step and he'd be close enough to bring them to life. And get walloped in the process. Along with looking crass. 'Sorry, I didn't mean to burst in on you.' He'd insisted she go first in the shower and now she was out here still getting ready. Turning away, he stepped back into the steamy bathroom. He was hardening fast. Hell, he needed another shower—a cold one. There wasn't time. But he couldn't walk back out there. She'd know he was hot for her. Bet that'd shock her.

'Leighton, I need the bathroom mirror as soon as you're done,' she called loudly. Too loud, as if she was embarrassed and trying to hide it.

'Sure. I'm finished in here.' He combed his hair with his fingers and headed back out to the lounge where his shoes were. Hopefully he looked all right. He wasn't hanging around in the cupboard-sized bathroom with Lyssa standing before the mirror fixing her hair or make-up or whatever it was she thought needed sorting. He couldn't fault a thing about her. She looked beyond beautiful. Her eyes were bright green and her face was open and happy. His heart went into overdrive.

'You've missed a button,' she said, looking anywhere but at him, but she had to have taken a look to know that.

So she wasn't entirely immune to him. He shouldn't give a damn, but unfortunately he did. She got to him far too easily, upsetting his equilibrium with a glance or a smile when he was determined to get through these few days without falling for her all over again. How was that going? Not so well if his erection was any indication. That had better back off, if nothing else. He had a wedding to attend. Time to get cracking. His brother needed him fully focused on the wedding and not taking an interest in one particular guest.

He cursed. He'd been adamant Alyssa would walk across to the venue with him. Going ahead without her now wasn't happening. Sitting down, he finished tying his laces.

'Let's go.' She headed to the door, her back ramrod straight and her head high. Not Alyssa as he remembered fondly, though her long thick blonde hair falling over her shoulders and down her back more than made up for that. He liked this tougher version a lot.

Swallowing hard, he followed and waited while she locked the door. Then, taking her elbow, he escorted her to the wedding venue, where he led her to a seat before joining his brother for his important day. 'Hey, man, you look very dapper.'

'Dapper? I was hoping for sexy.' Jamie shot him a nervous grin.

'If I'd said that you'd have been worried.' Leighton laughed. Though it sounded a little hollow, because his eyes were on Lyssa as she talked to Andrea. The years since they'd gone their separate ways had been good to her. She'd matured into a confident and strong woman and her beauty reflected the changes from the pretty girl he'd married. He'd loved her so much back then. What was to say he couldn't again? Or was that still?

Jamie nudged him none too gently. 'Glad you're with me, Leighton.'

Which brought him back to why he was here. This was

his brother's wedding day, and he shouldn't be thinking about his, no matter how hard it was to ignore. 'I wouldn't be anywhere else.'

The marriage celebrant, Clara, joined them. 'Collette's on her way. Time to get your special occasion under way.'

Collette was walking towards Jamie, holding her father's arm and beaming as though she couldn't be any happier.

Which he presumed she couldn't. Leighton felt a twang of longing in his heart and his eyes searched Alyssa's face as she watched her friend walk up the hibiscus-strewn aisle set between the guests' chairs. She brushed at her eyes and glanced his way, quickly looked back to Collette as colour stained her cheeks. Remembering their day too? Or was he making it up to suit his own feeling of missing out on love? Love that was all about Alyssa.

'Welcome to Rarotonga and this special occasion, everyone.' Clara smiled around at the group of friends and family. 'I am honoured to be marrying Jamie and Collette today.'

It seemed only minutes before Clara asked, 'Collette Brown, do you take Jamie Campbell to be your lawfully wedded husband?'

'I do.'

'Jamie Campbell, do you take Collette Brown to be your lawfully wedded wife?'

'I do.'

Clara nodded at Leighton and he dug in his pocket for the tiny box with the two rings. Opening it, he held it between the happy couple, and was stunned to see his hand shaking. From happiness for his brother, or because of the longing filling him, he didn't know. One thing he *was* sure of was one day he wanted to be standing in Jamie's place, telling the woman he loved how much he cared for her.

As he'd done once before. Look where that ended up. Not good. He'd been so sure he'd found his lifelong partner. His for ever love. Possibly he had and then thrown it away without thinking through the consequences of what he was doing. Leighton stared sightlessly at the ground. Was that true? Really? He had withdrawn from Alyssa when there had been more going on than just his reaction to Jamie turning up in his life. He'd found he had insecurities about trusting anyone with his heart after his parents showed their true colours. If only he'd realised back then, things might've been different now. Happier for one.

Loud clapping and cheers cut through his maudlin thoughts. Quite rightly too. He shouldn't be thinking about himself, today of all days. 'Congratulations, Collette, Jamie. I wish you every happiness.' He hugged Collette. 'Now I have a sister.' Then he slapped Jamie on the back. 'Well done.' He stepped away so others could move in and bumped into Alyssa. 'Sorry.'

She smiled crookedly. 'No problem. That was very moving.' Moisture sparkled at the corners of her eyes.

He nodded, afraid to speak in case he sounded too emotional. All very well feeling like this, but showing Alyssa would only make her see how much he cared and he needed her to think he was still an aloof man or else she might think there was more to his time spent with her than he intended.

'Leighton.' Her hand wrapped around his, warm and caring. 'You're allowed to be emotional. This is your brother's day, and you two are close.' She'd remember he didn't do showing emotion very well. Sometimes she'd complained that he was too aloof, and that protecting his feelings was unnecessary, especially with her. Even on their wedding day, he'd kept his feelings under control until they were alone in their hotel suite. Could be that deep down he'd always known something wasn't quite right between his parents no matter how hard they tried to hide it.

Right now, when he didn't need it, warmth spread through him from her touch and her understanding. 'You're right.' If only that were all this was about. But she'd only guessed the half of it.

'It's awesome you've got a sibling. I've always wondered what it would be like, though I never felt hard done by being an only child.'

'It's special.' He was having no trouble saying what he felt about Jamie, which was a worry. She'd better not ask how he felt about her, because she was still in his heart and there was nothing but trouble to be gained if he told her.

Her head dipped in acknowledgement. 'I imagine it is.'

'Here, you've smudged your mascara.' He dug in his pocket for a clean tissue and gently wiped the black stain from her cheeks. It would be too easy to drown in those beautiful emerald eyes. Stepping back, he pocketed the tissue. 'There you go.'

'Thanks.' She blinked twice, but not before he saw another tear appearing.

His heart expanded. How could they have broken up?

Then she looked to her friend. 'Hey, Collette, congrats. You look stunning. That dress is perfect for you.' Lyssa wrapped her arms around the bride and hugged her tight. 'You made me cry when you read your vows.'

Collette laughed. 'Nearly bawled myself. I am so lucky.'

'So's Jamie,' Lyssa returned. 'Be happy.'

'Where's the champagne? I could do with a cold drink now my nerves have calmed down.' Collette laughed some more.

'I'll get the waiter to bring some over,' Leighton said, needing to put space between him and Alyssa after touching her cheeks. That reminded him of the happiness and love that had filled him when Lyssa had said 'I do' to him. It had been the most wonderful moment of his life. Now *his* eyes were moist. If only he could find that love again, but it was unlikely.

With a heavy heart Alyssa watched Leighton stride away. On their wedding day she'd truly believed nothing could come between them, and she'd thought Leighton felt the same. He did. She was sure of it. Which only went to show even the strongest love could go sour.

'He looks gorgeous in that white shirt and black pants.' Collette stood beside her.

He certainly did. Especially that firm butt. 'Hey, concentrate on your man. He's pretty hot too.' Not a patch on Leighton though. She grinned. She felt good. The way he'd touched her face to remove the mascara was so soft she'd nearly cried.

Come on. You did cry.

'Yeah, I know.' Collette chuckled. 'Bring on the night games.'

'You're supposed to enjoy the wedding feast and all the speeches first.'

'Of course, but the anticipation will grow with each passing hour. Ah, just what I need.' Her friend took a glass from the tray a waiter was holding in front of them. 'Thank you.'

Lifting one for herself, Alyssa tapped it against her friend's. 'Congratulations again. You deserve to be so happy.'

'So do you.' Collette tapped back.

They sipped their drinks.

'Go mingle,' Alyssa said. 'Everyone wants to hug and congratulate you.' She turned away and wandered to the end of the deck to lean on the railing and stare across at the reef. It would be perfect if a whale leapt up high right now. Like an acknowledgement of the words the bride and groom had shared—life was wonderful if you trusted it.

Rarotonga was perfect for a wedding. Turning around, she leaned back and watched the happy couple being swamped by family and friends, and felt happy. Truly happy. Those two deserved this. Everyone did. Including herself. One day she'd try again.

Would she though? Did she want to take that gamble and risk being hurt again?

Her eyes sought out Leighton. He was with Dan and the other two doctors with their partners from Nelson. Yes, she did. Leighton was gorgeous. Hot as hot could get. Her breasts rose on a deep inhale. Nothing had changed there. He'd always turned her on in an instant without even trying. She'd never known a man like him for making her come alive, before or since. Definitely a hard act to follow.

He looked around, locked eyes with her and waved her over. 'Come and join us.'

Good idea. Standing here on her own wasn't the way to celebrate. Not when she had friends to enjoy the occasion with. Did that include Leighton? Were they friends? Or had too much water gone under the bridge for them to come back to friendship at least? 'I was taking a breather,' she said as she stepped up to his side. 'All those emotions are hard to shove aside.'

'Embrace them. It's all part of celebrating these two and their marriage.' He was watching Collette and Jamie make their way along the deck, stopping to talk to every person on the way. 'Glad it's not a huge wedding party or we'd be here all night.'

Laughter bubbled up. 'The sun is nowhere near the horizon, Late.'

'Late?' An emotion she couldn't recognise slipped through his eyes, and disappeared.

Oops. Damn. Her pet name for him when they were making out had come from nowhere, just spilled free, feeling natural. She stepped sideways, putting space between them. 'Sorry,' she whispered.

'Don't be.' He was watching her too intently for comfort. 'You're being natural. I like it,' he added with a twist of those delightful lips. 'I used to like how you'd say whatever popped into your head.'

Especially when they made love. Her face flamed. He remembered? Was he deliberately winding her up? Whichever, the temperature had just risen a lot of degrees higher than normal for this island. 'I need water,' she muttered and headed over to the table where Pepe was handing out glasses of champagne and sparkling water.

'You want more champagne?' Pepe asked, nodding at the glass she was carrying.

'Ah, no. Water please.' She hadn't even noticed she was still holding the glass. Leighton was getting to her too damned much. That was the problem because she was not getting together with him. She wouldn't even share a kiss with him. As much as she'd like to when she wasn't thinking about the consequences. Awkward when he lit up every nerve ending in her body just by breathing. But she could not be vulnerable again. She would not go through the pain of another break-up from him. Yes, it would be a break-up if they kissed and then turned their backs on each other.

'Looks like you're thirsty.' Andrea laughed as she waited for Pepe to pour her a champagne.

Alyssa shrugged away the problem of Leighton and laughed with her friend. 'I haven't had my H2O quota for the day.'

Andrea gave her the 'You're not fooling me' look. 'Let's go take a seat in the shade while those two get their wedding photos done.'

'Isn't it the perfect setting? I love how everyone's so relaxed and the sound of the waves crashing on the reef is a perfect backdrop.'

Talking too much, girl. Andrea's not stupid. She knows you're in a pickle and probably also knows it's all over Leighton.

'The photos will be awesome,' Andrea agreed.

Photos. Leighton would be in a lot of them. She looked around and sure enough, there he was, standing beside Jamie as the photographer made the wedding party smile and laugh. Her heart stuttered. He looked good enough to eat. Her mouth watered as she pictured herself touching his chest with her tongue, tasting and feeling that firm skin. How had she managed to walk away from all they'd had? It seemed impossible now. 'The people in the photo look pretty damned awesome, never mind the setting.'

'You think?' Andrea laughed and downed a large mouthful of her drink.

'I do,' she admitted. Hopefully Collette would give her a photo of Leighton to keep under her pillow. The water she gulped went down the wrong way. Everyone turned her way. Embarrassing, and made worse when Andrea slapped her back.

'You all right, Lyssa?' Leighton was there in an instant.

'I'm fine,' she managed through another cough. 'Carry on with the photo session. They're waiting for you,' she added gruffly, not needing his attention. Not when he'd been the cause in a roundabout way of her nearly choking.

'I'm done. It's time for Jamie and Collette to have some taken of them alone. Pepe, can I have a glass of champagne, please.'

Lifting both her glasses, she looked from one to the other, and shrugged. What the hell. It was her friend's wedding and she was going to have fun. She drained the water and put the glass on the table, then finished what was left of the champagne and held that glass out to Pepe. To heck with Leighton and the way her skin heated and her heart pounded when he was near. To heck with being careful. This was a day of celebration, not one to waste being serious.

'Alyssa, Leighton, over here,' Collette called. 'I want a photo of the four of us.'

Alyssa laughed. 'Yeah, sure.' Collette was deliberately causing trouble. For once she didn't care. She wanted a photo of her and Leighton together. Tucking her arm through his, she said, 'Come on.'

He didn't hesitate. 'Let's show her who's in charge.'

'Really?' Cool. He stayed at her side when they reached the happy couple and didn't go to stand by his brother. Then he put his arm around her waist and drew her closer. The photographer didn't need to tell her to smile.

CHAPTER FIVE

ALYSSA'S HANDS LAY on Leighton's chest as they swayed in time with the music coming from a guitarist and piano player. They'd stepped onto the dance floor with everyone else and initially kept apart, but the music had drawn them close and soon Leighton was holding her as she danced, and she hadn't been able to resist him any longer. His hands were on her waist, holding her ever so gently. Their movements were in sync as though they'd never been apart. This was bliss. She hadn't felt so happy in for ever.

Every breath she took filled her senses with Leighton: a new outdoorsy smell of the sea and sun, the feel of his muscles under her palms, the sound of his heart beating, the suntanned skin where the top buttons on his shirt were undone. This was Leighton. Familiar but different.

Brushing her lips on his neck, she inhaled deeply and closed her eyes and drank in the wonderful sensations rolling through her as his hold tightened.

'Hey,' he whispered by her ear.

'Hey, yourself.' They'd often said that when they were hugging one another. Nice to think some things hadn't changed.

The music ceased.

Their feet stopped moving, though their bodies still swayed to a beat of their own. Alyssa continued leaning against Leighton, reluctant to move away.

'Okay, folks, the bride and groom are leaving.' Pepe stood by the musicians. 'Let's give them a big send-off.'

Clapping and catcalls filled the night air as Collette and Jamie walked hand in hand towards the exit. They were laughing and looking so happy.

Alyssa's heart lifted and she ran after them. 'Collette.' Throwing her arms around her friend, she hugged her hard. 'Have an awesome honeymoon. Love ya.'

Collette hugged her back just as tight. 'Love you back. Make the most of the rest of your time here.' Her wink was glaringly cheeky.

'Yeah, right.' She turned away and bumped into Leighton, who placed a hand on her waist before reaching out to his brother.

'Enjoy yourselves. See you on your way home.'

Jamie nudged Alyssa aside to hug his brother. 'Thanks, man.'

Then they were gone.

'Feel like a stroll along the beach?' Leighton asked the beautiful woman beside him as Jamie and Collette disappeared from sight.

'Best offer I've had all night.' Alyssa chuckled.

He could think of a few more offers to suggest, but even he knew when to shut up. Sometimes. 'I thought they'd never leave.' It was nearly midnight and the bride and groom had finally left for the upmarket resort where they'd booked a room for the night before heading to Aitutaki in the morning.

'I reckon they were making the most of the occasion.' Lyssa kicked off her shoes. 'Am I glad to take these off. My feet are killing me.'

They did look red in places. He'd love to rub them. 'Let's go.' He could still feel the heat of her body as she'd danced with him. 'How long have you got the bungalow for?' he asked as their shoulders touched, sending a thrill of heat throughout him. This was Alyssa and he was happy.

'Until I go home next weekend. Management upgraded me until tomorrow, but I decided to splash out and continue staying in it. They had to shuffle guests around but they've been so kind.' She looked embarrassed.

'Why shouldn't they look out for you? You're part of a larger group and helped with the woman who fell off the bus.'

'It's still very good of them.' The embarrassment hadn't faded. 'I could've kept the booking the way it was, but I couldn't resist staying on in the bungalow.'

'Go you. Why not have a bit of luxury?'

'Because I'm saving hard for a house and it's hard to justify spending money on this.' She glanced at him. 'But I haven't had a holiday in for ever, and it's magical waking up in the morning and seeing the pool right there with the beach only a few metres beyond the boundary.'

She'd never had fancy holidays growing up. All her mother's earnings had gone on the basics, yet not once had he heard Lyssa complain. She said she'd had a wonderful upbringing and wouldn't swap any of it for a more comfortable lifestyle. 'Knowing you, you'll get that deposit no matter what.'

'It hasn't helped with house prices skyrocketing over the last couple of years but, yes, I will get there.'

'I believe you. Believe *in* you,' he added.

She tripped, straightened and looked directly at him. 'Thank you. Sometimes I wonder if I'm asking too much of myself, but then I remember how hard Mum worked to give me what I needed because it was important to her and she loved me, and I know I've got a great role model.' She blinked, and turned to walk along the beach.

It had been a day full of emotions. His heart felt lighter than it had in years. 'You only ever said good things about her.'

'I didn't tell you how she used to growl if I wore odd socks? Or when I left my broken hair ties lying around?' She giggled like the kid she must've been.

His heart swelled with longing. Alyssa could be so much fun when she forgot to worry about getting everything right. 'She sounds like a perfectly normal mother.' His used to throw paddies when he didn't keep his shoes in a straight line in the wardrobe. 'She'd be proud of you buying your own home.'

If he ever got to share a home with her again, he'd make certain he didn't stuff it up. As if that would ever happen. His stance sagged. What if they could put the past behind them and try again? What if it went belly up again? He couldn't face the thought of watching Alyssa walking away once more. But neither was it possible to walk along the sand with her and not have some connection. Holding his breath, he reached for her hand.

When her fingers tightened around his, his lungs expelled the air they were holding.

'Mum would've liked you.'

Knock him down. That was new. Alyssa never said things like that. 'You think?'

'I do.'

I do. The saying of the day. Except this one was a long way different from when Jamie and Collette said it.

'I'd like to have known her. She's such an integral part of who you are.' Alyssa had talked about her a lot when they'd first met, though over time she hadn't so much. He'd wondered, when they'd first started talking about getting married, if she'd hoped his mother might be as loving towards her. Not a chance. His mother was very guarded about who she loved. He had come to understand his mother a lot better since Jamie turned up in his life, but he'd never get his head around her staying with the man who'd been unfaithful to her. It was beyond comprehension.

Alyssa looked around as they continued strolling along the beach. 'Mum worked so hard to raise me and make sure I never went without the basics.' Another pause.

He sensed she wanted to get something off her chest, so he kept quiet, giving her time to put into words whatever was making her hand tighten around his.

'I always felt I had to emulate her. Had to be as focused, as determined, so that having fun came way down the list of what I was allowed to do.'

Light-bulb moment. 'So when you qualified as a nurse and could toss the study notes aside you wanted to let your hair down for the first time.'

'You're onto it.' She sounded surprised. Then she laughed. 'Of course you are. You're smart.'

'I wasn't at the time. At the time I only saw it as you not happy being stuck at home while I was working all hours to get through my rosters and studies.' Something else he'd let her down over.

'Don't start blaming yourself, Leighton. I never explained how I felt. I don't think I really understood myself back then. I'd always been a good girl, trying to please Mum because she worked so hard, and after she died nothing changed. I owed her for all she'd done for me, and when she left me the wherewithal to go to polytechnic and become a nurse there was no way I was going to let her down.'

'Eventually the bubble had to burst.'

'So it seems. Not that I became outlandishly bad, just started to enjoy partying and time at a bar with friends.'

'And now?' He hadn't seen her being outrageous or over the top or getting drunk and making a fool of herself while here.

'Now I work a lot of hours and play up very little. More like the old Alyssa with a few exceptions.'

Turning to her, he smiled as he tried to ignore the way her beautiful eyes were focused on him as if there were nothing else to be seen, tightening him where he shouldn't be. 'I could never imagine you not working hard, but I also see a more confident and relaxed Alyssa.'

Her laughter was a tinkling sound causing heat to rush up his spine. 'I've grown up.'

'And some. You know who you are now, and what you want from life.' Had she had another relationship after they broke up? He didn't want to know if the answer was yes. Just the thought of her in another man's arms had goose bumps rising on his skin. Which was way out of line, considering they were no longer a couple. Obviously he hadn't let go of her as much as he'd believed.

Lyssa was gazing at him, a small smile lifting her lips and tipping his equilibrium further. That mouth. Damn but he'd missed her kisses.

He leaned closer, needing to share the air she was breathing. She wound him up while making him wonder what it would be like to kiss her again. Give over. He knew what her kisses were like. Had never forgotten the hot, tantalising sensations that her mouth provoked. But that was then. This was now, here on the beach under a zillion twinkling stars.

Her arms were reaching around him, pulling them together, their bodies touching breast to chest, thigh to thigh. Mouth to mouth. Tongue to tongue. Deep and touching, hot and exciting. Memories mixed with this new kiss. Hot, caring. Sharing.

Exciting.

Yes, her fingers were caressing his neck as they used to do, teasing, loving, hardening him. Lifting his mouth off hers, he whispered, 'Lyssa?'

'Yes, Leighton. Yes.'

Need mixed with relief and longing as he lifted her into his arms and carried her up the beach to the bank below an empty section. With every step he took Lyssa was kissing his neck. And he'd thought he was turned on. He was getting tighter by the second. 'Stop,' he growled. Or he'd never make it.

She laughed against his skin, hot breaths adding to his heat. 'Like that's going to happen.'

'No, seriously, I don't have any condoms with me.'

'It's okay. I'm on the pill to keep regular.'

He lowered her to stand in front of him by the bank, his mouth covering hers, his hands sliding under the skirt of her dress, touching hot, silky skin. His groin pulsed hard, and heavy, and when he touched Lyssa's sex she was wet with need. He pulled his head back. 'You sure?' She had to be if she was that wet, but he needed to hear her say so.

'Absolutely.' Fingertips were tripping all over his chest, light as feathers, caressing, tightening him further as they headed south when he didn't believe it possible. 'Absolutely.'

He traced the outline of her breasts, first one, then the other, feeling her nipples harden under the light fabric of her dress. Sliding one strap down her shoulder, he followed it with his mouth, touching her there, everywhere. Feeling her skin heat and tiny bumps lift where he touched.

Lyssa worked at his trousers, undoing the front, shoving them down his thighs, over his knees to drop to his ankles. She sent his underwear in the same direction and he stepped out of it.

Hooking one leg over his hip, then the other, she wound her arms around his shoulders and opened herself to him.

He turned so he could lean against the bank, and breathed deep to absorb the scents that were Alyssa and the sea air. Magic.

'Make love to me, Leighton.'

Nothing could've stopped him from pushing into her warm, moist centre, and pulling back to push in again and again until he lost himself in her and felt her squeeze tight around his hard-on. When her heat increased and her body rocked, he waited for her to cry out as she always had. 'Leighton, now.'

Then he let go and joined her in forgetting everything but right now, this wonder that filled him with love. And then he forgot everything but being with her, and making love in this special place. It felt unbelievably good to be here. This was Lyssa, his woman, he was making love to and he couldn't be happier.

His chest rose and fell on harsh gasps for air. His head spun. Lyssa in his arms was special and wonderful, and he felt as though all his dreams had come together at once. Again.

'Let's go to my room.' Without waiting for his answer, Alyssa took his arm and headed back to the resort. Just as well they hadn't got far along the beach before they'd got caught up in each other and made love like something out of a dream because she could barely place one foot in front of the other. Her legs were weaker than wet bread. Thank goodness Leighton had his arm around her waist or she'd be a heap on the sand. Which wouldn't be too bad, given how warm it was out here. 'Why don't we go into the water and cool off?'

'Because we won't be able to see the rocks and coral in the dark and they can be seriously sharp if you kick them with your toes.'

'Sensible to the last.' She chuckled, not at all worried her idea had hit a wall. The bungalow was more comfortable and there was her spa pool to get into and cuddle up to him. 'There's champagne in the fridge.'

'Now you're talking. Though I have had a few today.'

'So have I.' It wasn't every day she attended such a romantic wedding. Or let her hair down and had so much fun and made love with a very sexy man. Another glass of bubbles, and maybe making love again, sounded ideal.

'What time are you taking Jamie and Collette to the airport?' How long could they stay in bed in the morning?

'Ten o'clock. But I'm going to call them an hour before to make sure they're awake and up, not lounging in bed together forgetting the time.'

They reached the steps up to her accommodation. Leighton turned and took her in his arms, held her tight. 'Let's not think about them. This is our moment.'

They were on the same page. She sagged against him, more than happy not to be thinking about anything or anyone but them. Stretching up, her mouth found his and she kissed him with all she had to give. This was special. Leighton was special. That was all she could think about.

When he swung her up in his arms again, she shivered with anticipation, her body already tingling with desire at the idea they'd make love again. On her deck, he paused. 'Want to sit out here? I'll bring the champagne out.'

'The key card's under the pot plant by the door,' was her way of saying yes, let's do this.

His smile made her heart swell. He was good-looking, but when he smiled that sexy smile he went beyond that to movie-star looks.

'Do you need me to undo your dress? It's very fitting.'

She could manage, but why give up an opportunity to have his hands on her? Spinning around, she lifted her hair and waited with her breath hitched in her throat.

When his fingers slid the zip down, as though one tooth at a time, tension tightened in her centre. She wanted him again. Already. It had been a long time since she'd known these sensations. With a quick flick of her head, she shoved that thought out of her mind. Now was for enjoying each other with no consequences.

'There you go.' His whisper against her neck sent shivers of longing all over her skin.

She'd only just had him and she was so ready again she ached. 'Leighton, please take me.'

He looked around. Her tiny deck was in darkness, the little spa invisible to anyone not in her unit. No doubt a deliberate move by the resort designers. His answer was to shuck off his trousers and toss his shirt onto a chair. Then he lifted her up and slid into the water.

She gasped. It wasn't too hot, but still a shock to her overheated skin. Under her hands little goose bumps rose on Leighton's arms. Seeking lower, she found his hard reaction and wrapped her fingers around him. Moving up and down in a slow, steady action, she leaned back and watched his eyes widen and darken as his need grew and grew.

Leighton pulled back. 'Wait, Lyssa. Not so fast. We've got all night.'

Magic to her ears. All night with this wonderful man. Her hand kept moving, up, down, up, down. But now it was hard to concentrate as firm fingers touched her, pushed inside her and found her button. Her back arched, her mouth dried and she cried out as everything came together and sent waves of desire rolling through her. 'Leighton,' she whispered through clenched teeth. 'Leighton.'

The sun was streaming into her room when Alyssa hauled her eyes open. Rolling over, she reached out for Leighton and came up empty-handed.

'Leighton,' she called.

No answer.

Where was he? Sitting up, she looked around for his clothes but they weren't there. So he'd left. What was the time? He had to take Jamie and Collette to the airport but it couldn't be that late. She never slept in past seven-thirty, even on the weekends.

Nine forty-nine.

Okay, seemed she could sleep past her normal time after a heavy night between the sheets. Leighton must've moved quietly. Or had she been that exhausted nothing would've woken her? Leaning back against the pillows, she grinned. It was possible. They'd had a big workout.

Coffee would be good about now, she decided. Picking up the phone, she called the restaurant and ordered one. 'Bacon and eggs too, please.' She was starving.

Leaping out of bed, she dived under the shower and washed away the night's activities. Next she put on a bikini and covered it with T-shirt and shorts, then made her way out to the deck with a book and sunglasses.

Life couldn't get any better, she decided as she sank onto a lounger. It was going to be hard leaving this to return to winter in Nelson. Not only winter, but the lack of a certain sexy man. Shoving those thoughts aside, she opened her book, but the words didn't make a lot of sense as memories of Leighton's hands on her body, his mouth covering hers, his sex pushing into her came to the fore. It had been a wonderful night. So good she wanted to do it all over again tonight.

'Here's your breakfast.' Pepe appeared at the side of the deck. 'Where do you want me to put it?'

'I'll have it out here, thanks. Do you know if Jamie and Collette have left for the airport?'

'Yes, Dr Leighton left to take them in his car about

fifteen minutes ago. They were excited yesterday about going to Aitutaki. It is very beautiful over there.'

'So I've heard.' She'd like to visit the island but not on her own, and definitely not while the happy couple were on their honeymoon. They wouldn't want to be bumping into friends over the coming days. From what Collette had said it was a small island compared to Rarotonga and catered mainly for couples. There was a day trip she could do, which meant flying in, going on a boat and swimming with the fish, eating a gourmet lunch, and flying back to the mainland at the end of the day. Perhaps one day she might go with someone special.

The coffee hit the spot and she sighed happily. Her body ached a little as muscles that hadn't had a workout in a long time complained. Last night it was as if everything had fallen into place and there was nothing to get in the way of having fun with Leighton. Who'd have thought? Not her when she was packing her bags to come here. Even if she had been aware he'd be in the same place, the idea they'd get together would never have entered her head.

Where did last night leave them? They'd been all over the place since meeting up the night she'd arrived. On edge, then relaxed and comfortable with each other, then wary again. Yet last night there'd been no hesitation when they'd kissed. They'd gone from a kiss to making love in a flash. Not just once either.

For her, the romance of the wedding had filled her with longing and hope for a brighter future. A future that included someone who loved her. But that hadn't been the reason she'd been intimate with Leighton. He wasn't the future. At least, she doubted he was, despite how often she'd thought she still had feelings for him. It had to be a two-way thing, and Leighton hadn't shown any signs of wanting her back in his life other than for a bit of fun between the sheets, and on the beach or in the spa. Whatever.

She wasn't convinced she was ready to try again either. Losing Leighton in the first place had been horrendous, knocking her low confidence further down and making her question what she wanted in the future. But she'd overcome everything to get back on track. To risk losing that would be a huge step sideways, and she wasn't sure she could take it, though she certainly was tougher nowadays.

Was today going to be one of the cautious times? It was a little weird to have slept with Leighton, considering how they'd broken up, hurt each other, and not spoken in four years. Did they have a future, or was this a final farewell? What did she want to happen?

As she munched on crunchy bacon, she pondered the question. She wanted happiness, and, if the few liaisons she'd had over the years since Leighton were anything to go by, it wasn't easy to come by. Happiness for her meant love and trust and commitment. The things she'd believed she once had with her husband, only to learn that wasn't true.

'Help.'

'We need a doctor.'

Shouts came from down the beach.

Jumping to her feet, she shoved her phone in her back pocket, locked the door to the bungalow and raced to the edge of the resort lawn. Looking along the beach, she saw three frantic-looking people grouped around someone lying on the sand under some palm trees. 'Coming,' she called back and leapt over the low bank to run along the beach. 'What happened?'

'A coconut fell out of the tree and hit Matilda on the head.'

'Are you a doctor?'

'Is she going to be all right?'

'She's not saying anything or responding to my touch.' A man looked up at Alyssa.

The woman's head was at an odd angle and blood poured from a deep indent on the right side. Alyssa dropped to her knees. 'I'm a nurse. Can someone run to the resort and ask them to phone for the ambulance and a doctor? Tell them it's urgent and that Alyssa is here, and if Dr Leighton turns up I need him.'

The woman's pulse was hard to find, and when Alyssa finally felt it her heart sank. It was slow and getting slower. The head injury was serious. The impact from a coconut falling directly onto her head would've been immense. What to do? There wasn't a lot she could do about the head injury, except keep it as clean as possible. Sand was a problem. Looking around, she said, 'I need a towel or scarf, something to cover her head injury.'

'I've got a packet of tissues.' A packet appeared in front of Alyssa.

'Thanks.' Better than nothing, though there was a likelihood the tissue would stick to the wound and need cleaning away before doctors could do anything else.

'Here, use my shirt.' A man handed her his top. 'It's clean.'

Better than tissues. 'Thank you.' She carefully placed the garment over the injury. Where was the ambulance when she needed it? Stop being impatient. The hospital was fifteen minutes away. Hard not to worry when the woman was in such a serious condition. Her pulse was not improving, though Alyssa would have been surprised if it did without any medical input. There was nothing she could do except keep monitoring the woman and be prepared to do CPR if the worst happened.

There were moments when being a nurse sucked. She hated feeling useless, and would feel worse if the woman didn't make it.

'Hey, give me the rundown.' Leighton had arrived.

'Phew.' Her heart thumped with relief and something more personal she didn't have time to think about. Though she was aware she was no longer dealing with a serious trauma on her own. 'Major head trauma, pulse weak and fading. Unconscious and no reaction when I touch her.'

'Straight to the point. I like that.' Leighton was down beside the woman, lifting the shirt to study the impact injury, already assessing everything thoroughly. As she'd expect of him. 'Pepe says the ambulance is less than five minutes away. The crew were on standby at the football field.'

'Thank goodness. This woman needs to be in hospital asap.'

Leighton's fingers were gently touching the woman's scalp everywhere. 'Agreed.' He met her gaze with a steady look that said he knew she'd understand. 'We can't do anything here, except be prepared.'

In other words that hopefully the onlookers didn't get, the woman was at risk of dying and needed a lot more help than was available. 'I'm ready to do CPR.'

His smile was tight as he nodded. 'I'll call the hospital, alert them to what's coming.' Standing up, he stepped away with the phone pressed to his ear.

'What's happening? Why isn't Matilda moving?' asked the woman who'd handed her the tissues.

'She's unconscious,' Alyssa explained. 'Her body is coping by shutting down everything but her vital organs to keep functioning.' Fingers crossed that was the case and those organs weren't shutting down too.

'Is she going to be all right?'

The dreaded question Alyssa hated. 'We're doing what we can.' Which was very little. 'The ambulance isn't far away and once she's in hospital she'll get the best care.' She'd probably be flown to New Zealand as soon as it was possible to arrange the medical aircraft to fly up here.

'The ambulance's here.' Leighton was back and tapped her shoulder lightly. 'I want you to come with us to the hospital, Lyssa. Just in case,' he added quietly so only she heard.

'No problem.' Of course she'd be there for him and their patient. 'Can someone follow us to the hospital? We're going to need your friend's details.' She didn't have time to put them into her phone.

'I'll go there now,' the man who'd handed over his shirt answered. 'Just need to get to the house we're staying in and get my motorbike. Her name's Matilda Maguire.'

'See you there.' She moved to take a corner of the stretcher once the woman had been shifted onto it.

It wasn't easy walking over the sand with a heavy weight balanced between four people trying hard to keep the stretcher steady so as not to move the woman at all, but finally they were on the path and heading to the ambulance. The heat felt intense and Alyssa could feel the sweat popping out on her forehead, but nothing mattered more than getting Matilda into Theatre without any further injury.

Two minutes down the road Alyssa called out, 'No pulse.'

Leighton was onto it, grabbing the defibrillator he'd already primed to save time if needed. 'Stop the ambulance,' he told the driver. 'Stand back, Lyssa.'

Matilda's body jerked as the current hit. The flat line rose and fell, albeit slowly.

'Better than nothing,' she muttered to herself.

'Agreed,' Leighton said.

The ambulance driver pulled out and drove carefully. It seemed to take for ever before they were backing into the parking space outside the emergency room at the hospital, and Alyssa could feel her muscles tightening all the way. She heaved a sigh of relief when they finally stopped. Now Matilda would get the help she needed. Or more than she'd received so far.

As Leighton climbed out of the back of the ambulance he told her, 'If I ever need a nurse to save my butt, I want you.'

Warmth spread throughout her. The compliment meant so much coming from him.

'Let's go to town for brunch,' Leighton suggested when Matilda was in hospital and there was nothing more they could do. 'I never got to have breakfast. Slept in and had to race to get the happy couple to the airport in time.'

'My breakfast's sitting on the table on my deck. I'd

barely started when I heard the shouts from the beach.' She shivered. 'It was awful seeing her lying there.'

Leighton wrapped an arm around her shoulders. 'It wasn't good. They've already arranged for the Life Flight to come up from NZ.' He'd felt so helpless not being able to do much for Matilda but at least she was in good hands.

'That's the best news. Who'd have thought a walk along the beach could go so horribly wrong?'

'I should've warned you. That's the second time I've attended a person hit by a falling coconut. The nuts are huge and hard as rock. There's nothing forgiving about their impact. Never lie on the beach beneath a palm tree.'

Another shiver rippled through her. 'Believe me, I won't. I heard it was wise to avoid going under the palms, but today was an eye-opener. The chances for Matilda of making a full recovery are slight.'

His hand tightened on her shoulder. 'I hate these cases. Which is why we need to do something to take our minds off it. Let's go relax over coffee and food, and then check out the market.'

'Why not eat at a stall in the market? I've been told the food's wonderful.'

He was more than happy to oblige. 'Waffles for me.'

'Make that two and we've got a plan.' She moved sideways out of his arm and took his hand in hers. 'Luckily I stuffed my phone in my pocket when I heard the shouts. There's a bank card in the cover. I might buy a few knick-knacks to support the locals too.'

'Things you take home and put in a cupboard never to come out again?'

She laughed. 'You're onto it.'

His heart soared. That was a sound he loved to hear.

He'd missed it over the years. Hell, he'd missed a whole heap of things about Alyssa. But they were rapidly making up for lost time. The lovemaking had been wonderful, and exhausting in a heart-shaking, head-softening kind of way. They'd gone from wary to fully involved in such a short time. He knew he should be cautious, but it'd been so long since he'd fully relaxed with a woman.

Since he'd last been with Alyssa in fact. The women he'd dated over the intervening years hadn't affected him in the way she did. Alyssa was no ordinary woman. She'd already stolen his heart once. Not that he'd let her get away with that again. He hadn't completely got over the feeling he might be pushed away once more if he made another faux pas. That didn't mean they couldn't have some fun while she was here. He might even feel comfortable enough to think about what he really wanted going forward.

'How do we get to town? I don't see a taxi anywhere.'

'Follow me.' He tugged her hand, and led her around the corner of the building where a guy sat in a van. He was a cleaner at the hospital, plus the on-hand driver for any of the staff caught out without a vehicle for whatever reason, and he also picked up freight from the airport and seaport whenever it came in. 'Hey, Tomo, can you give us a ride to the market?'

'Sure thing. Hop in.'

'Tomo, this is Alyssa. She's here for a wedding. She's also a nurse and was there for the woman hit by a coconut this morning.'

'Hi, Alyssa. I heard about that. Not good for lady, or Rarotonga. Are you all right?' he asked.

She nodded. 'Yes, but I don't like seeing anyone seriously injured. It's always hard to take in.'

'I could never be a nurse,' Tomo said. 'I cry when my dog gets hurt.'

'I totally understand.' Lyssa smiled and clambered into the back of the van. 'Sometimes I wish I was a florist or dug ditches for a living.'

'You been busy this morning?' Leighton asked Tomo.

'Nah. It's Saturday, man.' He laughed. 'Then again it doesn't really matter what day it is around here, they're all the same—quiet when they're not busy. It's not called Raro time for nothing.' He pulled onto the side of the road outside the market.

Leighton dug out his wallet and gave him some cash. 'Thanks, mate.'

Tomo shook his head. 'You don't have to pay me. I was bored.'

As if he'd take advantage of the guy. 'Sure thing, but take it anyway. I'll give you a call when we're ready to head back to the resort where my car is. If you're not available I'll grab a taxi.'

'I'll listen out for you.' Tomo waved and drove off.

Lyssa was looking around at the many tents and small buildings that made up the market. 'I can smell something delicious.'

'In other words, food. Come on. I know exactly which stall we're going to for our waffles.' He took her hand as they walked into the melee that was the Saturday market.

'Do you come here often?' Lyssa asked with a frown. 'I never knew you to be into shopping, let alone mingling with large crowds.'

'I often come for breakfast. It's good sitting back

watching the flow of happy tourists pouring through the area.' It was good to hear chatter and laughter and be able to talk to the people behind the counter when they had a moment to spare, as there were times when he got sick of his own company. The work in the medical centre didn't keep him half as busy as he'd thought he'd be so there were plenty of hours to fill in and not a lot to do.

'Are you enjoying working here?' Lyssa asked after they'd put in their orders at the waffle stall and grabbed an empty table.

'It's been an experience. The pace is way slower and everyone's friendly, but I miss having more to do at work and away from it.' He leaned back in his chair. 'I also miss the changing seasons. The temperature range is slight and when it rains it remains warm. Never thought I'd say I miss the cold.'

'What do you do when not at work?'

'Not a lot. I've done the sights, flown to some of the outer islands for a night or two, and climbed over the top of Rarotonga. That was fun. Very slippery and steep in places and when I was almost at the top I came across hens. Totally left field to me, but then this is Rarotonga.'

Lyssa looked pensive. 'I can see how you'd get antsy for some action. You never liked sitting around.'

'I'm not as obsessive about keeping busy as I used to be, but I don't like doing nothing either. I can't say I regret coming here though. It has been an experience I'll always remember fondly.'

'It might be a shock getting back into the rat race of home.' A smile broke out on her face. 'Here comes the food.'

It was only waffles, but they were damned good ones.

Alyssa's company was the best part of the meal. Funny how relaxed they were together despite their past. Probably because last night had been magic. Making love with Alyssa made him feel whole again. But one night of magic did not make a lifetime plan. His trust issues remained. Trusting her not to reject him wasn't going to be easy. But he'd have to get there if he wanted to take this further. It would be a struggle not to wonder if she might up sticks and pack her bags if something went wrong between them.

And you're open to talking about anything and everything that touches your heart?

'Where have you gone?' the woman slowing his appetite asked.

'Not far.'

You're right opposite me.

But she didn't appear to have figured out he was thinking about her, and them. 'Want another coffee?'

She stared at him with an intensity that brought back other, not so pleasant memories. She knew he'd dodged her question, and in doing so had answered one of his own for himself. He was not ready to be completely up front with her. It would mean putting himself on the line. Even after such a short time in her company, if she said he was too like his father for her to stay around his heart would break.

He waited for her to pounce with whatever was bugging her, but in the end she merely said, 'Yes, another coffee would be great.'

Getting up, he went to order two, feeling daggers in his back. Great. Now where were they at with their day? She'd probably tell him to leave her to get on with checking out the stalls alone. And if she did? Leighton drew a long breath, and made a decision.

'I'm coming with you,' he told her when she said exactly that. 'I haven't really looked at what's on offer before.' Souvenirs didn't interest him, but keeping Alyssa company did. He wanted to spend as much time with her as work allowed over the coming days. Last night had been too wonderful to turn his back on. It wasn't because the sex had been out of this world, it was more about who he'd shared it with. Alyssa had him in her hand once again, and at the moment he was happy to see where that led them despite the glitch over what he hadn't told her. He wasn't ready for a full relationship and might never be, but to be back on good terms with his wife held a lot of appeal.

'I'm sure you'll be bored,' she retorted as she headed over to a small shop full of floral sarongs in every colour imaginable.

'I doubt it,' he replied in a lighter tone. 'I might end up with a couple of bright floral shirts.'

A twinkle appeared in those heart-stopping eyes. 'Bring it on.'

He relaxed. He was back in favour, albeit only a little bit. It was progress. 'That colour would suit you,' he said when she lifted a red and white sarong off the rack. 'Or that yellow one.'

'Shut up.' She grinned. 'I don't wear yellow ever.'

'How about green and black?'

'How about you look at some shirts in the tent next door?'

'Yes, mam.' He went outside and stood watching people wandering around with bags in their hands or on their backs. Everyone was casually dressed, making the most of the warmth. This was what he enjoyed most living here. The relaxed atmosphere backed up by wonderful nature.

But he'd be glad to get home too. The restlessness that had him taking the job in the first place seemed to have left him since Alyssa had reappeared in his life. She gave him hope for a more grounded future, though he still wasn't one hundred per cent certain where he was going to work once back home. Auckland didn't hold any appeal, and while Nelson did tempt him there was a problem with that now. Lyssa living there would mean he had to be prepared to be a small part of her life even if they went no further with what they'd started last night, because she was close to Collette and Jamie. There'd be no avoiding her all the time.

Did he want to? No. So was he prepared to open up and expose his fears? That was the big question. The question he had no definite answer for, and wasn't ready to consider yet. If he ever would be.

'Next I want to find a sun hat.' Lyssa was swinging a bag at her side. 'Then maybe one of those small carvings to put on my sideboard. Or in the cupboard you mentioned, never to be seen again until I move into my house.'

Her house. Lyssa had moved on with her life better than he had. But she didn't have the distrust issues he did these days. 'Seems you've settled in Nelson for the long haul.'

She flicked him a wary glance. 'I have.'

He was pleased for her, and a little envious. 'I'm glad you've found somewhere you want to be, and that you're putting down roots.'

'I was always ready for that, Leighton.' There was an edge to her voice.

'You made our apartment look so homely it was always warm and inviting.' She'd repainted rooms and bought second-hand furniture that suited the place perfectly. He'd objected, saying they could afford new, but she'd claimed that she couldn't so when *she* was shopping second-hand was it.

'I had a lot of fun doing it up.' She looked wistful.

'Have you done the same where you are now?' He didn't even know if she lived alone or shared a flat with others.

'Not really. I haven't had a lot of time and I'm happy with most of the décor. I only rent anyway. Look at those.' She'd stopped at a stall selling colourful ceramic pictures of Cook Islanders going about their daily lives.

'Some of those would look good on your walls.'

'I reckon.' Lyssa held two in her hands and was looking at others. 'These are amazing. I love that one.' It was a picture of three women dressed in sarongs with hibiscus flowers in their hair sitting on a grassy bank while talking and laughing.

'It's one of our most popular tiles.' The woman behind the table smiled.

'I'll take it, and these two.' Lyssa was still looking around. 'Plus that one on the wall behind you with the fishermen. Oh, and the one with the whale leaping out of the sea.'

Leighton shook his head. 'You should've brought your backpack.' Turning to the saleswoman, he said, 'I'll get her a bag for whatever she buys.'

'You don't need to do that,' Lyssa said.

'No, I don't, but I'm going to. One of the hessian bags,' he told the other woman.

'I might not be allowed to take that back with me. They might not allow hessian into the country.'

'It's all right. Tourists buy these all the time,' they were told.

'Now what?' he asked Lyssa once she'd paid for her souvenirs. 'Want to wander through town or head back to your bungalow?' They could sit out on the deck and watch the world go by on the beach. Or go inside and make love again.

'How about both?' She grinned.

She'd read his mind? The beach and making love? No, she wanted to go through town. 'Give me that bag.' He reached for the one containing the ceramics.

'I wonder how Matilda is,' Lyssa said as they strolled along the pavement.

He'd been trying not to think about it. 'I hope no news is good news.' But it was doubtful the woman would have a good outcome.

Two minutes later his phone rang. He recognised the hospital's number. It was almost as though talking about Matilda had made this happen. 'Hello?'

'Leighton, it's Phil. I thought you'd want to know about the woman who was hit by the coconut. She didn't make it, I'm afraid.'

His heart plummeted. 'The brain injury was severe.'

'Yes. So much so I doubt whether she'd have ever recovered full cognition.'

'I'm sorry, Phil.' The surgeon would be hurting too. They all did when cases went belly up.

'Me too. Talk later.' He was gone.

Lyssa was watching him. 'Matilda?'

He nodded. 'She died.'

Lyssa blinked, looked away, drew a breath and looked back at him. 'That sucks.'

'It does. Terrible for the family. Here for a good time and this happens. Not fair.'

His hand was gripped tight. 'Let's go. Shopping doesn't appeal any more,' Lyssa said.

'I agree.' He looked around for a taxi. Nothing in sight. 'I'll call Tomo.' He wouldn't normally bother the man but right now he wanted to be away from the cheerful crowds. 'He's on his way,' he told Lyssa moments later. 'He'll meet us where he dropped us off.'

They turned around and headed back the way they'd come, hearts heavy.

Alyssa's arm brushed his. 'The joys of working in the medical environment.'

CHAPTER SIX

'IT'S STRANGE BUT those palm trees don't look so romantic now. The views are amazing, only there's a catch,' Alyssa said as she stood on the deck outside her room, then fell silent. Matilda hadn't lived to see another day, or any more amazing views anywhere.

Leighton came to stand next to her. 'Hey, it's all right. It's very sad, I know, but we can't watch every word we say because of it.'

'It never gets any easier, does it?'

'If it did then it would be time to get out of the medical profession.'

'True.' Move on. 'So whereabouts are you living?' She'd hoped they might've gone there rather than come back to the resort, but Leighton hadn't mentioned where he lived. Typical. Something else he wasn't sharing.

'In a small house about three kilometres back towards the hospital. It belongs to the family of the doctor I'm filling in for. It's great living with the lagoon only a few steps away and I can hear the surf pounding on the reef at night.'

'I haven't been off the main road yet. Bet there are some stunning views from up on the hills.' Hint, hint.

'You haven't exactly had a lot of spare time since arriving, what with the pre-wedding activities. Your hot little car hasn't done much mileage either.'

She gave up. 'It will over the coming days.' Andrea and Gina were flying out tonight to start back at work on Monday and she'd be on her own so she'd make the most of driving such a cute car. 'Are you starting back at work on Monday?'

'I am. It's going to be busy as there's a mammogram clinic happening over the week. A radiologist is due to arrive from home tomorrow and she'll read all the scans while here. There's no permanent radiologist in the country, all X-rays are usually read online, but they've done this so women will be more willing to come forward and be checked. At the same time, the medical centre runs a full medical check-up clinic for the women, many of whom don't visit a doctor unless it's urgent.'

'So the medical service here is tied into that back home?' It made sense since the Cook Islands were part of the realm of New Zealand.

Leighton nodded. 'Yep. Mostly it works except for serious illnesses and then the patient is flown to Auckland for treatment and follow up.' He paused to gaze out to the sand and lagoon beyond. 'Feel like a drink?'

'You know what? I'd love one.' It might help her relax after that awful news. 'But I haven't got anything in my fridge at the moment.'

'Take a seat and put your feet up. I'll go over to the bar. Be right back.'

It wasn't hard to do as she was told. The view was as stunning as the first time she saw it, and the air warm, plus she was shattered. They hadn't had a lot of sleep during the night, then throw in the shock of losing their patient and she was struggling to stay upright.

'Here, get some of this into you.' Leighton held out a glass of beer minutes later. 'Unless you don't drink lager these days.'

'Sometimes, and now seems like one of those. Thanks.' She took a sip and savoured the cold liquid on her tongue. 'I'll probably fall asleep next.'

'I have a plan.' Leighton laid a board on the deck table and then a small box. 'Remember one of these?'

'A chess set? Of course I do. We used to have a match whenever one of us was in the doldrums after losing a patient.' They'd played hard, winner take all, and it had helped negate the pain either of them had been in. 'That's a long time ago. I'll be rusty.'

He laughed. 'Good. I've played online occasionally but it's not the same as a current game with the opponent right here. Online games can take weeks and don't have the same buzz.'

She rubbed her hands. She was already feeling a little better. 'Let's do this.' Now was not the moment to let him know she'd played a few times recently with a patient who was on the ward for nearly four weeks and got bored easily. With a bit of luck she might've learned enough to beat Leighton for once. It didn't pay to get too cocky around him. He was smart and until she actually had him in a no-win position she'd stay quiet.

He tossed a coin and covered it with his hand. 'Heads or tails?'

'Heads.' Always.

'You win. But that's all you're winning.' He grinned.

'We'll see.' She made her first move, and sat back

to wait for Leighton to take his turn, enjoying the light breeze touching her hot skin. 'This is nice. We don't often get a breeze here.'

'It's not usually what the tourists want.' He made his first move. 'There you go.'

An hour passed before Alyssa finally sat back with a smug smile. 'Got you.'

Leighton studied the board then looked over. 'You're right. You win. Well done.'

'Go on. Admit it. You're peeved.'

'Of course I am. I hate losing, and I've never lost to you.' He shook his head. 'Guess I had it coming.'

'Dinner's on you.' She laughed, then stopped. 'Thanks, Leighton. That was just what I needed.'

'Me too.'

'Where did you get the board from? I don't imagine you had it in the car.'

'There's a cupboard with board games in Reception. I took a look on the off chance there might be a chess set and voila.' He looked pleased with himself. 'Feel like a dip in the sea?'

'Good idea.' She pushed up out of the chair. 'I'll change into a bikini.'

His eyes widened. 'Perfect. I'll stay as is.' He'd been wearing knee-length shorts all morning.

'You carry a change of clothes in the car?'

'I do have a change of clean clothes at the ready. Never know when I'm going to get messy while helping a patient.'

'It's happened three times since I arrived,' she admitted. 'Which seems a lot.'

'Tourists do get up to some mischief at times. I thought you were going to change.'

'Impatient, aren't we?' She headed inside. Which bikini? The red one was her favourite, but the white one looked pretty good on too. No, the red one was better against her still pale skin.

'Woo-hoo,' Leighton whistled when she joined him.

Obviously red was perfect if the sexy look on his face was anything to go by. 'You like?'

'Like? I'm struggling not to rush you back to bed.'

'What's stopping you?'

'The housemaid's in the next unit and I suspect yours is next to be tidied.'

Nothing like cold water poured on her hot skin. 'Glad you noticed.'

'So am I, considering how turned on you make me.'

Her chest swelled. 'Let's hit the beach.'

'Where's the sunscreen?'

'Right there on the table.'

'Have you put any on?' he asked, picking up the tube.

'I was going to after I'd eaten breakfast, but got interrupted.'

'Turn around.'

Firm hands rubbed cream over her back and shoulders, increasing the heat in her veins. It was as though she was making up for the lack of sex over the last four years in twenty-four hours. She hadn't been interested in getting down and personal with any man since splitting up from Leighton, always aware how good it had been with him. Suddenly her body was waking up, all because of him.

Leighton stepped in front of her and began covering her chest, neck and arms.

She groaned. She could not help herself. 'Stop or I'll drag you inside, to hell with the maid.'

He just laughed. 'Nope, we're going for a swim.'

She glanced down and laughed too. 'You can walk normally with that?'

'Damn you, Alyssa Harrison. I'll look like a waddling duck and everyone within sight will know why.' He dropped the tube on the table and swung her up into his arms. 'That bikini should come with a warning label.'

Harrison. No way.

'I'm Alyssa Cook.'

Leighton froze to the spot, then his arms loosened and she slid slowly down until her feet touched the deck.

A chill crossed her as she locked her gaze on him.

He looked bewildered and furious all in one.

She stepped back. 'Hello? You thought I'd be using my married name after all this time?'

'No, I didn't. I knew you weren't.'

'Then what's your problem?'

'I don't have one.'

'Try again, Leighton. Your body language tells a different story.'

Here we go.

'You won't talk about anything important, will you?'

'I got a surprise, that's all. It's a bit of a wake-up to what we're doing, despite being separated and all.'

She gasped. He didn't used to give sucker punches. But he might have a point. They had got down and sexy fast last night, with no thought about where it might take them. None on her mind, anyway. But still.

'We're having some fun, that's all.' Was it though? She wasn't looking for more? For something deeper to follow up on? Not likely considering they hadn't cleared the air between them. Sure, she'd heard how Jamie came on the scene and how that had affected Leighton to the point where he'd let her go, but he'd given her only a bare outline of what happened. Nothing about how deeply it affected him or what he hoped for moving forward.

'You're right, we were.' He moved further away.

'Were?' Time to draw a line in the sand. Except she needed to know why he was afraid to tell her everything that happened when Jamie turned up in his life. She needed closure, and suspected Leighton did too. 'Like we're not even going to see each other over the coming days?'

'It isn't that straightforward.'

'Meaning?' She'd make him talk, if at all possible.

He stared at her. 'You know exactly what I mean, Alyssa.'

It was impossible to get him to say what was really on his mind.

'We have a past.'

He didn't say a word.

'A past that blew up in our faces. But we still seem to connect when we're relaxed and not overthinking everything.' Like when they'd been making out on the beach or in her bed.

'I don't want to go there, Alyssa, so I'll head away now.' He was already turning away.

'Nothing's really changed,' she said sadly. 'Not that there's any reason it should've, I suppose.'

Leighton still kept personal issues close to his chest. If she got too involved it would only come back to hurt her. She could not face that for a second time.

* * *

She was right. Nothing had changed. He still hated opening up. Leighton slammed the car door shut. Even more so since he didn't know if he could trust her with his heart. Or if he even wanted to. Their marriage had failed, so what was the point? They weren't getting back together despite a fantastic time overnight and at the market.

His chest ached at the thought of not spending more time with Lyssa despite having walked away from her. He'd needed to clear his head and get over the hurt that slammed him in the heart when she said 'I'm Alyssa Cook' so fiercely. It was as though she was holding onto who she was and that she'd lost that when she went by his surname. It had meant so much when she'd taken it as hers. He'd never denied anything about her, always encouraged her to be herself so that was special. Now she'd reminded him that, while they were having fun, they were not a couple.

His foot pressed the accelerator hard and the car spun out onto the road heading in the direction of his temporary home. He did owe her an apology for being so abrupt and walking away. He also owed her an explanation, but first he had to figure out what was driving this need to get close to her and whatever it was preventing him making the move. Spending time with Lyssa felt good, and making love to her had been beyond wonderful. It had brought back happy memories and reminded him life didn't have to be so solitary if he opened up his heart.

If. It should be easier now she knew about his brother, but he was still afraid to let her see his fears, and that had become even harder after they'd made love. He felt close to her again, which only increased his worry.

I need to return to Lyssa and apologise.

The sound of a bird tweeting interrupted his dreary thoughts.

The caller ID on the screen of his phone said Amalie. He pulled to the side of the road. 'Hey, what can I do for you?' he asked the midwife from the medical centre.

'Mere Aro has been in labour for ten hours and now baby's the wrong way round.'

'I'll come. Where are you?'

'At the hospital.' Amalie hung up.

Yay, something to take my mind off Lyssa. He was almost grateful to Mere. Almost, but the woman would be desperate to give birth and worried sick that baby was stuck so he couldn't feel too pleased. Instead he needed to be the calm, confident doctor and not the man with a woman doing his head in.

Finally he laughed at himself, albeit a little sharply. As Jamie had said the other night, nothing ever went to plan. Though when it came to Lyssa, there weren't any plans other than to be friendly and try not to get too involved. Bit late for that after last night. He was already well on the way.

The road leading to the hospital came up on his right. Slowing to allow two tourists on mopeds to go past, he made a turn and headed up the hill.

'Glad you're here,' Amalie said the moment he stepped inside the birthing room. 'I think baby's getting desperate to come out.'

'Right, let's do this.' The sooner baby was here, the sooner Mere would be comfortable and holding baby to her breast. 'Hello, Mere. I hear you need some help.'

'You bet, Doc. I've had enough of this.'

'I'm sure you have.' Ten hours wasn't a long labour, but, as he'd been told in the past by various female nurses, he didn't know what he was talking about. He did know he'd hate it if his woman had to go through too many hours' labour. 'Where can I scrub up?'

Two hours later Leighton was home and mowing the lawn to keep busy. Baby Tepi weighed in at four and a half kilos and was very noisy. He was also very cute, and tugged at Leighton's heart strings when Amalie placed him on Mere's breast. If only he and Lyssa had stayed together, they might have had children by now.

The lawn done, Leighton went for a dip in the lagoon to wash off the sweat and cool down. He swam out to the inside reef and floated on his back, staring up at the endless blue sky. What a magical place. He loved it, but it wasn't somewhere to live permanently. Not for him. He needed more going on than happened here. Except for the past week. Plenty had happened. Where was Alyssa at the moment? Sunbathing in one of those erotic bikinis by any chance? She'd got him thinking about the future and how awesome it would be to have a life partner and even children. One look at her in that tiny red bikini and he'd wanted her. Just like old times.

Back on shore he walked the beach for a while, trying to ignore any thoughts about Alyssa. Finally he returned to the house and jumped under the shower, where he punched his fist into his other hand. 'Damn it. I give in. I can't ignore her any longer.'

Pulling on a white shirt and dressy shorts, he snatched up his keys and headed out. There was only one way to deal with the warring emotions going on between his head and heart. He had to see Alyssa.

Alyssa lay down on the lounger and closed her eyes. She stank of sunscreen but there was no way she was getting burnt.

She'd just returned from dropping Andrea and Gina at the airport for their flight home. On the way in they'd stopped at a popular bar on the beach for one final drink together in paradise. She'd opted for a soda as she was driving. Now she would relax and read the book she'd started on the flight over. So much for being a tourist and getting out and about, but it was nice to do nothing for a change. If only that included not thinking about Leighton's reaction to her putting the name she went by out there. Why wouldn't she go back to her maiden name?

Did she regret being so abrupt with him? No. She'd said it how it was. He wouldn't thank her for being a simpering idiot in an attempt to get on side again. It had come as a shock though, after how well they'd got on at the wedding and throughout the night. She'd begun to believe they might be able to make inroads into a deep and meaningful friendship. Silly woman. What was to be gained by doing that? They wouldn't pick up their marriage and carry on. It wasn't feasible. Leighton had to let go of his need to remain closed off to her because that said he didn't trust her. Until he talked she didn't fully trust *him* with her heart.

The gate leading into her area creaked. 'Hey, Alyssa, get your glad rags on. I owe you dinner, remember?' Leighton stood tall and proud, not showing a hint of remorse for what he'd said earlier.

She jerked in surprise. 'Really? After you walked out on me this morning?'

'Especially because I did. I'm sorry for acting like a sulky brat, Alyssa.'

But not sorry for not explaining himself. Did she bury this for now and enjoy an evening out with him? Or did she let her disappointment win and demand answers? It was a no-brainer. Making certain her bikini was in place, she sat up. 'Park your butt while I get ready.' She headed inside, paused and returned. 'There's a beer in the fridge if you want one.' Getting dressed and made up for a date took time. No way was she going out looking second rate.

His posture relaxed with those beautiful broad shoulders loosening and his chin softening with relief. 'Sounds good. I'll get it. Do you want a wine?'

'I'll wait until we're out wherever you're taking me.' Where were they going? There were a lot of great-looking restaurants all along the main road circling the island. Many of them were on the edge of the beach.

Leaping under the shower to remove the sunscreen, she tried not to smile too much. Leighton was taking her out. He'd also called her Alyssa. It had to be a good sign or he wouldn't have bothered to show up.

Which dress to wear? There was only one she hadn't used so far. Sky-blue and slinky, a perfect match for the cream high-heeled shoes she'd given into buying while she was filling in time at the international airport earlier in the week. They'd cost an arm and a leg but were worth it. Though she'd probably rue the decision when she returned home and checked her bank account, something she refused to do while on holiday.

At a restaurant on the beachside they were shown to

a table under the trees on a lawn that met with the sand. Terns danced along the beach and over the lawn, no doubt hoping for some crumbs from the diners.

'This is lovely,' Alyssa said as she gazed around. It got dark quite early but there were lights strung throughout the trees casting long shadows. 'Have you been here before?'

Leighton shook his head. 'I've thought about it but it's not a place to come on my own. I prefer company when going to a restaurant. That's not asking for sympathy. I'm just saying how it is. The locals I've got to know don't dine out often.'

'Aren't there quite a lot of expats here?' From what she'd read many of the bars and restaurants were owned by Kiwis and Australians.

'There are, and I've met a few, but they're usually working when I'm not.'

'Here you go. One wine and one beer.' Their waitress placed the glasses on the table. 'Ready to order?'

'Sorry.' Alyssa picked up the thin folder. 'I haven't looked at the menu. Too busy enjoying the scenery.'

'No problem. I'll give you a bit more time.'

Leighton handed her the glass of wine, and then tapped it with his beer glass. 'To making amends.'

She was over avoiding the issue. 'You believe it's that easy?'

He looked guilty. 'No, I don't.'

'Why is it so hard to talk to me?'

His fingers tapped incessantly on the table. Fear blinked out of his eyes, quickly covered by stubbornness then withdrawal.

Her heart went out to the only man she'd ever loved.

He was hurting. She wanted to help. But to push further when surrounded by other diners could lead to an embarrassing altercation there'd be no coming back from. Leighton hated being the centre of attention. She'd give him some space. *Again.* Coward that she was. But that look in his eyes said she wasn't going to win tonight so she'd go for showing how much she cared about him.

Taking his hand, she held tight and found a smile. 'What did you get up to after you left me this morning?'

'I mowed lawns after I helped deliver a breeched baby,' Leighton said. 'A cracker of a little guy.'

The last of the tension gripping her slipped away. No matter that there were issues between them, she liked being with him.

'Aww. He's all right? Mum okay?'

'Absolutely. Everything went well and was over quickly.' He sipped his beer, staring outward. 'Is it wrong to say that seeing a new life come into the world helps cope with losing one? I'm not saying the baby replaces Matilda, but I did feel a little bit better.'

'I believe it's a natural reaction, and I admit just hearing about it makes me feel all soft on the inside.' A pity she hadn't been there to help and see baby's arrival.

Leighton was still gazing towards the water. 'I think Jamie and Collette intend starting a family fairly soon.'

'Collette hasn't said anything but then she's not one for talking about personal things much.'

'I'll be an uncle.' Longing clouded his voice, but whether for nieces and nephews, or for children of his own, who knew? Not her. They'd occasionally talked about having a family in the future when he'd qualified and had more spare time.

'Uncle Leighton. Sounds good.' Had he been in a relationship since they'd broken up? If he had it must be over because he'd made love to her. He was a loyal man and would never be unfaithful. He was not his father. She changed direction. 'Are the golf clubs getting dusty back home?'

'A little. Everyone's busy with family commitments these days. Jackie and Cain have two kids, Jordan and Maggie one, with another on the way, and Chris and Vicki's children are teenagers needing lots of attention.'

'Teenagers? Already?' They used to babysit those two when Chris and Vicki went on a date night. 'Time flies.'

'Sure does.'

Her hand touched her stomach. Would she ever be lucky enough to have a family? Having a man at her side came first, and so far she hadn't done very well there. The chances she and Leighton could give it another go were slim, if at all possible. 'You mentioned settling in Nelson. Does me living there give you cause for concern?'

He winced. 'Would it bother you if I did?'

'Answer a question with another one, why don't you? Why can't you just say what's on your mind?'

Another wince. 'Fair enough.' He paused.

She waited him out. He could fill in the blanks this time. And if he didn't she would get up and walk away.

'I don't want to be in the way if we're not getting on. Chances are we'd always be crossing paths since you're friends with Jamie and Collette.'

'Then we'll just have to get along, won't we?'

'Are you suggesting I continue looking into moving to Nelson?' His eyes had widened a little.

'Hey, it's not a village. It's a small city, and there's

also Richmond and Stoke down the road. We wouldn't be bumping into each other every time we went out of our front doors.'

'Right.' Leighton set his glass aside. 'Want to go for a walk?'

This was going nowhere. 'No, thanks.'

'Then I'll take you back to the resort.' Standing up, he reached for her hand and tugged her up against him. 'Thanks for joining me.'

'No problem.' It was actually. She was fed up with going round in circles. And she was tired beyond belief. Leighton was sapping all her energy, physically and mentally. Sleep was next on her menu. Alone. She was not making love with Leighton tonight. She did not know what she wanted with him at this point so she would tread carefully. No one else was going to protect her as fiercely as she would.

Parking outside the resort, Leighton hopped out and went around to open Alyssa's door. His head was spinning. They hadn't caught up on much of what they'd done in the years since they'd last seen each other, but he was learning more about Alyssa all the time. She was stronger, fending for herself rather than looking to others for support. She also seemed focused on what was right for her. He couldn't fault that, whereas he still kept things close to his chest, afraid to be vulnerable. If anyone could hurt him, it was Lyssa. But he did want more time with her, and, yes, to explain himself. If only he knew how without seeming needy. Slipping his hand around hers, he started for the entrance.

'I'll see myself in,' she said as she pulled her hand free.

'I always see my date to her door.' Not that he'd had a lot of dates lately. Couldn't get enthused.

'Fine.'

When he reached for her elbow, she stepped sideways, increasing the distance between them in more ways than one, underscoring the fact he had to talk to her.

At the bungalow she swiped the key card and opened the door, then, instead of going inside, wandered over to the edge of the deck to gaze up at the star-studded sky. 'It's so clear.'

Tipping his head back, he could only agree. 'Magical.' As was the citrus scent wafting from Lyssa, stirring his blood. They could be so good together. And he wanted her so badly it hurt.

Slipping his arm around her waist, he drew her nearer. 'Alyssa, I am enjoying catching up and getting to know you again.' It was true. She was the same yet different. She seemed to have accepted who she was, and what she wanted. When he'd met her, she was still coping with the loss of her mother and wondering what was out there for her. Not any more. This was one determined woman.

'Have I changed that much you are starting at the beginning?' A wobbly smile appeared.

Don't stall now.

'Yes and no. You're still the same Alyssa with the quick smiles and wanting to follow your dreams. But I think you now know what those dreams are and have the strength and determination to follow through.'

She blinked. 'That's deep.'

Well, she had accused him of not opening up. 'I'm trying to answer your question.'

'Fair enough.' Her surprise remained. 'Honestly, you're

probably right. I do know what I want for my future, and in some areas I'm working hard to make it happen.'

'What about the others?'

'I'll have to wait and see.' She tipped her head back to look up at the stars again. 'That's so beautiful.'

So are you.

'I couldn't agree more.' Wrapping her in both arms, he dropped his chin on her head and breathed deep. Her warm body fitted against his as if she belonged there and made him feel he was finally coming home. Her hair brushed his arm and he held her closer, before leaning down to brush her mouth with his. 'Lyssa.' Then he kissed her.

She kissed him back. A chaste kiss.

Lifting his head, he looked down into those big eyes. 'Alyssa?'

Stepping out of his arms, she shook her head. 'Not tonight, Leighton. I would prefer to be alone.'

His heart stumbled. She didn't want him? 'It's all right,' he fibbed. The last thing he wanted was to leave, but he wasn't saying. She'd got to him without him realising just how much. She was probably doing him a favour by withdrawing. Except he wasn't happy. He wanted to be with her all night and into the next day.

'I need my sleep.'

He didn't believe that to be completely true, but he'd run with it. Arguing wouldn't solve a thing. If she didn't want to sleep with him, he had to accept that. 'Fair enough.' He turned towards the gate, then turned back. He felt vulnerable but the need to spend more time together was greater. 'How about we do something together tomorrow morning before I go into work to prepare for the coming week? I'd like to show you some sights.'

She hesitated, then nodded softly. 'That might be fun. Any idea where we'd go?'

Relief flooded him. And yes, he already had an idea. 'Leave it to me. I'll give you a call later in the morning, give you time to sleep in.' She never used to do that, was always up with the sparrows, but who knew now? Not him, but he was working on learning more about this wonderful woman.

'Leighton, dinner was lovely.' She placed her hand on his arm, setting his skin alight with longing. 'I just need space.' Then she placed a light kiss on his cheek. 'Until tomorrow.'

Again his heart lurched as lemons tickled his senses. It took all his strength not to haul her into his arms and kiss her senseless. But he couldn't. She'd said she needed time to herself and he would not intrude. 'Goodnight, Lyssa.' Yes, he used that name deliberately because he cared so much for her. 'Sleep tight.'

CHAPTER SEVEN

DESPITE THINKING SHE wouldn't sleep a wink, let alone tight, Alyssa woke late the next morning not remembering anything from the moment she climbed into her bed and switched off the light.

Stretching luxuriously, she grinned. 'Heck, I feel good.' The holiday was obviously having a good effect on her sleep pattern. As for Leighton, she wasn't sure if he was good or bad for her. How she'd managed to pull away when his mouth was on hers she'd never know. It had taken every last drop of determination, but she'd had to. Last night had proved once more he wasn't about to open up and tell her what she needed to hear. Sick of trying to force the issue, she'd backed off. Could it be that the harder she tried, the deeper he dug in to avoid the questions? But if she left him alone nothing would change. There'd be no future for them and she wanted one more than just about anything else.

It was hard to face. Leighton had always been quick to tell her he loved her, to show his pain whenever he lost a patient, talk about what made families special. She'd loved that about him. He had changed in that respect. And she'd changed by not being prepared to accept him keeping quiet about what was important to them as a pair. He couldn't keep doing this if they were to have a future. If he wanted one with her, that was.

After ordering coffee she leapt under the shower, humming to herself all the time. She opted for a sun frock over a bikini since she had no idea where Leighton intended taking her. He'd surprised her with suggesting they go somewhere today. She'd thought he might've stayed away after she pulled away from him.

Her heart softened. He was the only man she'd ever loved and now she wondered if she might not have stopped loving him. He made her feel so good without trying, just by being himself. Kind, funny, generous, gentle and tough. Yes, and afraid. He had the power to break her heart all over again.

So stand up and fight for him. Demand answers. Refuse to be ignored. Show him you care, that you won't hurt him.

Yeah, and get hurt in return.

Pepe knocked on the door, coffee in hand.

'Don't you ever stop working?'

He grinned. 'It's the family business and I'm the only son.'

'You've brought two coffees.'

'One for Doc Leighton.'

'He's not here.' Blimey, were the staff keeping tabs on them?

'He's on his way. He rang to order coffee for you and him.'

Alyssa scowled. Seemed Leighton was one step ahead of her. 'Typical.'

'So you're up.' The man messing with her emotions appeared on the deck. 'Sleep well?'

'Like a log. Everything's caught up.' Sipping her coffee, she shook away the thoughts plaguing her. 'What are we doing?'

'It's a surprise. You'll need your swimming gear, flippers and a snorkel. I've ordered a picnic brunch from here to have on the beach, that will be delivered once we've finished our excursion.' He looked pleased with himself, as though he'd done something out of the ordinary. Not a lot of dating been going on in his life? He'd always liked to spoil her whenever they went out, but that didn't explain why he looked so chipper this morning.

It wasn't until she saw the sign at a beach a few K's along from the resort pointing to Avaavaroa Passage that she knew what he had planned. 'Snorkelling with turtles.' She fist-pumped the air. 'Yes, that's on my list of things to do.' Doing it with Leighton added to the experience. 'This is amazing. Thank you so much.'

'Glad you're happy.'

'Are we doing it independently or with a group?'

'I've booked two places with the group as the organisers have lots of gear. Though the water's warm you may want the buoyancy of a wetsuit as it's quite deep in the passage.'

'No, I'll be fine.' She wouldn't be on her own if she panicked as she had the other day. Leighton would be keeping an eye on her. That was who he was. 'You're a gem,' she said with all her heart.

It was good to have someone with her instead of going it alone. Since she'd left Leighton, she'd never had someone at her side. She'd never met another man who understood her without having to be told every single thing. Throw in those sexy kisses and she'd been a goner from the get-go with Leighton. He was a hard act to follow, if it was even possible, which added to the feeling she still loved him.

'Let's do this.' He shoved his door wide and hopped out, swinging an underwater camera from his hand.

Her mind was so full of what to do next about Leighton she barely heard a word of the safety talk from the guides, nor the instructions on what to do when they reached the turtles. But once they made their way down to the water and slipped on their flippers and snorkel she began to focus on why she was here. As the water got deeper, Alyssa kept an eye out for Leighton, but she needn't have bothered. He was with her all the way.

Tapping her shoulder, he pointed. 'Look.'

A turtle swam beside them, totally unconcerned by all the humans flapping around nearby. 'Oh, my. That's beautiful,' she said around the mouthpiece. Not that anyone could hear her, but, hey, this was incredible. Rolling onto her side, she gazed around in awe. There were four turtles close to them. Big and cumbersome yet mesmerising as they moved along.

Leighton was taking photos of the turtles and her.

One of those might be the perfect photo of her dream holiday—if she accepted him back into her life. Something nudged her on the back and she turned to find a turtle merely inches away heading past. The creatures must be so used to people in their space it wasn't worrying them at all. How amazing. She rolled, and kicked and paddled, turning continuously to watch them. Every so often she bobbed to the surface and took a few deep breaths of air while checking on Leighton before dropping down again.

When the group leader called out that it was time to return to the beach she couldn't believe an hour had gone by. 'Surely not,' she said as she tore her mouthpiece off. 'We haven't been out here that long.'

'It's probably not an hour,' Leighton agreed. 'The time will include the talk and coming out here.'

Moving closer, she kissed his cheek. 'This has been the best.'

'You can come again during the week. I just wanted to be with you for the first time you got to see turtles close up.'

'Good. I thought I'd feel more comfortable in the deeper water knowing you were there but, to be honest, once I saw the turtles I didn't think about anything else.'

'I'm glad. Come on, brunch is waiting. I can see the resort's van by the tour site.'

She swam lazily towards the beach, happier than she'd been since they'd split up. The problems hadn't gone away though, would no doubt return before the day was over.

Idyllic didn't begin to describe the day. Leighton had got it perfect. She'd forgotten about the times he'd take her somewhere special and treat her like a princess. Careful. They might be having a wonderful reunion, but she was leaving in a week and then they'd be going their separate ways despite her new-found love for him. Did they have to though? They were older and wiser. Yet the problems were still the same.

'Where've you gone?' the man stirring her head—and heart, she admitted—asked.

'I'm right here with you.' That was how she wanted the rest of the day to go. Probably unrealistic but hope made her hide from her concerns. As they strolled up the beach, feeling so comfortable and at ease, she was tempted to take his hand, but it would only add to the confusion between them. She still wasn't ready to make love again. The past had to be resolved first.

'Those croissants look delicious,' she noted as Leighton unpacked the chilly bin containing their breakfast. Her mouth watered just looking at them with the raspberry jam and whipped cream oozing out of the sides.

'But wait, there's fruit first. Pawpaw, mangoes, bananas.'

'You're spoiling me.' He really had gone to a lot of effort today.

'I'm addicted to the fruit. Nothing like eating something that's straight off the tree. The bananas don't look wonderful but, believe me, they're tastier than most varieties we get back home.'

Leaning back in the beach chair, she sighed. 'I've never had a holiday like this. No wonder people rave about going to the islands to relax.' Would she do it again? On her own? Not likely. She'd spend the whole time thinking about Leighton, looking out for him while knowing he was back in New Zealand.

'Not bad, is it? I get to laze on the beach any day I like.'

'But do you?'

Tell me something about yourself.

'I prefer walking on the sand, not sprawling all over it.'

Alyssa watched two paddle boarders going past, their oars rising and falling in even strokes. 'Think they've done that before. I'm going to give it a go this afternoon. There are boards available at the resort.'

'Hope you've got good balance.'

'I'm sure I'll fall off lots, but it doesn't matter. Landing in the water isn't going to be painful as long as I stay clear of the rocky patches.'

'You're onto it.' Leighton sprawled out on the sand, hands behind his head. 'What else have you got planned for the week?'

'Not a lot. I'll go up to the Wigmore falls, browse the shops in town, swim and read, and just take it easy.' Nothing like what she'd ever done before, yet she was feeling chronically tired because of all the mental strain from thinking about Leighton and the future. 'I've been working long hours for what feels like for ever and it's hard to let go and do nothing.'

'Why the long hours?'

'Like every hospital up and down the country we're short-staffed. Being Charge Nurse, I feel responsible to take on the hours there's no one else to cover. I don't like patients not getting one hundred per cent care on my ward.'

Leighton looked at her. 'Yet it's not your problem to fix everything. You need to look after yourself too, Lyssa, or you'll end up not able to work at all because you'll be so exhausted physically and mentally.' The concern in his eyes nearly undid her resolve to remain cautious.

'I know, but it's not easy to turn my back on people.' She probably exaggerated the problems on the ward, but that was because she cared so much.

He didn't say anything more, so she closed her eyes, making the most of the warmth. 'I could get used to this.'

'The place or the lack of action?'

'Doing nothing.'

'Yeah, right. That'd last all of a couple of weeks and then you'd be beside yourself for something to do.' He sat up and stretched his arms over his head. 'I don't recall you ever not having more than one thing on the go at a time.'

'I still do. Work and more work.' She bit her lip. He looked good enough to eat. Or to make love with. Yes, definitely the better option and not happening until she knew her heart was safe. She clenched her hands at her sides to keep from reaching out for him. Making love after the wedding had been wonderful. She'd missed that so much, along with most other parts of their marriage. She'd had a few flings but not one man she'd met had flipped the switch the way Leighton always had.

He still does.

'You need some balance in your life. More holidays?' The cheeky smile he wore ramped up the desire filling her.

'I am enjoying this so much I might have to go on some more trips.'

Want to come with me?

Shuffling upright, she looked out towards the beach, but there was no ignoring Leighton. He took over the air she was breathing.

His hand closed over hers. 'I'm glad you're having a great time. It's wonderful catching up and getting to know you again.'

'You think?' She hadn't learnt much about him except how stubborn he was, and that he was as wonderful as ever.

'I do.' Leaning closer, Leighton kissed her. A slow, soft kiss, filling her with loving.

Leighton, you're making me feel whole again.

He pulled back, looked directly at her. 'Thanks for joining me today.'

'The turtles were amazing.'

So was the time with you.

'I'd better get to work.'

Standing up, she brushed sand off her legs. 'Fair enough.' Thank goodness one of them was being sensible.

Leighton turned on the fan in his room at the medical centre and sat down at the desk. Pulling the stack of patient files towards him, he sighed. It had been hard to leave Alyssa to come in here, but if he hadn't he might've given in and asked some personal questions about if she'd been in a relationship since they broke up and what that meant if she had.

Alyssa had turned his head and his heart the very first time he saw her, and he'd known right from the get-go she was the one. The women he'd spent time with over the last few years hadn't come up to speed. They didn't laugh like Lyssa. Making love hadn't held the awe and tenderness it did with her. The list went on. She wasn't easy to replace, and now they'd caught up again he doubted he ever would find another woman he'd love as he did her. He'd loved her with everything he had, and still did. She filled him with a calmness that was new, and a turn around on their old relationship.

He owned most of the blame for their separation by not trusting her with the truth about his father. Then when he'd learned she'd already dealt with his father's blatant disregard for others he had been ashamed. The shame remained. Though to move forward and try to reclaim the love of his life he had to come clean and accept the consequences, no matter what they were. Alyssa held his heart in her hands. He needed to know where their future lay.

There was a glaring problem with being in love with Alyssa. Needing to tell her everything didn't mean he could let go the fear that she'd find him lacking.

'Hey, man, what are you doing in here on a Sunday?' Henri, another doctor at the clinic, stood in the doorway. 'Nothing's that urgent it can't wait till the morning.'

Jerked out of his thoughts, he tossed the pen aside. 'You're right.'

'Good. Now get your butt off that chair and come around to my place for a feed. Got some tuna off the fishing boat this morning and Mela's making salad and doing something with potatoes.'

'Sounds good,' he admitted. Some company would stop him wondering how to approach Alyssa. 'I'll pick up some beers on the way.'

'You don't have to.'

Maybe, but he wasn't going empty-handed. 'What does Mela like to drink?'

'Buy her a bottle of Chardonnay and she won't let you leave the island.'

'Why don't you ask your friend if she'd like to join us too? I saw her walking along the road by the resort as I came into town so I know she's still here,' Henri added with a cheeky grin.

How did Henri even know he'd been spending time with Alyssa? 'I'll give her a call, but she's probably already got something on the go.'

'You will phone her?'

He picked up his phone and pressed her number, only to go straight to voicemail. Was that good or bad?

* * *

Alyssa wobbled as she tried to stand up straight on the paddle board. 'Whoa. This isn't as easy as it looks.'

'No, it's not,' returned the woman on her right. They'd met when she went to get a paddle board. Karin's partner, Jarrod, was out here too.

Splash. Karin was in the water.

Laughing, Alyssa forgot to maintain her balance and joined her. 'Oh, well. I knew I'd be falling in heaps of times. That's the first one out of the way.'

'Come on, you two. Get up.' Jarrod paddled past them, laughing his head off.

'I'll tip him in if he comes close,' Alyssa said. She wanted to paddle along the edge of the lagoon, but so far hadn't gone more than a few metres. She hoisted herself onto the board. 'I'm going to do this no matter how long it takes.' She began standing up, inch by inch, straightening until at last she stood tall. Slipping the oar through the water, she moved forward, wobbled, held her breath and paddled again. 'Woo-hoo. This is awesome.' Splash. She'd hit the bottom. 'Okay, I've made progress.'

By the time she made it back to her room she had aches in muscles she hadn't known existed, but felt really great. She was going to meet up with Karin and Jarrod for a beer and some nibbles by the resort pool. When she checked her phone, her heart sank. Leighton had called and she'd missed him. She'd been glad of the break from dealing with her mixed emotions and yet here she was wishing she'd answered his call and heard his sexy voice. Heat spiralled down to her sex. Damn him. This really was love all over again.

Except this time it was frightening. It could all fall apart too easily. Her heart had to be protected at all costs.

Her phone rang shortly after she sat down with her friends at the pool. The man himself. It seemed he couldn't stay out of touch for long either. 'Hey, how's things?'

'All good. How often did you fall off the board?'

'Countless times. I eventually managed to go a little way towards the other end of the lagoon and back.'

'Go you. I'm at Henri's, one of the doctors from the centre, and wondered if you'd like to join us.'

She'd love to. Wasn't she meant to be holding back? 'I'm with another couple I was paddle boarding with and we've already got food on the way.'

'Fair enough. How about we meet up tomorrow night for a meal?'

Her heart lifted. 'I'm on.' Despite the concerns about what was happening between them, spending time together meant possibly dealing with those concerns. It was a long shot but a necessary one. 'Did you get much work done?' She didn't want to hang up.

'Not really. Henri dragged me out of the office.'

'I can't imagine anyone dragging you anywhere.'

He laughed. 'You reckon? Anyway, I'd better get back to Henri's family. See you.'

'See you.' Why was it hearing his voice made her hotter than the warm weather did? Putting the phone aside, she picked up her beer and sipped the cold liquid. As for his deep laugh, that always tightened her on the inside. The very first time she'd met him, he'd laughed at a joke one of the other nurses she was with had said, and her tummy had knotted, and she'd been halfway to falling in love on that laugh alone. Warm, hot, exciting, suggestive.

The food was great, the company just as good, and when Alyssa finally headed back to her deck with a mug of tea in hand she felt so relaxed. Leighton mightn't be with her, but they'd spoken and he'd suggested hooking up tomorrow night for a meal. She'd agreed because she was over avoiding things.

She stepped onto her deck.

'Hey, Lyssa.' Leighton stood up from the sunbed and crossed over to her. 'Thought I'd drop by to say good-night.'

Tea splashed over her hand and her heart thumped. She wasn't ready, hadn't worked out what to say. Yes, she was. She'd had more than long enough. 'You should've joined me in the bar.'

'It's you I've come to see. Not your friends.' He took the mug out of her hand and placed it on the table. Then he wrapped his arms around her to draw her close to that wonderful body she knew so well, even after all the empty years. 'I wanted to hold you for a moment. Is that all right?'

Yes. No. Not sure, but she couldn't resist him. 'It's perfect.' Snuggling closer, she laid her cheek against his chest and breathed in his outdoorsy scent. Salt water and sunshine. Male skin. How had she ever left him? Because he hadn't been honest.

His arms tightened around her. 'Lyssa?'

She looked up, ready to tell him to leave, but her breathing stalled as his mouth touched hers ever so lightly. A feather touch that wound her up tight. She hesitated, afraid to kiss him back for fear of getting in too deep. If it wasn't too late. His eyes were focused entirely on her, sucking her in second by second. Heartbeat by heartbeat. Damn him. Stretching onto her toes, she kissed him back, harder, and deeper.

Leighton returned her kiss, touch for touch, pressure against pressure, heat on heat.

This was Leighton. This was them.

Then he stepped back. 'Goodnight, Lyssa. See you tomorrow.' And he was gone.

Feeling her lips with her fingertips, she sank onto the sunbed, smiling from ear to ear. 'Wow.' Every part of her was awake and quivering with need, and warm with love as well. 'Wow.'

Just like their first date, he'd left her with a kiss to remember him by, and a hint of more to come. Was he dating her now? That would be the way to go, exciting, interesting and allowing time to learn more about each other after their time apart.

Lying back, she stared up at the star-studded sky and smiled. Maybe that time together would allow him to finally open up to her. Bring it on.

Walking away from that kiss had been the hardest thing he'd done in a long time. Lyssa's mouth against his was a match to a firelighter. A conflagration of explosive heat. He hadn't been able to resist kissing her and, still, he'd known to leave before they went any further.

Because he still wasn't ready to have the conversation she was trying to dig out of him. He wanted to enjoy whatever time he had left with her before it all blew apart.

They'd fallen into bed fast the night of the wedding. If

they were to progress he had to go slowly and build up to making love so that it meant more and wasn't a quick coupling. Though those were always intense and satisfying with Alyssa. Mostly he needed to sit down and spill out how afraid he was that she'd say he was a replica of his father and she didn't want a bar of him.

Moments ago he'd been a hot mix of desire and love. The love was a worry with so much at risk. The desire, yes, he could feed that time and time again and he knew it wouldn't be enough. There was no such thing as having enough of Alyssa. Slowly was the only way to go to see if they were still compatible in every way.

The problem with that was time was running out. She was leaving on Saturday and he wasn't returning to NZ for another month, and then he had no idea where he was going. It was the first time he hadn't organised a position almost before he started the current one. He liked to know what lay ahead; needed to, if he was honest. That way life couldn't throw ugly surprises at him—at least that was what he always hoped.

Back home, he made a mug of tea and sat on the deck under the night sky and listened to the waves pounding on the reef. It wasn't a bad life. Could be better though. Let Alyssa right in and it could be perfect. How to approach this? Other than telling her how much she meant to him and still did? Even he understood that wasn't going to cut it. She wanted answers. Only revealing his fear that she'd believe he was too much like his father to be worth staying, and that she might think he hadn't believed in her love for him, would be enough. The worst scenario for him. But the only one.

Unfortunately now he knew how his father operated he half expected more trouble to arise. If Alyssa was back in his life he'd always be worried about her reaction. He knew the answer was being open and frank all the way, but it wouldn't be easy after having watched her walk away the first time. His lungs exhaled slowly. He could do this. He would do it. There was no other option.

But nothing was perfect. He and Alyssa had fallen in love, only to let each other down. They hadn't had what it took to work their way through the problems driving them apart. What was to say they were any different now? If they did get back together, how would they handle the next crisis? Because there would be one. That was a fact of life. Hopefully they would learn to be open with each other, especially him. He could not tumble back into his hole again.

His parents had undermined his ability to believe in people. If they'd lived a lie all his life, then how was he to know someone else wasn't doing the same thing?

He trusted Jamie, and still didn't talk about their father much with him.

Did he trust Alyssa? He wanted to. If he didn't, then what was the point?

He drained his mug and stood up.

Actually he did trust her, when he wasn't overthinking what might go wrong.

Hold onto that and stop procrastinating.

What about the fear of rejection? It might be getting smaller, but it was what could decimate him. So, slowly does it. One kiss at a time. His spirits lifted. Thank goodness Lyssa had agreed to dinner with him tomorrow night. He'd start with small steps in the right direction, convincing her she had to believe in him. Bring it on.

CHAPTER EIGHT

'WHAT DID YOU get up to today?' Leighton asked as they sat at an outside table at a restaurant overlooking the town and harbour.

'Paddle boarding with the two from yesterday.' She sipped her wine. 'When are you going to give it a go?'

'Probably never.'

'Wimp,' she teased.

His hair flicked sideways when he shook his head. 'It doesn't hold any appeal. If I want to be on the water there are things called boats. No getting wet or falling in.'

'Sounds boring.'

'Each to their own.' Suddenly he grinned. 'Tell you what. I'll go paddle boarding if you go fishing with me.'

She shuddered. She hated the smell of fish, the thought of winding one in and having to remove the hook from its mouth. But a challenge was a challenge. He did have a busy week ahead though, so she could accept and hope like crazy he didn't find the time. 'Paddle boarding first.'

He was laughing as he shook his head. 'You haven't won. I can do the board thing after work, and I have Friday afternoon off so I could arrange a fishing charter for then.'

Damn. She'd probably smell of fish all the way home the next day.

'Smile. You don't look good when you lose,' he teased.

'I'm thinking up ways to tip you off the board once you think you've got the hang of it.' Really, she was thinking about being in the water with him, and reaching for that gorgeous body to run her hands over his wet skin.

She gulped down the last of her wine and leaned back to study her husband. Ex-husband. Not quite. There was still a marriage certificate binding them together. But it wasn't the paperwork that mattered. It was their hearts, and she couldn't deny hers was well and truly caught up with Leighton's.

Swallowing hard, she said, 'Remember when we went fishing with your father and he got cross with me because I freaked out when a stingray got caught up in the net?'

John was a selfish man who expected everyone to go along with what he wanted to do, and he'd known she wasn't keen on fishing.

'I do.' Leighton looked annoyed as he stood up and pulled his wallet from his pocket. 'Let's go back to your bungalow for a nightcap.'

End of conversation. She'd deliberately raised the subject of his father, and therefore put a dampener on things, but she wasn't finished. 'I only went to be with you.'

'I figured that.'

'Leighton, relax. I'm not having a poke. I'm trying to get through to you that I struggled understanding what was going on and you didn't help.'

Anguish filled his face, and pain was in his voice. 'I get that.'

Still nothing of note. How much more could she take? She tossed her napkin on the table and stood up. 'Let's go.'

When they walked outside she slipped her hand in his to walk up the long pathway to his car, partly to save herself from tripping in the dark and partly because she wanted to reassure him she was here for him. It might help. 'Dinner was lovely, thank you.'

'Any time.' He leaned down and brushed her lips with his. 'We could do it again tomorrow?'

'Yes, please.'

Leighton pulled her into him to hold her close.

Instantly her body fired up. It hadn't got the message about going slow. 'Still want to come back to my room for a nightcap?'

'Yes, ma'am.' A sharp answer but vulnerability blinked out at her.

She half expected him to drop her off and head home like last night when he'd stopped kissing her and left. Instead he walked her through to the bar to order drinks, then took her elbow as they strolled to her bungalow. Though her attempt to stroll was tense, with her hormones in a tangle while relief warred with the fact she was meant to be resisting him until everything was clearer between them, but she couldn't. He was her man. She loved him. She wanted him so much it hurt. Whatever the future held she couldn't say stop now, broken heart or not.

Kicking off her shoes, she sank onto a chair on her deck, pulling the other one close.

Leighton sat beside her, holding her hand softly on his thigh.

They didn't talk as they sipped the nightcaps. Alyssa

gazed up at the sky and smiled, despite the heaviness in her chest. Everything was beautiful, magical. Except them. It felt as if this might be the end, not the beginning of a stronger, deeper relationship, so she wanted to reach out and grab whatever was on offer. Make some new memories to keep in the days ahead.

Some time later, Leighton stood up and reached down for her, enfolded her in his arms and kissed her. 'Goodnight, Lyssa.'

She sagged against him. She didn't want him to go. Though best he did if this wasn't going to end in tears. She whispered, 'Goodnight, Leighton.'

His mouth opened on hers, his tongue slipping inside.

Her knees softened as she clung to him, never wanting to let him go even when she had to for her own sake.

'Lyssa.' Her name was so sexy on his tongue. 'We need to stop.'

Or they didn't. 'Leighton, please take me inside and make love to me.' Probably for the last time.

He pulled back and stared down at her.

Her heart thumped with desire and fear he was going to walk away again.

Then she was being wrapped up into his arms and they went into the bungalow and over to her bed, sitting down together without letting the other go, Leighton leaning in to continue kissing her.

Leaning back on the bed, keeping her mouth firmly on his, she began undoing his shirt, one button, one caress, another button, another caress.

He began trailing kisses down over her neck, lower to her cleavage, heating her to simmering.

The next thing they were naked. Alyssa had no recollection of undressing, only aware of Leighton's firm body lying against her, his arousal pressing against her thigh as his fingers worked some magic on her hot spot. And then they were together in the only way possible to be really together, giving and taking the ultimate pleasure. When she climaxed it felt as though her world were imploding, her body quivering, her head light, and her heart racing. Arms around him, she held tight, knowing she had to let go, and the sooner the better.

'Lyssa, sweetheart, I've got to go.' Leighton leaned down to place a light kiss on her cheek. She was so beautiful it hurt sometimes. It was tempting to climb back in beside her but that'd lead to more lovemaking. He needed to get home and get some sleep before the sun rose over the horizon or he'd be a zombie at work.

Her eyes blinked open. 'Leighton?'

'I'm heading home.'

Another blink. 'Okay.' She sounded exhausted.

Resisting kissing her one more time, he headed for the door. 'Have a great day tomorrow.'

Hopefully they'd catch up later because, despite his determination to stay away, he'd come to understand that was impossible. Lyssa was a part of him. She'd never really left, had been there in his psyche all along. No wonder he'd never found another woman he wanted to get close to. His heart was already accounted for. Time to unlock it, take the risk that had crippled him, and hope Alyssa would give him a second chance.

'Night.' Sounded as though she was already back asleep.

Making sure the door locked behind him, he went quietly around the main building to his car and drove home. A week ago if someone had said he'd make love to his wife again he'd have told them they needed their head read, except it was him needing that.

Alyssa would be gone in less than a week, not a lot of time left to sort things out.

So get a move on, will you?

Alyssa stretched full length in her bed and yawned. Her body was tired and replete. Two nights in the sack with Leighton and she still hadn't had enough. She couldn't remember their lovemaking being quite so wonderful, which was why she kept giving in instead of insisting on talking.

Her head ached. The lovemaking wasn't resolving a single thing. Leighton still avoided talking about the past, and, to be fair, she let him get away with it because he distracted her so easily. One touch and she was gone. Also, she'd more or less given up on getting him to talk to her, so this was about making those memories to tide her through the coming months when she'd be on her own again, all her dreams destroyed.

Time to toughen up, Lyssa.

There was another choice.

Try again. Demand answers.

What, when she'd tried often already? What would change Leighton's mind about talking to her?

There were no answers, so she picked up her phone to check for messages, and gasped. Ten past nine. She was paddle boarding with the others at ten. She headed for the shower, then dressed in a bikini with shorts and T-shirt over the top and went to get some breakfast.

* * *

With boards under their arms Alyssa and Karin walked down to the beach. Alyssa dropped her clothes on a towel she'd collected with her board, and waded into the water. 'Where shall we go?'

'Let's head towards the turtles. Not into the trench where they swim but in that direction.'

'Sure.' She hopped on the board and stood up, oar in hand, pushing away from the beach. She'd got the hang of paddling on the board now and loved the sensation of bobbing over the surface while she looked around or down into the water at the fish swimming from coral crop to coral crop. She might get a board next summer. Lots of people used them at home but she'd never thought of giving it a try.

They reached the edge of the turtle area and paddled out towards the reef, where Jarrod joined them.

'Got tickets for dinner and the local show,' he told Karin. 'Hope you've got something fancy to wear.'

'For me to know.' His girlfriend grinned.

Alyssa's heart squeezed painfully. If only she could have love like that with Leighton, uninhibited and easy. When she'd first met Leighton she'd fallen for him hard without any hesitation. Not once had she questioned his love for her, or hers for him. It had been real and there had been no reason to doubt it. Her current feelings were similar but she'd learned her lesson. Falling in love didn't mean falling into a perfect world, but they could do their damnedest to come close.

A loud splash made her look around.

Karin was in the water, looking awkward.

'You all right?' Alyssa called out.

'No, I hit a rock,' Karin shouted back, holding onto the board with one hand. 'My arm hurts like stink. I'm bleeding too.'

Jarrod was paddling furiously to get back to her. 'Hey, babe, take it easy. I'll hold the board while you get back on.'

'I don't know that I can get on it.'

Alyssa paddled as fast as she could to reach them, wary of falling off herself. 'Let me see if I can take a look at your arm before you try to get on the board. I'm a nurse,' she added, in case she hadn't told them before. Getting off her board, she was relieved to touch the bottom with the water only reaching her armpits.

'She has to get back on it or how else are we going to get her to shore?' Jarrod sounded panicked.

'Karin, it's not so deep you can't stand and that would make it easier to check out the damage.'

'Okay.' Karin drew in a breath before easing down slowly until her feet were on the bottom. She continued to grip the board with her hand on the good arm.

'Tell me where the pain is.' There was a deep gash in the biceps with blood oozing fast.

'My arm's cut and I think I've scraped my thigh too.'

Carefully feeling around the gash on her arm, Alyssa noted Karin wince when she touched the bone. 'You might've broken it.' Which was going to make getting back to the beach difficult, and very painful. 'Jarrod, do you think we can lift Karin onto the board so she can sit while we tow her?'

'No way,' Karin cried. 'I'm not trying to climb onto the board. It'll hurt like hell. I'll hold one of the handle things and you two can paddle your boards while holding one side each and I'll kick as hard as I can.'

'You've got a cut above your eyebrow too,' Alyssa told her. 'Is your head throbbing?'

'A little but it's the arm that's really hurting.'

'Let's get ashore and then I'll drive you to the medical centre where Leighton works.'

'We don't have far to tow you, babe, before it's shallow enough to walk if you want.' Jarrod hugged Karin. 'Hang on tight. I'll get on my board first, then Alyssa can follow suit. We'll have to sit to paddle and hold your board.'

Once Jarrod was ready, Alyssa got onto hers. 'Let's go.' It felt like hours before they reached the beach. Collecting their clothes, she slipped into her shorts and shirt, then helped Karin into hers before walking up to the resort, where she grabbed her car keys and phone, and picked up a box of tissues to use to cover the bleeding. Looking around, she couldn't find anything that would be useful as a sling. 'I need something to hold your arm in place to prevent movement adding to your pain, Karin.'

'Here.' Jarrod unbuttoned his shirt and shrugged out of it. 'Use this.'

While Jarrod helped Karin into the car, Alyssa called Leighton and told him what had happened. 'Is it all right to come to the medical centre or should I take her to the hospital?' She was thinking of the night they helped the woman who fell out of the bus and how Leighton had said she was better off going to the centre.

'Bring her here for an assessment. Chances are she won't need to go to the hospital. We've got an X-ray machine and the gear to make a cast if needed.'

'See you shortly.'

At the medical centre the receptionist was waiting for them. 'Hi, I'm Charlotte. Leighton said to take you through to his room. He's grabbing a bite to eat in the lunch room but I'll tell him you're here.'

'This way, Karin, Jarrod.' Alyssa led them along the corridor to a room Leighton had used the other night and held out a chair. 'Take a pew, Karin.'

'Th-thanks.' She was shivering. The shock from the impact had caught up.

'Charlotte, can you get this lady something dry to wear?' Leighton had joined them. 'Whatever she finds won't be very becoming, I'm afraid, but I want you out of that wet swimsuit. I'm Leighton Harrison, by the way. I'm sure Alyssa has told you I'm a GP.'

'This is Karin and her partner, Jarrod,' Alyssa told him. 'As I told you on the phone, Karin hit coral when she came off the board.'

'Your left arm took the brunt of the fall?' he asked Karin as he carefully removed Jarrod's shirt from around her upper arm and neck.

'My thigh too.'

'Right, change of plan. Let's get you up on the bed.'

Alyssa took Karin's arm and led her over to the bed. 'I think the humerus is fractured. It doesn't feel even near the elbow,' she told Leighton.

He nodded. 'I'll take an X-ray shortly. But first let's check everything else.' His fingers moved over Karin's head.

She winced. 'Ouch.'

'Does it hurt when I press here?' Leighton asked.

'No.'

'Here?'

'Yes.'

'The bone doesn't appear to be fractured, but I'll X-ray that too to be certain. I'd say you've bruised it and because there's nothing between the skin and bone to absorb the impact you'll be sore there for a few days.'

'The bleeding stopped pretty much after we had her out of the water,' Alyssa told him. 'Same as with the thigh wound.' She removed the wad of tissues she'd placed there earlier. 'How are your sewing skills?'

'Excellent.' He smiled at her, making her uneasy about the confrontation she intended bringing about as soon as they were alone.

Keeping her face straight, she reached for the box of sterile wipes on the counter and began cleaning Karin's thigh. 'This is deeper than I first thought.'

'It's rough too, which is due to the coral. All those spikes cause quite a mess.'

'You'll have seen a few injuries like this, then?'

His smile faded. 'Yes, and, Karin, the biggest thing to be aware of with these abrasions is infection. Especially in the heat. When do you fly home?'

'Tomorrow,' Jarrod answered for his partner. 'We weren't looking forward to it, but it might be for the best now.'

Alyssa shuddered at the thought of sitting on a plane with someone in the seat beside that arm. It wasn't going to be a comfort trip home. 'Have you pre-booked your seats?'

'Yes. A window seat and the one beside it. Karin will have to use the window seat to protect her arm.'

'I agree.' At least her arm wouldn't be knocked by

passengers moving about or the trolleys being pushed down the aisle.

'Alyssa, can you come with me and Karin to the X-ray room? You can help with getting her arm in the right position.'

She was sure he could manage blindfolded, but she wasn't turning down an opportunity to work with him, however small it was. 'No problem.'

Once they had Karin on the bed under the X-ray machine, Leighton moved her arm into a position where he'd get the image he wanted. 'I'll check to see if that's clear enough. You might have to shift it a little to the right, Alyssa.' He went behind the safety window and looked at the screen. 'Karin, can you turn your arm slightly towards me? That's it. Alyssa, the shoulder needs to drop a little.'

She helped Karin move and stepped out of the room while Leighton took the X-ray.

'Now for the head. I need Karin to turn so that area where she landed is facing up to the camera.'

'Don't you have a radiology assistant in the centre?'

'No. We can call in the one from the hospital but all the doctors have had a crash course in taking X-rays for minor injuries.'

'Interesting. Right, Karin, we need you to turn your head to the side so the injury is exposed to the camera.'

Soon they were back in Leighton's room and he was stitching Karin's thigh, Alyssa helping by handing him whatever he required.

'You two have done this together a lot?' Jarrod asked.

'Never,' she said. 'Apart from those accidents last week.'

'Amazing. You work well together.'

Warmth stole through her. Yes, they made a great team without any effort in lots of ways, instinctively knowing what the other required. 'It's all part of the service.'

Working alongside Leighton was good, sharing the experience of helping Karin. All the misadventures in her time here seemed a lot for a small place, even filled to the brim with tourists. 'Blimey, am I bringing bad luck to visitors?'

Leighton's head tipped sideways so he could look directly at her. 'You'd better stay locked up in your room for the rest of your visit just in case.' Was he saying he'd keep her company?

No way. She had another agenda and this time she was not putting it off.

'We can't have too many tourists getting knocked about while enjoying their activities. It wouldn't be a good look for the island.'

Karin smiled for the first time since coming off her board. 'Believe me, this won't put me off getting back on a board.'

Leighton opened his mouth to answer.

'It's okay. I'm not paddle boarding while my arm's broken.'

Leighton relaxed.

'Might do the hike over the top instead.'

Alyssa said, 'I'll come with you.'

He shook his head at them. 'Next stop is the plaster room. Then you can go back to your resort. I'm going to prescribe strong painkillers and antibiotics. You'll need to start taking the painkillers straight away so there's a build-up for the trip home. It's painful now but the chances of getting a knock on the plane are high and will increase the pain.'

'Thanks, Doctor.' Karin's smile had disappeared. 'I appreciate all you've done.'

'I'll get one of the nurses to do the cast as I've got patients scheduled from ten minutes ago.'

Jarrod shook his hand. 'Thanks from me too. I'm glad Alyssa knew to bring us here. She saved us a lot of time and hassle.'

'That's Alyssa for you. Onto it.'

His smile lit her up on the inside, and on the outside. She turned away before making a fool of herself by ignoring the warning bells ringing in her head. Nothing more was happening between them until she knew what was really going on with Leighton.

'I can't believe how fast the week's going by. I'll be heading home before I know it,' Alyssa said as she and Leighton wandered along the beach back to the resort after dinner.

'It has been a bit of a whirlwind,' Leighton agreed.

'Will I see you when you return home?' There were a few ways he could answer.

'Do you want to?'

She spun around to stare at him. She hadn't expected that. 'Of course I do. Why would you ask?' Where had he been when they were together? Didn't he get that she was happy being with him? Or had her doubts come through and made him cautious?

'Because you know I haven't been upfront with you.'

That was honest. 'No time like the present.' A brick was forming in her stomach as tension rose.

Leighton stared back at her, his face grim. 'Lyssa, it's been wonderful spending time with you…' He paused.

Here it came. The but. Her breath stuck somewhere in the middle of her chest as she waited.

He took her hand in both his. 'I want to have more time with you.'

'But?'

'But nothing. That's the answer to your question about seeing you once we're both back on New Zealand soil. These past days have been wonderful. Being with you, getting close again, has made me want more. We're so good together.'

Her heart crashed. 'That's not the point. Why aren't we talking about the reason our marriage failed?'

Dragging his hand through his hair, Leighton stared out over the water. 'It's not that simple, Lyssa.'

'Try.'

He continued looking outward.

What was going through his mind? Coming up with excuses to avoid the truth? Touching his hand, she said softly, 'You can trust me, Leighton.'

A shudder ripped through him. 'I want to.'

Her head flew up and she stared at him. 'You want to? You have doubts?'

'Yes.'

'You can make love to me, kiss me blind, tell me you have a brother and that your father betrayed your love for him, and yet you can't trust me?' There must be something really bad going on if he didn't believe she'd be there for him if he asked.

Leighton pulled her against him and held tight. 'I'm sorry. I've thought about this from the moment I saw you in Reception the night you arrived and I still struggle with what needs to be said.'

Pulling back, she looked into the face she adored. 'Start with telling me more about what went down between you and your father when you learned about Jamie.'

Stepping back, he swallowed hard. 'No. I'm not going there. I've told you enough already.'

Trying to calm her nerves, she implored, 'Leighton, I need to understand why you wouldn't talk to me back then. I understand you were hurt badly by what John did, but surely you could've told me?'

'I couldn't. Understand that, Alyssa. Not then, and even now it's hard.' Regret filled his face.

Her heart pounded. He was going to walk away again. She'd seen that expression before when he'd refused to tell her what was worrying him, and knew the outcome. She took his hand. 'Come on, walk and talk.' It'd be easier than standing staring at each other. 'Leighton. I love you. We need to do this.' She hadn't said that the last time, too hurt and angry to make him see how she felt about him.

For the first few minutes they walked in silence, then suddenly Leighton began talking fast. 'It was a shock learning I had a brother and that he'd come about through my father having an affair with Mum's best friend, and how everyone covered up the fact that Dad paid Jamie's mother all those years to keep her quiet. Jamie and I missed out on so much. But while that was horrendous, for me the worst was realising I didn't know the man who was my father.'

He paused, breathing heavily, staring along the beach, away from her.

She waited, giving him space, still holding his trembling hand. Given how close they were, it must've been soul-destroying to learn his father's true colours. Her heart ached for him.

He began walking again. 'All my life people joked about how alike we were in all ways.'

She knew that, but didn't agree. Leighton was gentle and kind, cared about other people, something John never had.

Leighton sighed. 'I used to be proud I was like him. Until Jamie turned up, then I became ashamed.' His hand squeezed hers. 'Totally ashamed. I'd come home at night and look at you and know I couldn't tell you. I thought you'd leave me because I was my dad all over again. You'd think I could do the same horrendous things to you he'd done to Mum. I couldn't face that. You were the love of my life but I'd already lost the two other people I loved. I couldn't bear the thought of you walking out on me, or thinking I might betray you, so I pushed you away instead.'

'That's utterly ridiculous,' she snapped through the pain roaring through her. How could he believe that of her? 'I loved you with all my heart. I trusted you, believed in you.' Tugging her hand free, she stopped to stare at this man she'd thought she knew well. 'There's no way in hell you're your father. No way.'

'Easy to say now.'

'Because it's the truth. It was then and still is.' So much for moving forward with Leighton. They really were over because he wasn't giving her the benefit of doubt.

'You have to understand how messed up I became. There was Jamie, a brother I'd known nothing about, wanting to get to know me. As you've seen, we get on great, and did from the get-go, but deep down I still had to accept he was for real. It was hard, given the circumstances with my father. I even went to counselling.' He drew in a lungful of air. 'Throw in Dad demanding I have nothing to do with Jamie and instead support *him.* I fell apart. I was terrified you'd find out and leave me. Then I learned Dad tried to bribe you. I was so proud of you then, but it also increased my fear that you'd never fully trust me again.'

'Thanks a lot, Leighton.'

Calm down. Take this slowly.

A deep breath and she continued. 'I would've trusted you, and supported you.' Her mouth was sour, her head spinning. 'So you didn't trust me.' Without trust there was no relationship. Not for her, anyway. Or Leighton, otherwise they might've made it through the turbulence brought on by John Harrison. She rubbed the goose bumps on her arms. 'I need time on my own.'

'Lyssa, I let you down badly. I'm truly sorry. I just hope that one day you might forgive me and that we can at least be friends.'

Turning around, she headed for her bungalow. Friends? With Leighton? Not likely. With him it had to be all or nothing. Her heart wouldn't have it any other way. Right now she needed to work through all he'd said and figure out where to go from here.

CHAPTER NINE

SINKING ONTO A chair on the deck, Alyssa hugged the robe around her and let the tears flow. No point in trying to stop them. Her heart was broken into so many pieces there wasn't a quick fix. There wasn't anything that would put it back together. Leighton hadn't trusted her. Still didn't if he found it so hard to tell her after four years.

She loved Leighton. As much as, if not more than, she had when she married him. How could she have ever thought she'd got over him? It was so untrue. Within such a little amount of time she'd known he was still the only man for her. Trying to deny it had simply been to protect her heart, and now it lay shattered. There'd be no picking up the pieces and carrying on as if nothing were wrong. He'd undermined her love.

How could he not trust her and talk about his parents? Yet what else had they done to hurt him so much? He'd loved and believed in them. *Trusted* them. He'd been nothing but proud of his family and said he'd grown up happy and feeling loved, then to be treated so callously must've devastated him. No wonder he'd had counselling. Leighton was strong but he'd been dealt a huge blow. It made sense why he'd left the medical centre to work as a locum up and down the country. He was staying clear of involvement. Except with Jamie, which also made sense because that was where this all began and their father had betrayed them both.

If only she'd known, he'd never have been on his own.

More tears spurted down her cheeks. 'Leighton, why couldn't you trust me? I love you. I'd never deliberately hurt you.'

Cuddling further into the robe, she tucked her feet underneath her backside and stared unseeing at the edge of the deck. 'He's gone.' Her stomach ached as it squeezed in on itself. Her head was full of fog. Her hands clenched together. And inside her chest was a solid wall of pain pressing on her lungs and her heart. 'He's gone.'

The sun was lightening the sky when she finally dragged herself inside and onto the bed. Wrapping the pillows around her neck and tucking the sheet tight, she closed her eyes and pretended to sleep. There was nothing else to do.

She woke to the sound of knocking. 'Leighton?' Leaping out of bed, she rushed to open the door, and sagged. 'Karin.'

'Hi. You look wiped out. Big night?'

One way to describe it. 'Sort of. How are you feeling today?'

'Very sore. But never mind. I came to say thank you for all your help yesterday. It meant a lot to both of us.'

Yesterday was another world. Working alongside Leighton, receiving his smiles, looking forward to dinner. Not any more.

'Alyssa? Are you all right?'

Shaking away any thought of Leighton, she said, 'I'm good. As for yesterday, I'm glad I was there to help.'

'I'd better go. We're about to head to the airport. Keep in touch. We might visit you in Nelson in the summer.' Karin laughed.

'See you around.' Back inside she headed for the shower and a long soak while she mulled over what to do next.

Go home was the best she could come up with in answer to that and, once dressed, she went online to see if there was a seat available on any flight before Saturday.

The first available one was for the flight she was already booked on. So she was stuck here, like it or not. Why waste her holiday thinking about Leighton and what she'd lost? Because it was impossible not to think about him. She had to move on. He hadn't trusted her, and still didn't. That hurt bad. But if she left without a word he'd be right. She'd be deserting him and fuelling his distrust right when he'd finally told her everything.

Picking up her phone, she found Leighton's number. She'd talk to him, try to get him to understand she would've stayed. Her finger hovered over the icon. Press and hear his voice. Don't press and get on with filling in her day, wondering if he'd have talked to her or not.

Dropping the phone back on the table, she headed outside. She'd said it all last night. 'Leighton. I love you.' There was nothing to add to that. Not until she'd thought everything through again and was one hundred per cent certain they could make it work. Failing again would be horrific.

For a distraction she went to the resort café where other guests were lazing by the pool soaking up the sun.

The coffee went down easily, the croissant not so much, forming a lump in her belly.

Next she drove to Wigmore's Waterfall and walked a little way into the bush up the side of the main hill. When it got too steep, she returned to her car and drove to town to wander through the shops, buying T-shirts she didn't need. In the afternoon she took a board and paddled up and down the lagoon, though her heart wasn't really in it. Back in her room she ordered an early dinner with a glass of wine and sat on her deck reading. Except she read the same five pages numerous times.

Tossing the book aside, she gave in to the question continuously knocking at her. Was there another way to rebuild their trust and get back together?

'Your mammogram's normal,' Leighton told the woman. 'So is your blood pressure. Next we'll take some blood to check your haemoglobin, liver and kidneys, and you can go home.'

Unfortunately she was his last patient for the day.

He'd go home too. To do what? The lawns had been mowed to within an inch of the dirt, the house was spotless, and he'd even cleaned the car. He really needed to get a life, not this lonely facsimile of what he'd once believed in.

You could have one with Lyssa.

If she hadn't already run a mile when she heard the truth behind him getting into such a mess after his father's true self came to light. She'd never liked his dad, and he didn't think that was only because of the offer of money he'd made. He presumed she'd sensed that his father wasn't all he portrayed himself to be. 'I'm a good bloke who looks out for others,' was his constant saying. So untrue.

'Why didn't I see through him?' Leighton asked himself for the thousandth time. He knew there were no answers other than he'd loved his parents and believed in them. There'd been no reason to have gone looking for problems.

Alyssa had got to know his real father when he'd tried to bribe her to leave him, before they married. She hadn't rejected him over that. His heart lifted briefly. How did he make her see how much he loved her? Last night she'd said she had trusted him, loved him. Could she still? He had to convince her he trusted her with his heart and soul, that never again would he let her go to protect himself. He was better than that now. He had to ask for another chance so they could work through everything together. There could be a pot of love at the other end of this. Surely it was worth the risk?

Worst case—he'd be back where he was a week ago, except Alyssa now knew everything.

Best case? His heart would be full of love and he'd be so happy.

Suddenly it seemed so easy. He might have blinkers on but his heart was ready to face anything. Hope of winning back Lyssa was winning over his negativity. Hopefully she'd say again she loved him. If not, he'd set about wooing her. Because he wasn't giving up this time. They belonged together.

His change of heart had happened in a blink but only because the hope and love had been there all along, hidden beneath his pain and fear. If only he'd been able to admit it long ago. But maybe it had taken so long because he'd needed time to reconcile everything for himself. He'd acknowledged his love for Lyssa to himself over the past days, but there'd always been the handbrake in place. That was gone. He was free to love again. He was not going to live under a shadow a minute longer.

Hands in pockets, Alyssa kicked the sand as she strolled up the beach towards her room. Her last night in Rarotonga. It wasn't what she'd hoped for. Dinner in the resort restaurant and early to bed with the book she'd finally managed to get more than halfway through wasn't exactly exciting.

Reaching her deck, she stopped. 'Leighton?'

He turned from where he was leaning on the railing and came towards her. 'Lyssa, I'm sorry. For everything.'

She ignored the tightening in her belly and the sudden thumping in her head. 'I owe you an apology too. I should've stayed with you despite the tension and my bewilderment over what was going on. I'm truly sorry I let you down.'

'Thank you.' His smile was full of love as he pulled a chair out from the outdoor table. 'Are you ready to put it all in the past? To let it go and move forward with me?'

'It is the only way to go if we're going to be seeing each other back home.' Sinking onto the chair, she crossed her legs and placed her elbows on the table. And waited for him to continue. She wasn't trying to make it any more difficult for him, but she was afraid to say anything that might turn him away again.

'I handled everything badly. Sure, what happened was a shock.'

'How did you manage not to say anything to me when

I got home?' They had been married, in love. They had shared everything, or so she'd believed.

'With difficulty. I wanted to pour it out and hear you say it couldn't be true and that everything was a lie. Except I knew it wasn't. That's when I started sinking into despair, unable to grasp the fact my life hadn't been what I'd believed. It took the ground out from under me. I struggled with knowing who I was. Everything seemed wrong, even us. I was so afraid you'd leave me when I needed you the most that I put up the barriers that drove you away.'

Guilt hit her. 'I should've stayed.'

'We'll never know if that would've helped or driven a bigger wedge between us.'

'You're right. We can't undo what's happened.' What lay ahead was far more important.

'When did you learn John had offered me money to not marry you?'

'After you'd left. I'd gone to see Mum, naively hoping she'd answer some of my questions. Dad turned up and said you'd be regretting not taking the money because obviously you wouldn't want to stay with me after that.'

'Because I hadn't told you about his offer I inadvertently added to your pain.' It must've seemed she was hiding secrets too. 'I did hide it from you. I was disgusted with John and I also didn't want you choosing between family and me. I figured if you didn't know we could still get married and be happy.'

'It's all right, Lyssa. You told me that last week and I understand. It can't have been easy, especially now I know how manipulative Dad can be. I don't hold it against you, I promise.'

Her stance softened a little. 'Thanks.'

She took his hands in hers, holding tight. 'You are nothing like John. Nothing at all. You are kind and caring, loving and genuine. You don't put yourself first all the time. You never have. You were never anything but loving to me.' Until the end, but they were both off track by then. 'You're more than good enough. Way more.'

'Your words are a balm. After all this time I'm struggling to believe them.'

'I wasn't perfect either, Leighton. I did want to have some fun and you weren't available. I didn't play around, just partied with the girls from work, but it still wasn't the right thing to do. I realise I should've dug deeper into what was upsetting you, not put myself first all the time.' She had grown up since then. 'I'd never do that again.'

'Honestly I was just glad you were out and not demanding my attention.'

'I understand completely, but I mightn't have back then. I was too engrossed in what was going on in my life to think about what you were feeling.'

A silence fell between them.

Alyssa felt a new tenderness for Leighton growing inside. He was the love of her life, and now she could let go the past and move forward. With him. Or not, if he didn't love her back. She'd hurt, but there'd be no point arguing about it. That'd only increase the pain between them.

A scraping sound interrupted her thoughts. Leighton was standing up. Going? Her heart plummeted. No, please not that.

Then he was in front of her and taking her hands in his, and getting down on one knee. 'I love you, Lyssa.

Always have and always will. Will you stay married to me, live with me for ever, have our children?'

Her throat clogged with tears so she couldn't speak and had to nod. Bending forward, she brushed her mouth over those wonderful lips. 'Yes,' she squeaked. 'Yes.'

Before she knew what he was doing, she was being swung up into his arms and carried inside, where he kissed her so intensely she had to pinch herself to make sure it wasn't a dream.

When he stopped, so did her heart.

'Lyssa, let's renew our vows. Here in a month's time before I come home. We could have a honeymoon on Aitutaki too.'

Last time they'd spent a weekend in a high-end hotel in Auckland, then gone home and back to work. 'Sounds perfect.'

As perfect as the lovemaking that ensued.

EPILOGUE

Four weeks later

THE MARRIAGE CELEBRANT stood on the beach in front of Alyssa and Leighton. Beside them were Jamie and Collette, who'd flown over with Alyssa especially for this moment.

'Ready?' asked Clara.

'More than,' Leighton replied.

Clara cleared her throat. 'Alyssa Harrison, do you agree to continue your marriage to Leighton Harrison from this day forward and to stand by his side through everything life throws at you?'

'Try stopping me. Yes, I absolutely do.'

Leighton's eyes appeared bluer than ever as they twinkled at her with love.

'Leighton, I will do everything possible to be a great wife. There will be times I'll annoy you to pieces but always remember I love you with all I am, and I have since the day I first met you.'

A solitary tear escaped to run down his cheek. 'I believe you.'

'Leighton Harrison, will you remain married to Alyssa

for ever, and support her through every twist and turn life throws at you?'

'I most certainly will. I love you to the moon and back, Lyssa. Always have, always will. There'll be no more avoiding the tough stuff, and lots more making the most of the good times. You are my for ever woman.'

Clara looked to Jamie. 'You wanted to say something.'

Surprised, Alyssa glanced at Collette and got back a wide smile.

Leighton looked surprised too. 'Hope you know what you're doing, brother.'

'Who? Me? Not a clue.' Jamie cleared his throat. 'Alyssa, I've known you for a while now as a competent nurse and a good friend to Collette, and thought you were an amazing person. What I didn't know until our wedding is that you were my sister-in-law. Welcome back to the family. From the moment you walked into the resort that first night I've known Leighton loved you, even if he didn't. No one could be more glad that you two have found each other again.'

'Apart from me,' Collette added.

Alyssa smiled and smiled. This was perfect. Her marriage was back intact, and her friends were now her family. 'Thank you, guys.'

Leighton spoke up. 'I haven't finished.' He dug into his pocket and pulled out a tiny box. 'Lyssa, I know we agreed you'd wear the wedding band I gave you on our wedding day, and here it is.' He slipped it onto her finger, all polished and looking beautiful.

She stretched up to brush a kiss on his lips. 'Thank you.'

'I also want you to wear this. It's an eternity ring,

which seems appropriate.' He revealed a gold ring with a large sky-blue sapphire in the centre.

'Oh, my. That's beautiful. Which finger?'

'How about with your wedding ring? It's the same size.'

She held her hand out and as he slid it on love filled her for this very special man who did so much for her. 'I love you, Leighton. I always have and always will.' It never hurt to say that again and again.

'Here's to the future, to Mr and Mrs Harrison,' said Jamie as he handed glasses of champagne to everyone. 'Cheers to all of us.'

'Cheers and love,' Alyssa said before sipping her drink.

This was the best day of her life—better than the first time she'd swapped vows with Leighton. Now they were older and wiser…and happier than ever.

* * * * *

AN ER NURSE TO REDEEM HIM

TRACI DOUGLASS

MILLS & BOON

CHAPTER ONE

TATE GRIFFIN JERKED upright in bed, breath seizing in his chest as jagged lightning bolted across the sky. Sweating and trembling, he scrubbed his hands over his face, then shoved off the covers. The chilly night air, made chillier by the rare, raging mid-October nor'easter outside, cooled his heated skin. He fought the urge to fall back to sleep because if he did, he'd be right back there again, smack in the middle of the nightmare that had dogged him for four years now. But as he stared into the rain-lashed darkness the memories returned anyway.

"We can't get any lower!" the pilot yelled as the UH-60 Black Hawk tilted precariously above the churning Indian Ocean. "It's too dangerous!"

Three stranded airmen depended on his team to rescue them.

"We can't leave them!" Tate shouted back. "No one else will get here in time!"

Ten seconds later, lightning cracked and towering waves slashed the bottom of the helicopter, causing it to shake violently. Close. Too close. A sharp blast of light, followed by intense heat and excruciating pain, then...

Nothing...

Tate stared over at his window as raindrops pelted the glass and forced himself to take a deep, shaky breath. He wasn't trapped in the burning wreckage of that downed chopper anymore, choking on seawater and the horrible knowledge he was the only survivor.

He hadn't saved a single soul that night. In fact, his fateful decision to even go on the mission had cost the lives of his team as well.

Back then, he'd been young and cocky. They all were. Tommy and Brad were pararescue like him, eager to save the world. Kelly was pararescue too, one of a small, elite group of women to graduate from an Air Force Special Warfare pipeline, qualifying as an STO—special tactics officer—by passing the grueling Apprentice Course at the service's Combat Control School at Pope Army Airfield. She'd done it in two attempts. It had taken Tate and the other guys at least three.

Kelly had been a force to be reckoned with, both on duty and off. She and Tate had even dated for a while, but in the end, they'd made better friends than lovers. He still missed her and the others on his crew every single day. Each time he boarded the helicopter at Wyckford General, he said a silent prayer for them. Then another for himself. That maybe someday he could atone for his failures.

Tonight, with the storm raging and his tension high, all the horrors of the accident seemed far too close to the peaceful, tiny tourist town of Wyckford, Massachusetts. He'd come here on extended leave from the Air Force after additional surgery on his leg to remove some scar tissue because he'd thought it might give him a chance to rest and heal, both mentally and physically. But he'd quickly gotten bored just sitting around on his butt and had ended up taking a temporary job as an EMT on the hospital's new flight crew, doing his level best to put one foot in front of the other and not get lost in the guilt and grief and shame living in his soul now because of the accident. Because in Tate's mind at least, it was his fault all those people were dead. And at night, when he was alone, there was too much space to think about everything he'd done wrong on that last mission and the burden he'd carried every day since.

The next streak of lightning and crack of thunder had him jumping out of his own skin again.

Christ.

Angry at his own weakness, Tate got up. No more eating lobster rolls before bed.

But if he was honest with himself, he knew it wasn't food that brought on those nightmares.

It was his PTSD from the accident. Another reason why staying busy was the best idea for him. When his friend Mark Bates—a firefighter in Wyckford—had first mentioned the flight EMT job, Tate had been skeptical and more than a little worried it might be too much for him. But when the past started haunting him more and more in the quiet, uneventful days, Tate had decided helping others was the least he could do to keep those ghosts at bay. Plus, working in the private sector turned out to be a nice change of pace from his usual highly regimented existence in the military.

Standing, Tate winced as he stretched his stiff leg, then pulled on a pair of jeans and tugged on his shirt from earlier before pulling on his socks and shoes. He'd rented this ranch-style house when he'd first arrived but hadn't really done much with it yet. He went into the living room and turned on the emergency scanner in the corner, figuring if he was up, he might as well make himself useful. Medical emergencies happened 24/7, regardless of the weather or location, so there was a good chance the flight crew could use an extra set of hands tonight.

In fact, maybe he'd just drive into town anyway. Stop at that little diner with the funny-looking bird on the sign on the way, if they were still open in the storm, and get some coffee to fully wake him up before going in.

Tate grabbed his jacket, then walked into the attached garage. As he flipped on the lights the smells of motor oil, well-greased tools and rubber tires welcomed him. In the center of the space sat his baby, his restored 1970 Chevelle SS454. The one luxury he afforded himself, his car brought back fond memories of working on vehicles together with his dad when Tate was growing up. Both his parents were gone now, so the car felt like a little piece of home.

He grabbed the keys from a peg on the wall and slid behind the wheel. The garage door lifted as the engine purred, and Tate backed out into the tempest, eager to outpace his past and pay his debt to all those lives lost on that fateful night four years ago.

The nor'easter raged as Madison Scott ran the short distance from her Mini Cooper to the front door of the Buzzy Bird Café. Thunder shook the ground, and the wind nearly blew her over. She'd forgotten an umbrella that morning because of course she had, but it was just as well—in these gales she'd probably have taken off like Mary Poppins anyway.

A bright bolt of lightning cleaved the ominous clouds, and Madi gasped as everything around her glowed like daytime for an instant: the parking lot, Buzzards Bay across the road full of angry roaring whitecaps and the menacing sky above.

Everything went dark again as she burst into the café, feeling like the hounds of hell were on her very tired heels. Her rubber-soled white nurse's shoes squeaked on the linoleum floor as she stood near the entrance to catch her breath.

The tiny seaside town of Wyckford tended to shut down after 10 p.m., and the diner was deserted except for Madi's best friend, Luna Norton, behind the counter. Luna's parents owned the café and Luna filled in part-time when needed and when it didn't interfere with her regular full-time job as a physical therapist for the hospital. She'd always reminded Madi of a fashion model, tall and leggy, not exactly beautiful, but with an interesting face that made you want to learn more about her. She was also a fantastic artist and had a fearless, kick-ass attitude to life in general. Tonight, her short black pixie cut was tousled and her gray eyes amused as she watched Madi make her way over to the counter.

"Nasty out there," Luna said. "Like a Stephen King novel or something."

Madi nodded as she shook off the icy rain from her scrubs. She'd forgotten a jacket too, having been on the go since dawn and in a perpetual rush for the whole day. One incredibly long ER shift and seventeen hours later, her clothes were now stuck to her like a second skin.

Another gale howled against the building and something heavy lashed the windows. Madi frowned, squinting back at the glass door. No. It couldn't be. Not five minutes ago it had been raining and now... *Snow.* Coming down fast and furious. "This weather's nuts. It's only October."

"That's New England for you," Luna said, her expression disgusted. "Sixty degrees this morning, thirty now. I never know how to dress this time of year."

Speaking of clothes, Madi really needed to change. She bit her lip and glanced out the door again. Maybe if she left now, she'd be okay.

As if reading her mind, Luna said, "Wait it out. This storm will blow over quick enough."

Madi knew better, but it was her own fault. She'd ignored the forecast ever since last week, when the weather guy had promised seventy-degree temps and the day hadn't gotten above fifty, leaving her to spend a long day frozen in the ER. Man, all she really wanted to do was to go home and go to sleep. "My house isn't far. I can make it, I think. I just need to pick up something for dinner first."

"Sorry." Luna hiked her thumb at the pass-through window showing a darkness beyond. "Grill's closed. I can make you a PB&J if you want."

Madi exhaled slow. Dead on her feet, she'd only stopped because she didn't want to cook that night. Or ever. She was horrible in the kitchen and could burn water. "Sounds good."

She took a seat at the counter while Luna gathered the ingredients and made sandwiches.

More lightning flashed, followed immediately by a thundering boom. Great. Now they had thundersnow. The entire diner shuddered under the blast of frigid winds. Then glass shattered as an ear-splitting crack sounded. A giant tree limb now waved at them through the new opening where the front door and windows had been moments before. Then the lights flickered and went out as another hard gust of wind sent more sharp shards tinkling to the floor.

Madi scurried to join Luna, who was crouched behind the counter. "We're safest right here, away from flying debris."

Luna swallowed audibly. "Maybe we should both leave now."

"No." Madi shook her head, staring through the shadows at the blocked entrance of the café. "It's not safe. Let's call for help though." She slapped her scrub pockets. "Damn. I left my phone in the car."

"I forgot mine at my apartment earlier when I changed," Luna said.

Huddled together in the dark, illuminated only by the battery-powered green exit sign over the back door in the kitchen, Madi said, "Too bad we don't have a big, strong hero who'll come looking for us."

Luna snorted. "Don't need one. I do my own heavy lifting."

Madi glanced at her friend's camo cargo miniskirt, butt-kicking combat boots and snug long-sleeved tee. All topped by a bright pink apron with a cartoon buzzard on the front and the words Buzzy Bird Café emblazoned below it with their web address. One of Luna's designs, because on top of being a physical therapist and filling in as a waitress when needed, Luna was also a great artist. Madi would've been jealous if she didn't love her best friend so much.

She peeked over the counter again, hoping the snow had lightened up outside. It hadn't. In fact, the flakes were blowing sideways now, a constant icy bombardment against the remaining windows and flying in through the broken ones. Maybe if she went out through the rear exit, she could make her way around the building to get to her car. Madi peered up at the pass-through into the pitch-black space. Going through the obstacle course of the kitchen in the dark posed its own set of issues, but what else could she do? They couldn't just sit there all night and freeze to death.

Decision made, Madi climbed to her feet and started toward the swinging door into the back, only to halt as the sound of the two windows over the sink smashing echoed. Her heart stumbled. She sat back down beside Luna as the tree branch in the front entrance continued to wave at them tauntingly. Another escape attempt foiled.

The temperature inside the diner was dropping fast now as wind and snow gusted from two directions. Despite the situation, Madi was still starving. Her stomach growled, and Luna grabbed the sandwiches off the counter above them, handing one to her. They ate like it was their last meal, unnerved by the storm, huddled close to share body heat.

Eventually, Luna said, "If we survive this—"

"Hey." Madi scowled in concern. "We're going to be okay.

As soon as the storm lets up, I'll get to my car and call for help, and—"

Luna shifted her weight. "Well, even so, once we get out of here, I'm going to change things. Live my life instead of letting it live me. I suck at that."

"Me too." Madi sighed. Growing up, she'd always been the stable one, the only child in her family who never caused drama, who always followed the rules, who didn't color outside the lines, who supported everyone else. And she did do all those things. She had her reasons, of course, but sometimes—like now—she wished she'd loosened a little, stopped worrying about being the glue at work, in her family. But seeing as how changing the world's perceptions of her would take a lot more than wishing and hoping, Madi decided to go with a more realistic request. "I'd just be happy with a date to the free clinic fundraiser next weekend. I'm the only nurse in the ER without one."

"Okay then." Luna pulled her order pad and a pen from her apron pocket. "We're stuck here right now, so let's make a list of possible dates for you. And promise me you won't write off anyone too fast, even if he seems like Mr. Wrong."

Luna held out her pinkie for a swear. They'd done that since they were kids. Madi hooked little fingers with her bestie. "I promise—"

A loud thump sounded on one of the walls.

They went still, staring at each other with wide eyes.

"That wasn't a branch." A bad feeling came over Madi, the same one she got sometimes right before they got a serious incoming case. "It's a fist."

She rose to her knees and peered through the dim greenish light toward the direction where the sound had come from near the entrance. A snow drift now blocked the area. Incredible for this early in the season, but big, fat, round snowflakes the size of dinner plates piled up fast she supposed.

The thump came again, along with a moan. A pained one.

Madi stood. “Someone’s out there and they’re hurt.”

“It’s too dangerous to go out there right now,” Luna pleaded.

“I can’t just ignore them.” She sidled around the tree branches clogging the front door, arms wrapped around herself. Someone was in trouble, and it was her duty to help. The nurse’s curse.

Glass crunched beneath her shoes, and snow blasted her in the face, making her shiver. Amazingly, the aluminum doorframe had withstood the impact, and she was able to shove her way outside. She peered into the parking lot but saw nothing.

“Hello?” Madi called, inching farther out into the night. “Is anyone—”

A hand grabbed her ankle, and she screamed as she fell into the darkness.

CHAPTER TWO

MADI SCRAMBLED BACKWARD, but a firm grip around her leg prevented her from going far. The hand was attached to a big male body, sprawled flat on his back. The guy shifted slightly and groaned, and Madi's panic turned to concern. She leaned over him, brushing the snow away from his face to get a better look, despite the pummeling wind. "Are you hurt?"

He didn't respond, wet from the snow and shivering beneath his down jacket. Blood trickled down his temple from a nasty gash over his right eyebrow. His eye was swollen too, probably from being struck by the tree that had fallen. Lightning flashed once more, and his eyes flew open, green-gold and intense, unwavering on hers.

She knew him. Tate Griffin, one of the flight paramedics at the hospital. All the nurses and half the doctors—both female and male—lusted after him because he was so handsome.

They'd never been formally introduced, but Madi had worked indirectly with him at Wyckford General. He'd started a few months back and generally kept to himself. He was always cordial and well-prepared when giving rundowns on patients to staff, at least from what Madi had seen of him.

She'd sighted him in town too—here at the Buzzy Bird, at the local gym, buying gas for his muscle car. Tall and broad shouldered. She remembered how the muscles of his back strained his T-shirt as he moved, how long his legs were, how he looked in his dark sunglasses, jaw firm and mouth grim, lending him a hint of brooding bad boy that had always intrigued Madi—probably more than it should. Still, a little frisson of female awareness always skittered up Madi's spine whenever she saw him and tonight was no exception, even when he was wet and cold and hurt beside her.

"It's okay," Madi said to him. "You were hit by a large branch. You'll need stitches. I can—"

Before she could finish, Tate caught her by the wrist and rolled her beneath two hundred pounds of solid muscle, the entire length of her pressed ruthlessly hard into the snow by him, her hands pinned high over her head by his. He wasn't crushing her, or hurting her, but his hold was effective. In less than a second, he'd immobilized her between the ground and his body.

"Who are you?" he growled, his voice low and rough, raising more goosebumps on her chilled flesh.

"Madison Scott, RN. We've seen each other in the ER." She struggled to free herself, but it was like moving against a slab of cement. "You have a head injury. And you're hypothermic."

His chest heaved against hers, his breathing too rapid. It was hard to see anything, but she'd bet good money he wasn't fully conscious at that point. His grip was still strong though. He felt much colder now, and if that big branch *had* hit him, then he more than likely had a concussion too, in addition to the cut on his head and his swollen eye. She stopped squirming beneath him. "We need to get you inside."

Slowly the man drew back, pulling off her until he was on his knees, but he kept hold of her wrists in one hand. His eyes were shadowed in the darkness, but his tension came through loud and clear.

"Are *you* hurt?" he asked, his tone sluggish.

Madi sat up. "No. I'm fine. *You're* bleeding and—"

Tate interrupted her with a mumbled denial, followed by another groan before he toppled again. Madi barely managed to break his fall with her own torso, and they both fell back into the snow.

"That's a lot of blood."

She peeked out from beneath Tate to see Luna's face wedged between the fallen tree branches and the doorframe.

"Can you help me get him into my car?" Madi tried to sit up again. "My phone's there, and I can turn on the heater to warm him up while we call 911."

Luna eased fully outside, then came over to peer into his face. "Oh, gosh! That's Tate Griffin. He's one of my physical therapy patients."

"Really? Well, we need to get him out of this weather." Madi finally managed to extract herself from beneath his heavy weight, then wrapped her arms around him from behind, lifting his head and shoulders out of the snow and into her lap. He didn't move.

"It's karma. You know that, right?" Luna took Tate's feet and together they huffed and puffed as they dragged him to Madi's car. "He could be your date. I don't know why I didn't think of him."

"The last thing I'm worried about at the moment is the auction."

Squinting into the wind, they made it to her Mini Cooper and, thankfully, the keys were still in the ignition. They got Tate loaded into the passenger seat, bending his long legs to accommodate his torso, then she climbed behind the wheel and started the engine. Once the car was running and the heat was blasting, she dug her phone out of the console and handed it to Luna while she checked Tate's vitals. "Have them send an ambulance. Tell them we've have a male, approximately late thirties, unconscious with a head injury and possible hypothermia."

"Fifteen minutes because of the weather," Luna said after she ended the call, the snow glittering on her dark short hair making her look like a pixie. "They said to keep him warm and dry."

Madi nodded, then focused on her patient. Tate's brow was still furrowed and his expression troubled. Whatever he was dreaming about, it wasn't pleasant. Then his shoulders and neck tensed, and he went rigid. She cupped both sides of his face to hold him still, her voice soft and soothing. "Relax. Help is on the way."

He let out a low, rough wail. "They're gone. All…my fault."

"Shh." She knew not to wake him abruptly. "I've got you—"

Tate shoved her hand away and sat up fast, blinking at her, his gaze unfocused and filled with shadows.

"We've called an ambulance," she said, trying to keep him calm.

He swiped at his temple, then scowled at the blood on his fingers. "What the—"

"Stay still," she said, forcing him to lie back down.

"Bossy," he muttered, his eyes closing once more. "But hot."

Hot? Madi frowned down at her wrinkled scrubs and wet shoes. Her hair had to be a complete disaster by now. She was about as far from "hot" as a person could get, which only further confirmed his head injury in her mind. Madi looked down at Tate's handsome, bloody face, and remembered her promise to Luna earlier. She had to admit she could do worse for a date than Tate Griffin.

A female voice penetrated the haze in Tate's brain.

He took stock of himself before opening his eyes again. He wasn't dead. His legs ached from being stuffed into an awkward position in this tiny little clown car. He shifted slightly, but pain lanced through his skull. Nauseated, he licked his dry lips and tried to focus. “I’m okay.”

“Stay still,” the woman said, the same one who’d told him he’d been hit by a branch. It felt more like he’d been run over by a semi. Repeatedly. Her voice came from his left, so she must be sitting in the driver’s seat. Despite the bile scalding his throat, Tate managed to squint one eye open to see her. Tricky, that, since everything was doubled. Brown hair, long and wet and currently scraggly. Purple scrubs embroidered with the Wyckford General Hospital logo over the pocket on her chest. *A very nice chest too.* Her face was pretty in an understated way, her features delicate but set with purpose. No pushover then. Probably a nurse.

Yeah. She’d told him that, he vaguely remembered. Mary? Milly? McKenzie?

His temples throbbed as he recalled it. Madison. Yep, that was it. Madison Scott, RN.

He’d seen her before on his EMT shifts. Cute, but bossy.

And if she wanted to talk shop, well, unfortunately, Tate had dealt with more head injuries than she could possibly imagine.

Still, her warm hand stroked the side of his face and felt better than anything had in a long time. He turned into it without thinking, trying to figure out how he’d ended up there. He remembered having his usual nightmare, then driving into town to see if they needed him for a shift. Then the rain became snow, and everything went sideways. Literally. As conditions deteriorated into a blizzard, the lights of the diner had acted as a beacon. He’d parked safely and nearly made it to the door when something heavy slammed into him from behind and the world went black.

Unsettled, Tate tried to move, but Nurse Scott held him down. Focusing past the jackhammering in his skull was difficult, but if he squinted, the cobwebs in his vision weren't quite so bad. Behind her shoulder, another woman leaned over the backseat, staring at him. This face he knew. Luna, his physical therapist. He wondered what she was doing at the café on a night like this before he remembered she also worked here sometimes.

Tate gave in to the lethargy threatening to pull him under, sinking into her caring warmth. "Thanks for saving me, ladies."

Madison smiled down at him and despite his situation, a tingle of awareness spiked through his bloodstream. "The ambulance will be here soon. You've had quite a night."

So have you. He saw it in his nurse's pretty chocolate-hued eyes.

"They'll patch you up and get you some meds for your pain," she continued.

"No narcotics," Tate said, then gripped his aching head to keep it from flying off his shoulders. Stars danced in front of his eyes, turning to red and blue lights.

Madi looked down at her patient again. His complexion had gone a bit ashy beneath his light brown skin. Clammy too, but he was conscious. The ambulance pulled up near the Mini and two EMTs got out, then walked to the back of the rig for their gear and a gurney.

"What happened?" Tate ground out, his jaw tight, his big body a solid weight beside her.

Memory loss wasn't uncommon after head trauma. "Tree on the head."

"And my friend here came to your rescue," Luna told him. "You owe her a favor."

"Luna!"

"She needs a date this weekend," Luna continued as if Madi

hadn't spoken. "If you go with her to her charity event on Saturday night, you'd save her from merciless ridicule, so..."

Madi sighed. "This is completely inappropriate and—"

"Okay," Tate mumbled.

Wide-eyed, Madi looked at her patient, then Luna again. She normally dated men who were fine. Fine looking, fine acting, just all-around fine. No one to rock the boat. No one to cause disruptions to anyone else's lives or their perceptions of little "Miss Goody Two-Shoes"—a nickname she'd earned as a kid and still despised to this day. Fine was good. Fine was safe. Fine seemed to be her lot in life.

But Tate Griffin was *so* not her usual type. He was the kind of man who'd create waves in town if the two of them were seen dating. But Wyckford better hold on to their proverbial hats because it looked like they would indeed be going on a date together, even if it was fake. And if Tate looked this good while bleeding and semi-conscious, Madi could only imagine what he'd look like on his feet and dressed to the nines.

CHAPTER THREE

ONE WEEK LATER, Madi still walked around in a cloud of nervous anticipation. The charity auction was that night, and she'd spent the last seven days alternating between long ER shifts and working on the event. A large portion of the evening's proceeds would go toward her beloved Health Services Clinic where anyone in the county could go to get free medical treatment, community recovery resources, teen programs, crisis counseling and a whole host of other things. Hopefully, the money raised would keep them going until next year. It's what should have been foremost in her mind.

Instead, her thoughts kept returning to Tate Griffin.

She'd hoped to touch base with him at least once—either on a shift or around town—so they could work out the details of tonight, but, so far, he hadn't made an appearance. Then again, given his injuries that night, he'd probably been put on bed rest for a few days. It was possible he hadn't been cleared for duty yet. Whatever the cause, Madi hadn't gotten his phone number. And because Tate hadn't technically been her patient, looking up his files from the other night now would be a HIPPA violation. So, if she wanted his information, she'd have to ask for it. But with the rumor mill inside the hospital and in the town in general, that just wasn't an option. The two of them together at the auction would create a big enough stir tonight. She considered asking Luna but didn't want to add any more fuel to the fire. He'd be there, and if not, well, she'd survive. She'd survived much worse, after all.

Luckily, Madi had a full patient roster that day to keep her busy and stop her from spiraling into an anxious mess about the evening. Including a new arrival in the ER—a crotchety old man named Luther Martin. He had an arrhythmia complicated by vasovagal syncope, which caused dizziness and fainting. He also suffered from a terminal meanness.

"I brought your juice," she said, entering Mr. Martin's room.

"I asked for it three hours ago. What's wrong with you? You were always slower than molasses."

Madi ignored his complaint because it had been five minutes since he'd asked. And because he'd been her first-grade teacher at Wyckford Elementary thirty years prior, before he'd retired. The man was so difficult that even his own son, who lived an hour away in Boston, refused to call or visit.

"I remember you wet your pants in front of the whole class, missy," Mr. Martin said. "Don't act all superior with me now."

She'd been six at the time, but her face still heated with remembered shame. "Because you wouldn't let me go to the bathroom."

"Recess was five minutes away."

"I couldn't wait."

"So, you're making *me* wait now? You're a horrible nurse, letting what happened back then affect your treatment of me."

Madi could have argued she was the only one on staff willing to help the old coot, but she took the high road and set the cup, complete with straw, on Mr. Martin's bedside tray.

He picked it up, sniffed, then took a tiny sip, acting like it was radioactive waste. "I wanted *apple*."

"You asked for cranberry."

Mr. Martin cursed loud and threw the juice against the wall. The liquid splashed across the bedding, the floor, the IV pole, and Madi. Juice dripped off her nose, and she sighed. It took her and housekeeping twenty minutes to clean up the mess. Ten more to get the patient back into his freshly made bed. She huffed with the effort.

"Out of shape or just gaining some weight?" he asked, his tone snide.

Madi reminded herself she helped save lives, not take them, and walked out of the room.

Thankfully, a new patient came into the ER to distract her, a two-year-old with a laceration requiring stitches. Madi got him cleaned up and prepped the area for the doctor—lidocaine, a suture kit, four-by-fours—then assisted in the closing of the wound.

The rest of her morning followed much the same pattern.

At noon, she went to the staff break room and grabbed her lunch from the fridge. Her older sister, Toni, was there too. Once upon a time, Toni had been wild. So had her other two siblings: Jack Jr. and Karrie, Toni's twin. Madi had always been the good one, hoping to stand out.

Then, the one time when her goodness and support could've have made the difference between life and death, she'd failed. The night Karrie had taken a lethal dose of pills and died. Even all these years later, Madi felt guilty about it. If she'd just listened more, paid more attention to her, given her the support she'd needed, maybe Karrie would still be alive. It didn't matter that Madi had only been sixteen at the time and Karrie was eighteen and a lifetime apart experience-wise.

Some people might have gone the opposite route after that—drinking and partying to bury the hurt and pain and guilt. That's what Toni and Jack Jr. had done. But Madi had instead grown more terrified to do anything wrong, to screw up again and lose more people she loved. For all the good it did. Her parents had ended up divorced anyway, with her father moving to Hawaii and having no communication with the family again. Still, she was undeterred. Being good and dependable and supportive was who she was now, for better or worse. And if she sometimes wanted to break free of that, well, it was a nice fantasy, but she had a lot riding on her persona these days. Including the fate of her beloved clinic. She hoped it was enough to keep the lights on for another year.

Madi took a seat beside Toni at the large round table in the center of the break room, stopping to wave at Lucille Munson, one of the elderly volunteers from the local retirement home, who sat on a sofa along the wall sipping a cup of tea. No one knew exactly how old Lucille was, but before moving into Sunny Village, she'd run the town's art gallery. She was also a hub of all things gossip in Wyckford with Ben Murphy, the father of Madi's other best friend, Cassie Murphy. Cassie was a surgeon and had recently moved back to town from San Diego to be with Brock Turner, the resident GP and pediatrician.

Their second chance at romance gave her hope maybe she'd find her special someone someday too. If she was honest, that was what she wanted most, deep down inside.

Toni smiled and put down her phone. "Hey, sis. Heard you have a date to your event tonight."

Frowning, she froze as she pulled out her sandwich. "How did you hear that?"

"I'm psychic." Her sister stole Madi's chips from her lunch bag.

"Luna told you, didn't she?"

"Yep. When I grabbed breakfast at the café earlier." Toni munched away. "Can't believe you landed Tate Griffin."

Madi glanced around, all too aware of the other staff probably hanging on their every word.

"Seriously. I'm impressed. The last guy you dated was a

boring accountant from Providence." Toni laughed loudly, looking over at the sofa where Lucille was almost falling out of her seat trying to hear their conversation. "Are you catching all of this?"

"I am." The elderly woman pulled out her cell phone and started typing. "Good stuff. Keep going."

After her shift, Madi drove home and fed the ancient black cat who'd come with the house she'd inherited from her grandmother, the one who answered only to "Violet" and only when food was involved. Before she got ready for the charity event, Madi checked her social media—then wished she hadn't.

Because of course Lucille had tagged her in a post to the town's Facebook page.

Tonight's the big dinner and auction with all proceeds going to support the Health Services Clinic, organized by Wyckford General's own Madison Scott, ER nurse extraordinaire, who apparently has a date with…flight paramedic Tate Griffin!

P.S. If anyone snaps pictures of the couple tonight, please share here.

CHAPTER FOUR

TATE'S ROUTINE HADN'T changed much since he'd come to Wyckford. He got up in the mornings and worked out, either by swimming—when it was nice enough—or going to the gym, usually with Mark and sometimes Brock Turner, though he didn't come with them often anymore. Brock had gotten engaged a few months back to Cassie Murphy, a big-time surgeon who'd come back home to consult on a case. They'd supposedly found their happily-ever-after together.

If you went in for that sort of thing.

Tate didn't, but it was fine. He preferred keeping things light and friendly without too many messy connections. Connections only caused pain and suffering when they were gone, in his experience. Just look at his team, his parents. So yeah. He had lots of casual friends and a few best buds. Mark Bates was one of the latter. He'd moved to Wyckford from Chicago after his discharge from the Navy, so they had the military in common. He'd been the only person Tate knew in town when he'd arrived. And the first person to give him a run for his money at the gym too.

Today was warm for October, so Tate went swimming alone since Mark was busy. He put on his wet suit and used a small private beach not far from his rental house on Buzzards Bay, doing laps until exhaustion nearly pulled him under. Then he forced himself to walk along the rocky shore for about a mile.

At first, it was slow going, more like a crawl, but he went the distance, no problem. Quite the feat, given that four years ago he'd had a severe post-surgical infection in his leg after the helicopter crash. And while overall he'd recovered well from the ordeal within a year, except for a permanent slight limp, he'd had surgery a few months back to remove some excess scar tissue, thus this new leave from the Air Force. But things were improving daily and hopefully he'd be cleared to return to duty soon. He was building up his strength and endurance.

He should be grateful he still had a leg at all after the accident. And honestly, even if he'd had an amputation, it would still have been a far better outcome than the fate of the rest of his team that night. They'd lost their lives.

Why didn't I just postpone that flight a few hours? Wait for the storm to pass? Wait until daylight?

He knew the answer to those questions. They'd been stated clearly in black-and-white by the naval investigators who'd cleared him of any wrongdoing in that night's horrendous accident. Postponing the rescue would have been an absolute death sentence to the airmen trapped in the ocean. The cyclone hadn't passed for another day, and daylight wouldn't have helped anything in the situation, other than making it even more apparent what a dire mess it had been. His crew hadn't hesitated to follow him into the breach. They'd made their choice.

Now he had to live with the consequences.

Tate knew all of this, but still grief and guilt slashed through him again. He stopped to catch his breath. He hadn't saved any of them. Not his team. Not the victims. No one. Despite all his training as a trauma paramedic, despite all his para-rescue skills, despite all of it, he'd failed. He'd always prided himself on being a good leader—responsive, supportive, making the difficult decisions. But the accident had made him doubt everything.

So now, he worked twice as hard as everyone else on the crew at the hospital, double- and triple-checking it all to make sure he didn't screw up again. It was also why he kept the circle of people he let close to him small. Because if he couldn't protect those he cared for, what was the point? It felt like penance—the long hours, the lonely nights—because maybe if he punished himself enough, saved enough people, perhaps he could somehow earn the forgiveness of those he'd failed all those years ago.

Even if he'd never forgive himself.

Once he got back from his swim, Tate changed out of his wet suit, showered, then stared in the mirror, barely recognizing the man looking back. Brock had done his recheck from the head injury and mild concussion after the storm and had cleared him to return to the flight crew. But it took a bit to get back in the regular shift rotation, so Tate had mainly spent the week stuck at home, getting more restless by the second. Another reason he was glad to have an excuse to get out of his house tonight, beside the fact he had a date with Nurse Scott from the parking lot.

Was she as pretty as he remembered from that night or was that just another hallucination courtesy of the bump on his head? If Tate shut his eyes, he could still remember how she'd smelled, like bleach and flowers and crisp snow from the weather.

Enough.

Shaking off the silly thoughts, Tate stared in the mirror again and reminded himself this was a favor for her helping him that night, nothing more.

Even so, he looked a mess—as his mom used to say—with stitches over one eye and a yellowing bruise on his cheek from the tree branch that had hit him upside the head. His hair was on the wrong side of a haircut, and he'd skipped shaving that morning. He'd lost some weight too, making the angles of his face starker. His eyes looked...*hollow*.

There was no way cute, kind Nurse Scott wanted anything more than a favor from him tonight. She'd been a Good Samaritan who'd helped him when he needed it. That was all. This wasn't some grand romance. It was a business arrangement. Because while his body might have mostly recovered from the accident, there was work yet to do on his soul.

Without thinking he grabbed the empty bottle of Vicodin on the vanity and rolled it between his fingers. He'd quit cold turkey three years ago the minute he recognized his desperation to numb everything, but the craving remained. The pills made it all go away.

He finished getting dressed, then went out to his garage and the Chevelle.

The rest of the day passed with him under the chassis since he didn't have a shift that day. He thought about stopping by the hospital to see if he could find Madison and discuss their plans tonight, but then decided against. He was currently filthy again from working on the Chevelle's transmission. Plus, there really wasn't a reason to see her beforehand. He'd seen the flyers plastered all over town about the auction, so he knew where to be and when.

No sense making a bigger deal out of this than it was. Regardless of how his body reacted each time he remembered sitting beside her in that tiny car, the way her breath had hitched as she tenderly stroked his hair, her chocolate-brown eyes and her parted pink lips...

"Stop it, son." His dad's voice rang through his head, giving Tate advice when he was unsure about something. *"Mind*

on your work and hands busy. Stay out of trouble, and you'll be just fine."

After several hours more under the car, he finally rolled out on the creeper, rubbing his left thigh absently, determined to keep his end of the deal he'd made with Madison that night. It would be okay. They'd have a nice dinner, maybe he'd bid on some stuff at the auction since the proceeds went for a good cause, and then he'd come home and sink into his comfortable routine again.

No harm, no foul. His stupid reactions and thoughts about the sexy nurse would be over.

All he needed to do was make it through the next couple of hours with his head on straight and his heart tucked away safely where he'd locked it four years ago.

Resolved, he went back inside and showered again, then dressed in his best suit, before checking the clock and slipping his keys, cell phone, and wallet into his pocket and walking out to the Chevelle.

Tate had a fake date to keep.

Madi paced the lobby of the town's 1920s-era restored theater-turned-event-space in her little black dress and heels, nodding to the occasional late-arriving straggler. Through the doors into the large gathering room, the delicious smells of dinner made her antsy to get in there with her guests—to eat, smile, schmooze. Her job tonight was to get people fired up to donate and bid. But she was still missing her escort for the evening.

She'd been certain Tate would come, even though they'd not spoken since the night of the storm. After all, the charity auction was the hopping place to be. Well, she wasn't giving up hope yet.

It was all Luna's fault, Madi decided. Making her pinkie swear. Tate was hot and had that restless, brooding air about him that lit her up from the inside out for some reason. She'd never taken a walk on the wild side before, but he did make it look extremely appealing…

Whoops. No.

She quickly reeled those errant thoughts in fast. They barely knew each other. *Gah!* All this stress and nervousness was exactly why she didn't date outside her safe box of accountants and bankers. She should have never made that stupid pinkie swear.

"Hey," Luna said, coming up to Madi in the lobby.

Madi blinked at her best friend's appearance. Luna looked amazing, dressed to perfection with her hair and makeup done. Her slinky purple dress emphasized her curves and long legs, as did her stiletto heels. "Wow."

"Thanks." Luna shrugged, then looked away fast as Mark Bates walked by and waved to Madi.

Usually, the guy was in full firefighter gear. But tonight, Mark looked dapper in his suit. Six foot and rangy, the tailoring showed off his lean, muscled form, and the dark charcoal fabric highlighted Mark's sun-kissed blond surfer looks and light blue eyes. He flashed an easy smile as he passed, straight white teeth gleaming against his tanned skin. "Hey."

"Hey," Madi said.

Then he glanced at Luna, his eyes widening.

She kept her attention on Madi. "See you in there."

Mark watched Luna vanish into the gathering room, and Madi bit back a grin. The poor guy looked bewildered. Sharp, quick-witted, and tough as hell, he was one of five firefighters on the Wyckford brigade and handled everything from Jaws of Life rescues to removing kittens from trees. Nothing much ever seemed to rattle him.

Until tonight, apparently.

He shook his head as he walked off.

Alone once more, Madi looked around the lobby again. She'd been so busy earlier setting up and greeting people, maybe Tate had slipped in without her seeing him. But wouldn't he have come up to her and said hello at least? Ugh. This whole idea had been crazy from the start and reminded her of why she preferred her nice quiet life. It was predictable. Peaceful.

And boring.

Shaking her head at her own silliness, Madi walked over to peer out the large windows into the night, but there was no sign of Tate Griffin or his car. With a sigh, she squared her shoulders, then peeked inside the gathering room doors.

They had a sold-out crowd.

She wasted another five minutes tidying the already immaculate auction item displays on the table lining the back wall of the lobby, dawdling in front of a small silver bracelet. Each charm was handmade and unique to Wyckford in some way: a tiny buzzard, a miniature pier, a little fishing boat and an anchor. Normally, Madi only wore the infinity necklace her sister Karrie had given her. But this piece urged her to spend money she didn't have.

"Not exactly practical."

Mr. Martin stood behind her, leaning heavily on a cane, his wizened features twisted into an unfriendly smile.

Ignoring his statement, Madi asked instead, "Are you feeling better?"

"My ankles are swollen, my fingers are numb, and I'm plugged up beyond any Roto-Rooter help."

As a nurse, Madi was used to people telling her things they'd never mention in polite conversation. "Well, please stay hydrated. Are you taking your meds?"

"There was a mix-up at the pharmacy."

"Did you call Dr. Turner?"

"I tried. He's an idiot. And he's twelve. Tries to skate by on his looks and reputation alone." Mr. Martin sniffed. "Not like his father."

Brock was not, in fact, an idiot. He was thirty-six, and one of the best MDs in Massachusetts. Plus, he'd worked his ass off to save the practice his father had started and was a good man to boot. He always helped Madi out at the clinic whenever he could. Of course, she might be a bit biased since he was also engaged to Cassie, but now wasn't the time or place to argue with the crotchety old man. "I'll check into the meds issue for you first thing in the morning."

"See that you do." Mr. Martin glanced around, scowling. "Where's your date? Been stood up?"

Then, without giving Madi time to answer, he limped away.

She turned back to stare at the bracelet again. He'd been right about the jewelry though. It *was* impractical for a nurse. The charms would snag on everything from leads to the bed rails.

"Honey, what are you doing out here?" Her mother.

Ellen Scott was a nursing supervisor at the hospital. Tonight, she wore her Sunday best, a pale blue dress showing off an early season tan she'd gotten from her taking her breaks during the summer on the hospital's upper deck where the new medical flight service helicopter landed.

"Pretty," her mother said, looking at the bracelet. "I had the kitchen save your dinner for you. Dessert's next for the rest of us."

Her mom kissed Madi on the cheek, then returned to the event.

When the lights dimmed in the gathering room, and the PowerPoint presentation of the auction items started, Madi sneaked inside to take the only empty seat at one of the back tables. It was too dark to see the people sitting around her.

To her left sat a man facing the slide show. She squinted at his profile. He seemed vaguely familiar, but before she could figure out from where, someone tapped her shoulder. “Madi, there you are.”

She craned her neck and smiled as the lights came up again. “Hello.”

“I’ve been looking everywhere for you.” Judith Meyer was nursing director. “I’m glad you finally get a chance to rest and enjoy the fruits of your labor.”

“Thanks. I made sure everything was ready out front. We have a full house. We’re doing good.”

Her boss grinned. “Fabulous! And how are you, Tate?”

Stunned, Madi whirled around to find him next to her in the left-hand chair, a bandage above one eye and the small bruise on his temple yellowish purple against his light brown skin. His green-gold eyes were as gorgeous as she remembered and were now lit with curiosity.

Wow.

A spotlight hit the stage and the MC announced, “And now, let’s welcome the hardest-working nurse in Wyckford. Please give a round of applause for Madison Scott!”

CHAPTER FIVE

"GO ON." JUDITH GRINNED, nudging her from her seat before turning to Tate. "Escort your date up there."

"Oh," Madi rushed to cover. "It's okay, he doesn't have to—"

But Tate was already on his feet, his hand at the small of her back, gesturing for Madi to precede him, a smile curving his lips.

She did her best to exude confidence for anyone watching them—and *everyone* was watching them—then whispered to the man at her side, "I was worried you'd forgotten about me."

Something flickered in his eyes before he covered it and his polite mask fell into place. Madi wasn't sure how he'd managed to slip past her in the lobby without her seeing him, but it didn't matter. She was grateful Tate was willing to play her fake date in front of the whole town.

They threaded their way through the tables to the stage, the sea of faces nothing but a blur. All she could concentrate on was the big, warm hand at the small of her back attached to the gorgeous guy escorting her. Tate stood near enough now that his scent—woods and spice and everything nice—surrounded her. It nearly made her turn around and pull him away into a private corner where they could get to know each other better. A lot better.

But as they got to the stairs leading up to the stage, Madi

forced herself to focus on the task at hand. The auction. Raising money for the clinic. That was way more important than her neglected libido right now. She glanced over at Tate then and noticed for the first time his slight limp. Huh. She didn't remember him having a leg injury the night of the storm. She frowned. "Are you okay?"

Rather than answering, Tate nudged her up the steps. "Go. People are waiting."

With five hundred sets of eyes on her, Madi took the stage and grabbed the mic from the MC. "Good evening."

The crowd cheered.

Madi gave a genuine smile at their enthusiastic greeting. She'd grown up here, worked here, lived here. Even if she somehow ended up on the other side of the world, she'd always be from Wyckford. "Thank you all for coming and supporting such a worthy cause. Now, let's make some money for our free clinic tonight, eh?" Madi pointed to the big screen behind her where pictures of the items were being displayed. "Everyone, get your paddles ready because we have some great things for you to buy. Our favorite auctioneer, Harry Langston, is here from Boston, and I expect to see lots of bidding action."

"Let your date say hello too!" Lucille called from a table near the front, interrupting her. Dressed in a silver gown that resembled a disco ball, the older woman snapped a photo of Madi and Tate with her phone, then winked.

As Tate reached over to grab the mic, their fingers brushed and made her shiver. "Hello," he said, winking back at Lucille. "I'm Tate Griffin. The…date."

"And there you have it." Madi commandeered the microphone again, not wanting to give the old busybody even more to gossip about online. "Now let's get to the auction and have a good time."

After introducing the auctioneer, they stepped off stage

again, Madi focused on returning to their table and eating her dinner now that her speech was over, but she was waylaid by her mom, who pulled her down for a hug. Tate seemed to have disappeared, which was just as well because she wasn't sure she was up for answering any more questions about him just then.

Bidding began with her bracelet, and Madi quickly grabbed a paddle from her mom's table, considering it a sacrifice for the cause.

That's what she told herself anyway.

Someone else eventually won, and the auctioneer moved on to the next item.

"You did a great job tonight, honey." Her mother squeezed her hand, eyes suspiciously damp. "Out of all my kids, you've always been the good one. Running the clinic, organizing this auction. I'm so proud of you!"

They hugged again and Madi was glad for the support. "Thanks."

"Where's your date?" her mom asked, searching behind Madi. "I've seen him around the hospital. He seems like a nice young man. If a bit quiet and mysterious. How did you two meet?"

Nice wasn't the first word that popped into Madi's head when she thought of Tate.

"Oh, look. Here he comes now." Her mother beamed at someone over Madi's shoulder. Tate, of course, returning with two glasses of wine. He handed one to Madi.

"I'm Ellen Scott, Madi's mother." She held out her hand.

"Tate Griffin," he said, shaking her hand. "Pleasure, ma'am."

"I love your accent," her mother said. "Where are you from?"

"All over really." Tate sipped his wine. "My dad was in the

Air Force. But we spent the most time in Louisiana when I was growing up. Barksdale AFB. Guess I brought a bit of the south with me."

"I'd say so." Her mother was a shameless flirt. Madi secretly wished she had even half of the woman's skills in that department, but she hadn't inherited that gene, apparently. When it came to social interactions, most people described her as sweet and kind and polite, but not flirty. Her mother patted Tate's hand. "You are a charmer, aren't you?"

"Mom!" Madi scolded, her face heating. The last thing she needed now was Tate thinking this was a setup for more than just the one evening. And while she wouldn't be opposed to seeing him again after tonight, she wouldn't go there.

"What?" Her mother smiled. "Fine. Well, you two have a good time. I need to start spending some money."

Tate looked at Madi, giving her a sardonic half toast with his glass. "Cheers."

They both returned to their own table. Madi caught one of the wait staff and had them bring out her dinner that had been held in the kitchen for her. While she ate her yummy baked chicken and veggies, she monitored the room around her. The space was filled with happy, well-fed people, but they seemed to be doing more socializing than buying. When a Patriots game package came up and no one lifted their paddle, Madi's heart sank. And when a bid did finally come in, it was far less than expected.

The next item was another big-ticket one—an expensive night on the town in Boston, including a limo, a fancy dinner and an orchestra concert. The bids started low again. They had to do better. Three-quarters of their budget for the free clinic came from these donations.

Then Tate offered two hundred dollars higher than the previous bidder.

Madi stared at him. “What are you doing?”

He eyed her with a wicked, devious smile. And when someone joined him in a bidding war from across the room, Tate continued raising his paddle. Unbelievably, the battle for the “Night on the Town” continued for five more minutes, until the final sum was nothing short of dazzling.

Tate won.

Apparently satisfied, he set down his paddle and stretched his long legs out in front of him to watch the proceedings. Madi should have been watching the auction too, but now she couldn’t take her eyes off him as the night kicked into full gear. The whole place went crazy, everyone bidding on all the items, playfully outdoing each other.

It was…*wonderful.*

But she couldn’t stop thinking about how much money Tate had spent to get it going. She wasn’t sure what a flight paramedic’s salary was, especially a temporary one, but she didn’t think it was enough for him to have that kind of extra cash just lying around. “What are you going to do with that package you won?”

“Have a night on the town, apparently.” He grinned at her, then hiked his chin toward the front of the room. “Trouble at six o’clock.”

Lucille again, this time with another older gal from the retirement home’s blue-haired posse. They both bid fiercely for the next auction item—a date with Arthur Schmidt, the elderly owner of the local hardware store.

“That guy has got to be ninety, right?” Tate frowned, watching them up their offers alarmingly. “Can he handle that much excitement?”

Thankfully, the auctioneer suggested the two women share the date, and things ended peacefully.

Tate winced in clear sympathy for Arthur, who now had not one, but two, dates.

"Don't feel sorry for him," Madi said. "Yes. In fact, Arthur's probably loving it."

He slid her a look. "Seriously?"

"Oh, yeah." Madi couldn't help laughing at the shocked look on Tate's face. "Sex doesn't stop just because you get older."

"I suppose it doesn't." Then Tate's gaze dropped from Madi's eyes to her mouth, and suddenly she felt like climbing into his lap and kissing him silly. Which was totally unlike her. But then, this whole night seemed like something out of a wacky rom-com movie, so…

Madi hadn't realized how much she'd leaned into him until she nearly fell against his chest. She quickly straightened and sipped her wine before laughing low. He was good. Really good. *Charmer indeed.* "Save the flirting for my mother. I'm immune."

He gave her a long look, then said, "Okay. But explain something to me. How does a woman like you not have a real date tonight?"

She blinked at him, part stunned, part sad. "Suffice it to say I work a lot."

"I've seen that," Tate said, still watching her with those too-perceptive green-gold eyes.

Madi reached for her wine, wishing it was something harder.

Tate's hand sat beside hers on the table, and as she watched, his thumb glided over her fingers, a small, casual touch that sent a naughty shudder of awareness through her. His dark brows drew together as he stared down at their hands, the air between them shimmering with possibilities as his tone shifted from flirty to something far more raw and real. "I've been known to work too much myself. It's a good way to escape."

Unsure how to respond to that, Madi sipped more wine,

watching him over the rim of her glass. He was so close now she felt the warmth of his breath at her temple. In the crowded space, their nearness was no different from any other couple in the room, but butterflies swarmed inside her.

CHAPTER SIX

TATE HAD NO idea what he was doing, opening up to Madison Scott.

Getting in way too deep, way too fast, that's what.

Which was not like him at all. He was not a sharer, as his previous partners had always told him. Flirting was one thing. A distraction. A diversion. It came second nature to him. He used it like a shield to keep anyone from seeing what a complete mess he really was. But somehow, Madi seemed to cut through all his BS and get right to the heart of him. Scary, that.

And oddly exhilarating too.

She looked amazing tonight. Her deceptively modest black dress had little crisscross straps across her back and fell to midthigh, molding her curves and making him want to see more. High, strappy heels emphasized a world-class set of legs he'd only ever seen hidden beneath scrubs. And her hair, twisted up in some loose bun with a few tendrils falling around the nape of her neck looked sexy as hell. Her only jewelry was a gold necklace—no earrings.

Madi was everything he liked in a woman. Soft, sweet, smart. But he could also tell just by looking at her that she was the kind of woman who deserved the whole package—white picket fence, diamond ring, promises of forever. A partner who could protect her and love her unconditionally—without baggage.

She was someone's keeper.

But not his.

Yet, sitting there with her he…*ached.* Ached and yearned for more with her.

To hold *this* woman and lose himself in her.

Which was ridiculous. This was all fake. He knew it. Hell, he'd agreed to it.

So, why was he so tempted to break all the rules now?

Before he could contemplate that too much, Judith tapped Madi on the shoulder, interrupting them.

"I'm sorry," she said. "But could I have a moment, Madi?"

"Sure." Madi excused herself, then joined her boss in the foyer.

The auction moved ahead at full steam without her, people jumping up and waving as they bid. Telling himself he needed to stretch his aching leg and wasn't being nosy, Tate followed the two women. He lurked in the entranceway as he listened to their conversation.

"Absolutely," Madi said. "I'll go upstairs and get it right now. Thank you for the addition."

Then they parted ways.

Let it go, man. Let her go.

Tate knew he should go back inside and wait for her at the table. That would be the logical, sensible thing to do. They could finish out a nice night and then be done with it. Madi wasn't for him.

Except she was clearly under a lot of pressure here and she was still doing her best to keep everyone happy and supported. He felt that to his soul. He admired her for it, maybe because he'd done the same so many times himself.

Part of him screamed for him to walk away. Madi deserved *way* more than he could offer.

But the other part of him—the one that had been lonely too long—won out, and he followed her down the hall anyway.

Madi walked up the stairs, cursing the shoes pinching her toes as she searched for the antique Judith had so graciously donated to try and raise even more money for the clinic tonight.

Judith's family had built this theater in the early 1940s and apparently the "missing" vase had sat in the entry for years, until last spring when the theater had been renovated. It had never been put back on display and was worth several thousand dollars at least. Now all Madi had to do was find it.

The second story ran the length of the building. On one side was a series of rooms used by the rec center and various groups like the local Booster Club. On the other was one big closed-off storage area. Madi let herself in and flipped on the lights. Far above was an open-beam ceiling and a loft where more stuff had been haphazardly shoved away. Hopefully, she wouldn't have to climb up there in her dress and heels.

Warm and stuffy, the place smelled like neglect. She took a good look around and panicked at the idea of finding her way out of this maze, much less locating her quarry. She walked around a shelving unit stuffed to the gills with play props and background sets.

Past two huge fake potted Christmas trees. Large stacks of boxes. Madi kept searching. Near the center of the room were more containers of office equipment and furnishings, and miraculously, all by itself in the corner, a tall vase exactly like the one Judith had described. She grabbed it and turned to go, only to run into a brick wall of man.

Startled, she screamed and jumped back. The vase flew from her hands and would've smashed to the floor except Tate caught it and grinned. His dimples made him look boyish, except Tate Griffin was one hundred percent man.

"What are you doing?" Madi pressed a hand to her pounding heart. "You scared me half to death."

"Sorry." He winced slightly. "Anything I can help with?"

She snatched the vase from him. "No. This was all I needed."

He opened his mouth to say more, but the storage room door creaked open again and a voice called from somewhere far behind them, "Madi, dear? Are you in here?"

Oh, no. No, no, no.

This was not good. If Lucille found them in here, it would be all over social media by morning. She wanted to keep the town's focus on the auction, not her personal life. She glanced around for a place to hide.

Tate seemed to be on the same page because he held a finger to his lips, then took the vase in one hand and her wrist in the other to tug them into the shadows. Madi walked on tiptoe to avoid her heels clicking on the floor as they weaved through the shelves, his big body beside her, his breath in her ear. Stealth. Got it. Got something else too, an unexpected zing of wildfire through her blood as he leaned in to whisper, "She's persistent, isn't she?"

Madi nodded, biting her lip to keep from laughing.

Lucille called out for her again.

Scanning the area around them, Tate opened an electrical panel and the next second the lights went out. Madi gasped as Tate pressed her into the wall, his lips on her cheek. "Don't move."

Then he crouched before her and removed her shoes one by one. Madi grasped his shoulders for balance, unable to see a thing. Tate, however, didn't seem to have that problem as he led her through a maze of more storage shelves with apparent ease. They turned corners and squeezed into spots, his hands sliding to her hips, guiding her where he wanted her to go, taking care she didn't bump into anything. She had no idea where they were headed now, but she followed him anyway, trusting him for some reason she didn't really understand. Then there was the fact that each time they stopped, he pressed against her again until she began to anticipate it. Crave it.

"Madi?" A small beam of light now accompanied Lucille's call. She had a flashlight.

"Oh, for the love of—" she started before Tate's warm lips silenced her. Her knees melted then, and if he hadn't been holding her up, she would've fallen. That's why she put her hand around his neck. For balance. Yep. That's the excuse she was going with anyway.

"How badly do you want to hide from her?" Tate asked when he finally pulled back a few millimeters, each word rumbling from his chest through hers. He'd set the vase on the floor beside them now, freeing up both hands to stroke her arms, her hair, cup her face. Madi rocked into him, unable to help herself, tightening her grip, her kiss-frazzled brain struggling to process words. It had been so long, too long since someone had touched her like this.

"Madi?" Tate whispered; his own voice laced with need.

She liked how he said her name. Liked how he made her feel too, languid yet throbbing. "Hmm?"

When she didn't continue, he huffed a small laugh against her jaw, then spun Madi away, nudging her up a nearby ladder, his biceps on either side of her arms, his chest pressed to her back. "Climb."

Good thing it was dark because her face felt hotter than the sun. Madi did as he asked, aware her butt was in his face as they went. And if he *could* see, then Tate had a great view right up her dress. Thankfully, she'd worn new lacy underwear tonight, but still. Not her best angle.

They reached the loft at the top of the ladder. Moonlight

slanted in from a sole round window, revealing more stored items, a couch and a large table stacked with more stuff. There were also rows of framed pictures and empty planters. Everywhere.

Madi moved aside, but the space was so small she lost her balance and fell onto the couch.

Tate followed her down.

On the night of the storm, Madi had been beneath him too, but this time felt different. Sexy different.

He shifted a little to get the bulk of his weight off her. One of his thighs pushed between hers, and an involuntary, accidental moan escaped her, needy and wanton.

And horrifyingly loud.

They both stilled, peering down at the little beam of light as Lucille weaved through the aisles below.

"Unless she can climb a ladder, we're good here until she gives up and leaves," Tate whispered.

Yes. They were good here. Or very bad, depending on how you looked at it.

He went still, a solid heated package of testosterone and sinew pressing her into the sofa cushions. She felt a little helpless and every time he breathed, his leg shifted against her, sending shimmers of need through her whole body.

"She won't give up," Madi whispered back, more than a little breathless.

Tate pulled a coin from his pocket, then threw it. It landed with a ping all the way across the huge storage near the entrance.

"Oh!" Lucille's beam whipped toward the noise. "There you are!"

They watched as the older woman wobbled through the room to the door, then vanished.

Silence reigned, except for Madi's thundering pulse. She was in an attic loft, with her fake date. Common sense screamed for her to leave. But her heart wanted him, just once.

"Okay?" Tate asked.

Loaded question. "You have some impressive skills, Mr. Griffin. I feel like a Bond girl."

His smile made her toes curl. "The way you shimmied up that ladder will fuel my fantasies for some time."

So he *could* see in the dark. And now that they were here, with bright moonlight streaming over them from the window, she saw him too. Felt him. *All* of him. He dropped his head, his lips barely brushing her exposed skin, and she sucked in a breath.

"I have lots of practice," she said for lack of anything better.

"Yeah?" he asked, sounding intrigued. "I haven't seen a lot of ladders in the ER."

"Oh, uh, no." Nerves had her laughing. And babbling. "But I cleared the gutters on my house last fall and nearly fell when I found a fist-sized spider waiting for me. Luckily, I managed not to accidentally break my neck."

Another chuckle escaped him.

"And thanks, by the way. For saving me." *Again.*

He slid a hand down her arm, squeezing her hip before cupping her butt. "My pleasure."

Her body liquefied at his touch, making her want to squirm closer to him. She felt things she hadn't in far too long and intended to go with those feelings.

"Hey." His low, sexy tone held a warning.

She'd wanted another kiss and more. She wriggled, hoping he got her message. "Yeah?"

"Are you coming on to me?"

"Well, technically, you're on top, so… I think that means *you're* coming on to *me*."

He pressed his forehead to hers and swore beneath his breath. Not the good kind of swear either.

Horrified and humiliated that he didn't want her after all, Madi pushed at him. "Sorry. I got caught up in the moment. I'm not very good at this, obviously. Excuse me."

"Not good at what, exactly?" Tate asked, loosening his hold on her so they could both sit up.

She sighed. "Men."

Tate looked over at her. "What's happening here?"

He was giving her an out, putting the power back in her hands. She appreciated it and somehow it made her want him even more. She wasn't sure of a lot of things at that moment, like how she'd deal with the fallout of all this tomorrow, but tonight, she was sure of one thing. She twined her fingers around his neck once more, leaning in to kiss him. "I want you, Tate."

He groaned low and deepened the kiss.

Things went a little crazy after that. His mouth firm and hungry, his tongue sliding against hers. Madi had almost forgotten what it was like to be kissed like this, like there was nothing on earth more important than her. The thrill of feeling soft and feminine rushed over her. She'd experienced it a few times in her sporadic dating life, but nothing like this. Nothing like this overwhelming need for another person, like she'd die without having him. This felt new and intoxicating. Inevitable.

Then Tate lifted his head. She touched his face, the stubble on his jaw scraping against her fingers. "To be clear, this is still just a fake date, right?"

"Right."

Then Tate's mouth was on hers again, and while alarm bells went off deep inside Madi's brain, she was tired of thinking, couldn't think anymore because man, Tate was good at this too. Even better than his charm and flirting. She lost herself in his lovemaking, how he didn't seem to be in a hurry at all, like kissing her was an act all unto itself. She panted for air when they finally broke apart, Tate shifting to pull away, and Madi reflexively clutched at him. "Wait—we're stopping?"

Dropping his head, his jaw rubbed hers. "Yeah."

"Why?"

He let out a low groan. "Because you're not the one-night-stand-in-a-storage-room type of woman."

Well, when he put it like that…

She always put other people's wants and needs ahead of her own. But now, here, maybe she could have this just for herself. Besides, while she didn't know Tate well, she trusted him. He worked at the hospital. He was a medical professional like her. She knew he was polite and kind, and he'd spent time in Louisiana growing up. She knew he'd stepped in when she'd needed him, both as her date and with the auction, bidding on that expensive trip to Boston. And he'd just given her the most amazing kiss of her life. Maybe Tate Griffin wasn't her forever person, but he sure fit the bill for tonight.

"C'mon," she said, wrapping herself around him. "Please?"

This won her another long look. She ground against him, trying to sway the game in her favor.

After a huffed breath, Tate said, "You're sure?"

"I'm sure." Madi closed her eyes as his mouth blazed a path over her throat and collarbone. "I'm very, very sure."

When he encountered the material of her dress, a quick tug had the straps sliding down her shoulders to her elbows, trapping her hands at her sides and baring her breasts all in one movement.

Tate growled his approval, then paid careful homage to her body until she writhed beneath him as he moved down her stomach, taking her dress with him.

"So soft," he murmured across her skin, his breath a warm caress. But there was nothing gentle about him pushing the hem of her skirt up to her waist. He looked down at her thong, then slid the tiny slip of lace to one side, exposing all her secrets to his hot gaze. Lowering his head, he used his lips and tongue on her until Madi cried out her release, her hands gripping his head as stars exploded behind her eyes.

Before she'd stopped shuddering, he'd shoved off his jacket, then unbuckled and unzipped his pants and put on a condom. The sight of him ready for her made her moan. As he slowly pushed inside her, Madi lost her breath. Tate gave her a moment to adjust to his size, then his mouth found hers again. It was wildly sensuous, and all she could do was dig her fingernails into his back and hold on.

He swallowed her cries as he thrust, running a hand beneath her knee, lifting her leg up to wrap around his waist so he could go even deeper. Tate took her right out of herself, and Madi thrilled to it. He was powerful and primal, and she was there with him, meeting him halfway, unable to do anything but feel as he pushed her over the edge again. She was deep into another climax when he joined her, shuddering in her arms, his fingers digging into her hips as he lost himself in his pleasure.

Finally, tearing his mouth from hers, Tate dropped his head into the crook of Madi's neck, his shoulders rising and falling beneath her hands as he caught his breath and lifted his head to see her face.

"What?" she whispered.

"You're smiling."

Yes, she was. And probably would be for days. She'd just done something selfish, completely against her usual good-girl persona. She'd had sex. In a storage room. And it felt fantastic. Madi ran a finger over the bandage on his forehead, then along the bruise on his cheek. "I'm sorry you got hurt in the storm."

He shook his head, grinning. "I'm good."

They lay there like that for several long moments until thunderous applause rose in the distance, reminding Madi of where they were. Reluctantly, she nudged Tate, but he didn't move. "We need to go. Hurry. You first."

"I'm not leaving you up here," he said.

"Yes, you are. We can't be seen together." She pushed him again. "Go. Before Lucille comes back."

Not hurrying at all, Tate looked at her for another long moment, then pressed his lips to her damp temple and finally pulled away. He helped Madi straighten her clothing before taking care of himself.

Once he disappeared down the ladder again, Madi sat there alone, sated and introspective. Tate had given her exactly what she'd wanted tonight on all counts, fulfilling her fantasies and breaking her out of her self-imposed mold for a little while. They'd agreed to keep it simple. Just a fake date.

And now it was over.

CHAPTER SEVEN

TATE SLEPT HARD that night and didn't dream. His morning went pretty much status quo. Mark met him on the beach, and they swam several miles before Tate went home to get ready for his shift. Because they were shorthanded, Tate also filled in on regular ambulance runs when needed, like today.

The shift was mainly of the normal variety. Chest pain call from Sunny Village Retirement Home that turned out to be gas. A kid who'd broken his arm during sports practice. Concussion on a construction site when a bucket of debris fell off a second-story roof and hit someone on the ground. Thank goodness for hard hats.

Then there was the baby. A five-month-old infant who needed flight transport to Wyckford General from a rural farming community due to a possible RSV infection. Since the local hospital was also a designated children's trauma center, they got a lot of transfers from other area hospitals for cases that were too much for the smaller places to handle. Normally, these runs weren't a problem for Tate. He kept focused on the job and blocked out everything else. But this patient was so small, he could hold her tiny body basically in one hand, and the bed in the chopper all but swallowed her whole.

The pilot, Rita, worked the controls while Tate stayed in the back of the chopper. The mom was quiet, her eyes never leaving her daughter as they hurried toward Wyckford General. The father drove himself in the family SUV. From what Tate had gathered at the scene, the couple had moved to the US from Somalia a few years back, fleeing war and starvation and looking for a better life. He hoped they'd find one and that their baby girl would live to see it.

Respiratory syncytial virus, RSV, was a common contagion that normally caused either basic cold or flu-like symptoms and generally people recovered within a few days. But this baby girl also had an underlying heart problem and her case had turned severe, her condition deteriorating rapidly and requiring flight transport.

Luckily, since they'd picked her up, the baby's blood pressure had improved and her O2 sats were at eighty-nine to ninety, which was an improvement. Tate kept a close eye on all the monitors and IVs hooked up to their tiny patient as Rita landed on the helipad atop the hospital, then came around to help Tate get the patient and her mother out of the back.

Brock was there to meet them. He also pulled shifts in the ER when he wasn't holding office hours or home with his fiancée and daughter. Honestly, Tate wasn't sure how the man did it. But Brock looked happier than Tate had ever seen him, even though he was worked to death, so the man was obviously doing something right these days.

"What have we got?" Brock asked as they wheeled the tiny patient into the hospital and onto an elevator headed down to the first floor.

Tate gave him the rundown on the baby's stats and condition on the way, telling him about the case. As they reached their destination and rushed their tiny patient toward an open trauma bay, Tate helped lift the infant girl from the gurney to the bed. "She's currently got an open port in her left femoral for medications, if needed, and a PIV in her right hand. There were some ST elevations during transport that were concerning."

"Okay," Brock said, already moving, checking the baby's vitals and neurological responses. "Team, let's have some epi, just in case, and a resus cart if she codes."

Tate stepped back to let the ER team take over, noticing Madi there too. She caught his eyes and held a moment before looking away and concentrating on their new little patient. He got it. When you worked under emergency conditions you had to be at the top of your game and keep your focus where it belonged because things changed in an instant and you didn't get a second chance. Tate knew that all too well.

But this patient was safe, for now, and in the best possible hands, so he could step back and take note. Every movement Madi made was part of a well-choreographed routine the analytical part of him appreciated and admired. Almost as much as he'd admired how she'd felt in his arms last night.

Whoops. Nope. Not going there, dude.

"Her blood pressure's falling," Madi said, jarring Tate out of his thoughts. "Sixty-six over fifty-three. End-tidal CO2 is seventeen. Heart rate's one hundred and nine. O2 sats at eighty-eight."

"Get her on a ventilator," Brock said. "And get cardiology down here stat."

Madi assisted with intubating the tiny patient to help her breathe.

Tate and Rita were free to go, but he couldn't seem to tear himself away from the scene just yet. He needed to know the baby would be okay. And he liked watching Madi work. Maybe a bit too much.

"Since we're taking a break," Rita said, "I'm gonna go call Maureen. She's been texting me all morning about the kids' softball lessons. Be back in a few."

Tate hiked his chin in acknowledgment, his gaze still locked on the medical scene before him. “Tell your wife I said hi.”

“Will do,” Rita said as she walked away.

Brock glanced at the patient’s chart on the large wall monitor. “She’s stable for now. Looks like the patient is on dopamine, ketamine and fentanyl. Possible hypoxic heart event on the ride over here…”

“How is my daughter?” a voice asked from behind Tate.

He turned to find the mother and father in the hall behind him. After a final glance into the trauma bay, Tate led them down to a private waiting area, out of the hustle and bustle of the ER. He didn’t have kids of his own, but serving in conflicts around the world and talking to survivors of horrific ordeals, he knew how to comfort people. Even if those skills didn’t extend to himself.

They sat down, the mother and father on one side of the small room, and Tate in a chair across from them, as he explained what was happening with their infant daughter. “She’s not in any pain. Her condition is the same as when we left the other hospital earlier.”

“Will you be here with us?” the father asked him.

“I’ll be going back on my shift as soon as my partner gets back. We’re paramedics. We go out to the scene and bring patients into the doctors and nurses here who’ll care for them.”

“Oh.” The mother looked disappointed. “I thought you were the doctor.”

“No. I’m a first responder. An emergency medical technician. I’m also in the military, Air Force Pararescue. I’m home on extended leave right now.” He left out the rest of story because they didn’t need to know about the accident, about his failure. “And I’m glad I was here to help your daughter today. I know what it’s like to be on the other side of things.”

"Thank you." The father shook Tate's hand. "You did a very good job."

After that, Tate went back upstairs to check on Rita and the chopper. His leg bothered him a bit, but he ignored it. He deserved the pain, to remind himself of his guilt, instead of thinking about Madi and how sweet and warm and giving she'd been in that loft.

She'd been…*amazing*, revving his engine good. Every time he thought about how she'd looked spread out for him on that couch, his body reacted.

Which was stupid.

Yes, last night with Madi had been great. But that's as far as it went. They'd agreed.

He hadn't acted honorably when he'd slept with her, but he could now.

The less contact they had going forward the better. It was a one-night stand. Time to move on.

The rest of the day went smoothly with no major issues.

He checked in on the infant patient after their final run of the shift, and she was holding steady, which was about the best they could hope for at that point.

By the time Tate got home that evening, he took a long, hot shower, then pulled on clean clothes while eyeballing the empty Vicodin bottle on his dresser. This was his ritual, the stare-down. In the end, he shoved the thing into his pocket like he always did, wanting the reminder to keep his head on straight.

Then he drove the Chevelle into town for dinner. Wyckford was one of those storybook seaside towns where tourists flocked in the summer, and everything went quiet and still in the winter. Set on the rocky shores of Buzzards Bay, Wyckford offered a quirky, eclectic mix of old and new architecture. Victorian buildings painted in bright colors lined the main drag, housing the grocer, post office, gas station and hardware store. Farther down was a turnoff to the beach itself, where a long pier jutted into the water, with more shops, an arcade and Ferris wheel. Before you got there though, you got to the Buzzy Bird Café.

It was like something from the 1950s, all black-and-white tiled floors, red vinyl booths and chrome accents. Tate walked in, noting a new front door and windows had been installed since the storm. He took a seat at the lunch counter where his physical therapist poured him a mug of coffee. He'd had this same nightly routine for months. Luna didn't ask questions, and Tate really appreciated that.

Tonight, she dropped a tablet computer in front of him and cocked a hip.

Tate gave her a level look. Her expression had unhappy written all over it. She was dressed in a black shirt, black pants, black boots, all topped with a frilly pink apron with a cartoon buzzard on the front. She pointed toward the screen with a raised brow, and Tate finally read it.

Annual Hospital Auction Huge Success!

So far so good. Then he read the first paragraph, which credited it all to Madison Scott, who'd attended the event with her new boyfriend—Tate Griffin.

Boyfriend? Yikes. Still, it wasn't a big deal. Stuff like this blew over. When the next scandal hit, they'd be old news. He passed the tablet back to Luna and shrugged. "What's the special tonight?"

Luna crossed her arms. "The special is what's going on between you and my best friend?"

"Nothing," he said, unsure where this was going or why it was any of her business.

"Look. When I suggested she ask you to be her date, I figured it was a win-win situation. Madi gets a hot guy to parade around on her arm, and you get a fun night with no strings attached. But the title 'boyfriend' means something. How did that happen?"

"I don't know." He didn't like being put on the defensive here, especially because he kind of wondered the same thing himself. How had he let things go so far? And sure, Lucille was a gossipy old biddy who'd probably make up salacious stuff about the Pope if she thought it would increase her follower count but still. Tate had been raised by two parents familiar with the military. His dad had been gone a lot, serving as a pilot in the Air Force. And his mom had worked as a secretary at the Pentagon. And his job in pararescue had required knowledge, skill, discipline, the ability to think on your feet and be decisive and honorable.

The honorable part troubled him now.

Because despite being up-front about it all, he'd somehow managed to care about Madi and convinced himself that having sex with her last night was an easy fix for them both. She was lonely. He was lonely. But in hindsight, their choice was a bad one. Because while he'd move on to his next deployment someday soon, Madi lived here and had more at stake.

God, I'm such an idiot.

Luna continued to stare a hole in his head until he shrugged and said, "I won't hurt her. I promise."

The words tasted bitter on his tongue, probably because he knew they weren't true. Madi was an adult, yes, but even knowing just a little about her, he could see how good and softhearted she was. No way she'd make it out of this unscathed. On the flip side, neither would he. Because despite his best intentions, Tate had let his emotions and his heart get involved where Madi was concerned.

As if reading his mind, Luna muttered something under her breath and walked away.

He ate dinner fast, then returned to his big, empty house to work in the garage some more. He'd seen the Chevelle in the newspaper right after he'd arrived and hadn't been able to resist her.

He'd never been able to resist a sweetheart of a car.

Or a sweetheart of a woman either, apparently...

The next day, Madi sat in a hospital board meeting surrounded by a bunch of administrators who included her boss and her mother. Her mind, however, was a million miles away. Or, more accurately, in the trauma bay where she'd seen Tate Griffin.

Obviously, they'd run into each other at work, but even so, she hadn't been prepared for him. It had taken everything she had not to go after him in the hall after he'd left with the infant's parents. Just to say hello. Just to—

Gah!

She had to forget about their night together. Forget the fact she'd never gone up in flames for a man so fast in her entire life. Then, yesterday, he hadn't even said a word to her. He'd obviously moved on. She should too. That'd teach her to have inappropriate sex with a man she worked with.

But all it had really taught Madi was that she'd been missing out. Worse, the magnitude of her attraction for Tate Griffin had her afraid the next time they crossed paths at work or anywhere else, she might shove him into the nearest closet for round two.

"Madison? The amount we raised?" Judith repeated.

"Uh, eighteen thousand." Madi looked down at the paper in front of her to be sure. "All of which will go toward the Health Services Clinic budget for the year."

"Unfortunately, we may have to make some adjustments going forward," Bud Lofton, head of the board and chief hospital administrator, said. Tall and fit, he looked younger than his fifty-five years. With sharp eyes and a sharper mind, he was all about the bottom line. He did listen though, which Madi appreciated.

"Adjustments?" She knew better than to show weakness. "But we need the money to support our programs. People rely on those services in this town."

"Be that as it may, we've encountered some unexpected financial constraints," Bud said, "that require us to take another look at the budget and where funds are allocated."

Madi glanced at the other board members to see their reactions. Brock looked rumpled and gorgeous as usual. His blue eyes warmed when he met her gaze. No one else made eye contact with her though, which meant they all probably knew this news already. Great.

"But the free clinic is more important than ever," Madi said. "Nowhere in this entire county provides drug addiction and teen pregnancy counseling or an abuse hotline. We give necessary health care to an underserved population."

The HSC was important to her, and not just because Karrie had died because she'd had no place to get the services she'd so desperately needed. Madi intended to make sure that no other scared eighteen-year-old girl felt the helplessness and terror her sister had.

"We understand the importance of the clinic's mission. But we must also balance that with what benefits the whole medical center. There won't be a clinic if the rest of the facility goes under, Madi."

"Our numbers are good, Bud. Within our budget," she said, needing his support. "Plus, we're eligible for grant programs and funding. And because we're located in the old west wing of the hospital, one hundred percent of any money we do bring in goes directly into the services we offer. Why is this even being discussed?"

"Because the full liability for the HSC is the hospital's as well," Bud said.

That was true, unfortunately. Madi tried again to appeal to Bud's fiscal side. "But we've run in the black for the last two years. We've never had an incident. We make sense for our community, Bud, and it's the right thing to do." She paused, then added, "And I'll continue to champion it until my dying breath."

He shook his head. "Madi, I admire your tenacity and your belief in the clinic's mission. I want to be on your side here. But let's look at the other aspect of it—the clinic also brings a certain demographic to Wyckford, and a portion of the town isn't really behind this." Bud sat quietly a moment. "But I'll make you a deal. At this week's town meeting we propose our budget for next year. I'll give everyone a formal spiel about the clinic and the challenges we face, then ask for public thoughts."

Madi stifled a groan. Everyone went to the town meetings in Wyckford. If Bud wanted opinions, he'd get them—in droves.

"If there's a positive response, the HSC continues as normal," Bud concluded. "If not, then we'll reevaluate. Acceptable?"

Since Madi didn't have much choice, all she could say was, "Yes, sir."

"Oh, one more thing. When did the clinic's budget include a pharmacy delivery service?"

Bud must be referring to Madi picking up Mr. Martin's meds that morning and bringing them to the old man's home. It wasn't a mystery how he'd found out. Wyckford had one pharmacy, located in the only grocery store, which everyone in town used often. Anyone could have seen her, and Madi hadn't made a secret of what she was doing.

She felt an eye twitch coming on, but she didn't let it deter her. "I did that on my own time, sir."

An hour later, Madi was back to work on the ER floor, thankful the meeting and a crazy shift had at least given her something to think about other than Tate. She hadn't seen him since yesterday and assumed he wasn't working. Or maybe he'd start after she was gone for the day. Either way she wouldn't ask because that would be too pathetic.

Instead, she concentrated on the many new cases coming in. A stroke victim, a diabetic with gangrene in his toes, a guy who'd been stabbed in a bar in Boston and made it all the way to Wyckford before deciding he should get treatment. Plus, two drunks, a stomachache and a bad case of poison ivy.

When she yawned for the tenth time, Madi went in search of coffee. As she stood in the break room, her mind wandered again to that storage room loft and Tate's warm hands, rough and gentle at the same time, stroking her—

"Honey?"

She blinked and the daydream faded, replaced by the sight of her mother.

"I called your name three times. What in the world are you thinking about today?"

Madi couldn't tell her mom her X-rated thoughts, so she said, "Dessert."

"Madi," her mother murmured, giving her a skeptical look. "This isn't like you. Allowing yourself to get distracted by a man."

"I'm not distracted," Madi said even as her face heated. "I've just got a lot on my plate right now."

"And that's different from any other time how?"

"Can you please just drop it? I'm fine, okay?" Madi said.

"Are you sure?" her mother asked.

"Yes. You're worrying about nothing."

A fellow nurse named Camilla, twenty-two and fresh out of school, ran in, all but quivering with excitement. "He's here. In the waiting room."

"Who's here?" Madi frowned.

Camilla gave her a pointed look. "Him."

"Does 'him' have a name?" her mother asked dryly.

"Tate Griffin. That hot flight paramedic!"

Her mother slid Madi a look, but she was too busy trying to keep her heart from pounding out of her chest. "Tate's here to see me?"

"No. He asked for Dr. Turner," Camilla said in a rush. "But Dr. Turner's been called away."

"I'll tell him." Madi headed down the hallway toward the ER. At least her scrubs were stain-free, always a bonus. But she couldn't remember if she'd put on makeup that morning, and really wished she'd had time to brush her hair.

Tate sat in the waiting room, head back and eyes closed, one leg stretched out in front of him. Today he wore faded Levi's and a black T-shirt, looking like the poster boy for Tall, Dark and Mysterious. Anyone would assume he was asleep, but Madi sensed Tate was about as relaxed as a coiled rattler.

As she approached, he opened his eyes and looked at her but said nothing. His piercing green-gold gaze sent her nervous system haywire. She'd just handled three emergencies in a row without a blip, but now her blood raced like the Indy 500.

He didn't come here to see you. Act cool.

The air-conditioning blasted over her skin, which in no way explained why Madi felt like she was in the throes of a sudden hot flash as she stopped before him and bit her lower lip.

Tate rose from his chair and Madi's breath caught. Which wasn't good.

She needed to get a grip.

No one else was in the waiting room, for once, but just

across the hall at the sign-in desk sat Camilla and her mother, neither pretending to do anything other than stare at them in open, rapt curiosity.

Madi ignored their audience as best she could. “You’re here to see Brock?”

“Yeah. I need to get my stitches out. I’d do it myself but the angle’s awkward, so…”

“I’ll remove them for you,” Madi blurted before she could think better of it. “Brock got called out.”

Her mother and Camilla were still watching, now joined by additional staff who apparently had nothing better to do than eavesdrop. She’d lay odds this meeting would go public by the end of her shift, but there was nothing she could do about it now. “C’mon. Let’s go.”

She looked at Tate from beneath her lashes as they walked toward an open exam room in the ER—at his big, tough body, and the way he limped ever so slightly on his left leg. Then she hazarded another glance at his face and found him watching her too, looking bemused. She showed him into the room, then pulled the curtain. “I’ll grab a kit and be right back.”

CHAPTER EIGHT

In the Air Force, Tate had learned defense tactics and ways to conceal information. He excelled at both. As a result, concealing emotion came all too easily to him. There wasn't much room for emotion in the high-stress, high-stakes world of emergency medicine. So, he'd long ago perfected the blank expression, honed it as a valuable tool. It was second nature now or had been.

Until Madi, it seemed.

Because he was having a hell of a hard time pulling it off with her. Like now, for instance, when he was relieved to see her again today and yet struggling to hide that very fact.

She was a great nurse. He'd seen it firsthand yesterday with the infant. Also, on the night of the storm, she'd been extremely levelheaded and composed. And she looked cute in her purple scrubs with the tiny red heart embroidered over the front pocket. He especially liked her air of authority.

Honestly, he liked everything about her so far, including how she'd tasted.

Tate didn't get to think about that long though because someone moaned from the exam space next door, the sound laced with both fear and pain. He stood, reacting on instinct to the call to help.

The moan came again. He stuck his head around the curtain and saw a guy hooked up to a monitor, fluids and oxygen.

He was maybe in his early fifties, smelled like a brewery even from several feet away and either hadn't showered this month or rolled in garbage. The man's gray hair stuck out all over, some missing in clumps. Homeless, by the looks of him. He seemed small and weak and terrified.

"You okay, buddy?" he asked, staying where he was. "You need a nurse?"

The man shook his head, eyes wide, his free hand flailing. His pupils were dilated, so he was probably high on something.

Cursing, Tate moved to the bedside and checked the IV. They were hydrating him, which was good. Catching the guy's hand in his, he squeezed lightly. "What's going on?"

"My stomach hurts."

The filthy sleeve of the man's shirt had torn away enough to reveal an eagle seal tattoo on his arm. Tate let out a slow breath, feeling raw. "You were in the military?"

"Army," the man slurred, clearly still heavily intoxicated.

Tate might have turned away then, but the guy clung to his hand like it was a lifeline, so he slowly sat on a stool instead.

"I'm Air Force. Pararescue." Tate exhaled slow. "I'm on leave."

"You never leave," the man said.

True enough.

"They should pay us for the nightmares," the guy continued, his voice rougher now, like it took more effort to speak. "They should give us extra combat wages for all the ways they messed up our lives."

Silence settled, the man looking half asleep now, and Tate felt a little sick. In his gut. In the depths of his soul.

"I still think about them," the man whispered out of the blue.

Tate didn't have to ask who. All the dead. He swallowed hard and nodded.

The man stared at him, glassy-eyed but coherent. "How many for you?"

"Four." But there'd been others, too. *Way* too many others.

The man let out a shuddery sigh of sympathy, sliding a shaky hand into his shirt and coming out with a flask, which he held out to Tate. "Here. This helps."

Madi chose that moment to return, pulling back the curtain. "*There* you are," she said to Tate, then smiled kindly at the man in the bed. "Better yet, Mr. Ryan?"

Mr. Ryan didn't meet her gaze as he gave a jerky nod.

"Why don't I hold that for you, okay?" Gently, she pried the flask from his fingers.

Tate didn't know what he'd expected from her. Maybe annoyance—or resentment for having to care for a guy whose wounds were clearly self-inflicted ones. But instead, she ran a hand down the old vet's arm in a comforting gesture, not shying away from touching him.

More than duty. Much more.

"I've called your daughter," she told the man. "She'll be here in ten minutes. We'll let the IV do its thing, refilling you with minerals, potassium, sodium and other good stuff. You'll feel better soon." She patted his forearm over the tattoo, then checked his lead before gesturing to Tate to follow her.

"Is he okay?" he asked quietly on the other side of the curtain.

"He will be once he sobers up."

"I could tell from his eyes he's on something besides alcohol."

"Yes."

"Does he have a place to stay?"

She gave him a pointed stare. "Look at you with all the questions."

"Does he?"

She sighed. “I’m sorry, but I can’t discuss his case with you. I can tell you he’s taken care of. Does that help?”

Tate had no idea what the lump in his throat was doing or why his heart hurt. Or why he couldn’t let this go. “He’s a veteran. He’s having nightmares. He—”

“I know.” She touched him too, soothing him as she had Mr. Ryan. “And like I said, he’s being cared for.” Madi paused then, studying Tate for a disturbingly long beat. “Not everyone would have gone in there and comforted him.”

“I’m not everyone.”

The phone at her hip vibrated. She looked at the screen and let out a breath. “Sorry. Sit tight for me for a few minutes. I’ll be right back.”

Then she strode off again.

In the exam space on the other side of Tate was another patient. The curtain between them was shut too, but it suddenly whipped open as another nurse talked to the patient in the bed. “Change into the robe. I’ll go page your doctor.”

This guy had clearly walked in under his own steam but wasn’t looking good. Big, midthirties, dressed in coveralls with the Wyckford Public Utilities Department logo on the front. He was filthy from head to toe, clearly just off the job. As Tate watched, the man went from looking bad to worse. Then he gasped, clutching at his chest.

Christ.

Tate hurtled back in time to the open ocean, squinting against the brilliant fireball of wreckage. He’d clung to a piece of floating door, praying help would arrive in time…

Now, a million miles away and four years later, the guy in the next hospital bed groaned, dropping his gown as he slithered to the floor, his eyes rolling up in his head.

Tate yelled, “He’s coding!”

And the dance to save the man’s life began. Madi rushed

in, assisting Tate with CPR, checking the patient's vitals and finally shocking him with a defibrillator to get his heart started again when all else failed. It went on for maybe five minutes but felt like a lifetime. Finally, they had the patient stabilized and a cardiologist took over. Madi led Tate back to his exam space and shut the curtain, a suture removal kit in her hand.

She gave him a sharp look. "Thanks for your help there."

He didn't respond. Didn't move.

So she pointed to the bed and said with soft steel in her voice, "Sit."

He did, but on the stool. The bed was for patients, and Tate wasn't a patient. Not really.

Madi washed her hands thoroughly, then pulled on gloves and opened the kit she'd brought. She stood in front of him and carefully removed his bandage, yawning.

He smiled. "Tired?"

"I passed tired three hours ago." She soaked a gauze pad in rubbing alcohol and cleaned the area around his sutures, then picked up a pair of tweezers. "Don't worry. I'm an expert at getting these out quickly and relatively painlessly."

He wrapped his fingers around her wrist, stopping her. "Why are your cheeks flushed?"

She hesitated, then finally admitted, "I'm embarrassed, okay?"

This stopped him cold. "About what?"

"What do you think?" She looked confused. "What happened the other night."

"Why?"

She sighed, her warm minty breath tickling the hair near his temple. He suppressed a shiver of awareness.

"Because I'd never done the whole casual sex thing." She lowered her voice to a soft whisper. "And now..." Her eyes slowly met his. "I'm thinking I should have requested a two-night stand."

Her candor left Tate speechless.

Madi winced and shook her head, then laughed as she leaned in close to examine his stitches. "Brock does nice work. But you'll probably still have a scar. Shouldn't be too much of a problem for you though. Women like that. Fall all over themselves."

Except he wasn't looking for a woman. He wasn't looking for anything.

Right?

Madi used the tweezers to pull up a stitch, then snipped it with scissors. "A little sting," she warned, then pulled it out. "Do you like being a paramedic?"

He shrugged.

Madison continued working, her gaze steady on him. She had great eyes. Warm brown and sparkling with humor and intelligence.

The nurse from the front desk he'd talked to when he came in poked her head around the curtain, her eyes on Tate as she asked, "Need any help?"

"Nope." Madi kept working. "I've got this, Camilla."

The woman's face fell, and she left without further comment.

Two seconds later Madi's mother appeared. She waved to Tate, then yanked the curtain shut again, leaving them alone once more.

"Your mom's nice," Tate said.

"Yep." Madi pulled another stitch, and he barely felt it. She was right. She was good at this.

He stared at her, truly fascinated in a way that surprised him. Madi was supposed to be just a cute nurse in a small town he'd soon forget.

Except…he wasn't forgetting her. Not at all.

"Hey, Madi." Yet another woman peeked around the curtain, this one wearing a housekeeping outfit. "Need anything?"

"No," Madi snapped.

"Fine," the woman said, clearly insulted. "You don't have to take my head off."

When she vanished, Madi took a deep breath and turned away to dump her used instruments into the sink. "That was my sister. Toni. What about your leg?"

Tate scowled. "What about it?"

She looked at him over her shoulder with an expectant air, saying nothing. It made him smile. She said, "You can't use that silence thing against me. I invented it."

"What silence thing?"

She shook her head. "Some secrets are toxic if you try to keep them inside. They eat you up. You aren't married, are you?"

"No."

"Attached? Have a girlfriend? Or boyfriend?"

"No." Tate waved her questions away, changing subjects as she pulled off her gloves and tossed them in the biohazard bin. "Does your whole family work here?"

"Just my mom, my sister and me," she said. "And I also run the Health Services Clinic."

"Is there a need in a town this small?" Tate ran a finger over his now stitch-free cut.

"A huge one. We have a high teenage pregnancy rate, and drug abuse is on the rise everywhere. So is homelessness. Counseling services and advocacy and educational programs are vital. And we have weekly free office hours for those who can't afford medical care."

She sounded so fierce his heart ached all over again. He'd once had that same fire. Hopefully she'd never lose her genuine compassion to jaded cynicism like him. "What made you take on all that extra work?"

Madi cleaned up the counter. "Someone had to."

"Ah," he said. "You're one of those."

"One of those what?" She glanced at him, eyes narrowed. "Look. How about we make a deal? I'll answer one of your questions for every one of mine you answer for me."

He knew better than to go there. By all appearances, she was pretty and sweet and innocent, but beneath that guileless smile, Madison Scott held all the power, and Tate knew it. She'd have him confessing his sins with one warm touch.

When he didn't respond, she shook her head. "Figured that'd be too much for you."

It was. Tate should leave…but he opened his mouth anyway. "What time are you off?"

From the surprised look she gave him, he'd shocked her. Fair enough. He'd shocked himself too.

"Seven," Madi said. "Why?"

"I'll pick you up."

"For what?"

"A date."

She seemed to consider that a second, then said, "No. You know the pier?"

"Sure. Isn't it closed this time of year?"

"Some things are still open. I'll meet you there. In front of the Ferris wheel."

"Okay. I'll be there."

CHAPTER NINE

As Madi got into her car after her shift, her phone rang.

"Tate came to the hospital to see you?" Luna asked.

Madi didn't bother to ask how she knew. Honestly, she wouldn't have been surprised to see it as the leading headline in the paper. "Yes, he did. I'm meeting him in about fifteen minutes. Any words of advice?"

"Just be careful. Make sure you're both on the same page."

"I will," Madi said. "I need to go."

When she got to the pier, Madi took a moment to inhale the crisp, sea air while the sound of waves lapping the shore soothed her antsy nerves. Flyers were posted for an upcoming event at the local high school—a play the following week—and another for the town's monthly Interested Citizens Meeting where Bud Lofton would share the hospital's budget.

Her stress levels rose again, but she didn't have time to dwell on it. She had other things to think about now. She'd changed out of her scrubs before she'd left work, into jeans and a cute, pink sweater that brought out the copper highlights in her brown hair.

As she walked to the now dormant Ferris wheel, Madi checked her reflection in the back window of a closed food truck. The night was chilly, and the power of the water rocking gently against the pylons far below made the pier shudder faintly with the push and pull of the tide, matching the anticipation drumming through her.

You're not going to sleep with him again. It was a one-time thing. You're only here because you're curious.

Curious, yes. But also, she had a problem. A big, moth-to-a-flame type of attraction. Why? Madi had no idea. Their goodbye in the loft on the night of the auction had been…abrupt. But everything before then had been…*amazing.*

She stopped just past the Ferris wheel, and the hair at the back of her neck prickled. Madi turned to find Tate watching her as he leaned back against the pier railing, his long legs casually crossed at the ankles, looking for all the world like a guy who made a habit of hanging out on piers and strolling lazy beaches.

They both knew that wasn't true.

And man, he looked good. Stubble darkened his jaw, and his firm, sensuous mouth held a faint hint of a smile. The new scar above his brow was still shiny and only added to his whole ruffian look. He'd changed from earlier too, into dark jeans and a black sweatshirt with the Air Force insignia across his broad chest. He looked bad and built and dangerous as hell.

And he was hers for the evening.

Mine.

And Tate Griffin made Madi feel. A lot. Curious, annoyed, frustrated and—aroused.

That last one topped the list presently. She wanted to lick him head to toes.

His green-gold gaze held steady. Madi couldn't guess what he was thinking, but she flushed a little anyway for where her own thoughts had gone. Right into the smutty pool.

He pushed away from the railing and strode toward her, the slight limp only making him sexier and more intriguing.

When he got to her, Tate took her hand and pulled her around to the side of the pier, out of view, between two storage sheds.

"W-what are you doing?" she asked.

Instead of answering, he lifted her up on her tiptoes and kissed her.

Madi slid her fingers into his hair. And when his tongue touched hers again, all her bones melted away. Then, before she knew it, it was over and she was back on her feet, weaving unsteadily as she blinked him into focus. "What was *that*?"

Tate shrugged. "Sorry. Been thinking about that since earlier. You're distracting."

"And you're not?"

His eyes heated. "We could fix that."

"Oh, no." She stepped back. "You said you weren't a long-term bet. Not even a short one."

He pressed her into the railing and kissed her again. Apparently, discussion time was over. Which was okay because Madi couldn't form words when he touched her like this. His tongue in her mouth, her hands cupping his head, their bodies mashed together. She'd have climbed him like a tree if she could. Then his muscled thigh slid between hers. He felt so...*good.*

Then, drawing on some reserve of strength she didn't know she had, Madi pushed away. For a beat Tate didn't budge, then he moved back slowly, his eyes heavy lidded and his lips parted.

"Okay," she said shakily. "Let's try something that's *not* going to lead to round two of sex in a public place. Talking. Were you in the military?"

Besides the sweatshirt, she'd noticed how he carried himself. Calm, steady, ready for anything. Then there was his bone-deep stoicism. And the way he'd interacted with the old, homeless vet Mr. Ryan—like he knew to the depths of his soul what the other man had felt.

"I still am. Addicted to the adrenaline rush," Tate said, then crossed his arms as he leaned his hips back against the railing. "Now it's my turn. Why me?"

"Why you what?" Madi squirmed a little under his scrutiny. They both knew what he was asking and playing coy didn't do her any favors. He already knew that what they'd done that night at the auction had been a first for her because she'd told him as much, but what he didn't know, *couldn't* know, was that she'd only been able to do it with him at all because she'd felt something for him. She shrugged too. "Like I said, it'd been a long time."

"But you don't sleep around."

It wasn't a question.

"No. I felt…connected to you," she admitted.

He looked serious now as he slowly shook his head. "You don't want to feel connected to me."

"I can't help it. And there's more."

"You used me to chase away your restlessness," he said quietly.

"Yes." Madi winced, not sure how he knew, but it wasn't really a well-kept secret that she had no life, so… "I'm sorry."

"Don't be. You can use me any time."

"But we agreed it was only a one-time thing," she reminded him, her throat suddenly very dry. "I think I need a drink."

Tate smiled but didn't challenge her. They walked toward the arcade down the way. He watched her, his look hot and dark, causing another of those tingles inside her to start up again.

"Back to our question game," she said to distract herself. "Are you going back to the Air Force when your leave is over?"

"Yes." His eyes stayed on her lips. She was playing with fire, and she knew it.

"You know this whole man of mystery thing isn't as cute as you might think," she said.

"I'm not trying to be cute." A smile curved his mouth as he seemed to come to a decision. "You already know everything you need to about me, Madi. I'm in the military. I'm a thrill seeker. I'm on leave. Eventually I'll go back. Small-town life isn't really for me."

"I doubt that's everything about you." She eyed him skeptically. "How'd you hurt your leg?"

"An accident."

He hadn't hesitated to say it, but Madi sensed his big-time reluctance to talk about it further.

"I'm sorry." She didn't want to push, knowing exactly how it felt to *not* want to discuss something painful, but she wished he'd say more about himself. She was curious, that's all. "What brought you to Wyckford?"

"Mark Bates told me about it. He said he thought it would be a good place to relax and recoup."

"And is it?" she asked softly.

"It has its moments."

Madi fought the ridiculous urge to hug him but stopped herself. They didn't know each other well but she wasn't sure Tate would welcome it just then. "From the limp I'd guess your leg still bothers you. Are you taking anything for it?"

"No." He placed his hand at the small of her back and steered her into the indoor arcade. Conversation over, apparently. Tate gave the guy behind the Shooting Duck Gallery some money, then picked up one of the toy guns like he knew what he was doing and sighted and shot, hitting every duck and destroying the entire row.

"Show-off." Madi tried it herself, but she didn't know what she was doing and didn't hit a single thing. She sighed.

"Pathetic. Pick up the gun again." Tate handed over more cash, then stood behind her, correcting her stance by nudging his foot between hers to move her legs farther apart. Then he steadied her arms with his own, practically wrapping himself around her, surrounding her. If she turned her head, she could kiss his rock-solid bicep. And it shocked her how much she wanted to do just that. Madi bet he'd taste better than any drink she could order.

Tate went still, then let out a low breath, the side of his face brushing her jaw. "I know what you're thinking."

Madi hoped not. Then he pressed more firmly against her, and yep—he knew. Her face heated, and her throat constricted.

"Shoot the ducks, Madison," he growled.

With him guiding her, she hit one, and her competitive nature kicked in.

"Again," she demanded.

With a grin, Tate slapped more money onto the counter.

"Show me what you've got." He stepped back this time, leaving her to do it alone.

She took out one from the entire row. So annoying. "How do you make it look so easy?"

"Practice." His tone said he'd had lots. "Your concentration needs work."

Her concentration wasn't the problem. She was just focused on the wrong things. Like how his arms felt around her, how his hard body had been pressed to her back. Awareness shimmered through her bloodstream. Far too much for her liking. "Maybe I don't care about being able to shoot a duck."

"Then don't." He tossed down another few bucks and obliterated another row of ducks himself.

"Dude." The guy behind the counter looked impressed as he presented Tate with a huge teddy bear.

"Thanks," Madi said as Tate handed her the prize. She hugged the bear close, the silly gesture giving her warm fuzzies. Which was ironic because nothing about Tate Griffin should have given Madi warm fuzzies.

He clearly didn't want to be her hero.

They went to the squirt gun booth next, where Tate proceeded to soundly beat Madi three times in a row. Apparently, he wasn't worried about her ego either. He won a stuffed dog, then laughed out loud as Madi attempted to carry both animals and navigate the aisles without bumping into anyone.

It was ridiculous. *She* was ridiculous. Because no way would she fall for a guy just because he won her silly stuff she didn't need.

You're not supposed to fall for him at all…

They competed in a driving game next, side by side, fighting for first place. Tate handled his steering wheel with easy concentration, paying Madi no attention whatsoever. But she was too busy watching him out of the corner of her eye and fell behind as a result. Tate grinned, which meant he was paying attention to her.

Just to make sure, she nudged him with her shoulder.

His grin widened, but he didn't take his eyes off the game. "Won't work. You're going down."

Never one to turn down a challenge, Madi let her breast brush his arm.

"Playing dirty," he warned, voice low, both husky and amused.

But she absolutely had his attention. She did the boob thing again, her eyes on the screen, so she didn't notice when he leaned closer. Then he nipped her earlobe, soothing the tiny ache with his tongue. That's all it took. Her knees wobbled and her foot slipped off the gas.

Her car crashed into the wall while Tate sped across the finish line.

"Cheater!" she complained. "You can't—"

Tate kissed her until she couldn't remember what she'd been saying. When he pulled away finally, Madi rested against the booth because her legs felt like jelly.

"You started it." Tate kissed before taking her hand and leading her over to the snack bar in the arcade. He bought them both dinner, and she and Tate—with the two huge stuffed animals—sat there to eat.

"You're doing PT for your leg, right?" she asked, still curious. "With Luna at the hospital?"

"Yeah." Tate swallowed another a bite of hot dog. "But I still work out on my own to keep limber. Swim with Mark almost every day. And beat him." He finished his food, then asked, "Who gave you that necklace you always wear?"

Madi's appetite suddenly vanished. She set the rest of her meal aside and stared down at the table. "Karrie. My sister. She died when I was sixteen."

Regardless of how many years had passed, it never got easier to say.

"I'm sorry." Concern flashed in his eyes, stirring feelings she didn't want to revisit. Thankfully he didn't offer the usual platitudes, for which Madi was grateful. But he did take her hand. "How?"

"Overdose."

His long fingers entwined with hers were warm and callused.

He squeezed her hand, and Madi blew out a breath. "You ever lose anyone?"

Tate didn't answer right away. She looked over at him and

found him studying a map of Wyckford on the wall. "The last mission I led, there was an explosion. I lost all my team members; plus the people we were sent to rescue." He met her gaze at last. "That was four years ago now. I live with those memories every day."

Throat tight as she struggled to process what that must have been like for him, she said, "I'm sorry."

"The weather conditions were awful that night, and the investigation done after the accident confirmed we had no choice but to go… But still," he continued, "it shouldn't have happened. It was my fault."

Madi frowned. She didn't know a lot about him, but she was sure of one thing. "I'm sure that's not true."

He didn't answer, just stared at the map on the wall. When Tate finally turned to her again, Madi could tell from his closed expression the walls had come down again. He scrubbed a hand over his face. "Look. I'm about as unsafe a choice as you can possibly get for this…" He gestured between them. "Whatever this thing is. You know I'm leaving soon. Wyckford's too quiet."

Yeah. But for some reason, she trusted him. Both the night of the auction and now. She changed subjects to safer topics. "Do you like working on the flight crew?"

"It's what I know." He looked into her eyes, his own unapologetic. "People always need help. When I go back to the Air Force, I'm sure it'll be the same."

When I go back...

Her heart lurched. Which was silly because it wasn't like they were in a long-term relationship or anything. Hell, they'd only had sex once. But the fact he clearly wouldn't be in Wyckford forever was like a bucket of icy water over the head. And a reminder to herself that this was just an interlude.

Her disappointment was undeniable and shockingly painful. Madi had really thought she could do this, keep things casual, but that wasn't the case apparently. She wasn't built for flings. With a sigh, Madi stood. Tate did as well, gathering their garbage and taking it to a trash bin before coming back to stand beside her at the table.

"I can't do this," she whispered.

He nodded. "I know."

"I want to, but I—"

"It's okay." Tate brushed a kiss over Madi's temple. Then he was gone, proving for the second time he was, after all, her perfect Mr. Wrong.

CHAPTER TEN

TWO DAYS LATER, Madi entered the town meeting for the budget presentation in the big central meeting room at Wyckford General. It was full, as they all tended to be.

God forbid anyone in Wyckford miss anything.

Palms sweaty and heart racing, she bit her fingernails through discussions on putting sports and arts back in the schools, getting parking meters along the sidewalks downtown and whether the mayor would run for another term.

Finally, the Health Services Clinic budget was up on the agenda. Bud Lofton stood and reiterated the bare bones of it all and then asked for opinions. Two attendees immediately rushed up in the center aisle to the microphone. The first was Mr. Martin.

"I'm against this idea and always have been." He gripped his cane in one hand and pointed with a bony finger of the other. "It costs us—the hardworking taxpayers—money."

"Actually," Bud interrupted. "The clinic runs mainly off grants, plus donations from the auction and other events throughout the year. Like next week's pumpkin carving contest." He smiled at Madi. "Nurse Scott talked everyone on the board into entering, so I'm expecting you all to come out and support us."

There was a collective gasp of glee.

People *applauded*, and Madi relaxed a bit. Bud's announcement had just guaranteed them a huge showing at the contest. Wyckford was sweet that way.

Still in the aisle, Mr. Martin tapped on the microphone, his face pinched. "I'm still talking! The free clinic brings too many *undesirables* to our town. Addicts. Criminals." His gaze found and zeroed in on Madi in the back. She sank deeper into her seat. "You all need to think about that."

Mr. Martin hobbled back to his chair.

Next up was Sarah Gordon, the town clerk and manager. With what sounded like genuine regret, she said, "I'm also against the clinic, but not for the reasons Mr. Martin stated. I just don't think we need to deplete our limited hospital resources with the Health Services Clinic. While Bud is right about grants and donations making up the bulk of the clinic's budget, it doesn't cover it all. Wyckford General is responsible for the rest of it. And when our library has no funds and our schools are short-staffed due to enforced layoffs, I think we need to take a close, hard look to see if these funds are allocated in the best way possible. I'm sorry, Madi, but it's true."

Some in the audience murmured agreement, and Madi's panic soared.

She couldn't lose the clinic. She'd worked so hard to get it running. It helped so many people who needed it. People like Karrie. There was nothing she could do to save her long-lost sister, but maybe she could prevent someone else from following the same fate…

Then Lucille Munson, in her bright pink tracksuit and brighter white tennis shoes, took the mic. A matching magenta headband held back her steel gray-blue hair. She was so short the microphone stood about a foot above her head. This didn't stop her. She tipped her head up toward the mic, her bun all aquiver. "The HSC serves a very specific and needed function in our community. Because if I thought I had the clap, I have a place to go."

The audience erupted in laughter.

Lucille continued. "And the clinic is in the best hands with Madison Scott. She's a wonderful nurse and has her degree in business as well. She's one smart cookie. I know some of you might think Madison's too sweet to handle such a big responsibility as the HSC." She glared at Sarah Gordon first, then Mr. Martin in the front row. "Or that her programs for drug rehab and teenage pregnancies will cause Wyckford to be overrun by dealers and pimps. But if she can't control the riffraff, then her new boyfriend certainly can."

By this time, Madi had sunk so low in her chair she could hardly see when a tall, broad-shouldered guy in faded jeans took the microphone, which came up to his chest.

Tate.

He spoke in a clear, unrushed tone. "The Health Clinic will improve the quality of life for people who'd otherwise go without assistance."

Another murmur passed through the audience. One naysayer called out, "There's other places for people to get that kind of help."

"Yeah," someone else called out. "People here don't need the HSC."

"Wrong," Tate said bluntly. "On every flight crew and EMT shift, I encounter townsfolk in Wyckford who *do* require exactly the sort of services the HSC provides. Veterans, for instance."

No one said a word now, though it was unclear whether they were scared into silence by Tate's quiet intensity or simply acknowledging the truth of his words.

"There are people right in your own neighborhoods who need help managing their addictions," he went on. "People who don't have a safe place to go away from violence or teens who can't get STD education or birth control. These problems are real and growing, and the Health Services Clinic is an invaluable resource for the entire county." Tate paused and you could've heard a pin drop. "And Lucille's right. You couldn't have a better person running that clinic than Madison Scott. Each of you should be trying to help. I support this budget and I'll even add to it by donating enough money for a program for veterans, where they can get assistance in rehabilitation or job opportunities or simply to reacclimate to society."

Madi gaped.

The place went silent. A real feat when it came to Wyckford. No one even blinked.

As if sensing her scrutiny, Tate turned and met her gaze for one charged beat, then left.

He'd stood up in front of the entire town and defended her. The knowledge washed over her, as she craned her neck to watch him go.

The meeting ended shortly after that, and people rushed Madi with questions. It was another hour before she was free, and as she left, she looked for Tate, but he was long gone.

That night another storm broke wild over Buzzards Bay. He'd had the day off, so Tate had worked on the Chevelle after he'd gotten home. Then he'd decided to take a drive into town to clear his head of a certain warm, sexy nurse.

He'd learned to shelve his emotions when he'd joined the Air Force, long before he'd ever met Madison Scott. But no amount of training could have prepared him for her.

She was a one-woman wrecking crew when it came to the walls around his heart, laying waste to all his defenses. Only a few weeks ago, no one could've convinced him she'd have the power to bring him to his knees with a single look.

And yet she had.

Tate ended up at the café again, thankfully without large trees knocking him in the head. Luna was there also, watching some reality singing competition on the TV mounted high on the café's wall in the far corner. "Come on, judges! Tell it like it is."

She met Tate at a booth with a coffeepot. Normally she looked alert and on guard, but tonight her face was pale and her smile weak. "What can I get you?"

"What kind of pie do you have left?"

She rattled off the selections, then returned two minutes later with a huge slice of apple for him. "Enjoy. Best on the planet, trust me."

Quite the claim, but one bite proved it was true. Tate stopped midway through his second mouthful when he noticed the bloodstained towel wrapped around the palm of Luna's left hand as she refilled his coffee. "Are you okay?"

"Fine."

But her other hand shook, and she looked miserable. "Do you need a doctor?"

"No."

He nodded and continued eating. But when he was done, he cleared his own plate, bringing it to the kitchen, unable to stop himself from helping. "I'm going to ask you again. Do you need a doctor?"

"It was a silly accident with a knife."

Not an answer. Tate unwrapped her hand and looked down at the cut. "You need stitches. And a trip to the ER."

"No, I don't."

"You have a first aid kit?"

"Yeah."

He nodded. "Get it."

Unfortunately, the Buzzy Bird's supplies consisted of a few

Band-Aids and a pair of tweezers, so Tate got his own medic bag from the Chevelle, then returned to the kitchen to tend to Luna's wound. He had Steri-Strips, but the laceration was a little too deep for that.

"Sit down," he told her.

"The café's still open. People might come in."

"They'll wait." She looked a little greener now, so he pushed Luna onto the lone stool in the back. "Put your head down."

She dropped it to the counter instead with an audible *thunk* while Tate disinfected the wound, then opened a tube of skin glue. The stuff stung like hell but would do the job. Luna sucked in a breath as he worked, finally covering her hand with a large waterproof bandage.

"Thanks." Luna let out a shuddery sigh once he was done.

"You're welcome." Tate gestured toward her hand. "How's that feel?"

She opened and closed her fist, testing it. "Better. Thanks." She watched him put everything back into his kit. "You and Madi make a pretty good team."

Before Tate could answer, Mark Bates walked into the kitchen, then stopped, his eyes narrowed on the blood-soaked towel on the counter. "What happened?"

"Nothing." Luna turned her back on him.

Mark looked at Tate then, expecting an answer. "What happened to her?"

"She's declined to say."

"A knife," Luna said over her shoulder. "It was an accident. No big deal. Go away."

There was definite tension in the air between his good friend and Luna. Usually, his friend was affable and easygoing, but now Mark had all sorts of tense body language happening.

Then Luna made an annoyed sound and opened the door,

gesturing for them both to leave. For emphasis, she jerked her head, making her wishes perfectly clear.

Mark waited a beat, then walked away, muttering under his breath.

Tate followed, telling himself this was none of his business. She wanted him. He wanted her right back, more than he could have possibly imagined. Right this minute, he could be wrapped up in her sweet, warm limbs, buried deep.

He strode out to the parking lot after Mark, both silent and brooding.

CHAPTER ELEVEN

ON SATURDAY, the free clinic opened as usual. The budget had passed, barely, and Madi knew she had Tate to thank for it. After the town meeting, a handful of locals had pledged more money for certain programs, including one called Drink Responsibly and another for art for seniors. Even one to help counsel the chronically ill. If things kept going the way they were, they might have enough funding to open five days a week to provide crisis counseling. And of course, the Saturday free clinic.

They saw patients nonstop, and later, as Madi closed at the end of the clinic hours, their attending physician for the day, Brock Turner, came out from the back.

After their long day, he looked more rumpled than usual and still had his stethoscope hanging around his neck. His dark hair was tousled too, and his blue eyes lined with exhaustion. But there was also a constant readiness about him that said he wasn't too tired to kick ass if needed. If Madi remembered right, he'd worked a double shift in the ER and a full day of office hours in his own clinic prior to filling in today when their other scheduled volunteer physician had canceled unexpectedly. He'd told Madi before that he did it out of love—both for the job and for taking care of those in need. She was so happy he and Cassie had found each other. They were both wonderful people and made the best parents to Brock's young daughter, Adi.

"Nice job today," he said to Madi.

"Thanks to you."

He shrugged like it was no big deal. He was about the same height as Tate, over six feet and muscled. He might be a workaholic, but he was also the most approachable doctor she'd ever met. And treated the nurses with respect. Such behavior should be automatic, but so often wasn't.

"You're doing something really good here, Madi," Brock said.

She glowed over the compliment later as she locked up. As the last staff member on the premises, she'd walked through each of the rooms, cleaning up a little as she went. They had two of them, plus a small kitchen, and a front reception area large enough for groups to rent when the clinic was closed. They were also in the process of renovating a back storage closet to house the controlled drug lockup, but for now those medications and samples were kept in one exam room in a secure cabinet.

Tomorrow night they'd hold the regularly scheduled AA meeting. Monday night would be Narcotics Anonymous. Wednesday nights hosted a series of guest speakers for teen advocacy programs. All of it made Madi feel useful. Helpful. She hadn't been able to save Karrie, but she could save others.

By the time she locked the front door and got to her car, thunder rolled in the distance. Night had fallen, and the lot wasn't as well-lit as she'd like. She was parked on the back side of the hospital in a narrow side street. She slid behind the wheel just as the rain started and inserted her key in the ignition. Turned it but nothing happened.

Madi tried again and nothing. Dead battery, probably. She peered out and sighed. She was far too tired to walk home in the deluge, plus her feet ached from being on them all day. So, she pulled out her phone and called her brother.

"Yo," Jack Jr. answered. "Bad time."

"I need you to come jump-start my battery. You owe me, Jack. I let you and your idiot friends borrow my car, remember? Maybe this is somehow your fault."

"No, the windshield is my fault. Not the battery."

She noticed a small crack in the glass on the passenger side and felt another eye twitch starting. "Come on. Please. I could really use your help tonight."

"Hang on." Jack Jr. covered the phone and murmured something to someone. A muted female voice laughed, then he was back. "Madi, I'm on a date. With *Allie*."

Then he hung up.

Grinding her teeth, Madi called him back.

He didn't pick up.

"Dammit." She scrolled through her contact list again. Her mother was out of the question. She didn't own a set of jumper cables, let alone know how to use them. Madi dropped everything to help everyone else, and none of them could return the favor. This depressing thought didn't change the fact she was still wet, cold and stranded in a dark parking lot. She thumbed her contacts again, then stopped.

Tate Griffin.

She had his number from the other day when she'd gotten into his records to type up her notes on his suture removal. But she shouldn't call him. For one, they'd had a one-night stand. For two, she liked him. A lot. And for three, she'd started fantasizing about sleeping with him again.

All great reasons not to call him.

But then he *did* know a thing or two about fixing his own vehicle…

With a sigh, she dialed his number, then held her breath. He answered on the fourth ring. “Griffin.”

“It’s Madi.”

He seemed to absorb that information for a moment before she rushed on. “I’m at the clinic and my car won’t start. I’m the last one here, and I’ve tried calling my brother but he’s not available and—”

“Lock your doors. I’ll be right there.”

Madi slipped her phone into her pocket and rested her head on the steering wheel. She was tired. She could really use a foot rub. And a body massage, come to think of it. She’d gotten one at the lovely day spa in town for her birthday last year from Toni. It had been fantastic, but Madi now wondered what it would be like to have Tate work her over instead.

She pictured them on a deserted beach at sunset, Tate in a pair of low-slung board shorts and nothing else, his big hands all over her bikini-clad body, his eyes creased in that way he had of showing his feelings without moving his mouth. Madi smiled up at him as he flipped her over to lie face down on her towel. She felt breathless for him to touch her again. His lips brushed her shoulder, and she wriggled for more. He groaned her name, a whispered warning as he ran a finger down her spine, then between her legs until she writhed with need. She moved with him, seeking more. Then he entered her, and she cried out as he shuddered in pleasure, then collapsed on top of her and—

Rap. Rap. Rap.

Madi jerked upright and banged her head on the sun visor. Tate waited while she rolled down the window, her face hot.

“Hi,” she said. “I was just—”

Dreaming about sex on the beach with you.

“Sleeping?” he asked when she hesitated, one brow quirked.

She nodded and looked away. “Guess I’m tired.”

"You look flushed. You're not getting sick, are you?"

She shook her head. "I'm fine."

"Pop the hood for me, and I'll get started." He moved back to the front of the car, seeming not to care that he was getting soaked by the rain.

Madi was glad for a second alone to collect herself. But it didn't take long before Tate was back at her window again.

"Try starting it again," he said. "You'll need a new alternator sooner rather than later."

Whatever that was. "Is it expensive?"

"Not for the part." He wiped his hands on a towel he must've brought from his vehicle. "The labor's what will cost you, but it shouldn't. It's easy enough to replace." He held up a metal stick. "You need oil too." He disappeared back beneath her hood again, asking, "When's the last time you had anyone look at this poor baby?"

"Uh..."

The sounds of him fiddling with her engine were interspersed with mutters of "the lack of respect for the vehicle" and "even if it *is* a piece of crap."

"Who taught you how to do all this car stuff?" she asked, hoping to learn more about him.

"My dad. When he wasn't flying planes for the Air Force. And my mom was a secretary at the Pentagon."

Madi smiled. "A military brat through and through, huh?"

"All I ever knew," he agreed, returning to work on some part under her hood.

"Is that why you wanted to start a program for veterans at the clinic?" she asked. His check had arrived, earmarked for that purpose. Madi had already contacted a good counselor about getting involved, one who could help people like Mr. Ryan. "Where are your parents now?"

"Both gone. My dad died in Desert Storm. My mom a couple of years ago from pneumonia."

"Oh." Her smile faded as he continued to inspect—whatever he was inspecting. "Do you have any siblings?"

"Nope. Just me now." Tate straightened, then closed her hood. "Everything else looks okay, but I'll follow you home just in case."

"There you go again," she said softly, still thinking about him being all alone in the world. "Acting like a hero."

"Make no mistake," he said quietly as he started back to his Chevelle. "I'm nobody's hero."

CHAPTER TWELVE

MADI WATCHED WITH satisfaction as the citizens of Wyckford lined up in the high school gymnasium for the pumpkin carving contest on Sunday. The schedule had been set in advance, and as heavily advertised, every board member had agreed to participate.

They charged a twenty-five-dollar entry fee for everyone and that included your pumpkin, a carving tool, and a T-shirt. Big price tag, but people were paying for the joy of seeing their town hotshots get covered in goo like regular Joe Schmos.

Madi had picked out a medium-sized pumpkin for herself and stood now behind the table near Mark Bates, Brock Turner and Judith. They all were dressed in jeans and Pumpkin Contest T-shirts with a logo designed by Luna as people registered and filled the other tables in the gym.

Mark had brought along his earbuds and was currently bopping to his music as he drew a face on his pumpkin with a black marker.

Luna walked up to Madi, a large pumpkin tucked under her arm and her carving tool in her hand. "How's it going?"

"Good," Madi said, glancing over at Mark. "Go see what he's drawing."

Instead, Luna cocked her head toward the door. "Maybe you should see what your new boyfriend is up to."

"What?" Madi frowned as she looked over to see Tate walking in, hot as ever with his dark stubble and plenty of attitude.

Tate had been awake since before dawn. He'd gone for a punishing swim with Mark at the beach. Afterward, he'd run, falling only once, and only because a crab had come out of nowhere and startled him. Then, on his way back into town just now, he'd seen a sign for the pumpkin carving contest in support of the clinic and decided to check it out. Seeing Madi in her formfitting orange T-shirt and jeans made it more than worth it. She looked like a girl-next-door-meets-*Maxim* photo shoot.

Drawn like a magnet, Tate got in line and registered. As he collected his T-shirt and carving tool, something loosened deep within him. Tate couldn't have explained the feeling to save his own life.

She'd piled her hair on top of her head for the contest, but it wasn't holding. Loose strands had escaped and curled next to her temples and cheeks and down the back of her neck. He knew how soft her skin was there, and if he put his mouth to the sensitive area, she'd make a little sound that went straight through him. He was crazy in lust with a woman he had no business wanting.

Not that *that* seemed to deter him in the slightest.

"Hey, there!" Madi called as he picked out a pumpkin, then walked toward her table. Before he reached her though, Lucille stopped him.

"My neighbor's got a Charger," the older lady said. "1970, I think. Front-end problems. Told him you might be interested in looking at it. Are you?"

That vintage vehicle was a sweet old thing. Tate wouldn't mind getting his hands on one. "Yep."

"Good." Lucille smiled. "That's right nice of you."

That was him, a right nice guy.

Madi waited until he stopped in front of her, then said, "Thanks for coming."

He smiled, slow and suggestive. Madi went bright red.

"Best get changed," she warned. "You don't want your regular clothes ruined by pumpkin guts."

He laughed and set his pumpkin down, then pulled off his sweatshirt, enjoying her fluster as she tried to look anywhere but at him.

By the time he had the T-shirt on, Madi was busy drawing, so he moved on down the long table until he found an empty spot at the end. Pumpkin carving wasn't something he had much experience with, but he did the best he could and by the time the buzzer went off and he'd gotten elbow deep in gourd guts, he was happy with how his creation had turned out. He'd ended up with a creation that looked like a cross between Freddy Krueger and Kermit the Frog. And if that wasn't terrifying, he didn't know what was.

After grabbing some wet wipes and a towel to clean himself up, he strolled around the tables looking at the other pumpkins, gradually making his way over to where Madi was talking with some of the other townsfolk about the contest. Behind her was a large plastic bucket full of pumpkin guts. Tate walked up and tapped her on the shoulder, and she turned fast. Too fast.

"Oh!" Madi said as she jumped back.

"Watch out." Tate reached for her, but it was too late.

She tripped over the bucket and went down with a little squeal of surprise—straight into the vat of goo.

"Oh, God!" Madi flailed. "Help!"

Brock and Mark, who stood nearby, rushed over, but Tate got to Madi first.

"Are you all right?" he asked, pulling her up.

She stepped back, her hands going to her own butt, now

covered in slimy muck. "No worries. I have lots of padding back there."

"You sure?" Brock asked, frowning at her ankle. "You didn't reinjure the one you broke last year, did you?"

"No." Madi laughed a little, obviously embarrassed. "Just please tell me no one took my picture."

Someone from the other end of the place yelled, "Say cheese…"

Brock swore beneath his breath, making Madi laugh. "Oh, well. What's a little public humiliation for a good cause, eh?"

Then everyone went back to the contest.

Tate waited until they announced the winner—which unsurprisingly wasn't him—and would've said goodbye to Madi, but she was already busy talking to the judges. So, he changed direction and started to walk out, but something made him look at her once more as he left. From across the gym, Madi watched him too, her gaze long and thoughtful.

After the accident, Tate had tried to live with no regrets. But this time, when he left Wyckford, he'd regret leaving Madi Scott behind.

That night, Madi met her friends in their usual booth at the Buzzy Bird, forks in hand.

"So." Cassie licked frosting off her lips. "Arthur Schmidt at the hardware store asked me out the other day."

Madi and Luna busted out laughing.

"Good thing you're engaged to Brock, huh?" Madi winked.

"Yep." Cassie ate another bite of chocolate decadence cake. "How's the drawing coming, Luna?"

Luna shrugged. "Between my schedule at the hospital with PT patients and filling in here when needed, there's not a lot of time for me to do art these days." Then she eyed Madi, changing the subject. "You want to talk about today?"

Madi frowned. “What about it?”

“Gee, I don’t know—how you drooled over Tate Griffin at the pumpkin carving contest earlier.”

“I did not drool.”

“BS,” Luna said.

Madi sighed and set down her fork, shrugging. “I like him.”

“And that’s a bad thing why?” Cassie’s brow furrowed. “You’re both single, right?”

“Because he’s not exactly a forever kind of guy,” Madi said. “He’s made that clear.”

Tate went swimming that night by moonlight. Then he hit the beach for another run. This time he didn’t fall. Not once. When he was done torturing his body and his every muscle quivered from exertion, he went home and showered, then went back to bed, hoping he was too tired for nightmares.

Things started out good too. He dreamed about a time his team had been assigned to rescue the passengers of a sinking reconnaissance vessel off the coast of Istanbul. Then the dream shifted to another mission, where they’d used a local fishing boat in Cambodia to reach a stranded airman, which then transitioned a third time to when they’d managed to save a bus, loaded with recent recruits, that had somehow gone off the road and into the Gulf of Mexico.

All successful rescues.

But before long everything went straight to hell once more.

Tate had been thrown from the burning wreckage by the force of the helicopter’s explosion. Darkness followed. When he opened his eyes again, his ears rang so loud he couldn’t hear anything. A silent horror as wild flames surrounded him.

He swam with all his might, trying to reach what was left of the chopper. On the way, he found Kelly, but she was already dead. Located Tommy and Brad too and did what he could for them, but they passed as well. Then he'd discovered Trevor, their pilot, floating on the other side of the wreckage, gasping for air, his chest crushed and bloody. By the time Tate reached him, all he could do was hold Trevor's hand as his life slowly faded away…

Drenched in sweat, he woke up alone in bed, far from the black churning ocean. He inhaled deep and shoved his fingers through his damp hair. A glance at the device on his nightstand showed it was eight in the morning now. His next shift didn't start until that afternoon, but Tate got up again anyway, tugging on his jeans and shoving his phone and empty Vicodin bottle into his pocket.

It wasn't even dawn yet, but he was too restless to sit still. He grabbed the part from the shelf in his garage, then fired up the Chevelle and drove into town. To Madi's house, a ranch in an older neighborhood with a fresh coat of paint, and her junky car in the drive. Which was why he was here.

Or that's the excuse he was going with anyway.

It took him all of six minutes to replace her alternator with one he'd brought.

Maybe he needed to pick up more shifts with the flight crew or ambulance service to stay busy and feel useful. But there were only so many emergencies in a town the size of Wyckford. He put his tools away and started to get behind the wheel of the Chevelle when he heard the garage door open.

In the lit interior Madi stood with her long brown hair in a wild cloud around her face and shoulders and her bare feet sticking out from beneath the hem of her robe. "Tate? What are you doing here?"

Honestly, her guess was as good as his.

But then, he found himself climbing out of the car and walking up to her.

"Tate?" She frowned up at him, clearly confused. He knew the feeling.

He didn't answer. Waiting to see if she'd tell him he was crazy or gave him the slightest indication he wasn't welcome. If so, he'd leave.

He was good at leaving.

But instead, Madi surprised him by stepping closer, meeting him halfway. Her hand trembled slightly as she reached for him, making him feel very useful indeed.

In the back of his mind, he'd told himself if Madi hadn't started things up between them at the auction, he'd have never slept with her. But deep down he knew that was a lie. It was supposed to have been just one night, but they kept getting in deeper.

She was like a drug. The most addicting kind. He craved her like he'd never experienced before. Tate was pretty sure Madi felt the same about him. He had no idea what to do with that or with his emotions, which got in his way. His whole "no attachment" thing had gone right off the rails, and he felt disconcerted, discombobulated, like his world had turned upside down.

But then his thoughts stopped entirely because her parted lips and flushed cheeks and bedroom eyes told him he affected her every bit as much as she did him. Helpless against the riptide of desire pulling him in, Tate caught Madi to him and stepped over the threshold back into the house, slamming the garage door button and then kicking the door closed behind him.

They staggered into the entryway, mouths fused, bumping into something and knocking it over as she tripped and slammed into the coat rack. They both laughed as Tate spun Madi away from danger, pressing her against a little cherrywood desk. He trapped her there with his body, all amusement fading as she gasped, the sound full of desire.

He wanted to hear it again. Lowering his head, Tate kissed the sweet spot beneath her ear, along her jaw, then the column of her neck. He spent a long moment at the hollow of her throat because, oh yeah, she made the sound once more, her shaky hands clutching his shoulders.

"I dreamed about you," Madi said softly.

Tate was glad, even more so since he had no idea how much he needed this, *her*, until this very minute. "Tell me."

"We were back at the auction." Her fingers glided through his hair, making him shiver. "Working our way through all the furniture."

"Where did we start?" he asked, nibbling her earlobe.

She gasped. "A table."

"Nice." He was hard as a rock. Maybe distance wasn't the way to go. Maybe they could get each other out of their systems. Tate turned her so she faced the small mirror over the desk. Madi watched the reflection as his hands ran down her arms.

The air crackled with electricity. And need. So much need.

"What are you wearing beneath the robe?" he asked.

She bit her lower lip. "Nothing."

Her body was so close to his that a sheet of paper couldn't fit between them. Tate reached her belt. "Do you want this?"

"Yes."

One tug and the robe opened. She didn't take her hungry gaze off their reflection, her eyes glued to Tate's fingers as they bared her body.

"Madi. You're so beautiful." He stroked her stomach, then cupped her breasts, his thumbs brushing her nipples, wringing another gasp out of her. He did it again, his touch light and teasing before he let her go.

She whimpered.

He pushed the robe off her shoulders. Then he pinned her hands in front of her on the desk, which forced her to bend over. He gently squeezed, signaling he wanted her to stay like that.

"Tate—" she choked out, holding the position with a trusting sweetness that nearly undid him, especially combined with the sexy sway of her breasts and the helpless grind of her hips back against him. He cupped those gorgeous full breasts again before skimming one hand south, between her legs, where he found her wet and ready for him.

She gripped the table tight, eyes closed and head back. Then he slid a finger deep inside her, and she gave an inarticulate little cry, straining.

"Tate—" she gasped, breathless. "Please."

Madi trembled as Tate added some pressure with his thumb, kissing along the nape of her neck to her shoulder. She panted, arms taut and face a mask of pleasure.

"Tate."

Madi skittered over the edge, crying out as she shattered, her knees wobbling. Tate caught her, then stripped, putting on a condom before pushing inside her. Her body still quivered from her orgasm, and he bent over her, pressing his torso to her back, brushing his mouth against her neck, giving her a moment. Then she ground against him, restless, and he moved, pushing them both close to the edge again. She met his thrusts, arching her back, demanding more.

His hunger surged, along with a rather shocking, scary, sizzling shot of adrenaline-fueled possessive protectiveness.

You can't protect her.

Still, despite his anxiety, he couldn't stop. Couldn't tear his eyes from their reflection either. He was too far gone. Every nerve ending in his body screamed at him to let go. The fire she'd started inside him flashed bright, a tight ache in his gut. He couldn't hold on much longer. Then Madi went over the edge again and Tate followed, burying his face in her hair as he climaxed so hard his legs buckled.

It was not enough.

It was too much.

It was everything.

He made sure his knees hit the floor and not hers, turning Madi to face him and pulling her in. After a minute, he leaned back to see her face. Her helpless smile tugged one from him as well.

"Good?" Tate asked.

Madi traced a finger along his lower lip. "So much better than good."

CHAPTER THIRTEEN

SHE WASN'T SURE what had brought Tate to her so early in the morning or what he'd been doing out in her driveway, but sitting with him now, naked in her entryway, was a pretty good start to the day.

Madi blushed as he bent in to kiss her. She traced her hand down his torso, over a hip to his upper thigh, and found an unnatural ridge. A jagged scar ran the length of his left leg from groin to knee, and she stilled in horror for what he'd suffered. Their position, with her cuddled up against his chest, couldn't be comfortable for him. "Are you all right?"

"I'm numb from the waist down right now."

She gave a breathless laugh, relieved to feel the usual tension in his big, battle-scarred body lessen. "Good. I know it gives you pain from the accident."

"It wasn't an accident." He paused, then grimaced. "I mean it was, but it was preventable."

She frowned. "Preventable how?"

"If I'd chosen not to go out there in the first place, my team would be alive today."

Her throat tightened at the guilt and remorse edging his tone now. "But didn't you say those airmen would've died if you hadn't gone?"

"Yes, but they died that night anyway. I could have at least saved my team."

Madi took that in a moment, letting the silence settle around them for a while. Finally, she said, "That must have been awful for you. Alone out there, injured."

"It was. I had cracked ribs, a broken wrist, and a collarbone fracture. Some internal injuries and the leg. All survivable." He paused again. "Unlike everyone else."

Survivor's guilt. I know it well.

Aching for the physical and emotional pain he'd endured, Madi ran her fingers lightly over his chest, feeling the fine tremor of his muscles. Aftershocks of great sex or bad memories, it was hard to tell.

"It wasn't your fault, Tate," she said softly. "You were forced to make an impossible decision."

"Madi." He shook his head. "I *really* don't want to talk about this."

"I know." She clutched the infinity charm around her neck. "I don't like to talk about what happened to my sister Karrie either. For a long time after she was gone—after I failed to save her—I couldn't bear to remember her, much less talk about her."

He gave a long, shuddery exhale, then drew her in closer, burying his face in her hair. "You said she overdosed?"

"Yeah. She was eighteen," she said, closing her eyes against the sting of tears. "And pregnant."

"Oh, Madi." He tightened his grip on her. "Please don't tell me you think what she did was your fault."

"We were sisters. I knew she was having problems. I should have—"

"No." He pulled back to look into her eyes. "There's nothing you could have done. *Nothing.* You were just a kid yourself."

She could barely speak. "How do you get past it?"

"I'm still figuring it out. But you keep going. You keep moving. You keep living."

* * *

Tate woke up a little while later, on his back, the wood floor stuck to his spine and a warm, sated woman curled into his side. Somehow, he staggered to his feet, then scooped up Madi. The first rays of sunlight were just visible over the horizon.

"No," she murmured, her words slurring from exhaustion as she stirred in his arms. "Not time to get up yet."

He'd seen the rosters in the ER the other day and knew she'd been working around the clock, twelve hours and more at a time. "Shh," he whispered against her temple. "Sleep."

"Tate?" Groggily, she slipped her arms around his neck. "Where are we going?"

"Bed." He planned to tuck her in, then get the hell out of there before he did something stupid like fall asleep with her. Sex was one thing. Sleeping together afterwards turned it into something else entirely.

You idiot, it's already something else...

On her bed were the two big stuffed animals he'd won for her at the arcade. An odd feeling went through him, warm and cozy, followed closely by wry amusement. He put her down and started to straighten, but she tugged him down with her.

"Cold." She shivered and tried to burrow against his body.

Giving in, Tate pulled her close for a minute, yanking the comforter over them. He'd share his body heat until she fell back to sleep, then he'd head out.

Madi pressed her face into his throat, tucking her cold toes behind his calf. "Feels good."

"I'm not staying," he warned, not knowing which one of them he was telling.

Two minutes later, her breathing slowed into the deep slumber of the exhausted.

She was out for the count.

And all over him.

Her hair was in his face, her warm breath puffing gently near his jaw, her bare breasts flattened against his side and chest. She had one hand tucked between them, the other low on his stomach. Plastered to him like a second skin.

Lulled in by her soft, giving warmth, he closed his eyes and fell asleep.

At some point, the nightmare gathered, pulling him in. Luckily, he woke up before he made a complete ass of himself. It was still early by the sunshine slanting in through the blinds. Rolling off the bed, Tate walked out into the entryway to grab his jeans when he felt the hand on his arm. He jumped and whipped around to face Madi. Unable to help himself, he twitched free, and the front doorknob jabbed him hard in the back. "Ouch."

"Sorry. Didn't mean to startle you." Silhouetted by the rising sun behind her, Madi stayed a short distance away, concern pouring off her in the same way passion had earlier. "Okay?"

He could've lied. Added a small smile and a kiss, to make sure she bought it.

But he didn't want to get close. He shoved his feet into his shoes and grabbed his wallet and keys as he saw Madi put on his shirt.

"Tate?"

He opened the front door and headed outside. She padded after him onto the porch, her fingers running down his bare back.

"Did you have a bad dream?"

He stilled. "No." *Yes.*

"The night in the storm," she said quietly. "You had a nightmare. Did it happen again here?"

"No." He dropped his head to the door. "That's not it."

"Then what's wrong?"

He straightened. "I have to go, Madi."

"Stay. Sleep with me. I won't tell."

Tate knew she only wanted to help. But he didn't want it. He was fine. All he needed was to be left alone. That was for the best. "Can't."

"But—"

He pulled open the door and stepped into the chilly morning, leaving before he couldn't anymore.

Madi plopped back onto her bed and stared up at the ceiling, haunted by Tate's expression when he'd left. This whole thing with him was supposed to have been fun. A little walk on the wild side. But it had become so much more. She was good at healing people.

But with Tate… She couldn't heal him, any more than she'd been able to heal herself.

Madi showered and changed, then went to work. A few hours in, she was paged to the nurses' station.

"What's up?" she asked Camilla, who sat behind the desk when she got there.

Camilla hiked her chin toward the hallway. Madi found a familiar man propped against the wall, his stance casual, his body relaxed. But she knew better.

"I'm on break," she said, then walked toward Tate. "Hey."

"Hey." His eyes never wavered from hers. "Got a minute?"

"Sure." All too aware of Camilla's eyes—and ears—on them, Madi gestured for him to follow her to the staff room where they sat in the corner. It was too early for the lunch crowd, so they had the place to themselves, except for a janitor working his way across the floor with a mop.

Tate's knee brushed against hers beneath the table. He was dressed in his flight crew uniform now, probably on his way to work.

He looked edible.

And she was afraid he was here to tell her he was leaving.

"You want anything?" she asked, pointing to the vending machines. "Coffee? Tea?" *Me...*

"No, thanks. Listen, Madi." He stared at her, his green-gold gaze fathomless, giving nothing away. "I wanted to apologize for earlier." He caught her hand. "I acted like an idiot."

She sank back into her seat. "I understand, you know."

"I'm sorry about Karrie," he said. "But you deserve better from me."

Before she could respond, the elevator music on the overhead PA system was replaced by an authoritative male voice. "Code Red."

They both jumped up. Code Red meant there was a fire, and personnel were to report in immediately. Today was a scheduled drill but Madi hadn't expected it now. Great timing.

"Code Red," the voice repeated. "All personnel respond immediately. Code Red. *Repeat, Code Red.*"

CHAPTER FOURTEEN

WITH THE HOSPITAL in temporary lockdown because of the fire drill, Tate went to his appointed station and waited. Soon, firefighters and other emergency personnel came pouring in. Ten minutes later, the hospital employees reappeared, without Madi.

Two women in scrubs stood near him, looking at him, then whispering to themselves, clearly gossiping, probably about him and Madi. Perfect. He'd tried to make her life easier while he was here, and all he'd done was make things worse.

He shouldn't have messed around with her life. He'd be gone soon, but Wyckford was Madi's home, her world. Tate felt confused and uncertain, two foreign emotions for him. He'd started to believe *he* was the one giving here, the experienced one imparting a little wildness and the dubious honor of his worldly ways. How magnanimous.

Especially since the truth was Madi had done all the giving, schooling him in warmth, compassion and strength. In the process, she'd wrapped him around her little finger with her soft voice and a backbone of steel.

Dammit. He headed out, slowing at the front entrance. A donation box had been placed there for the Health Services Clinic. He'd given money for the veterans program already, but he knew now exactly what he'd do to give back to the woman who'd given him so much.

* * *

The next day Tate brought the sick vet, Mr. Ryan, dinner. He'd found the man out on the street, having left his daughter's somewhere in the night, and—per Mr. Ryan's wishes—moved him into a halfway house outside of town instead. Mr. Ryan had said he didn't want to be a burden on his family anymore, so Madi had arranged a room for him at the halfway house through HSC. It was infinitely better, and safer, than being homeless.

After they ate, Mr. Ryan asked Tate for a ride to the free clinic.

"What's going on here?" Tate asked as they pulled up to the hospital.

"A meeting."

The sign on the front door of the west wing read Narcotics Anonymous.

As he walked the old vet up to the door, Tate noticed someone had attached a sticky note to the sign that said EMPHASIS ON THE "A", PEOPLE!

Tate didn't know whether to be amused that only in Wyckford would the extra note be necessary or appalled that the town could not keep anything *anonymous* at all.

But part of any twelve-step process was learning to trust, so…

He turned to Mr. Ryan, who'd gone still beside him, seemingly frozen in place.

"I'm too old for this," the vet muttered.

"How old *are* you?" Tate asked.

"Two hundred and fifty."

Tate snorted. "Then you're in luck. They don't cut you off until you're three hundred."

A ghost of a smile touched Mr. Ryan's mouth. "I'm fifty-eight."

Twenty years older than Tate. The vet's body trembled from

detoxing. Not good. Tate would've paid big bucks to be anywhere else right now but figured if Mr. Ryan was using him as a crutch, he had to be in a bad way. "How long since your last hit?"

"I ran out of OxyContin four days ago. Doctor says I don't need it anymore."

Without thinking, Tate slipped his hand into his pocket and touched the ever-present empty bottle of Vicodin there. Three years, two weeks, and counting. He thought about saying he'd wait outside, but that felt cowardly, so he went in.

They both survived the meeting. An hour later they exited in silence. Tate didn't know about Mr. Ryan, but he was more than a little shaken by the stories he'd heard, the utter destruction of the lives those people in there had been trying to reboot and repair. He felt grateful he hadn't been one of them. Not completely anyway.

He was almost back to the halfway house when the old vet finally spoke again. "Are you and that cute ER nurse a thing?"

"Madi, you mean?" Tate had been asked this so many times since the auction. By the clerk at the grocery store. By the people he helped on his EMT runs. By basically everyone who'd crossed his path. The very same people who—until he'd met Madi—had been content to just stare at him.

She was the heart and soul of this town, or at least what it would look like in human form. And maybe Tate had thought she'd be someone he could easily walk away from. But he knew now, deep down, that wasn't the case. *She* was different. The big problem was, Madi was grounded here in Wyckford, while *he* would need to decide about leaving soon. The one-night stand had been Madi's idea. Though she'd also accepted his latest visit as an addendum to the original deal. And she'd let him off the hook for being an idiot.

"No," he finally said to Mr. Ryan, hoping to squash any further interest the man might have. "We're not a thing."

"Huh." The vet scratched his scruffy jaw. "Does she know that?"

"Yeah. She knows."

But do you?

"She's a real nice lady," Mr. Ryan continued. "When I was living on a bench at the park, she brought me food at night. Did she ever tell you that?"

Tate shook his head, his chest a little tight at the thought of Madi, after a long day in the ER, seeking out Mr. Ryan to make sure he was fed.

"She can't cook," Mr. Ryan told him with a small smile. "But I ate whatever she brought anyway. Didn't want to hurt her feelings."

Tate shook his head, grinning to himself.

"If I was younger and—" Mr. Ryan shrugged "—*different*, I'd try for her. She's something special. Way too special for the likes of me, though, you know?"

Yeah. Tate knew. He knew *exactly*.

"One time she came to the park and some kids were throwing rocks at me. Madi chased them away. I still think I looked better than she did. Her hair was all over the place, and she was in her scrubs. She looked like a patient from the place I'd stayed in after I got back from my third tour."

A mental facility. Tate pictured Madi furious and chasing off a bunch of bullies.

"You've seen the stuff on Facebook, right?" Mr. Ryan asked.

Tate slid him a side glance. "How are you getting on Facebook?"

"There's a community computer at the halfway house." The old vet smiled. "The town has a homepage. There's a pic up of you two. You two seem awful cozy for not being a thing."

Yeah. Except what he'd had with Madi was the opposite of cozy.

It was hot. Bewildering.

Staggering.

He dropped Mr. Ryan off at the halfway house, then went back to his rental place. He showered and changed, then saw a missed call on his phone and got a little rush at the thought maybe Madi had called him, or they needed him for an extra shift with the ambulance service.

But the message wasn't from either of them. It was from Brock, reminding him he was due in for a recheck of the scar tissue in his leg, per his VA medical records.

The next morning, Tate got his scans, then went to Brock's GP office on the same grounds as the hospital. He checked in at the front desk and was told to wait. He'd perfected the art of hurry up and wait in the Air Force, so when he was finally led back to the office and then the man himself strode in carrying a thick file containing Tate's medical history, he didn't react.

Brock was in full doctor mode today. Dark blue scrubs, a white coat, a stethoscope around his neck, and his ID clipped to his hip pocket. Hair rumpled, eyes tired, he dropped Tate's chart on his desk and sprawled out into his chair. "God, I'm exhausted."

"Long day already?"

"Is it still morning? I don't know anymore." Brock scrubbed his hands over his face. "Adi has started asking questions about where babies come from, and if you know anything about my daughter, she's persistent as hell."

"Oh." Tate grinned. "So, what's the verdict on my scar tissue?"

"Scans show improvement. I think all the exercise you're getting with Mark helps. Keep it up."

Another month in Wyckford might kill him. "I have to let the Air Force know if I'm re-upping for another stint soon."

Brock gave him a look. "You're not planning on leaving, are you?"

"I was *always* planning on going eventually."

"But *now*?"

Tate sighed as Madi's face flashed in his mind. Her looking up at him while lying snuggled against him in her bed, wearing only a soft, sated smile and a slant of moonlight across her face.

"Does Madi know about your plans?" Brock asked quietly.

"This has nothing to do with her," Tate lied.

Brock shook his head, looking baffled. "And reenlisting is what you want to do?"

Tate didn't know. He didn't know much of anything anymore. This thing with Madi had rattled him to his core.

"You know," Brock said in his infuriatingly calm, professional voice. "I'm on the hospital board and there's talk of making your flight paramedic position permanent and giving it a title. Team Leader. The board wants to expand the service to more rural areas and even transfer cases between Wyckford General and Boston. I could put your name in if—"

"I'm not interested."

Brock stared at him.

Tate held the other man's gaze steadily.

With a shake of his head, Brock stood. "Then I guess we're done here for now."

Tate spent two days *not* making any plans for his future. First, he needed to finish up the Charger for Lucille's neighbor. Then he made some easy repairs around the rental home. After that, there were no excuses left and Tate decided to give himself a day off from thinking at all.

Which turned into yet another day…

Then he woke up to a message from Brock to stop by his office at ten that morning. Tate swam. Then he ran, hard. Then he worked out with Mark at the gym for an hour until they were both sweating and exhausted. Finally, Tate took a shower and drove to Brock's office.

When he was led back to the office, Brock looked up from the mountain of paperwork on his desk and scowled at Tate. "You give word to the Air Force yet?"

"No."

Brock gave him a long look, steepling his fingers as he studied Tate like a specimen on a slide. "Why not?"

"Haven't had time." Tate straightened his leg, then winced.

"Hmm." Brock's tone was dry. "I was at the gym this morning too, but you never even noticed me. You were too busy wiping the floor with Mark. You overdo it there?"

"I pulled something."

Brock shook his head. A silent beat passed, then two. Finally, he said, "Maybe I spoke too soon about your scar tissue. I think I should check you one more time in a week before I clear you to return to duty."

Tate agreed, then left by the back exit, which meant he stood in the bright late autumn sunshine in the hospital parking lot staring at Madi's car. He wondered what was wrong with him, but since that was too big of a problem to solve in this decade, he went home. He hadn't been called in for any extra shifts in a while now because things were slow. So, he went out to the garage and fiddled with the Chevelle until it was dark. He'd just gotten back inside when someone knocked on his door.

Madi.

She gave him a small, sweet smile. "Hey."

Chronic idiot. That's me.

"Hey yourself."

She stepped over the threshold and bumped into him since he hadn't moved. He thought it was an accident, but then her hands brushed over his chest and abs. No accident there.

Nor was the fact that she wore that fuzzy pink sweater again, with low-riding jeans and a pair of high heels that brought her up enough to perfectly align their bodies. Her pulse beat like a drum at the little dip in the base of her throat. Tate ran a finger over that spot now, feeling her heart race even faster.

"I talked to Mr. Ryan this afternoon."

Tate lifted his gaze.

"He was back in the ER," she said.

Concerned, Tate frowned. "What happened? Is he all right?"

"Someone caught him wandering around on the highway last night and brought him in. He had a bottle of whiskey and some dope he'd scored somewhere." She put her hand on Tate's, squeezing reassuringly. "He's fine. He's sleeping it off, but before that…he was talking. He said you took him to the NA meeting. And you stayed."

Tate could've lied and said the old vet needed assistance, but he didn't. He waited for Madi's expression to change but she only nodded. No leaping to conclusions, no trial and jury, no pity, nothing.

"Why don't you just ask me what you really want to know, Madi."

"Okay." She drew a deep breath. "Are you an addict, too?"

Tate slipped his hand into his pocket to touch the ever-present Vicodin bottle. It was empty and weighed nothing. Both those things reassured him. He'd messed up plenty, but not that way. "I had a lot of pain and they put me on heavy narcotics after the accident four years ago. I was a wreck."

"You'd just lost your team," she said softly.

Something warm inside him unfurled. Madi was defending

him. To *himself.* "I knew if I wanted to have any kind of life again, I had to get off the pain meds, especially to work as a paramedic." He paused, remembering. "It was hard though. I liked the oblivion. Too much."

Her eyes stayed steady on his as she absorbed his words, seeming to take them in without judgment. "That's why you refused narcotics the night of the storm."

Tate nodded. "I stopped taking Vicodin three years ago because I found myself living for the clock again, just waiting for the minute I could take another pill. That's when I quit."

"You went cold turkey?"

"I did." He flashed a grim smile and blew out a breath. "And I still crave it sometimes."

She went quiet for a moment, then said, "The craving part is normal. I gave up chocolate once and the cravings *sucked.*"

He choked out a laugh. "I don't think it's exactly the same, Madi."

They both smiled now.

Madi sighed. "I think it helps to keep busy. I know that much."

"I've been distracted plenty lately." Tate rocked back on his heels and her cheeks flamed.

"You must be Wyckford's new go-to mechanic. Lucille said you're helping a friend of hers with his Charger," she commented, glancing at a grease stain on his T-shirt. "Were you working on your own car just now?"

"Yep. Want to see?"

She nodded, and he took her hand and guided her out to the garage.

"What were you doing?" Madi asked as she looked around at the Chevelle and the slew of tools scattered across his worktable.

"Brake lines."

"Show me," she said.

"You want to learn how to put in new stainless steel brake lines?" he asked, heavy on the disbelief as he looked pointedly at her high heels again. "Madi, those shoes aren't meant for working on a car."

"What are they meant for?"

"Messing with a man's head."

Then he figured, what the hell. She saw blood and guts every single day. A little dirt wasn't going to bother her. He grabbed a forgotten sweatshirt off the bench and handed it to her. "Put this on to keep from getting dirty."

She did and it fell to her thighs. "It smells like you."

The odd pressure in his chest increased to a yearning ache that had everything to do with the woman standing in front of him. "And now it's going to smell like *you*."

He kicked over the mechanic creeper, then his backup creeper, and gestured for her to lie down on one of them. When they were both flat on their backs, she grinned over at him. "Now what?"

"Under the car."

She slid herself beneath the Chevelle, and he joined her. Side by side, they stared up at the bottom of the chassis. Then he looked over at her sweet profile and reminded himself he was leaving Wyckford soon. Tate handed her a roll of brake line. "Bend it to fit the contours of the frame as you go." He pointed out the route, and Madi began to work.

"It's peaceful under here," she said. Tate slid her a dubious look, and she laughed. "I'm serious. You don't think so?"

It was grimy, stuffy…and yeah. Peaceful. "I do. I'm just surprised you think so too."

"You don't think I enjoy getting dirty once in a while?" She bit her lower lip as her cheeks flushed pink, and she laughed at his raised brow. "You know what I mean."

When she had trouble bending the line, he put his hands over hers to help. "Unravel another foot or so."

They worked in companionable silence until she asked, "What was the first car you fixed?"

Tate smiled at the memory. "When I was fourteen my dad bought a Pontiac GTO. Man, she was sweet."

"She?" Madi turned her face to him, and he stroked a rogue strand of hair from her temple, tucking it behind her ear.

"Cars are always female. Do you want to hear this story or not?"

"Yes." She nudged his shoulder with hers. "Go on."

"I took apart the engine."

"Oh, my God." Her brown eyes widened. "Was he mad?"

"It was a classic and in mint condition. *Mad* doesn't even begin to cover my dad's reaction."

Madi blinked at him. "Why'd you do it then?"

Tate still remembered the look on his father's face—the complete shock at the empty engine compartment, the horror that his baby had been breached and violated and then the sheer fury. "I liked taking things apart and putting them back together again. I hadn't meant to take it so far, but I kept undoing and undoing..."

"What happened?"

"I thought my dad would kill me." Tate smiled. "But we ended up rebuilding it together."

She touched his jaw, cupping it in her palm and lightly running the pad of her thumb over the stubble on his chin. "I like being under a car with you."

Working on cars was familiar ground. His constant. But Madi had squeezed herself right into his safety zone, then into his heart. Because no matter what he told himself, he liked being here with her, too.

"What are you scared of?" she asked.

You, he nearly said. And it was true.

Instead, he let out a short laugh. “In general?”

Her eyes softened, and she slid her hand around his nape, bringing him a full-body shiver of pure pleasure. “Yes.”

“Being trapped.” He rolled out from beneath the Chevelle, then crouched beside Madi’s creeper and yanked her out by the ankles.

She sat up and pushed her hair back to meet his gaze. “I know this isn’t your home, Tate. That you’re going back to the Air Force soon—”

“Madi—” He put his finger over her lips.

She pulled his hand away, keeping a hold on his wrist. “No, it’s okay. You’re not the small-town type.”

And yet here he was, still here in Wyckford.

CHAPTER FIFTEEN

THE NEXT MORNING, Madi woke to Violet's disgruntled *meow*, letting the world know it was past time for her breakfast. When she ignored this, the cat batted her on the forehead with a paw. "Shh."

Meow.

Madi stretched, her body sore from being with Tate the night before. She sighed blissfully and rolled over. She hadn't gotten home until late. Or early, depending on how you looked at it. She'd have liked to stay at his place all night, but that would have been too much.

Not for her. For *him.*

She'd promised him this was a simple fling. No use telling him she'd broken that promise. Besides, she loved being with him. That was the bottom line. The only line. There were no preconceived notions on how they should behave. It was freeing, exhilarating.

Amazing.

Also unsettling. Madi was playing in the big girls' sandbox now with Tate, and she was going to get hurt. Nothing to be done about that though, so she got up and got ready for her workday. When she went to the closet for her white nurses' shoes, she pulled them out, then sniffed, wrinkling her nose, then scowling at the cat. "Oh, no, you didn't."

Violet sat in the middle of the bed, daintily washing her face. She had no comment.

"You *pooped* in my shoe?"

Violet gave her a don't-come-home-late-again look, then continued grooming herself, completely unconcerned about ramifications because they both knew there wouldn't be any.

Madi cleaned up the mess, then grabbed her phone off the nightstand and headed out to her car.

Her brother stood in her driveway with her car hood open, frowning. "Who did your alternator?"

"No one." Madi frowned. "What are you doing? You said you were busy."

"And now I'm not. I picked up a used one for you this morning, but someone beat me to it."

"What?" She peeked at the thing he pointed at, the one shiny, clean part of the whole engine.

"Brand new too," Jack Jr. said.

Her mind flashed back to finding Tate in her driveway in the middle of the night. She'd never questioned his reasons for being there, figuring it had been about sex. But she got a little warm fuzzy now knowing it hadn't been *all* about sex.

Madi drove to work smiling. She parked and went into the ER.

Five minutes into her shift, Judith called her into her office and laid a piece of paper on her desk, a receipt for ten grand. "Anonymous donation for HSC."

"Wow." Madi sank into a spare chair. "Am I looking at all those zeros correctly?"

"Yes. Well done."

Madi glanced at her boss again, astonished. "How do you know I had anything to do with this?"

Judith smiled. "Because without you there would be no free clinic."

The words rang through Madi's head for the next few hours as she dealt with her patients. Tate was working today too. She saw him several times with the regular ambulance crew when they brought in a new case. First up was a bad case of food poisoning. Then a teenager who'd let her new tattoo get infected. And a woman who was eight months pregnant and ate a jar of pickles, putting herself into labor with gas pains.

They didn't have time to talk though, since Madi was pretty much run ragged for the rest of the day until there was finally a lull in the afternoon. She used the rare quiet time to sit at the nurses' station and catch up on charting.

"Madi!"

She looked up to find one of her regular patients, Jodi Larson, beaming from ear to ear. Jodi was ten, a leukemia patient, and one of Madi's all-time favorite people. She'd been upstairs to the oncology department for her six-month check and based on the smile also on Jodi's mom's face, the news had been good.

"Officially in remission," Jodi said proudly.

Her mom's eyes shone bright as she nodded affirmation of the good news. Thrilled, Madi hugged them both tight, and Jodi presented her with a plate of cookies. "Chocolate chip and walnut. I baked them just for you."

They hugged again. Before Madi could say much else, she got paged—by her own mother.

"Madison." Her mother dragged Madi into a far, quiet corner of the staff break room. "Are you still seeing that man?"

Lucille walked by in her volunteer uniform. "I hope so. Tate Griffin's the hottest thing you've dated since…well, ever. And it's about time Madi stops being the one everyone depends on and finds someone to depend on herself."

Her mother stared at Madi for a long beat, looking stricken. "Is that what this is about?"

Before Madi could answer, Lucille said, "Your next patient's ready for you."

Mr. Martin. Again.

"You," he said when Madi entered his room.

"Me," she agreed and reached for the blood pressure cuff. "Your chart says you passed out after your bath today. Did you take your meds at the right time?"

"I did. I'm not a complete idiot. They didn't work."

"Did you space them out with food, as explicitly instructed on the bottles?"

Mr. Martin glared at her.

"I'll take that as a no." The man's color was off, and his blood pressure was far too low. Both red flags for Madi. "When was your last meal?"

"Hmph."

"Mr. Martin." She put her fingers on the man's narrow, frail wrist to check his pulse. "Did you eat lunch today?"

He straightened in his bed, quivering with indignity. "I know what I'm supposed to be doing."

Madi glanced into his rheumy, angry eyes and her heart clenched. Her instincts said the real problem was the older man didn't have any food, and he probably wasn't feeling good enough to take care of himself, since he'd long ago scared off family and friends with his mean, petty, vicious ways. Madi picked up the phone attached to his bed rail and called the cafeteria. "I need a full dinner tray for trauma room three in the ER."

When the food came, Madi stood beside her grumpy patient. "Eat."

Mr. Martin tried to push it away, but Madi held it still this time. The man's eyes burned bright with temper, which she was happy to see because it meant he already felt better. She leaned closer. "I'm stronger, and *I've* eaten today."

"Well, *that's* obvious." Mr. Martin sniffed at the juice on the tray. "Hmph."

"It's apple."

"I have eyes in my head, don't I?" He sipped and within sixty seconds, his color improved. "You didn't used to be so mean. I'm ready to leave now."

"You can't go home until you eat."

"You're making that up. This cafeteria food isn't fit for a dog," Mr. Martin complained.

"Fine." Madi went to the staff kitchen, pulled out her own lunch and brought it back to the room. "Try my sandwich. Turkey and cheese with spinach. There's a little bit of mustard and probably too much mayo on it, but cholesterol is the least of your problems." Madi also tossed down a baggie of baby carrots and apple slices.

Mr. Martin took a bite of the sandwich first. "Awful," he said, but took another bite. Then another, until there was nothing left but a few crumbs.

"The carrot sticks too," Madi said.

"Are they as horrid as the sandwich?"

"They're as horrid as your bad attitude. And you will eat it all, even if I have to make you."

"Nurse Scott!" a shocked voice said from the doorway.

Judith. *Perfect.*

Madi turned, but not before she saw the evil glee in Mr. Martin's eyes. She jabbed a finger toward the carrots. Mr. Martin meekly picked one up.

In the hall, her boss led Madi out of hearing range of the patient. "What are you doing?"

"Trying a new tactic," Madi said, channeling her inner Tate. He was always so confident and assertive. It made her want to emulate that herself. "Did he finish it all?"

Judith went back to peer around the door, then returned, shaking her head and grinning. “Every bite.”

By the time Madi left work that day, she was starving and dead tired. She solved the first problem by eating a handful of Jodi’s cookies. Then she eyed the remaining ones before driving to Tate’s.

His garage door was open, and the man himself was flat on his back beneath his car, one long denim-clad leg straight out, the other bent. His black T-shirt had risen or maybe his Levi’s had sunk indecently low. Either way, the revealed strip of washboard abs and vee of muscle at his hips made her mouth water. She thought about standing there and watching him all night, but after the day she’d had, Madi couldn’t imagine he’d enjoy looking at her in return.

Not that Tate had ever said she looked anything other than beautiful. She was stymied. His attraction to her was apparently based on some intangible thing she couldn’t fathom. She couldn’t get used to the fact that no matter what she did or what she looked like, he seemed to want her. And the feeling was far too mutual.

CHAPTER SIXTEEN

TATE SAT UP on the mechanic's creeper and took in the sight of Madi standing there with a plate of cookies he hoped were for him.

All he could think about was her face down on his bed, boneless and sated with bliss. He'd stroked the damp hair from her face, and she'd smiled in her sleep. His heart had constricted at her arrival, and he'd thought, *Christ, I am in trouble.*

He'd been torn by the urge to tug her close and the urge to retreat. In the end, it hadn't been his choice at all because she'd awakened and gotten dressed to go. He'd followed her home to make sure she got there safely, then driven back to his place and missed her.

Clearly, he was losing it.

He had no idea what she was thinking now, but he hadn't expected her to smile at the sight of him, a smile filled with…

Relief, he realized, and surprise that he was still here.

Yeah, join the club. He was surprised, too.

She still had on her purple scrubs and white Nikes from the ER. She had two pens sticking out of her hip pocket, one red, one black, with corresponding ink marks on the material. She followed his gaze and sighed. "I'm a mess. Don't ask."

"Not a mess," he said. "Are those cookies?"

"Yes. And I had to fight off the staff to keep them for you."

She crouched at his side, holding the plate out for him. He took a big bite of one and moaned in deep appreciation.

"Did you give the HSC ten thousand dollars?" she asked.

He'd hoped she wouldn't find out, but that was unrealistic in a town like Wyckford. Taking his time, Tate ate cookie number two, then reached for a third, but she snatched the treats away.

"Did you?"

He eyed her for a long moment. "Which answer will get me the rest of the cookies?"

Madi looked worried as she lowered the plate for him again. "You already gave a donation."

"Your clinic needs it, right?" he asked around another bite.

"But it's *so* much money."

"Don't worry. I can afford it." She just stared at him, so he shrugged and continued. "I can. I get good pay from the Air Force, plus disability from the accident. I'm thrifty and I save."

Madi huffed, then kissed his cheek, but he turned his head and caught her mouth with his. They were both gratifyingly out of breath by the time they pulled apart.

"Thank you," Madi whispered.

"You're welcome," Tate said, as she rose and went to sit on the stool at his workbench.

"Don't let me keep you from what you were doing. I'll watch."

He arched a brow at her, surprised. "You want me to get back under the car?"

"Absolutely."

Humoring them both, he lay back down onto the mechanic's creeper and rolled back beneath the chassis. Tate heard Madi get to her feet and walk closer, peering into the opened hood above him as she said, "There was another board meeting today at the hospital. They approved making your position permanent on the paramedic flight crew."

She was as see-through as glass. Which in hindsight made her a hell of lot more dangerous than he'd thought. "Yeah? Good for them."

She squatted at his side. "Sounds like the perfect job for you."

Her hand settled on his bad thigh. It'd been only recently that he'd even gotten more sensation back in it, but he was having no trouble feeling anything now. An odd mix of anxiety and anticipation flooded his system. He didn't like where this was going.

"I know Brock gave them your name to consider," she said. "I told Bud you have my vote too."

That had him setting down his wrench and pulling himself back out from beneath the car. Madi was still crouched low as he frowned up into her face. "Why?"

"Because you're probably the most qualified person I know. And if you wanted choices then—"

"I don't want choices. I'm going back to the Air Force."

Madi went still, staring at him with those eyes he'd never been able to resist. "You don't have to."

He met her expressive gaze and felt a stab of pain right in the gut. He'd survived pararescue training. He'd lived through a plane crash. He'd kept on breathing when the rest of his team and the victims they'd been sent to save hadn't done the same. But he didn't know how to do this. "I can't do this, Madi. I'm sorry."

"Why?" she asked in disbelief. "Because you've never explained it to me."

Well, hell.

Chalk it up to the panic now fizzing through his veins like sparklers. Whatever he did here, whatever he came up with, he needed her to want to keep her distance. Except Madison Scott was incapable of distance when her heart was involved. That was both painfully attractive and terrifying. "Madi, I was up-front with you from the start about me and about all this being temporary. I'm not a good fit for you or for that job. Trust me."

She sucked in a breath like he'd slapped her. "So, what? You'll just keep running back to the Air Force for the rest of your life?"

"Maybe."

Madi stared at him, then turned away again.

Tate rose to his feet and walked around to see her face. "C'mon. Let's finish this."

With a sigh, Madi shook her head and put a finger to her twitching eye. "Dammit," she muttered, then looked up at him. "Don't you get lonely, being on your own all the time?"

"But I'm not alone. Not with you around, anyway," he said, and made her laugh.

"Stop it," she said. "This isn't funny."

He drew her closer. "Done being mad at me?"

"Yes."

"Good." Tate knew he had no right to touch her, crave her like air, but he did. And when he kissed her, tasted her, he knew she'd been made for him. Which meant he was far more screwed than he'd even imagined.

But suddenly Madi pulled free, shaking her head. "Tate—stop. I can't. I can't do this and keep it…not real."

"It's real."

"Yes, but real for you means sex with no strings. Real for me means…" She rubbed her chest as if it hurt, then closed her eyes. "Never mind." She took a step back and then another. "I'm sorry, this is my fault. I shouldn't have—"

"Madi—"

"No, it's okay. I'm going now."

Tate watched her get into her car and drive off and knew it was time to make that call to the Air Force. Past time.

CHAPTER SEVENTEEN

AFTER A SLEEPLESS NIGHT, Madi worked a long shift, then took a detour home by Mr. Martin's house. Last night the HSC had hosted a healthy living seminar given by a local dietician, and he'd promised to go. But when she'd looked over the sign-in sheet from the event this morning, Mr. Martin's name wasn't on it.

She pulled into the older man's driveway and saw the neglected yard and house. The bad feeling in the pit of her stomach grew. Madi got out of her car, grabbed the bag of groceries she'd picked up for him and knocked at the front door.

No one answered.

Madi tried again, but something felt off. She wriggled the handle and the door opened. "Mr. Martin?" she called. "It's me, Madison Scott."

"Go away!" a feeble, yet somehow still arrogant, voice called.

Ignoring the command, Madi walked inside the dark house, flipped on the lights and saw Mr. Martin sprawled on the wooden floor at the base of a set of stairs. She dropped everything and rushed to the older man's side. "You got dizzy and fell down the stairs?"

"No, I like to nap here," Mr. Martin snapped. "I told you to go away. You have no right to be here."

Okay, so at least he was conscious, with no obvious disorientation. Probably vasovagal syncope then. Madi checked his limbs quickly and found nothing obviously broken. "Can you stand?"

"Sure. I just chose to be the rug today. Why the hell are you here? Don't you ever get tired of saving people?"

"And miss your charming wit and sweet nature?" Madi retorted. "Never. Can you sit up for me?"

Mr. Martin slapped Madi's hands away but didn't move.

Question answered. Madi sat on the floor next to him as she called an ambulance, then rifled through the bag of groceries she'd brought. "While we wait for the EMTs to arrive, how about a snack? I bought soup, or I could make you a sandwich, or—"

"Go away! I'm old. I'm alone. I'm going to die any second now. Just *let me*. Why did you have to call the EMS? Do you have any idea how expensive that is?"

"I do. And I called because you need help. I can't move you myself. Also, you're not that old," Madi said. "You're just mean. And *that's* why you're alone. You could have friends if you'd stop snapping at everyone. Lucille would take you into her posse in an instant if you were even the slightest bit less evil. She *loves* snark."

"I'm *alone*."

"You have me," Madi said. She pulled out a kid's box of apple juice and shoved the attached straw through the foil-covered hole in the front. "Here. Drink this. It's your favorite."

"Not thirsty."

"Then how about I make you some chicken soup?"

A slight spark of life came into Mr. Martin's eyes. "Is it from a can?"

"No," Madi said, her tone dripping with sarcasm. "I spent all day cooking it myself. After raising the chickens and growing the carrots and celery in my garden. What do you think?"

The older man sniffed disdainfully. "I don't eat food from a can."

"Fine." Madi pulled out a bag of prunes as sirens wailed in the distance.

He snatched it from her and opened it with shaking fingers.

Madi smiled.

"You're enjoying my misery?"

"I knew I'd get you with the prunes."

After a minute or two, with the sugar in his system, Mr. Martin glared as the ambulance pulled up in the driveway. "I'd have been fine without you."

"Sure. You'd be even better if you took care of yourself."

"What do you know? You're not taking care of yourself either."

"What does that mean?"

"The *boyfriend.*" He said the last word like a curse. Mr. Martin gave her a snide stare as the ambulance crew, including Tate of course, rushed inside with their medical packs and gear. Tate looked at Mr. Martin, then Madi, a brow raised. Mr. Martin continued. "Yes, I heard about you two at the auction."

Good Lord.

While Madi prepped the older man's arm to insert an IV, Tate checked his vitals, not missing a beat as he said, "I'm not her boyfriend."

Madi bit her lip and cleaned up the mess she'd made when she'd dropped the bag of groceries.

Mr. Martin sneered at her. "So, you're giving away the milk for free then?"

"First of all, I'm not a cow," Madi snapped back. "And second of all, we're *not* discussing this."

"Vitals good. BP's normal, O2 sats normal, pulse good,"

Tate said, slinging his stethoscope back around his neck. "Do you have pain anywhere, Mr. Martin?"

"Besides my butt from dealing with you people?" the older man growled. "Leave me alone! Ow!"

"Can't do that, Mr. Martin," Tate said. "IV in. Let me put on a cervical brace just in case, then we'll get him on the gurney."

"I don't want a brace or a gurney! Which part of 'get out' don't you people understand?"

When no one responded to his nastiness, Mr. Martin seemed to refocus his efforts on Madi as Tate put on his neck brace. Then together with his EMT partner, Tate hoisted the man up and onto the gurney they'd rolled into the room when they came in. Mr. Martin narrowed his gaze on Madi as he was buckled in. "I know what you're trying to do, missy," he snarled, his gaze darting to Tate, then returning to Madi. "You're trying to save him. Like you try to save everyone. But even you must realize he isn't interested in settling down with a small-town nurse, not for the long term."

The jab hit a little close to home because it was true.

Am I trying to save him? Because I couldn't save Karrie?

"Watch it," Madi said, deflecting. "Or the prunes stay with me."

"Hmph."

It took a few more minutes for Tate and the other EMT to roll Mr. Martin out to the ambulance. Madi followed them to the door. The older man's vitals were stronger now, which was good because Lucille, who'd apparently walked up from Sunny Village a few doors down, joined them.

The elderly woman stepped inside the rig, her eyes on Mr. Martin. "Luther, are you all right?"

The oddest thing happened. Right before Madi's eyes, Mr. Martin seemed to soften a bit. Even...*smile.* Or at least that's what Madi thought the baring of his teeth meant.

Mr. Martin flushed and looked away. "I'm fine."

"Liar." Lucille moved in beside his gurney. "You get dizzy again?"

"Of course not."

"Luther?"

"Maybe a little," Mr. Martin said sheepishly. "But only for a minute."

Lucille nodded to Madi. "I'm glad you checked on him then. He doesn't make it easy I know. But we take care of our own here in Wyckford, even the prickly ones."

Madi smiled, knowing Lucille was right. Then she gave Mr. Martin a pointed stare. "It's good to know he's not *alone*."

The older man rolled his eyes, but shockingly not a single mean thing crossed his lips.

Lucille had on a neon green tracksuit that clashed horribly with her pink lipstick and her black-and-yellow tennis shoes. Madi practically needed sunglasses to look at her.

Mr. Martin narrowed his gaze. "You can leave, Lucille. These people insist on taking me to the hospital."

"Then I'm coming too." Lucille smiled.

Tate gave Madi one last unreadable look as he closed the doors on the rig. Then they took off, lights and sirens going.

Madi went home and unlocked her front door. She glanced at the little foyer desk—where she and Tate had made love—and sighed.

Meow.

"I hear you." She fed Violet, then glared at her foyer desk, telling it, "This is your fault."

The table had nothing to say in its defense.

She ached for Tate with her whole mind and body.

Madi showered and changed, then headed over to the Buzzy Bird, needing an immediate infusion of chocolate cake. As she entered the diner, the comforting sounds of people talking and laughing washed over her, and her stomach growled.

With everything that had happened with Mr. Martin, she'd missed dinner. Cassie was there too, alone. Madi knew Brock was working a shift in the ER that night. She slipped into the booth and eyed the empty spot on the table in front of her. "You not eating?"

"Nah. I'll eat with Brock later," Cassie said, her cheeks pink.

Madi's teeth ached. She was so happy for her friend and so sad for herself. She'd made a horrible mess of things with Tate.

Then Luna appeared, holding a slice of cake so dark it was almost black, and three forks.

"Five customers have already tried to buy this from me, so you're welcome." After locking the door, Luna returned and sat with a sigh. "God, it feels good to get off my feet. This day has been nuts. They repaired all the damage from the storm, but now the sprinkler system in here has been acting wonky. The men have been out a couple times to look at it, but so far, they haven't pinpointed the problem yet. Like strange noises from the pipes and stuff. It's weird."

Madi didn't respond. She was still too busy stuffing her face.

Luna frowned at her. "What's wrong?"

"Nothing." Madi shrugged.

Not letting her off the hook that easy, Luna continued to push. "Something's wrong. I can tell."

Cassie sipped her water, then asked Madi, "Trouble in paradise?"

"No." She finally set her fork down, unable to eat another bite. "Tate and I… It was just fun. That's all."

"Really?" Cassie asked. "Because it looked like more than fun to me."

Madi sighed, then shook her head. "I don't want to talk about it."

"But we *do*." Luna smiled. "C'mon. Maybe we can help."

"It was a fling. That's all. That's what we agreed on from the start. But then I took it too far..." She bit her bottom lip. "You guys know I'm not hardwired for that. I like strong and stable. But there's something about Tate. I know he's leaving. I know this thing between us is only temporary. But every time we are together, I want..." She closed her eyes. "More."

"Sweetie." Cassie squeezed Madi's hand.

Luna put an arm around Madi. "I'm so sorry. I tried to tell you."

Madi slumped forward. "I know. And I appreciate that. I do. I tried to follow your advice, but I couldn't keep things light. I tried, but... I think I love him and he's leaving and—"

Someone knocked on the door.

Madi looked over to see Tate and her traitorous heart clutched at the sight of him.

Their gazes held for an unfathomably long beat, and as always, she got a little thrill. He always seemed bigger than life, and a whole lot more than she could handle. Especially in his EMT uniform. But there was something different about him now. He looked weary and a little rough around the edges.

She loved him. And she missed him. Even though it had only been a few hours since they'd seen each other. Madi wanted to kiss away his problems. Hold him.

It made no sense because he was leaving. He'd been upfront and honest about that with her. And he'd take a big piece of her heart along with him when he went, but it was a done deal. Madi also knew she wanted whatever he had to give her in the meantime. Because with him, she wasn't Miss Goody Two-Shoes. She wasn't always thinking, planning, overseeing.

With Tate, she was just...*alive.*

He smiled, touching a finger to the glass.

"Sorry." Madi slid out of the booth, ignoring her gaping friends. "I have to go."

Outside, the stars were bright, like scattered diamonds on the velvet night sky. The waves from Buzzards Bay lapped against the shore in the distance. They walked along the pier in the chilly air, past the dark arcade and the closed shops. Past everything until there was nothing but emptiness and water ahead.

Madi stopped and leaned over the railing facing the bay. "I'm sorry about earlier," she said quietly. "Mr. Martin can be super mean." She sighed. "And I'm also sorry for seconding your name for that job without asking you first. I had no right to do that."

When Tate didn't answer, Madi searched his face in the shadows, hoping for understanding. Forgiveness. Or at the very least, a sign that he'd heard her.

She got nothing, and her heart sank.

After a minute, he leaned on the railing beside her to stare out at the water. "You said before you didn't understand my situation, why I am the way I am, because I never explained it to you. So, I want to tell you now." He took a deep breath before continuing. "After the accident, I was a mess. Saving lives is my job, it's my life. It's who I am. But after what happened with my team, I don't trust myself. Not completely."

She placed a hand on his arm. "Tate…"

"No. That night in the helicopter…" He hesitated. "It was my fault. Those people died because of my bad decision. I can't ever change that. I can't ever atone for it."

Madi waited a few beats, letting his words hang in the air, then drift away with the tide. "Tate, you may not want to hear this, but you're smart and strong and kind and generous. You protect people. You heal people. That's who you are. I trust you with my life. You don't have anything to atone for. That accident wasn't your fault."

He was quiet, seemingly absorbing that, then he turned to her and ran a finger over the infinity charm around her neck, looking at it in the moonlight. "I've spent the last four years believing that I didn't deserve comfort. Punishing myself, trying to pay for what I'd done." He let out a breath and dropped his hand from her. "I didn't want anyone close. Because I *can't* protect the people I care for, Madi. I tried with my team, with those victims in the ocean, and I failed."

She couldn't imagine what losing his team, his friends, the people he'd been sent to rescue must've been like for him, trapped out in the ocean, hurt and alone, grieving and helpless.

Or maybe she could. She'd felt much the same after she'd lost Karrie.

Madi held the charm in her hand and closed her eyes for a minute and pictured her sister's laughing eyes. "My sister gave me this the night she died. She told me we'd be forever connected because of it. She wore it all the time, and I always used to bug her to let me borrow it. I wanted to be just like her. It used to drive her nuts. Then, that last night, Karrie came to my room. She kissed my cheek and told me to be good, that being good would keep me out of trouble. She made me promise. Then she said she'd watch over me, guide my way, make sure I was okay." Her throat tightened painfully. "The next day they found her body."

Tate pulled Madi against him. She fisted her hands in his shirt as she cried. She was supposed to be comforting him here, but she was the one breaking down.

"I know you're hurting, but you're not alone, Tate," Madi managed to choke out against his chest. "And you're not responsible for the death of your team or the victims. You were in a terrible situation, and they made their choices. Please stop punishing yourself."

They stood like that, locked together, a light breeze blowing her hair around. A strand of it clung to the stubble on his jaw and Tate left it there, bound to her.

"How's Mr. Martin?" Madi asked at last.

"Doing well when I checked before leaving after my shift," Tate said.

He'd left a message at the Air Force recruitment office, but hadn't gotten a call back yet.

Madi finally lifted her head and looked at him. "I'm glad you're still here."

He held her gaze, his own steady. "For now." Then Tate pressed his forehead to hers. "You should walk away from me right now and avoid any more heartbreak. I'm not worth it. You deserve better."

Instead, she pushed him up against the railing and kissed him. Took full advantage of his surprise, opening her mouth over his, causing a rush of heat and the melting of all his bones. In less than a single heartbeat, Madi had stolen his breath and his heart.

"If the decision is mine to make," she said breathing hard, her voice utterly serious once she'd pulled back, "then I'm staying with you, for as long as I can have you."

CHAPTER EIGHTEEN

THE NEXT MORNING, Tate woke with a gloriously naked Madi sprawled over the top of him. He'd always valued his own space. He was a big guy and didn't like to feel crowded. Madi was half his size, and as it turned out, a bed hog. She was also a blanket hog and a pillow hog.

But that was okay. They'd made love again the night before, both knowing what this was and wasn't. Then they'd fallen asleep together. Didn't mean anything. If it happened again… well, *then* he'd panic. "Madi."

She snored softly, and his heart squeezed.

"Are you working today?"

He had one hand on her butt and squeezed lightly. She froze and jerked upright. "What time is it?"

"Seven." Tate nuzzled his face in her crazy hair.

"*Seven?*" Madi leapt out of the bed, frantically searching for her clothes.

Enjoying the show, Tate leaned back, hands behind his head, as he grinned.

"Where are my panties?" she demanded.

"Under the chair."

She reached for them, giving him an amazing view that made him groan.

"Not here!" she yelled; her voice muffled from her position.

"No? Check beneath my jeans then," he said.

She straightened, blowing the hair out of her face, her gaze narrowed on him.

He smiled.

She crawled there, another hot view, and snatched her panties, then disappeared into the bathroom. Five minutes later she reappeared, freshly showered and dressed, looking thoroughly flustered.

"Come here," he said, waggling his fingers at her.

"No. If I come over there, we'll never get out of this bedroom."

"True." He laughed, feeling lighthearted and...*happy.* "I want to put my mouth on your—"

"Stop." She shook her head and grabbed her keys, her still-wet hair pulled back into a sloppy braid. "I have to go!"

"Come on," he said. "It'll be the best part of your day, I promise."

She hesitated, biting her lower lip, looking tempted, then rushed to the door. "Bye."

Tate stayed there for a while after Madi left. Then his phone beeped. Rolling out of bed, he accessed his messages and saw one from the recruitment office. That one could wait for later. The next was from Mr. Ryan.

"Hey, man," the vet said. That was it, the full extent of the message. It could mean anything from "let's have dinner" to "I'm jonesing for a fix and need someone to talk to."

There were two others as well. One from Mark looking for a gym partner and another from Brock asking if he'd given any more thought to the flight crew job.

Tate stared at his phone, realizing that while he'd been busy trying to keep to himself in this slow-paced, sleepy little town he'd made ties to people, connections he hadn't known were there.

He got up and showered, then got dressed. After running

some errands, he called in to the ambulance service for his updated schedule, then worked on the Chevelle for a while. By the time he was done in the garage, it was past dinner time. Too late to call back the recruitment office, so he drove into Wyckford, thinking he'd stop by and see Mr. Ryan at the half-way house and take food from the café. But as he passed the hospital, he saw Madi through the glass and before he knew what he was doing, he'd pulled into the lot and parked. Tate got out of the Chevelle and walked into the empty clinic lobby. From the hallway, he heard voices from the open exam room door—Madi talking to whoever was in there with her.

From outside, he'd seen her purple scrubs. It was a good color for her. Her hair was still in the braid, but a few strands had escaped over the hours they'd been apart. He inched down the hall a bit more to get a better look at her. She wasn't good at hiding her feelings, and right now she looked on edge, tired and frustrated.

A long day, no doubt made longer because they'd spent most of the night tearing up his sheets. Tate still couldn't say he regretted it, and he knew exactly what he'd do to relax her, but he had to remind himself she wasn't his to take care of. By his own choice.

Once he talked to the recruitment office and his reenlistment paperwork was filed, he'd be out of Wyckford in no time. Then Madi would stay up all night with someone else. Someone who'd take care of her, help her unwind at the end of the day. Someone not him.

And whoever she chose, he had nothing to say about it, because it was none of his business.

But it still sucked.

"Just trust me," she was saying to the patient in the room with her, pulling a set of keys from her pocket and opening the medicine cabinet, eyeing the samples there before grabbing a box. "Take these. One a day."

"What are you poisoning me with now?" the man asked. Tate recognized his voice. Mr. Martin.

"Vitamins," Madi said.

Mr. Martin took the samples. "Vitamins are a sham. A way for the drug companies to make money off us unsuspecting idiots."

She crossed her arms. "Your bloodwork after your fall shows you're anemic. These will help. Or you can keep passing out and waiting until EMS finds you on the floor again. Your choice."

A long silence followed. Then Mr. Martin said, "You used to be afraid of me. You used to tremble like a child."

"Things change." Madi's tone was mild. No judgment, no recriminations. "Take the vitamins. Don't make me come over every night and make you take them."

"Well, if you're going to out-mean me."

"I am," Madi said firmly. "I don't want to be mean to you, but if that's what it takes for you to take care of yourself, then that's what I'll do."

Turning from Mr. Martin, Madi caught sight of Tate standing there. Her surprised smile only added to the ache inside him, but he nodded and stepped back, leaning against the wall to wait.

She looked at her patient once more. "I have something else for you—hold on." She came out into the hall, shutting the door behind her. She flashed Tate another smile, then vanished into the next room. When she returned, Madi handed Mr. Martin a flyer before guiding him from the clinic.

A few minutes later she returned to Tate. "Hey."

"Hey." He hiked his chin toward the lobby. "You should lock the front door when you're alone."

"I wasn't alone, and this is Wyckford. I'm as safe as it gets."

"Not with that medicine cabinet you're not. Someone could break in. Someone desperate."

"It's only temporary. We're getting a much better setup next week." She smiled, still not taking her safety seriously enough for Tate. "What brings you here?"

"I was on my way to see Mr. Ryan," he said. "Are you done for the night?"

"I am."

"Good. Then I'm going to collect on a favor."

Madi sputtered, then laughed. "What exactly *is* this favor?"

He pushed off the wall and came toward her. "I need the same thing you needed the night of the auction. A date."

"To the halfway house?"

"No. I just remembered I have other plans tonight." He brought her hand to his mouth, brushing his lips against her palm as he watched her over their joined fingers. "Say yes, Madi."

Staring at him, she cupped his face. "Always."

His heart rolled, exposing its underbelly. He was equipped to deal with emergencies, to serve. Not to love.

Never to love.

Madi had no idea what his plans were. Tate had made some phone calls before they'd left the clinic, but she hadn't been able to hear anything and he wouldn't tell her where they were going. Now on the highway, heading toward Boston. Once there, he drove to a block lined with designer boutiques and parked.

He pulled her out of the car and into a dress shop. "Something for the theater," he said to the pretty saleswoman who came forward. Then he turned to Madi. "Whatever you want."

Confused, she asked, "Whatever I want? I don't even know what we're doing here."

"The night on the town package from the auction. Tonight's the last night of the orchestra. I thought you could use a night off." He looked endearingly baffled. "Don't women like romantic surprises?" For the first time since Madi had known him, Tate looked uncomfortable in his own skin. "You're right. This was a stupid idea. Let's go get a pizza and beer. Whatever you want."

Madi knew he was far more at ease in the role of tough guy than romance guy and he'd probably certainly have preferred pizza and beer over the orchestra. And yet he'd thought of her. He'd wanted to give her a night off, even if it was last minute, and he'd brought her to a place filled with gorgeous, designer clothes so she wouldn't stress about what to wear. Madi also knew, deep down, that this was goodbye. But she wanted this. With him. She went on tiptoe to whisper, "Thank you."

Tate claimed her mouth in one quick, hot kiss. "Take your time. I'll be waiting."

He walked out the front door and drove away in the Chevelle.

She stared after him. "That man is crazy."

"Crazy *fine*," the salesclerk murmured, then gestured around them. "What would you like to try on?"

Thirty minutes later, Madi was decked out in a silky siren-red dress that made her feel like a sex kitten. She tried to see the price tag, but the clerk had hidden it. "He said you weren't allowed to look at the prices."

Good Lord.

By the time Madi exited the shop, she felt like Cinderella. And her prince stepped out of the Chevelle to greet her in a well-fitted, expensive tux that nearly made her trip over her new strappy high heels. She'd seen Tate in a suit before at the auction. Since then, she'd seen him in jeans, in his uniform and in nothing at all. He always looked mouthwateringly gorgeous. But tonight… "Wow."

He took her hand and pulled her in. "You take my breath away."

That's when Madi realized he was looking at her differently. Heart-stoppingly so.

Dinner was at a French restaurant so amazing she started to regret not going one size up on the dress. But the wine quickly reduced any lingering anxiety. The problem was, combined with a long day at work and almost no sleep the night before, her eyes were drooping by the time they got to the orchestra. Still, she accepted another glass of Zinfandel as they found their seats. The curtain went up.

And that's the last thing Madi remembered.

When she woke, the theater was quiet, and Tate leaned over her with an amused smile.

"What?" She blinked, confused.

His smile spread to a grin. "You snore."

"Do not!" She straightened, staring at the empty stage and the few people left around them. "It's over? I missed the whole thing?"

He pulled her to her feet. "That's okay. You didn't miss the best part."

"What's that?"

"Wait for it." He drove them home and after they walked into her house, Tate slowly stripped Madi out of her new dress and bra and panties, groaning at the sight of her in just the heels.

"You are the most beautiful woman I've ever seen." He carried her to the bed. "I know how tired you are, so let me take care of you for a change."

"I'm not tired," she said. "I took a very nice nap at the orchestra."

With a soft laugh, he crawled up her body, kissing and nipping as he went. “I’m offering to do all the work here. And I’m ready for the best part.”

“What’s that?” she panted against his cheek.

He gently bit her lower lip and tugged, then soothed the ache with his tongue, making every single nerve ending in her body beg for more. “You. You’re the best part.”

Her heart caught. “Me?”

“Always,” he breathed, then set about proving it.

CHAPTER NINETEEN

THE NEXT AFTERNOON, Madi was in the ER doing her damnedest not to dwell on the fact Tate would probably be leaving town soon. She was just checking in a patient who'd been brought in after breaking up a fight when a call came in from Camilla.

"I'm at the clinic," the young nurse said. "And we have a problem."

She finished up with her patient, then hurried over to the old west wing. "What's wrong?"

Camilla showed her the medicine lockup. "Four boxes of OxyContin are missing."

Madi's heart sank. "What?"

"A month's supply."

"What?" She stared at the cabinet in shock.

"Yeah. I was just closing after the teen advocacy meeting when I found it like this. I called Judith already." Camilla looked a bit sheepish. "I didn't want to cause problems for you, but I also didn't want to not report it, then have it come out later and for anyone to think I tried to cover it up. I never even got into the lockup today at all."

"No. It's fine. You did the right thing." Madi nodded even as her mind raced. If Camilla hadn't been in the lockup today, that meant the last person in there had been Madi yesterday when *she'd* been in charge. She remembered getting into the locked storage cabinet several times for different patients—once for birth control samples and another time for smoker's patches. And then for Mr. Martin's vitamins. A tight feeling spread through her chest. There were only two reasons to take OxyContin.

To sell or to use. Stealing them was an act of desperation, and addicts were desperate.

Karrie had been desperate too, and Madi had failed her.

Who else am I failing now?

She returned to the ER heartsick and found herself almost immediately summoned to Bud Lofton's office. When she arrived, several board members were there, including Judith and her mother, waiting.

"How could this have happened?" Bud asked, his tone stern.

Madi took a deep breath. "We received samples early yesterday for the weekend health clinic, as usual. I stocked the cabinet myself and locked it afterward."

"Exactly how much is missing?" Judith asked.

She had to have already known. Camilla had told her she'd called their boss and reported it. "Four boxes. Each one is a week's supply. So, a month total."

She'd gone over the inventory a hundred times in her head, hoping she'd just miscalculated.

She hadn't.

Someone had stolen those meds from right under Madi's nose. An anguished, distraught, frantic act, by a person she most likely knew by name because everyone knew everyone else in Wyckford.

"We'll need a list of who came through the clinic yesterday for the police," Bud said.

This was what she'd dreaded. "But the patient rosters for the clinic are supposed to be anonymous."

"I know, but this is out of our hands now. I'm sorry," Judith said. "The list, Madison. By tomorrow morning at the latest."

"Please. I can fix this," Madi begged. "Let me—"

"The only way to fix this now is by trusting the police to do their jobs," Bud said. "This is a legal matter now. A felony has been committed and that puts the entire hospital under a huge burden of liability. Understand?"

"Of course. But—"

"No buts, Madi." Bud cut her off. "Don't put your job on the line as well by making this more difficult."

Her heart lurched, and she ground her teeth to avoid saying something she'd regret later.

"And until this is resolved," Judith added, looking regretful, "the clinic stays closed."

Another stab to Madi's gut. "Understood."

Somehow, she managed to get through the rest of her shift. All she wanted to do was get home and be alone, but her mother caught her in the parking lot. "What's going on here?"

Madi frowned. "What do you mean?"

"Honey, you're the most conscientious person I know. I don't believe for a second that you don't have some idea of who's behind this. Why won't you tell them?"

"Mom, I honestly don't know who took those drugs. Your guess is as good as mine. I just want to leave now, okay?"

Her mother looked deep into Madi's eyes, then shook her head. "Madi, this isn't your fault."

"Really?" She pulled free and opened her car door. "Because the hospital board seems to think it is. Someone has to take the fall, and since I'm in charge of the clinic, I guess that person will be me."

"Unless you can find out who took the pills."

Exhaustion took over and Madi slammed the door, then leaned back against it, all the emotions she'd buried earlier rushing to the surface and overwhelming her. "I don't know what happened yesterday, but it *was* my fault. The board is right. I allowed that to happen on my watch. But what bothers me even more is the fact that someone I know is in trouble and I can't help them." A sob choked her, shutting off her words, and Madi slapped a hand over her mouth. "I hate feeling helpless like this. It reminds me of what happened to Karrie. I didn't know she was floundering so badly, Mom. How did I not know?"

"Oh, honey," her mother said, pulling Madi into a hug. "You should have talked to me about this. None of what happened with Karrie was your fault. None."

Madi buried her face against her mother's shoulder. "I just keep thinking that if I'd cared more, done more, she wouldn't have..."

"Honey, listen to me," her mother said fiercely, pulling back to look in Madi's eyes. "You were sixteen. None of what happened was your fault. It wasn't anyone's fault. It took me a lot of years and heartache to realize that and if I can save you the same trouble I will. You are not responsible for other people's actions, Madi. Understand?"

Madi let out a shaky breath. "But I still feel like I failed her. And now with this situation, I don't want to make the same mistake, Mom. I can't let anyone else fall through the cracks like she did. That's why I work so hard. That's why I started the clinic. To help people like Karrie. To make up for not being able to save her."

Her mother pulled her close again and whispered against the top of Madi's head, "Sometimes people must do for themselves. Find their own will, their own happy. Their own path. You can support them with that, but you can't do it for them, honey. You know that."

Madi sniffled in response. She *did* know that, deep down.

She'd just forgotten with everything that had happened. And regardless of why she'd started the clinic, it was a part of her now. A vital one she wanted to keep going. She pulled back and gave her mother a weepy smile. "Thanks for the pep talk, Mom. But I'm willing to fight for the clinic and whoever took those drugs because they need help. That was a desperate act, not a malicious one. This is my hill to die on."

A beat or two passed before her mother gave a reluctant nod of understanding.

Afterward, Madi got into her car and drove straight to Tate's house.

He didn't answer her knock. The place was quiet. Empty. She put a hand to her chest, knowing last night had been a goodbye. For a minute, she panicked. Would he really disappear without a word?

Frustrated and annoyed, mainly with herself, she went home, intending to get into bed and tug the covers over her head and have a good, long cry. She dropped her keys on the foyer table, then kicked off her shoes in the hallway and walked into her bedroom as she struggled to pull her scrub top off over her head. But it caught in her hair and pulled painfully. "Dammit!"

She stood there arms up, face covered by scrubs, when two strong arms enveloped her.

Madi gave a startled scream before she was gathered against a familiar warm, hard chest. "Tate?"

He chuckled. "Expecting someone else?"

"I wasn't expecting anyone at all. Please help me get this shirt off."

Instead, he slid a thigh between hers.

"*Tate...*" She squirmed and only succeeded in getting herself tangling up more and cursing a blue streak as a result.

Laughing, Tate finally freed her from the offending garment

and tossed it over his head while still pressing her against the door. "Where'd you learn such filthy words?"

"Just because I live in a small town doesn't mean I'm sheltered," Madi said, not in the mood to play.

"Got it." His voice sounded dark and edgy tonight. Apparently, he wasn't feeling playful either. A chord of need struck deep inside her despite the awful day. "I've been looking for you."

Her heart yearned to let him take all her worries and woes away. In the back of her mind, an image of that empty Vicodin bottle from his pocket flashed before she dismissed it entirely. Tate wouldn't do that to her. He was a paramedic. A medical professional just like her. Never mind the statistics that said ten to fifteen percent of health-care professionals would abuse drugs in their lifetimes. Tate was a good man, an honorable man. He'd been clean for three years. Yes, he'd been through tough times recently, but hadn't they all? He wouldn't do it. Didn't do it. She believed that to the bottom of her soul.

They could discuss it later. Right now, their time together was limited. Too limited. Between kisses, she said, "I want you."

In the shadows, his eyes gleamed with heat and intent. She kissed him again, swallowing his rough groan, savoring the taste of him, done with waiting. "My bed. Now."

They staggered farther into the room and fell onto her mattress.

"Take the rest off too," he demanded right back in that quiet voice that made Madi go weak in the knees. She unhooked her bra and wriggled out of her panties, then got distracted by watching him strip. Tate tugged his EMS uniform shirt over his head. His hands went to his fly, his movements quick and economical as he bared his gorgeous body. In two seconds, he was naked, one hundred percent of his attention completely fixed on her as he put on a condom. And apparently, she was moving too slowly because he took over, wrapping his fingers around each of her ankles, giving a hard tug so she fell flat on her back. He was on her in a heartbeat. “All day while I was working, all I could see was you.”

She slid her hands down his sinewy, cut torso, planning on licking that same path as soon as she got a chance. “Yeah?”

“Oh, yeah,” he said silkily. “You’ve had me in a state all day, Madison Scott.”

The air crackled with electricity, and he kissed her again. His touch as demanding as his mouth, his hands finding her breasts, teasing her nipples, sliding between her legs. She was ready for him. He groaned and pushed inside her with one hard thrust. “You feel amazing.”

Madi felt him to the depths of her soul. She wrapped her arms around his broad shoulders and melted into the hard planes of his body. Emotion welled within her, and she bit her lip closed to hold in the words that wanted to escape.

She stared up into his eyes, her heart aching. His hands slid up to her hips, positioning her exactly as he wanted. Wrapping her legs around his waist, she whispered his name, needing him to move.

His fingers skimmed her spine, leaving a trail of heat she felt all the way to her toes, taking her exactly where she needed to go without words. And that was the point of no return for her. Tate was what she wanted, what she’d never had the nerve to reach out and grasp for herself before. He didn’t want her to depend on him, and yet he’d given her the security to be who she was. If only he’d stay.

It wouldn’t happen, she knew. So, she had to settle for this, for the right now.

* * *

Sometime in the night, Tate woke up wrapped in warm woman. He had one hand entangled in Madi's crazy hair, the other on her bare butt, holding her possessively to him.

Jesus.

If he stayed with her tonight, it would be a mistake, and Tate didn't make mistakes, much less the same one twice. With more effort than it should have taken, he finally managed to get out of bed without waking her. Gathered his things, he left her, quietly shutting the door behind him.

In the hallway, he dumped his stuff on the floor and started dressing, hesitating once to look back at the door. He wanted to go back in there.

Don't do it, man.

He reached for his shirt and realized it wasn't there and he also only had one sock. He stubbed his toe on his own shoe and swore softly, then kicked the thing down the hall.

Tate froze when the bedroom door opened, and the light came on.

Madi blinked sleepily at him, tousled and adorable wearing nothing but his missing shirt. "Everything okay?"

"Sorry. Didn't mean to wake you."

"Are you leaving?"

"Yeah, I… I'm going." He needed to. Before he couldn't leave Wyckford at all.

She looked down at his lone sock, the things that had spilled out of his pants pockets he hadn't picked up yet—his keys, his wallet, the empty Vicodin bottle.

She bent and picked that up, staring at the label on the meds for a long time—the three-year-old date of the prescription, the refills available to him which he'd never used. Finally, she handed the bottle back to him with a gentle smile. "Stay. Just tonight."

He couldn't. "Madi—"

But she covered his mouth with her fingers, took his hand, and drew him back into her bedroom, into her bed and into her warm, soft heart.

CHAPTER TWENTY

THE NEXT MORNING Tate and Mark went for a hike after the gym. They walked a well-worn trail until they reached a plateau about the size of a football field, with a decent view of Buzzards Bay in the distance.

"Good spot," Tate said.

"Lot of stupid teenagers come here." Mark shrugged. "Four-wheeling in Daddy's truck or messing around. Then they get lost, and we rescue them. Still beats fighting a fire in Chicago in high summer in full tactical gear though." He laughed, then stared out at the horizon. "You hear what happened at the clinic?"

Tate frowned.

"Someone stole Oxy samples from the locked cabinet."

Tate's gut tightened, remembering how Madi had studied the empty Vicodin bottle that had fallen out of his pocket. "When?"

Mark watched him carefully. "Not sure, but probably the night before. Police are still investigating."

The night he'd taken Madi to the orchestra. Which meant she'd known last night and hadn't said a word to him about it. He tried to think of a reason she wouldn't have mentioned the missing meds that didn't involve her thinking it was him but couldn't. Tate forced words past his constricted throat. "Is she in trouble?"

"The clinic's closed down until the cops find the perpetrator. And depending on what they find, it might stay that way. Madi accepted the blame, of course."

"How do you know all of this?"

"Because I'm the fire department rep on the hospital board." Mark eyed him. "Law enforcement wants a list of patients there on the day the pills went missing. Madi objected because the clinic's services are supposed to be anonymous. But the board wasn't happy with her decision, which puts her job as an ER nurse at risk too."

Christ. Tate let out a breath and closed his eyes. "I was there that night. At the HSC." He looked at Mark, then pulled out his phone only to see no bars of reception. "I need to go."

Without waiting to see if his friend followed, Tate started back down the trail toward his house. He needed to see Madi. Halfway home, he finally got a decent signal and dialed her number. She didn't answer.

Mark called to him from farther back. "I know where she is."

Tate looked back at him.

"At the diner with Luna and Cassie. I was there earlier because their sprinkler system was acting up again," Mark said. "Should be fine for now, but eventually they need to replace it."

They reached Tate's house and rather than going inside, he went directly to the garage and grabbed the keys to the Chevelle, climbing behind the wheel while Mark slid in the passenger side. They took off in a squeal of tires, heading for town.

A few minutes later, they parked in the Buzzy Bird's lot. The place was decorated for Thanksgiving with papier-mâché turkeys and pilgrim hats hanging from the ceiling tiles and streamers around the windows. It didn't match the fifties decor but was definitely eye-popping.

The noise level was high from the full breakfast crowd.

Tate recognized most of the faces now, which meant he'd been there far too long. Madi was at the counter, and he sidled past a small group of people waiting to be seated. Cassie sat beside her, and Luna stood behind the counter from them. As Tate got closer, he heard Luna ask, "What did your boss say when you quit?"

Oh, God.

"Not much really." Madi shrugged. "They were going to have to fire me anyway. Bud had no choice, so I just saved them the trouble."

"Wow," Cassie said. "I'm so sorry all this happened."

Madi let out a combination laugh-sob. "Me too."

"What are your plans now?" Luna asked. "We can always use more help around here, if you need something to keep you busy until you get another nursing job."

"I'm thinking I'll work for a quiet little doctor's office somewhere and forget about all this." Madi shook her head. "I don't want to talk about it right now, okay?"

Tate moved in beside Madi. "You'd wither up and die of boredom in a quiet little doctor's office."

Madi whirled on her stool to stare up at him, her eyes shining with unshed tears. Everyone in the diner froze, watching them. Except Luna, who stared at Mark as he took a seat at the counter to watch the circus.

Tate narrowed his eyes at all the nosy folks of Wyckford. No one took the hint. His glare used to terrorize people. But it hadn't worked for him in this town, not once. Giving up, he looked at Madi again. "Why didn't you tell me about the missing drugs?"

"Because I know that you didn't take them." Madi said.

"Excuse me," Lucille said from a nearby table. "Did someone take medicine from the clinic?"

Madi pinched the bridge of her nose. "Which part of private matter don't you understand, Lucille?"

The older woman blinked at her, apparently astonished. "Are you sassing me, Madison Scott?"

"No." Madi grimaced, then added politely, "But stay out of my business, *please*."

"All you had to do was ask, dear." Lucille smiled. "And I'm glad to see your backbone emerging. Looks great on you."

Madi stared at the older woman, then back at Tate who'd been rendered speechless.

Because I know you didn't take them.

Somehow, despite his best efforts, Madi knew him, inside and out, and accepted him. Faults and failures and all. And she'd believed in him, no questions asked.

This didn't really help now though since someone *had* taken the meds under her watch.

Tate could tell by looking at her that she *knew* who the responsible party was but didn't want to say. Even now she was still trying to save people. "If you know I didn't take the pills, then why didn't you turn over the list of people at the clinic to the police?"

Madi's temper ignited in her eyes. She stood and poked him in the chest with her finger, her cheeks flushed. "Because maybe you're not the only person I care about around here."

She still had on purple scrubs with a long-sleeved T-shirt beneath—*his* shirt if he wasn't mistaken. There was a mysterious lump of things in her pockets, and a red heart drawn on one of her white tennis shoes. Her hair was completely out of control, as usual, and she seemed ready to take down anyone who got in her path. She'd never looked more beautiful to him.

"Madi," Tate said, knowing how much her work meant to her. How much the clinic meant to her. How much Wyckford meant to her. "You quit your job."

In that moment, he made his decision. He'd take the fall, for her. He'd failed to save the people he cared for once before. He refused to fail again. "It's my fault," he said loud enough for all the eavesdroppers to hear. "I took advantage of you, Madi."

Two stools over, Mark groaned and shook his head. "Aw, man. Don't do it."

Madi scowled. "What are you doing?"

"Telling these folks what happened with the missing meds at the clinic," he said carefully.

"Hold it!" Mr. Martin moved in, jabbing his cane toward Tate. "Yeah, I'm talking to you, punk."

Punk? Tate stood a foot and a half taller than the old man and outweighed him by at least a hundred pounds. He stared down at Mr. Martin in shock.

Mark laughed. "Punk. I like it."

It'd been a long time since anyone had gotten in Tate's face, even longer since he'd been called a punk, and by the looks of him, Mr. Martin wasn't done with him yet.

"What the hell do you think you're doing?" the old man demanded.

"Confessing to a crime," Tate said.

Mr. Martin banged his cane onto the floor three times, then glared. "No! You have no right to confess to something you didn't do. You're trying to be the big hero, and you don't want her hurt." Apparently, he was sharper than he let on.

Madi looked up at Tate. "*Is* that what you're doing?"

Before he could respond, the older man rose to his full five-eight height and said, "It was me. *I* took the meds." He eyeballed the entire crowd in the diner. "Not this—" he gestured toward Tate with his cane "—*punk*. He didn't take the pills. That was me."

"No." A young woman stood from a table across the room.

The clerk from the grocery store. “It was me. I was at the clinic for birth control. *I* took them.”

“Liars.” This came from Mr. Ryan, at the far end of the counter. “We all know I have a problem. It was me.”

Madi gaped as the entire town rallied around her. Tate had never seen anything like it.

Luna wolf-whistled loud to get everyone’s attention. “Hey, I was there, too. I took the pills.”

Madi glanced at her friend. “You weren’t there—”

“Oh, no, you don’t!” Mr. Martin yelled. “Listen all you—egocentric, self-absorbed, narcissistic group of *insane* people. Don’t make me smack all of you!”

And with that, he pulled a small box from his pocket. A sample of OxyContin.

“See?” He held it up triumphantly. “I have them. I have them all. I took them because I thought they were for my constipation. It’s the same color. My insurance is crap, and even if it wasn’t, I hate to wait in line at the pharmacy!”

Before Madi could respond, a huge squeal sounded, followed by a *whoosh* as the overhead sprinkler system came on out of nowhere, raining down on the entire diner and everyone in it.

CHAPTER TWENTY-ONE

TOTAL CHAOS REIGNED as the sprinklers drenched the diner with icy water. People yelled and screamed, pushing and shoving to get out. Adding to the insanity, the decorations hanging from the ceiling soaked up the water and fell, pulling down the tiles with them. A papier-mâché turkey hit Madi on the head. She saw stars for a second. Someone would get seriously hurt in this mess. She blinked through the downpour to check the crowd for anyone needing assistance but could hardly see two feet in front of her through the frigid torrents. *Everyone* needed help. People were either running or down for the count. Utter mayhem.

Madi gulped a breath and swiped her wet hair out of her face. Her hand came away bloody. She was bleeding. Then she was grabbed and steamrollered her toward the door.

Tate.

"Forget me," she said, struggling against his steely grip. "Get Mr. Martin and Lucille!"

"You first." He dumped her outside, then went back in for more people.

Soon he returned with Mr. Martin and sat the old man down beside Madi on the curb. Lucille was nowhere to be seen though. Mark shoved Luna and Cassie out the door, then went back in for others alongside Tate.

She couldn't just sit there. She had to help. So, despite

Tate's wishes, she dove back into the chaos. The sprinklers still poured down water. Madi herded several more people outside before she ran into Tate again. He had two of Lucille's blue-haired posse by the hand, but he stopped to stroke the wet hair out of Madi's face to check her bloody cheek, making sure she was okay.

Warmth washed through her, knowing he cared. It was in his every touch, every look.

And he was still going to leave.

By the time the fire department arrived and shut off the sprinkler system, everyone had been evacuated. Several people were injured enough to require a visit to the ER, and Madi helped triage those people on the sidewalk. Near her, Mark and Tate assisted the paramedics. Mr. Ryan had gotten a nasty laceration down one arm, and Tate was crouched at the vet's side, applying pressure to the wound.

Brock was on the scene now too and rushed first to Cassie's side, then once reassured, moved on to Mr. Ryan.

"He's in shock," Tate said quietly.

It was true. The veteran shook, looking glassy-eyed and disoriented. Brock went to his car and returned with a medical kit. Together, he and Tate wrapped Mr. Ryan in an emergency blanket to get him warm until an ambulance could take him to Wyckford General. Madi helped get the vet settled inside the rig, then jumped back down to assist other people in time to hear the tail end of a conversation between them.

"The least you can do is consider the position," Brock said to Tate. "You're the perfect person to be flight crew team lead. We'd be lucky to have you. And look at all this. We can be exciting for an adrenaline junkie like you too."

Tate shook his head, then crouched at Lucille's feet as Brock stalked off to help another patient.

Madi moved in to ask Lucille, "Are you okay?"

"Oh, sure, honey." The older woman patted her arm, then gazed at Tate adoringly. "He's a good boy."

Tate smiled, then tended to Madi's wounded cheek. "You need that taken care of. Let me—"

"It can wait." She sank to the curb as the crowd began to disperse, dropping her head to her knees, exhausted to the bone and far too close to losing it. Tate ran a big, warm hand down her back, then wrapped an emergency blanket around her.

"I'm fine," Madi muttered.

He sat at her other side and pulled her in against his warmth. "That's not what's in question here."

She lifted her head. "I don't get why you don't trust yourself—you just saved the entire town."

He shrugged. "Probably for the same reason you quit your job. Old demons are hard to beat."

She looked away, and he tugged on her ponytail until she met his gaze again.

"Madi," he said softly. "Please don't do this."

Suddenly, it was all too much. The clinic, the diner, Tate knowing how she felt about him and his leaving anyway. Her head hurt. Her cheek hurt. Her heart hurt too. When her eyes filled with tears, Tate kept his arms around her, and she buried her face in the crook of his neck.

How had things gotten so out of control?

All she'd wanted was to stretch her wings. Live for herself for once instead of for others. "I screwed up," she said into his chest. "I always wished I could go a little crazy, but as it turns out, I'm not a good rebel."

"I think you're better at it than you give yourself credit for."

She choked out a laugh. "I just wanted something for myself."

"You deserve that," Tate said with absolute conviction. From the beginning, he'd treated her like someone special. He'd shared his courage, his sense of adventure, his inner strength. Once, she'd been out of sync with herself and her hopes and dreams. That had changed. Because of him.

She was in balance now, but it wasn't enough. Loving him wasn't enough either because he was going back to the Air Force, and she'd be alone. Again. The smart thing to do would be to cut her losses before it got worse, but how could she? "Tate."

He looked into her eyes and time seemed to slow.

"I love you." She covered his lips with her fingers when he started to interrupt. "Don't worry, I know you don't feel the same, and I know I screwed up because this was all supposed to be a fling, but I can't do this anymore. I'm sorry."

"Are you dumping me?" His whisper sounded sharp and brittle.

Madi shook her head. "You were never mine to dump."

He nodded and stroked his thumb over her cheekbone in a gentle gesture that made her ache. Madi started to say something more, but someone tapped her on the shoulder.

"Madison Michelle Scott."

Her mother. The only person who ever used her middle name. She stood, and Tate wisely wandered over to talk to Mark and Brock.

"I heard about the diner on the radio in the ER and I came to help." Her mother took Madi's chin in her fingers to assess her cheek. "You're hurt? And you quit your job?" Her mother stared at her for a long beat, during which Madi did her best not to look as utterly heartbroken as she felt. Finally, her mom nodded. "Well, they overworked you anyway."

"You're not upset?" Madi was taken aback.

"The hospital has taken advantage of your skills for years. The board's already banding together to get you back. I suggest you turn them down. According to what I overheard the second offer will be a much better deal."

She choked out a shocked breath. "Mom!"

"I'm proud of you, honey. And now I need to go invite that nice young man of yours over for dinner tonight. He's been good to you. I want to thank him. You go home and take a hot shower and put something on your cut cheek."

Her mother hugged her tight, then pushed her toward her car.

Madi took a last look at the scene. Firefighters were hauling water damaged items out of the wrecked diner.

"Madi?" Brock waved her over to where Mr. Martin still sat huddled on the curb. "He's refusing to go to the hospital. He doesn't have any serious wounds requiring ER treatment. Mostly, he's just shaken up. If you're leaving, could you maybe drive him home?"

In the end, Madi ended up chauffeuring the entire senior posse since Lucille was the only one of them still in possession of her license, and she'd gone to the ER for X-rays. It took nearly an hour to drop everyone off because they all took forever to say their goodbyes and get out of the car. When Madi had finally gotten rid of them all, she drove to Tate's instead.

Still working on adrenaline, frustration and a pain so real it felt like maybe her heart had split in two, she stormed into his open garage and over to where he stood at his worktable. "Are you coming to dinner at my mom's?"

He looked at her, not commenting on what had to be her ghoulish appearance. She'd been hit with the sprinklers, then dust from the ceiling tiles, and now the whole mess had dried into a white, sticky paste that covered her pretty much everywhere.

"I am," he said. "Is that a problem?"

"Yes, it's a problem!"

"Why? I didn't want to be rude. And she said she'd make meatloaf. I don't think I've ever had home-cooked meatloaf. I thought it was a suburban myth."

Madi had never wanted to both hug and strangle someone at the same time before. He was killing her. She pressed the heels of her hands to her eyes but couldn't rub the ache away. Spinning on her heel, she stalked out of the garage, but Tate caught her at her car, pulling her back to him. Madi felt the rumble of his chest and realized he was laughing at her. At least until he saw her face. Then his smile faded.

With a frustrated growl, Madi shoved him away and got into her car. But before she could shut the door, Tate blocked it by crouching beside her, his muscled thighs flexing under the worn denim of his jeans, his expression unreadable. "Why are you shutting me out?"

"That's rich," she managed, throat inexplicably tight. "Coming from you."

He studied her for a long moment. "You don't really love me, Madi. You love this town. You love all these people. And they all love you."

Madi dropped her head to the steering wheel. "Don't tell me what I feel. I know my heart and I know I'll be okay."

"You'll be so much more than okay. You're the strongest woman I've ever met, Madi."

"I'm not strong at all. I thought I could save everyone if I was good enough. That if I was good, nothing bad would happen."

Tate's stroked his hand up and down her back, calming her. "And how did that work out for you?"

She tightened her grip on the steering wheel like it was her only anchor in a spinning world. Nothing was working out. Not her job. Not the way she wanted people to see her. And not things with Tate.

"It wasn't your fault. You did the best you could. Stop carrying all the responsibility for everyone else," he said quietly. "Let it go and be whoever the hell you want to be."

She looked at him a long beat, then asked, "What about you?"

"What about me?"

"Are you going to take your own advice?"

Rather than answer her question, Tate pulled Madi from the car, then led her inside. After making sure she took a nice hot shower to remove the caked-on dust covering her from head to toe, he wrapped her in a towel and sat her on the counter. He rooted around in a drawer and came up with a first aid kit, which he set near her hip.

Then he pushed her wet hair from her face and eyed the cut on her cheek. He disinfected the area, and when she hissed in pain, he leaned in and kissed her temple.

"Nice bedside manner," she murmured. "You kiss all your patients like that?"

"Almost never." He smiled as he carefully peeled back the plastic packaging on a pack of sterilized butterfly bandages and used them to cover her wound.

"Have you reenlisted already?" she asked.

"Not yet. I left a message for my detachment officer, that's all."

He continued tending to her, concentrating on his task and leaving her free to stare at him. His mouth looked both stern and generous at the same time, his jaw square and rough with a day's worth of scruff she knew would feel deliciously sensual against her skin. A tiny scar marred one side of his face and another on his temple, signs of a life filled with adventure and danger.

"Do you miss it?" she said softly. "The action."

"Once an adrenaline junkie, always one, I guess." He finished with the cut on her face, then lifted her hand, turning it over to gently probe her swollen wrist.

"It's not broken," she said.

He nodded, brushing a kiss over her bruised skin before expertly wrapping it in an Ace bandage. Then he moved on to her bleeding shin. She hadn't even realized she was hurt there.

"Why did you stay so long?" she asked.

He looked up into her face. "I think you know why."

There were some advantages to changing her life, to living for herself instead of for the expectations of others. For one thing, it gave her new confidence. She accessed some of that now by unwrapping the towel around her and letting it fall to the counter at her hips.

Tate went still, and a sensual thrill rushed through her.

He let out a breath and slid his hands up her legs, his fingers rough and strong but tender at the same time, and she quivered, rejoicing in the rightness of his touch. He murmured something against her skin and Madi urged him on, clutching at his shoulders until her toes curled, until she cried out his name, until there were no more thoughts.

Tate had wanted to get his hands on Madi again since he'd heard about the missing drugs from Mark. Hell, he'd been wanting to put his hands on her since—well—*always*.

As they sprawled in his bed later, he stared up at the ceiling, trying to figure out what the hell to do while Madi snoozed beside him.

"Tate?" she murmured; her voice groggy with sleep.

He ran his fingers through her hair and drowned in her eyes. "Yeah?"

"I meant it when I said I loved you."

He knew that too. Knew it to the depths of his soul.

He'd been a military brat who'd never landed in one place for long, then a soldier himself. After the accident he'd steered clear of anything that even remotely sounded like a real connection. He was fine with that. Or so he'd thought.

Until Madi…

In his heart of hearts, he'd known from the first stormy night that his tie to her had been undeniable and unbreakable, no matter how he might have wished otherwise. It'd happened in an instant and had only strengthened with time. Tate couldn't imagine a future without her now. Talking, touching, kissing—whatever he could get because she beat back the darkness inside him. But being with her was also a double-edged sword. Because every minute he spent with Madi absolutely changed his definitions of—*everything.*

She made him feel differently about the past. Made him realize, hope, maybe that tragic night in the ocean hadn't been his fault. That maybe he'd been caught up in circumstances beyond his control and he'd done the best he could with what he was given. Madi also made Tate yearn for things he'd not experienced in a long time—home, family, love. She made him yearn to put down roots and make a life for himself. With her. Here in Wyckford.

His entire universe had gone topsy-turvy and that scared him most of all.

The only thing he was certain of was being with her felt right. *Real.* "Careful." He shifted slightly to kiss her swollen cheek, then her wrapped wrist. "Don't hurt yourself."

Madi smiled, then nuzzled into his side again and went back to sleep.

Her hair was in his face, her body plastered to his. She had one leg thrown over him, her face stuck to his pec, her hand over his heart like she owned it.

She did own it. His soul too.

Jesus. All this had started out so innocuously. Innocent, even.

Okay, not innocent. But that night at the auction he'd not been in a good place. Hadn't felt good enough for his own life, much less anyone else's. Certainly not for a woman like Madi, who'd give a perfect stranger the shirt off her back.

But being with her made him feel good.

Worthy.

He'd never intended to be anything to her except a good time, but best-laid plans…

Maybe he should've run hard and fast that first night, but something about her had drawn him in.

His arms involuntarily tightened around her, and although Madi gave a soft sigh and cuddled deeper into him, she didn't waken. Nor did she stir when Tate forced himself to let her go and slip out of bed. He needed some time to think and work out his next steps. But first, there was something else he had to do. And he had to do it alone.

Madi awakened slowly, thinking about the day before—the clinic being shut down, her quitting, the chaos at the diner—and Tate making it all okay. Responsive but not smothering, encouraging her to talk when necessary and letting her be quiet when it'd counted.

She stretched, her muscles aching in a very delicious way.

In truth, it hadn't been just sex for her since their first time, but she hadn't been sure how he felt.

Until last night.

The way he'd touched her, the way he'd looked at her, how he'd responded, had been lovemaking at its finest. Smiling, she rolled over and reached for him, but found only an empty mattress.

Something inside her went cold.

She sat up and grabbed her phone off the nightstand. A text flashed on-screen. She squinted, thinking it might be Tate—maybe he got called in for a shift—but it was from Judith:

The board refused your resignation. The clinic is back open. Your next shift is tomorrow at eight. See you then!

Wrapping herself in a sheet, she walked through the house, searching for Tate, but he was gone.

Madi got to the garage and flipped on the light. The Chevelle was missing too.

Heart in her throat, she ran back to the bedroom to get dressed, then figure out what the hell was going on. He couldn't leave now. She wouldn't let him. But first she had to find him.

She'd just finished putting on her shoes when she noticed something on the floor. A small, carefully wrapped gift. It must've been knocked off the nightstand when she'd reached for her phone. Madi picked it up.

Pulse racing and face hot, she sank down on the edge of the bed to open it. Inside was the bracelet she'd so coveted from the charity auction all those weeks ago. She had no idea how Tate had known she'd even wanted it, but maybe he'd overheard her talking with Mr. Martin that night in the lobby…

Tears stung her eyes as she stared down at it. He'd even added another charm to it, this one of a car that looked suspiciously like the Chevelle. That was it. That was all she needed to know.

Throat tight, she put it on and shored up her determination to continue stretching her wings. She'd done as she'd wanted. She'd stepped out of her comfort zone. She'd lived her life the way she saw fit, and it'd been more exciting than she could've imagined.

But how did she go back to being her old self again?

You don't.

She'd laid her heart on the line for the first time in her life, and Tate loved her, even if he might not admit it. To her or to himself. And she refused to let that go.

Not yet.

Maybe not ever, if she had her way.

CHAPTER TWENTY-TWO

TATE SAT IN an uncomfortable chair in front of Bud Lofton, administrator, and head of the board of directors for Wyckford General Hospital. He'd faced down the worst firefights and snipers in the world during his time in the Air Force, but he'd never felt more nervous in his life. He resisted the urge to fidget as the other man assessed him from across the desk.

"Tell me why we should hire you as permanent leader for the flight paramedic team," Bud said, holding the résumé Tate had hastily put together before he'd left his house earlier. "I know what's on here, and your work for us thus far speaks for itself, but tell me what's not on this résumé. Tell me who you are, Tate Griffin."

On his first mission, and on every assignment up to the accident, Tate had thrived on what he'd been doing. He'd believed in his work and understood he'd belonged out saving lives. After the crash, he hadn't just lost four friends. He'd also lost something of himself. His ability to connect. To get attached. His trust in his instincts.

Until the nosy, pestering people of this small town, who cared about everyone and everything in their path. Including him.

And Madi. She'd been the last piece of his shattered soul fitting back into place.

Tate cleared his throat, then said, "I'm a hard worker, dependable, loyal. I've got the experience and the drive and the knowledge to lead this team, and I have the foresight to keep it going to serve the people of Wyckford and the surrounding areas. I promise you that while there might be a few hiccups on the way and things might not always be perfect, I will always strive to do the best I can in every situation, sir."

Bud watched him closely for a moment, then picked up another paper from his desk. "I have a letter here from Dr. Brock Turner, speaking very highly of your capabilities and skills as a paramedic. He recommends you for the job."

Not sure what to say about that, Tate just nodded.

"And another from one of our firefighters, Mark Bates. He too gives you a glowing review."

For the first time in four years, Tate's chest tightened with something other than stress when he realized these people had gotten close to him. They knew him and cared about him, and he about them. He forced words out of his suddenly constricted throat. "Thank you, sir."

Since the accident, he'd thought keeping people away would help him forget and keep him safe. But now he knew the opposite was true. Being alone had only made him miserable.

Happiness had arrived when he'd come to Wyckford. The town and all the nosy folks here and one special woman who'd destroyed the carefully constructed barriers around his heart.

Brad, Tommy, Kelly, and Trevor's deaths would *always* mean something to him. And maybe forgiveness had to start with himself first. Yes, he'd given the order to go on that rescue mission that night, knowing the conditions, knowing how dangerous it was. But Madi was right. His team had known all the risks and they'd still chosen to follow him. They wouldn't want Tate to suffer endlessly for a decision made with no good choices available. They'd want him to be happy. Deep down, he'd probably always known that, but he hadn't had his head screwed on straight for a long time. It was now.

"No need to thank me." Bud stood and extended his hand to Tate. "Especially since you're going to have your hands full with the new flight crew. Congratulations and we're glad to welcome you as a permanent member of the Wyckford General Hospital. HR will contact you to sign all the paperwork."

Tate left the interview more determined than ever. He'd gotten his professional life back on track.

Now to focus on the personal one.

Driving past the parking lot of the Buzzy Bird Café, Tate saw the café was boarded up, but there were still a few cars there, people helping to clean the place up and get it back open again in time for Thanksgiving next week.

Heart pounding, Tate parked, then walked to the entrance. Amidst the wreckage from the sprinklers, he spotted Luna and Cassie and Madi near the counter, mops and brooms in hand.

He stepped inside and all three women turned his way. Madi froze, the charm bracelet glinting on her wrist.

Tate had absolutely no idea what she was thinking since her expression was carefully blank.

A lesson she'd probably learned from him.

CHAPTER TWENTY-THREE

MADI STARED AT TATE, her breath held.

He wore dress pants and a white button-down shirt with a tie, looking very professional.

Heart pounding, she said to her friends, "Give us a minute, please."

Luna looked at him, using her first two fingers to point at him, going back and forth between his eyes and hers, silently giving him notice she was watching and not to even *think* about misbehaving.

Cassie dragged Luna through the door leading into the kitchen.

Madi waited until they were out of earshot, then walked over to where he stood near the door. Her entire being went warm as she drank in the sight of him.

"You still trying to save me?" he asked quietly once she reached him.

She shrugged. "I can't seem to help myself."

"I don't need saving."

No. No, he didn't. He was strong and capable and more than able to take care of himself. "What *do* you need?"

"You," he said simply. "Only you."

"Oh," Cassie said softly through the kitchen pass-through window. "That's good."

"So good," Luna agreed.

Madi turned and glared at her friends until they disappeared again.

"Sorry." She refocused on Tate. He took her hand in his, entwining their fingers and bringing them to his chest, his heartbeat a reassuring steady thump beneath her palm. "I know you've looked for a hero," he said. "But how about a regular guy?"

Her throat went tight. "That'd be great. But I don't see any regular guys in front of me."

The corner of his mouth tipped up, but she wasn't going to be distracted by his hotness yet. "What about your reenlistment?"

"I thought that's what I wanted, but I was wrong. The only thing I want now is you, Madi. *You* fulfill me. You make me whole. You're the greatest rush I've ever known."

Sniffling echoed from the kitchen.

She ignored it, even as her own tears welled. "Does this mean you're staying?"

"It does. Bud Lofton just hired me permanently as the flight crew team leader. And I'd also like to volunteer to run some of the veterans' programs at the clinic too, if it's still going."

Madi absorbed all this with what felt like a huge bucket of hope on her chest. "It's still going."

Tate smiled, his voice sounding raw and staggered and touched beyond words as he said, "God, I was so stupid, Madi. I didn't know what to do with you. I tried to keep my distance, but my world doesn't work without you in it."

She melted. And given the twin sighs echoing from the kitchen, Madi wasn't the only one.

Tate cupped her cheek, careful of her wound, then kissed her. "I love you too, Madi," he said very quietly. "So damn much." Then his eyes went dark as he murmured against her lips, "How do you feel about sealing the deal with a ring?"

"What?" she squeaked, pulling back. "You want to get engaged? To be *married*?"

"You're it for me." Tate tipped her chin up and looked deep into her eyes, and there she found the truth. He stroked a finger over her temple, tucking a loose strand of hair behind her ear. "The best choice I ever made."

"Yes!" Heart full to bursting, Madi kissed the man she'd spend forever with.

* * * * *

COMING SOON!

We really hope you enjoyed reading this book.
If you're looking for more romance
be sure to head to the shops when
new books are available on

Thursday 25th April

To see which titles are coming soon, please visit

millsandboon.co.uk/nextmonth

MILLS & BOON®

Coming next month

DATING HIS IRRESISTIBLE RIVAL
Juliette Hyland

The mood around the table was far too tight.

Leaning across, he made a silly face. 'I read one self-help book. It was all about keeping lists and staying organised. I mostly remember the raised lettering on the cover. It felt nice.' Knox shook his head, horror at the memory of trying to read it returning. It had been recommended by one of his teachers, a way to focus his tasks.

She'd meant well. One of the few adults in his young life who saw through the mad-at-the-world kid to the well of potential beneath it. *If* he turned in his assignments.

If it was surgery or medical knowledge, he kept everything locked in. If it was something else, there was a good chance that he'd forget. Thank goodness for auto bill pay and a monthly subscription for Post-it notes.

'I take it from the sour look on your face you were not a fan.' Miranda tapped his knee.

Knox looked down. Her fingers had already disappeared but part of him still felt her touch. 'I prefer fantasy. Wizards, dragons, magic.'

'Wizards and dragons?'

Her smile made his heart leap. 'Yep. The more fire magic the wizard uses, the better!' He made a few motions with his hands and she giggled.

He finished his coffee, hating the sign that their outing was nearing an end. 'I can't listen while running, though. For that, I have to have a beat. I tried listening to podcasts that I enjoy since there never seems to be enough time for all the ones I love, but I couldn't make myself actually run at a good clip.'

'Why do you have to run at a good clip?' Miranda raised her eyebrow as she used her straw to pull the last of the whipped topping from the bottom of the cup.

'I—' Knox sat there, trying to figure out the answer. 'I—'

'You already said that.' Miranda laid her hand on his knee and this time she didn't pull it away. 'Just something to think about.'

'Want to get dinner Sunday?' The question popped out, and he placed his hand over hers on his knee. He had no idea what this was, but he wanted to spend it with Miranda.

She looked at his hand then back at him. Her dark eyes holding his. 'Like a date?'

'Yeah. Exactly like a date.' He watched the wheels turn in her eyes. Saw the heat dance across her cheeks.

Say yes.

'All right.'

The urge to pump his fist was nearly overwhelming but he kept it in check. 'I'm looking forward to it.'

Continue reading

DATING HIS IRRESISTIBLE RIVAL

Juliette Hyland

Available next month

millsandboon.co.uk

JC Harroway
Tempted by the
REBEL SURGEON
Breaking the
SINGLE MUM'S RULES
THE BABY the Desert
KING MUST CLAIM
BOUND by the
ITALIAN'S 'I DO'
JESSICA GILMORE
It Started with a
Vegas Wedding
The CEO and the
Single Dad